LIBERATING

ATLANTIS

HARRY
TURTLEDOVE

A ROC BOOK

ROC

Published by New American Library, a division of
Penguin Group (USA) Inc., 375 Hudson Street,
New York, New York 10014, USA

Penguin Group (Canada), 90 Eglinton Avenue East, Suite 700, Toronto,
Ontario M4P 2Y3, Canada (a division of Pearson Penguin Canada Inc.)

Penguin Books Ltd., 80 Strand, London WC2R 0RL, England

Penguin Ireland, 25 St. Stephen's Green, Dublin 2,
Ireland (a division of Penguin Books Ltd.)

Penguin Group (Australia), 250 Camberwell Road, Camberwell, Victoria 3124,
Australia (a division of Pearson Australia Group Pty. Ltd.)

Penguin Books India Pvt. Ltd., 11 Community Centre, Panchsheel Park,
New Delhi - 110 017, India

Penguin Group (NZ), 67 Apollo Drive, Rosedale, North Shore 0632,
New Zealand (a division of Pearson New Zealand Ltd.)

Penguin Books (South Africa) (Pty.) Ltd., 24 Sturdee Avenue,
Rosebank, Johannesburg 2196, South Africa

Penguin Books Ltd., Registered Offices:
80 Strand, London WC2R 0RL, England

Published by Roc, an imprint of New American Library, a division of Penguin
Group (USA) Inc. Previously published in a Roc hardcover edition.

First Roc Mass Market Printing, December 2010
10 9 8 7 6 5 4 3 2 1

continued . .

"Engaging. . . . The story line is fast-paced and gripping with strong characters, especially the reluctant hero Radcliff. However, what hooks the audience is the obvious comparative analysis to the American Revolution as subgenre fans will relish figuring out what is identical, similar, and radically different in the birth of a nation. Mr. Turtledove provides a refreshing middle tale." —Alternative Worlds

"Readers familiar with the American Revolution will find analogues to Benjamin Franklin and Benedict Arnold as well as real figures, such as Marquis de la Fayette and Thomas Paine, and elements of real battles of the American Revolution." —Publishers Weekly

"*The United States of Atlantis* is at its heart an adventure against foreign tyranny. . . . Come enjoy the turmoil and pain that forming a new country entails. I look forward to seeing more adventures set in Atlantis." —SFRevu

"In this fantastic journey into revolutionary history on an undiscovered continent, the characters are as magnetic and resourceful as true historical heroes should be. Readers will be delightfully drawn to the newly forming country of Atlantis as they mark and compare our own American history with the progress of our 'sister' colony. This is an engaging read, cover to cover." —Romantic Times

Opening Atlantis

"An interesting, alternative version of our own world. . . . Turtledove's development of it allows him to look not only at political, but also geographical and evolutionary differences between his world and our own." —SF Site

"Imaginative." —Don D'Ammassa

"I enjoyed this book. . . . The exploration and in some cases defiling of this new land [are] interesting. . . . I look forward to the further adventures of the Radcliff(e)s." —SFRevu

"The book itself is quite readable: Each vignette is based around a military conflict, and the author has his usual eye for appropriate detail and ear for authentic historical attitudes. Turtledove has been generally unwilling to warp his characters to the point where they are twenty-first-century Americans in funny clothes, and keeps to that tradition here: The viewpoint characters judge themselves by their standards, not ours . . . makes for a more internally consistent novel." —Collected Miscellany

BOOK I

I

*I*f not for the floorboard that came up at one end, it might all have happened differently. Or it might never have happened at all. How do you measure might-have-beens? Frederick Radcliff never found an answer to that, and the question was in his mind much of the time. He'd never known a slave in whose mind that question had not taken root and flourished.

Frederick Radcliff was a slave himself: a house slave on Henry and Clotilde Barford's plantation, thirty miles outside of New Marseille. He was of middle height, but uncommonly broad through the shoulders. By his complexion, he was somewhere between griffe and mulatto—he had more than a quarter white blood in him, but less than half.

He never used his surname where the master and mistress could hear him do it. Legally, the surname didn't belong to him. Legally, nothing belonged to any black or copperskinned slave in the United States of Atlantis. Legally, the whites (and the occasional free blacks and copperskins) who owned them also owned everything that was theirs.

Regardless of what might be legally true, plenty of slaves claimed descent from Radcliffs or Radcliffes. The great white clan, descendants of the English fisherman who'd founded the first settlement in Atlantis, had flourished mightily in the four hundred years since. Henry Barford claimed a Radcliffe connection on his mother's side. (Clotilde, *née* Delvoie, claimed a Kersauzon connection on *her* mother's side. The descendants of the Breton fisherman who'd led Edward Radcliffe to Atlantis, but who'd settled here after him, had also done well for themselves.) The Radcliffs and Radcliffes (and, indeed, the Kersauzons) had been fruitful and multiplied. And they hadn't been shy about lying down with slave women to do it.

After four centuries in Atlantis, some of Edward Radcliffe's descendants had flourished more mightily than others, of course. There were Radcliff and Radcliffe drunkards in the gutters of towns all over the USA. There were Radcliff and Radcliffe butchers and bakers and candlestick makers—and farmers, always farmers. There were Radcliff and Radcliffe doctors and lawyers and preachers. And there were Radcliff and Radcliffe leaders, as there had always been in Atlantis. More than a quarter of the Consuls who'd headed the United States of Atlantis since the War for Freedom were Radcliffs or Radcliffes, and quite a few others had the blood without the name.

Victor Radcliff had commanded the Atlantean Assembly's army in the war against England. After the war was won, he became one of the two First Consuls. (Isaac Fenner, the other, was descended from a crewman on Edward Radcliffe's fishing boat.) Every Atlantean schoolboy knew the First Consuls' names as well as he knew his own. So did Frederick Radcliff, although slaves, to put it mildly, were not encouraged to acquire an education.

And Frederick Radcliff had a stronger reason to remember the First Consuls' names, or at least one of them, than a schoolboy's fear of the master's switch.

Victor Radcliff was his grandfather.

So his mother had told him, over and over again. The story was that Victor Radcliff had come down into southern Atlantis to join up with the Marquis de la Fayette's French army, and that Frederick's grandmother's owner lent her to the general so he wouldn't have to sleep in a cold bed. Nine months later, his father was born.

Frederick didn't remember his father. Nicholas Radcliff had died when he was three years old. He'd stepped on a rusty nail outside, and lockjaw set in—so Frederick's mother said. She'd been a house slave, too, and taught Frederick what he needed to know so he wouldn't have to go out to the fields and work under the hot sun and the overseer's lash.

He knew he lived pretty soft ... for a slave. He was friends with the cooks—also slaves—so he got plenty to eat. Maybe he didn't dine quite so well as the master and mistress and their children (now married and out on their own), but he knew how the field hands envied his rations. He slept in a bed one of the master's sons had used before him. His bedclothes were ones the white folks had almost but not quite worn out. All that use only made the linen softer. No, not bad at all ... for a slave.

But if his grandmother had been white ...

No wheedling cooks then. No hand-me-downs—no stuff other people didn't want any more, or didn't need. No swallowing his pride to keep from angering people who could do anything they wanted with him, including putting him up for sale like a horse or an anvil. If he were the *white* grandson of one of the First Consuls of the United States of Atlantis, he would be a rich man. He would be an educated man. People would respect him, admire him, because of who his grandfather was. He might be getting ready to stand for Consul himself. He might already have served a two-year term. Instead ...

Instead, he had a meeting with that floorboard. He was never the same afterwards. Neither were the United States of Atlantis.

Henry Barford didn't have many friends. He would hunt with his sons or other neighboring planters every now and then. He would drink with them every now and then, too. Frederick had learned just how much brandy to pour into his coffee the morning after one of those drinking parties. A shot and a half was about right to take the edge off the pain in the master's hair.

Clotilde, now, was social butterfly, not social caterpillar. She was always clattering off in the carriage to visit the neighbor ladies. They gathered to sew or read books together, to stuff themselves with fried chicken or starberry pie, to pour down barrel-tree-rum punch (they didn't drink as hard as their husbands, but there weren't many teetotalers among them), and, always, to gossip.

And, when Clotilde wasn't clattering off to visit the neighbor ladies, they were clattering in to visit her. Frederick supposed she made a good guest. He knew she made a good hostess. She was as plump as a pillow and as friendly as a puppy—to her equals, anyhow. She wasn't especially hard on the house slaves . . . not so long as everything went well.

Sometimes only a few neighbor ladies visited the plantation. Three or four times a year, though, Clotilde would invite everybody from miles around. If you were doing well for yourself, you were expected to show off a bit, or more than a bit.

Whenever one of those grand convocations came along, Henry Barford would take a jug and either secrete himself away in an upstairs bedroom or go pay a call on the overseer. The next morning, Frederick would make a point of correcting his coffee.

It was a sultry, sticky summer's day. People who knew said the weather in the southeast, on the other side of the Green Ridge Mountains, was even worse. But this was bad enough for all ordinary use.

Frederick woke with the bedclothes sticking to him. In weather like this, he slept bare but for drawers. Helen, his woman, had on only a thin cotton shift. A slave preacher had made a marriage ceremony for the two of them—more than half a lifetime ago now—but it had no force of law. The Barfords could sell or give away either one of them any time they chose.

With a sigh, Frederick said, "Hate to climb into the monkey suit today. Gonna roast my bones for the sake of swank."

Helen looked at him. "You sooner go out and weed amongst the cotton plants? How'd you like to swing a hoe all day?"

"Oh, I'll wear the monkey suit," Frederick said, resignation in his voice. "But I don't have to like it."

"If the other choice is worse, you better like the one you got," Helen said. She was in no way an educated woman—she could barely read, and could not even sign her name—but she had her share of common sense and then some.

Frederick, stubborn and more hot-tempered, had just enough sense to realize Helen had more. He sighed again. "Reckon you're right," he said, and leaned over to give her a kiss.

She brought up a hand and rubbed first her cheek and then his. "Better shave, too—you're all scratchy. Miz Clotilde, she'll yell at you if she got to tell you that."

Once more, it wasn't as if she were wrong. "I shaved yesterday," Frederick protested feebly. Helen just looked at him. He let out another resigned sigh and scraped his cheeks and chin smooth with a straight razor. He had a heavier beard than most Negro men did, and as for copperskins. . . . That probably came down from his white grandfather. Like the rest of his inheritance from Victor Radcliff, it did him no good at all.

He kissed Helen again after he finished. She smiled and nodded. That was worth a little something, anyway.

Then he put on the white shirt with the tight collar, the cravat, the black wool trousers, the black wool jacket, the black socks, and the tight black shoes that pinched his feet. "Don't you look fine!" Helen said.

Sweat was already running down his face. "Maybe I do," he said, "but I sure won't be sorry to take this stuff off again come the night." He left it there. His woman was right: wearing the monkey suit had to be an improvement on a field hand's shapeless, colorless homespun.

An early-rising woodpecker's drumming punctuated the dawn stillness. The cooks already had coffee boiling in the kitchen. Frederick and Helen gulped big, snarling cups only partly tamed by sugar. A cook gave them bowls of cornmeal mush and chopped salt pork. A couple of young colored maids were in there eating, too. Soon they'd be off on one last orgy of sweeping and dusting. Everything today had to be *right*.

Feathers flew in the kitchen—literally. Black hands plucked chickens, ducks, a Terranovan turkey, and a couple of oil thrushes the master had shot in the woods the day before. The worm--eating Atlantean birds made mighty fine eating. They couldn't fly, and they had no great fear of man. They were so tasty, and so stupid, they grew ever scarcer.

In a way, Frederick pitied them. How could a man who dared not run away not pity a flightless bird? Pity them as he would, though, he ate of them whenever he got the chance.

And if that doesn't suit me to be a slaveowner, may I be damned if I know what would, Frederick thought. He poured himself more coffee.

Outside, another rhythmic thunking noise joined the woodpecker's percussive syncopation. One of the field hands was chopping firewood. As Frederick poured down the strong, brown brew—darker than he was, if not a great deal—he nodded to himself. No matter how warm the day, the kitchens would go through a great plenty of pine and cypress today.

He'd heard white men newly come from England complain about the lack of hardwoods. Oak and maple and hickory, they said, burned longer and hotter than Atlantean lumber. He hadn't noticed that the lack made them pack up and go back where they came from. All it did was give them something to complain about. He understood that. Everybody needed something of the sort.

A slave, by the nature of things, had plenty to complain about. The only trouble was, complaining didn't do him any good.

Clotilde Barford swept into the kitchen in a rustle of silk. The dress she wore was a pretty good copy of what had been almost the height of fashion in Paris eight or nine years earlier. She wasn't yet attired for receiving company. Before her guests arrived, she would put on a pretty good copy of what had been almost the height of fashion in Paris year before last. That would be plenty to let her keep up with the other women.

Now she was dressed for cracking the whip. "Get moving, you lazy niggers!" she snapped. Almost all the house slaves *were* Negroes; whites trusted them further than copperskins. That shamed Frederick more than it pleased him. The mistress didn't care one way or the other. "Sitting around lollygagging! The nerve of you people!"

Frederick glanced over at Helen. Helen's eyes had already swung his way. They carefully didn't smile. The mistress was in a state, all right. She got this way every time her friends and neighbors gathered here. The abuse mostly didn't mean anything. Mostly.

She pointed a pale, pudgy forefinger at Frederick, aiming it as Henry Barford must have aimed his shotgun at the oil thrushes. "Everything better be perfect when they get here. Perfect, you hear me?"

"Yes, ma'am." He scooped up his last few spoonfuls of mush double-quick so she could see he was hurrying. Like any sensible slave, he moved no faster than he had to. Why should he, when he was working for someone else's benefit rather than his own?

Sometimes, though, you had no choice. If the mistress or the master stood over you, you had to step lively. And Clotilde was liable to have her beady little blue eyes on him every livelong minute till her gathering proved the triumph she'd known all along it would be—known all along it had better be, anyhow. Frederick took a heroic swallow that drained the coffee mug and almost drowned him. He hurried out of the kitchen. Helen wasn't more than half a step behind him.

He wondered if the mistress would pursue them. Not yet. She stayed in there and laid down the law to the cooks as if she were Moses and they the children of Israel. Most of them had heard the speech before. Frederick certainly had. That didn't stop Clotilde Barford from coming out with it again. Stop her? It didn't even slow her down.

"She does go on," Helen said.

"And on, and on, and on," Frederick agreed, rolling his eyes. They both smiled. But they also both spoke in low voices, and neither one of them laughed. You never could tell who might be listening. You never could tell who might be tattling, either.

The house slaves had been scouring the big house—so called in contrast to the overseer's cottage and the slaves' shacks—for more than a week now. Wood glowed with oily, strong-smelling polish. The good china had been scrubbed and scrubbed again. Even the silver had been polished, and shone dazzlingly in the sun and more than well enough in the shade.

But, of course, everything had to be done one more time on the day itself. The housemaids bustled around, dusting and shining. They slowed down whenever they didn't think Frederick could see them. As he feared they might tell on him for saying unkind things about the mistress, so they worried he would tell on them if he caught them slacking. As coal and wood fed a steam engine, so fear and distrust fed the engine of slavery.

"Careful, there!" one maid warned another, who was swiping crystal goblets with a rag. "You drop one of them, it'll come out of your hide."

"Don't I know it?" the other one replied. "Now why don't you find somethin' for your own self to do, 'stead of standin' there playin' the white man over me?"

Playin' the white man over me. Frederick's mouth twisted. Overseers who were slaves themselves commonly failed, and often ended up hurt or dead. Negroes and copperskins didn't care to follow orders from their own kind. They thought their fellows who tried to give those orders were getting above their station.

They were right about that. What they didn't see was that whites who ordered them around were also above *their* station. Whites had more than looks on their side, of course. They had the weight of centuries of tradition behind them. And, if that weight turned out not to be enough, they also had whips and dogs and guns.

With such cheerful reflections spinning inside his head, Frederick nodded respectfully, as he had to nod, to Henry Barford as his owner came down the stairs. "Mornin', Master Henry," he said.

"Mornin', Fred," Barford replied. He was dressed in a shirt that had seen better days and trousers that had seen better years—they were out at both knees. He hadn't bothered putting on shoes or stockings. He often didn't. He seemed happy enough to let his hairy toes enjoy the fresh air. Maybe his wife would talk him into dressing up for her guests. More than likely, he'd stay comfortable and sit this one out with a jug, the way he did most of the time. He caught Frederick's eye again. "Clotilde's already in the kitchen checkin' up on things, is she?"

Even if he hadn't known her habits, anyone not deaf as a stump would have had no trouble figuring out where she was and what she was doing. Frederick nodded economically. "Yes, sir."

"Well, she'd better turn Davey loose long enough to sizzle me some bacon and fry up a couple of eggs in the grease, that's all I've got to tell you." Barford hurried past Frederick. The view from behind showed his pants were out at the seat, too. Frederick couldn't imagine how much trouble *he'd* get in for wearing such disreputable clothes. No, he could imagine it, much too well. But the master did as he pleased. That was what liberty was all about. Henry Barford took it for granted.

Back in Victor Radcliff's day, the Proclamation of Liberty had announced to the world that Atlantis was free from England. Had the Atlantean Assembly, convening in the little town of Honker's Mill, noticed how many people the Proclamation of Liberty left out? Not many of the laws the United States of Atlantis had passed since gave much sign of it.

There had been uprisings, here in the southern parts of Atlantis where slavery remained a legal and moneymaking operation (assuming there were differences between the two). Planters and farmers and white townsfolk put them down with as much brutality as they needed, and a little more besides to give the slaves second thoughts next time. Once or twice, the Atlantean army helped local militias smash revolts. What were the odds the army wouldn't do the same thing again?

Frederick sighed one more time. You couldn't win, not if you were colored. You couldn't even break even—not a chance. And they would hunt you with hounds if you tried to run off to the north, where Negroes and copperskins were free. They weren't sure to catch you, but they had a pretty good chance.

He'd never had the nerve to flee. Things weren't *too* bad

where he was. He could tell himself they weren't, anyhow.
The top circle of hell wasn't supposed to be *too* bad, either.
Good pagans went there, didn't they? The only thing they
were missing was the presence of God. Frederick nodded
to himself. Yes, that about summed things up.

The first carriage rattled up to the big house before ten in
the morning. A black man in clothes as fancy as Frederick's drove it. A frozen-faced Negro in an even more splendid getup—he looked ready to hunt foxes—rode behind.
When the carriage stopped, he jumped down and opened
the door so Veronique Barker could descend.

Like Clotilde Barford, she was from an old French
family that had married into the now-dominant English-
speaking wave of settlers who'd swarmed south after
France lost its Atlantean holdings ninety years before.
Henry Barford wasn't a bad fellow. By everything Frederick had ever heard, Benjamin Barker was a first-class son
of a bitch.

Sure enough, Clotilde had changed into her new gown
by the time Veronique arrived. The mistress swept down
to greet her guest in blue tulle and a cloud of rosewater almost thick enough to see. "So good to have you here, dear!"
she trilled. Then she switched to bad French to add, "You
look lovely!"

"Oh, so do you, sweetheart," Veronique answered in the
same language, spoken about as well. Frederick could follow them—his own French was on the same level. Here in
the southern Atlantean states, most people had at least a
smattering, though English gained year by year.

Arm in arm, chattering in the two languages, Clotilde
and Veronique went into the big house. Veronique thought
nothing of leaving her driver and footman standing there in
the hot sun. Frederick's mistress probably would have been
more considerate, but there were no guarantees.

Pointing, Frederick told the driver, "Why don't you put
the carriage under those trees? Horses can graze there if
they want, and they won't cook."

"I do that," the driver agreed. "Marcus and me, we won't
cook in the shade, neither."

"That's a fact," said the footman—presumably Marcus.

"Before too long, we'll bring you out something to eat, something to drink," Frederick promised.

"Got me somethin' to drink." The driver pulled a flask from one of his jacket pockets, then quickly made it disappear before anyone white could see it. "Food'd be mighty good, though. When the white ladies gits together, all the niggers who takes 'em gits together, too."

"That's a fact," Marcus said again. When he reached into *his* pocket, he pulled out a pair of dice instead of a flask. "Me, I aim to head on back to Master Barker's with some of their money."

"Good luck," Frederick said, wondering how much luck would have to do with the dice games ahead. Maybe those were honest ivories. Then again, maybe the footman had reason for his confident smile. Frederick decided he wouldn't risk any of his small, precious hoard of coins against Marcus.

Odds were he'd be too busy to get the chance even if he wanted it. Here came two more carriages, almost bumping axles as they rolled up the narrow path side by side. They rode that way so the women inside them could talk together. A handkerchief fluttered from a carriage window as one of those women made some kind of point.

Out came Clotilde Barford again to greet the newcomers. The women went in talking a blue streak. They hadn't even begun on the punch yet—though the guests might have got a head start before leaving home.

One driver had another flask. The other produced a deck of cards. The practiced way he shuffled them made Frederick leery of getting into a game with him, too. Were there no honest men anywhere any more? Once upon a time, Frederick had read a story about a Greek who'd gone looking for one—and ended up with nothing but a lantern to light the way and a barrel to sleep in. That didn't much surprise him. The world would have been a different, and probably a better, place if it had.

Carriages kept coming. Before long, Clotilde got tired of going in and out to greet each new arrival. That happened every time she threw one of these affairs. She told Frederick, "You just send 'em on into the house, you hear? I'll say hello to 'em when they come in."

"Yes, ma'am," he answered. She said that at every gathering, too. As long as he could stay in the shade on the porch between arrivals, he didn't mind.

In their dresses of white and red, blue and green, purple and gold, the women might have been parts of a walking flower garden. Some of them were young and pretty. Frederick carefully schooled his face to woodenness. Helen would tease him about it tonight. He knew that, but it was all right. But if any of those young, pretty white women noticed a black man noticing them . . . that was anything but all right. An incautious Negro could end up without his family jewels if he showed what he was thinking. But when a well-built woman was about to explode out of the top of her gown, what was a man of any color supposed to think?

Whatever Frederick thought, it didn't show on his face.

One of the housemaids tried to sneak past him to join the colored men under the trees. He sent her back into the big house, saying, "Wait till the white ladies are eating. The mistress won't pay any mind to what you do then."

"Spoilsport," she said. Gatherings like this let slaves from different plantations get to know one another.

Frederick only shrugged. "Don't want you getting in trouble. Don't want to get into trouble myself, either." She made a face at him, but she went inside again.

He watched the sun climb to the zenith and then start its long slide down toward the western horizon. The broad Hesperian Gulf lay in that direction, but Frederick had never once glimpsed the sea. Dinner was set for two in the afternoon. He figured just about all of Mistress Clotilde's guests would be there by then. Chatter and punch were good enough in their way, but he didn't believe any of the local ladies wanted to miss a sit-down feast.

When the sun said it was about one, he went back into the house and sidled up to Clotilde Barford. "How we doin', ma'am?" he asked.

"Everything's going just the way it ought to," she answered. She didn't say things like that every day. The gathering had to be doing better than she'd ever dreamt it could. What juicy new tidbit had she just heard about some neighbor she couldn't stand?

"Good, ma'am. That's good." On the whole, Frederick meant it. If she was happy, everything at the plantation would run more smoothly for a while.

She glanced at the clock ticking on the mantel. It said the hour was half past one. Frederick didn't think it was really so late, but that clock, the only one on the plantation except for Henry Barford's pocket watch, kept the official time. The mistress said, "You'll start bringing in the food right at two."

"However you want it, that's what I'll do," Frederick said, which was the only right answer a slave could give. He didn't like playing the waiter; he thought it beneath his dignity. To a white woman, a slave's dignity was as invisible as air. She'd want to show off to her guests, and a well-dressed slave fetching and carrying was part of the luxury she was displaying.

As if to prove as much, she said, "They'll be so jealous of this place by the time I'm through, their eyes'll bug right out of their heads. So you make a fine old show when you lug in the big tray, you hear?"

"Yes, ma'am," Frederick said resignedly. She'd want him to load it extra full every time he brought it in, too, so he could show the ladies he was not only graceful but also a nice, strong buck. One arm and shoulder would hurt tomorrow, but would she care? Not likely! She wouldn't feel a thing.

In the kitchen, they were straining broth through cheesecloth. More swank. It would taste the same either way. But the mistress wanted it clear, so clear it would be. If that made extra work for the cooks, what were they there for but work?

"You watch those oil thrushes!" the head cook—Davey—called to a scullery maid who was turning the birds' spits over a fire. "Watch 'em, I tell you! Anything happens to 'em, I'll serve them fancy ladies a roast nigger with an apple in her mouth, you hear me?"

Eyes enormous, the maid nodded. She couldn't have been more than twelve. Frederick wouldn't have been surprised if she thought the cook would really do it. Frederick knew Davey might be tempted, at that. The kitchen was his domain. The mistress might intrude here, but only in the way storms or fires intruded on a bigger domain. Once the storm blew over or the fire went out, the place was his again.

"How soon you be ready?" Frederick asked Davey. "She wants me to start serving at two o'clock sharp—two by the clock."

The head cook looked outside to gauge the shadows. Then he looked up at the roughly plastered ceiling, adjusting between what the sun said and what the clock claimed. The whole business took no more than a few seconds. His gaze came back to Frederick. "We make it," he said.

"That's all right, then." Frederick asked no more questions. When Davey said the kitchen would do this or that, it would.

And it did. The cooks put chopped scallions and bits of spiced pork back into their marvelously clear broth. The tray Frederick used to carry the bounty into the dining room was at least three feet across. Grunting, he got it up on his left shoulder and steadied it with his right arm.

"Watch the doorway, now," Davey warned as he headed out. One of the undercooks held the door open for him.

"Oh, I'm watching!" Frederick assured the head cook. "Obliged," he added to the undercook as he eased by. He tried to imagine what would happen if he stumbled just then. His mind shied away from the notion—and why wouldn't it? He'd give the white women something new to talk about!

He was similarly careful easing into the dining room. He had no actual door to worry about there, but the doorway was just wide enough for him and the tray both. All the ladies broke off their talk and stared at him as he came in. "That's a fine-looking nigger," one said to her friend. The other woman nodded. Frederick felt proud, even though he knew she might have said the same kind of thing about an impressive horse or greyhound.

He went around to the head of the table so he could serve Mistress Clotilde first. He stood a couple of steps behind her for a moment. Did he *want* the assembled white ladies of the neighborhood to notice him, even to admire him? He supposed he did. He never would have admitted it out loud, though, not unless he wanted to hear about it from Helen for the next twenty years.

Pride goeth before destruction, and an haughty spirit before a fall. Frederick often read the Bible. He knew that was the proper line, though even preachers often clipped it. He'd always thought the Good Book was full of good sense. Now he found out how very full it was, but in a way that made him wish he'd stayed ignorant forever.

After posing for the ladies—most of whom, sadly, paid him no more attention than the furniture—Frederick slid forward so he could start serving. And, as he slid, the toe of his left shoe unexpectedly came up against the end of that loose floorboard.

Had he stumbled in the course of his ordinary duties, that would have been bad enough. It would have humiliated him and infuriated his mistress—she would have lost face in front of all her neighbors. She would have found some way to make him pay for his clumsiness. She had her good points, but she'd never been one to suffer in silence. Henry Barford could testify to that.

Yes, an ordinary stumble would have been a mortification, a dreadful misfortune. What did happen was about a million times as bad. Everything seemed to move very slowly, as it does in some of the worst nightmares. Frederick's foot met the floorboard. He thought it would keep sliding ahead, but it suddenly couldn't. The rest of his body could . . . and did.

Of itself, his torso bent forward. He tried to straighten—too late. The heavy tray lurched forward on his shoulder. He tried to steady it with his left hand. He couldn't. He grabbed for it with his right hand. Too late. Instead of the edge of the tray, which might have saved things, his hand hit the bottom. That made matters worse, not better.

A back pillar on Mistress Clotilde's chair caught him in the pit of the stomach. "Oof!" he said as the breath hissed out of him. And he could only watch as the tray crowded with bowls of soup flew out of his hands and fell toward the fancy lace tablecloth that had been in Clotilde's family for generations—as she would tell people at any excuse or none.

It seemed to take a very long time.

It seemed to, but it didn't. Frederick hadn't even managed to grab at his own abused midsection before the tray crashed down. Bowls full of hot soup went every which way. A few of them flew truly amazing distances. Frederick was amazed, all right. Appalled, too. Some soup bowls smashed. Others landed upside down but intact in well-to-do ladies' laps—or, in one disastrous case, in a busty lady's bodice—thereby delivering their last full measure of savory liquid devotion.

Dripping women shrieked. They sprang to their feet. They ran here, there, and everywhere. Some of them ran into others, which sent fresh screams echoing off the ceiling. Others swore, at the world in general or at Frederick in particular. He'd heard angry slaves cuss. He'd heard white muleskinners and overseers, too. For sheer, concentrated vitriol, he'd never heard anything like Clotilde Barford's guests.

His mistress didn't jump up and start screaming. Slowly, ever so slowly, she turned on Frederick. Soup soaked her hair. Half her curls had given up the ghost and lay dead, plastered against the side of her head. A green slice of scallion garnished her left eyebrow. Another sat on the end of her nose. Imperiously, she brushed that one away. She couldn't see the other, so it stayed.

She pointed at Frederick. He noted with abstract horror that the soup had made the dye in her almost-up-to-date fashionable gown run; blue streaked the pale flesh of her arm. "You God-damned *clumsy* son of a bitch!" she snapped: a statement of the obvious, perhaps, but most sincere.

"Mistress, I—" Frederick gave it up. Even if he hadn't had most of the wind knocked out of him, what could he possibly say?

The crash and the screams made slaves from the Barford estate and those gathered under the trees rush into the dining room to see what had happened. One of them laughed on a high, shrill note. It cut off abruptly, but not abruptly enough. Whoever that was, he'd catch it.

And so would Frederick. Veronique Barker fixed him with a deadly glare. "You'll pay for this," she said. She wasn't his mistress, which didn't make her wrong.

II

The morning after: one of the more noxious phrases in the English language. It must have seemed pretty noxious to Henry Barford. He'd come downstairs the afternoon before to view the catastrophe. Unless you were dead, you couldn't help coming to take a look at something like that. He hadn't been dead, but a wobble in his walk said he'd already been tight. He'd looked, shaken his head, and gone back to his bedroom. And he'd finished the serious business of getting drunk.

And now, on the morning after, he was suffering on account of it. His skin was the color and texture of old parchment. Red tracked the yellowish whites of his eyes the way railroads were starting to track the plains of Atlantis east of the Green Ridge Mountains (only a few reached across them; the southwest was the USA's forgotten quarter). His hands shook. His breath stank of stale rum and of the coffee he'd poured down to try to counter the stuff's effects. His uncombed hair stood up in several directions at once.

He looked at Frederick with a certain rough sympathy on his face. The Negro felt at least as bad as the white man. But what Frederick knew was fear for the future, not regret for the past.

"Well, son," Henry Barford rasped, "I am afraid you are fucked."

"I'm afraid so, too, Master Henry," Frederick agreed mournfully. He was a year or two older than the man who owned him, but that had nothing to do with the way they addressed each other. The brute fact of ownership made all the difference there.

"Matter of fact," Barford continued, "I am afraid you fucked yourself."

"Don't I know it!" Frederick said. "That God-damned floorboard! Take oath on a stack of Bibles piled to the ceiling, sir, I didn't know the end had come up."

"I believe you," Henry Barford said. "If I didn't believe you, you'd be dead by now—or more likely sold to a swamp-clearing outfit, so as I could get a little cash back on your miserable carcass, anyways."

Frederick gulped. Slaves in that kind of labor gang never lasted long. The men who ran the gangs bought them cheap, from owners who had good reason for not wanting them any more. They fed them little and worked them from dawn to dusk and beyond. If that didn't kill them off, the ague or yellow fever or a flux of the bowels likely would. And even if those failed, the swamps were full of crocodiles and poisonous snakes and other things nobody in his right mind wanted to meet.

Barford paused to light a cigar: a black, nasty cheroot that smelled almost as bad as his breath. He sighed smokily. "I believe you," he said again. "But no matter how come it happened, what matters is, it *did* happen. My wife, she's mighty mad at you—mighty God-damned mad."

Frederick hung his head. "I'm sorry, Master Henry. I'm sorrier'n I know how to tell you. I tried to apologize to Mistress Clotilde last night, but she didn't want to listen to me. Honest to God, it was an accident." He hated crawling. If he wanted to save his own skin, though, what choice did he have?

"One more time, Fred—I believe you," Barford said. "What I believe right now . . . don't matter one hell of a lot. Something like that happens when we're sitting down to dinner by our lonesomes, maybe you can say 'I'm sorry' and get away with it. Maybe. Shit goes wrong. I know that. Everybody knows that. When you go and ruin somethin'

Clotilde's had her heart set on for months, now, and when you make her look bad in front of all of her friends . . . And we ain't even talking about how much all the fancy dresses that got ruined cost, not yet we're not."

How close *had* he come to selling Frederick—and maybe Helen, too—for whatever he could get? (This was the first time in his life Frederick was halfway relieved none of their children had lived—they would have been sold, too.)

Gowns of silk and lace and endless labor didn't come cheap. Frederick knew that, all right. He remembered his mistress complaining about how expensive the dress she'd worn to the gathering—only one of the gowns Frederick had wrecked—was. All the money he'd saved . . . He didn't offer it. It not only wouldn't be enough, it would be so far from enough that the very offer would seem insulting.

Henry Barford blew out another ragged puff of smoke. "So I got to make you sorry for real," he said. "Won't be any peace in this house till I do. And you know you've got it coming. Can't hardly tell me you don't."

"Reckon I've got somethin' comin'," Frederick said cautiously, "but what do you mean, 'make me sorry for real'?"

"Well . . . " His master stretched out the word in a way he didn't like. "My wife and me, we spent some time last night talkin' about that." Most likely, Clotilde had spent the time talking and Henry listening. He stared at the coal on the end of the cigar, and at the thin column of smoke rising from it. *He doesn't want to tell me*, Frederick realized, and ice spidered up his back. At last, Barford spoke again: "What we decided was, we got to give you five lashes and send you out to the fields. Don't like to do it, Fred—wish like hell there was no need. Got to, though. Damned if I can see any way around it."

"Ohhh!" The air wheezed out of Frederick as if he'd been hit in the belly. He'd known they would have to punish him, but. . . . "Is that really fair, Master Henry? I didn't hurt anybody, and five lashes're sure gonna hurt *me*."

"Got to do it." Barford didn't sound happy about it. To give him his due, he didn't enjoy hurting his animate property, as some masters did. But he did sound very firm, and he explained why: "Isn't just on account of you mucked up Clotilde's fancy gathering. Those dresses you ruined . . . Only way I can keep some of those damned biddies from going to law with me for hundreds and hundreds of eagles is to show 'em I made you sorry. Clotilde wanted I should give you ten, but I managed to talk her down some."

"I'll—" Frederick bit down hard on what was about to come out of his mouth. *I'll run off* was the last thing a slave wanted to tell a master, especially when it was true.

Biting down hard didn't do him the least bit of good. "You'll do no such damnfool thing," Henry Barford said, as if Frederick had shouted the words in his face. As if to underline that, Barford drew a flintlock pistol from his belt. It was an over-and-under affair, with a bullet in the top barrel and a charge of buckshot in the lower one. Percussion revolvers could fire many more rounds, but at short range a piece like that one would kill a man quite nicely. "Now you come along with me. We'll stash you away till tomorrow mornin'. Don't do anything stupid, or I'll be out even more jack."

"What about me?" Frederick asked bitterly as he got to his feet.

"Hey, I wish you didn't do it," his master said. "But you did, so this is what you get. Step lively—but not too lively. You don't want to know how good a load of double-aught buck'll ventilate your carcass. Believe you me, you don't."

Frederick did believe him. A bullet as fat as a finger wouldn't do a body any good, either.

Tied to the whipping post. The plantation had one. Frederick couldn't imagine a plantation without one. But it didn't get used much. Yes, Henry Barford might have made a much crueler master. Which, of course, did Frederick not an eagle's worth of good, or even a cent's.

I should have tried to run away last night, he thought as the overseer stripped the shirt off his back and shackled his wrists to the post. But the slave cabin where they'd stuck him was fixed up to make it next to impossible—and it had been guarded, too.

House slaves and field hands watched the proceedings with wide eyes. Frederick didn't want to think about the expression on Helen's face. And he especially didn't want to think about the expression on Clotilde Barford's. He understood Helen's anguish. But the master's wife looked as if she was right on the point of reaching a climax. Would she, when the lash began to bite? Frederick feared he'd be too busy to notice.

After he'd been manacled, Henry Barford slipped a thick piece of leather into his mouth—cut from a belt, or maybe from a harness. "Bite down on that there," the master said. "It's supposed to help a little."

How do you know? Frederick wondered. He couldn't even ask, not unless he spat out the strong-tasting leather. He didn't. Instead, he settled it between his jaws as best he could. Anything to distract him from what was about to happen.

Barford stepped away. "Reckon all of you've heard why we got to do this," he said to the assembled slaves. "Doesn't make me happy. You know me. I like it when things go smooth. But when they don't, you got to set 'em to rights, and that's what we're gonna do here. You ready, Matthew?"

"Sure am," the overseer replied. He didn't sound pantingly eager, the way some men in his line of work would have. Instead, he was as matter-of-fact as if Barford had asked him if he were ready to shear a sheep. *Whip a nigger? All part of a day's work*, his voice seemed to say. That might have been more daunting than if he had seemed to look forward to it.

"All right, then," Barford said. "Five lashes, well laid on."

Frederick closed his eyes. *Well laid on.* Why say such stupid things? What else was Matthew going to do? Tap him with the whip? Frederick wished the overseer would, but what were wishes worth?

Snap-crack! Frederick jerked and groaned. That wasn't a lash, was it? It had to be fire across his back. Without the rude leather mouthguard, he might have broken teeth biting down. For some reason, he wasn't much inclined to be grateful to Henry Barford.

"One," the master said solemnly.

Snap-crack! Frederick had told himself he wouldn't

scream. So much for good intentions. The leather muffled his howl, but didn't block all of it.

"Two," Henry Barford intoned.

Snap-crack! More of the shriek escaped this time. Frederick wanted to die. And he wanted to kill everyone who'd had anything to do with this. Clotilde Barford, Henry Barford, Matthew . . . They could all perish. Horribly.

"Three."

Snap-crack! As these things went, Matthew was merciful. He didn't lay stripe on top of stripe, which would only have added to Frederick's torment. But these things didn't go very far in that direction. Frederick howled like a dog run over by a brewery wagon.

"Four," Henry Barford said.

Snap-crack! Shrieking louder than ever, Frederick hardly realized it was over. The flames consuming his back ate up the whole world. He slumped against the post, utterly exhausted. Tears and snot and sweat ran down his face. Something wet ran down his back, too. He barely cared if he was bleeding to death back there. If he was, everything would be over soon.

"Five," Barford said. "That's the end of it. Let him loose, Matthew, and help him to the cabin. I expect his woman'll take care of him from there."

"Right you are." Matthew was as businesslike unlocking the manacles as he had been fastening them or delivering the whipping. When Frederick spat out the piece of leather Henry Barford had given him, he didn't quite spit it at the overseer's feet. "You need to lean on me to walk?" Matthew asked him.

"Let me see." Frederick managed a couple of steps away from the post. The world swayed around him. Seeing him so shaky on his pins, Matthew grabbed his elbow with a strong right hand to steady him. *The hand that whipped me*, Frederick thought. He was glad for its support even so.

The overseer steered him toward one of the field hands' cabins—not the closest, but one that had stood empty since the old man who'd lived there gave up the ghost. "Show's over," Henry Barford told the rest of the slaves. "Get on back to work. It ain't like you got nothin' to do." Frederick heard him as if from very far away.

Three rickety wooden stairs. If not for Matthew's hand under his elbow, Frederick might not have made them. But he did. It was dark and musty inside the cabin. A couple of stools, a cot, and a chamber pot—that summed up the furnishings. "Lay down on your belly," the overseer said. "Your gal, she's got a pot of ointment to slather on you. You'll be ready to go out and weed in a couple of days."

Frederick wouldn't have lain down on his back for all the gold in Terranova. The straw and maize husks in the mattress rustled and crackled as his weight came down on them. The bed creaked. He wondered if it would break, but it held. The musty smell got stronger. Sharp things poked him through the worn-out mattress ticking. *So this is how field hands live*, he thought dully.

"I got to go keep an eye on things," the overseer said. "Soon as you're up and about, I'll be keepin' an eye on *you*."

He clumped across the floor and was gone. Softer footsteps came across the cabin toward Frederick. "You were brave," Helen said. "You stood it as good as anybody could have."

"I'll kill them all," Frederick whispered in a voice no one who wasn't right beside him could have heard. "Every last one of them. You see if I don't."

"'Course you will, sweetheart," Helen answered, as if he were a little boy. "Now you hold still while I put this stuff on you."

She dabbed it on with gentle fingers. It hurt anyway. Frederick jerked and twitched at every touch, almost as if he were under the lash again. "What's in it?" he asked, as if he thought it hurt him because of what it was made from.

"Lard and honey," Helen said. "Got it from one of the cooks. He said it'd soothe you—some, anyways—an' it'd make the stripes less likely to fester."

"Maybe," Frederick said through clenched teeth, meaning, *You must be joking*. Nothing could soothe his poor, abused flesh. Wishing he could drown the plantation in white men's blood came closest, but even that was no more than a momentary distraction. "How bad does it look?"

"How bad does it feel?" Helen countered one question with another.

"Couldn't feel any worse," Frederick said, which wasn't quite true. This ache was bad. The venomous sting of the lash striking him . . . that had been even worse.

"You're gonna have scars," Helen said sadly. She made haste to add, "Ain't like you'd be the only one. Plenty of slaves do."

"Scars . . . They'll pay for every damned one. So help me God, they will." Yes, rage was almost enough to vanquish pain. What would Victor Radcliff have thought if he could have seen his grandson's split and bleeding back? Would he have been proud of the United States of Atlantis?

"Hush," Helen told him. "Just you hush, now. Don't go talking crazy talk—don't go talking *stupid* talk. You land yourself in even more trouble than you're in already."

That was good, sensible advice. Good, sensible advice came easy when you hadn't just taken five lashes, well laid on. Frederick didn't want to listen to it. Whether he wanted to or not, some sank in. "Didn't only get me in trouble," he said dully. "Got you thrown out of the big house, too."

"I could go back. Mistress Clotilde ain't mad at me, 'cept 'cause I'm attached to you. Master Henry, he ain't hardly mad at me at all. Yeah, I could go back." Helen set a careful, gentle hand on Frederick's shoulder, well away from any of his welts. "Sooner stay 'longside of you, though."

Tears welled up in Frederick's eyes. Pain? Weakness? Fury? Love? All of them together, probably. Even so, he said, "You won't think that way when you got to start doing a field hand's work."

"It won't kill me," Helen answered, her voice calm. And she was likely right. A smart planter and a careful overseer didn't work field hands to death. What was the point of that? You couldn't get any more work out of them if they died, and you wouldn't be able to sell their corpses, either.

"God bless you," Frederick said.

"I love you."

"You must." Frederick didn't say what they both knew.

Work in the fields might not kill a slave, but it was harder than any job in the big house. And they wouldn't be eating pretty much what the Barfords ate any more. Maize meal, barley meal, molasses, bitter greens, every once in a while some smoked sowbelly or bacon . . .

It was enough to keep a body going. It wasn't much more than barely enough. Over the years, slaveowners had learned exactly how little they could get away with feeding their two-legged property. You heard about fat house slaves all the time. You even saw them every so often. But Frederick would have bet all the little he owned that nobody in the history of the United States of Atlantis had ever seen a fat field hand.

"Sooner or later, they'll call you back to the big house. When they do, I'll go, too," Helen said. "Me, I bet it's sooner. Ain't none of the damnfool niggers there can do for the Barfords like you do. They'll see. They can't help but see, once they get over bein' mad with you."

Frederick hoped she was right. But hoping wasn't the same as believing. What he believed was that Clotilde Barford wanted him dead. Five lashes weren't enough to make her happy. Ten lashes wouldn't have been, either. He'd humiliated her in front of all the ladies for ten, maybe twenty, miles around. They'd seen her sit there dripping, with a scallion on her eyebrow. After that, she probably figured even killing was too good for him. Maybe she'd enjoy watching him sweat and fumble in the fields till he finally wore out. He was sure she'd enjoy it more than recalling him to the big house.

"How's your back?" Helen asked.

Worrying about Mistress Clotilde had almost let him forget his pain for a few seconds. Almost—but not quite. "Hurts," he said.

"Well, I reckon. You don't care to know what it looks like—best believe you don't," Helen said. "Want I should put on more ointment?"

"Let it go for now," he answered. The less she touched it, the less he would be reminded of it. "Maybe I can sleep."

If he could sleep, he wouldn't feel a thing . . . unless he started to roll over onto his back. Try as he would, though,

he couldn't make his eyes stay closed. He hurt too much
for that.

An undyed, unbleached cotton shirt, loose enough so it
wouldn't cling to the wounds on his back. An undyed pair
of trousers of wool homespun. Thick wool socks, undoubt-
edly knitted by one of the slave women on the plantation.
Stout shoes that were more than a little too big. A ratty
straw hat. Put it all together, and it was the outfit a field
hand wore. Matthew the overseer delivered it to Frederick,
and its feminine equivalent to Helen.

"Here you go," he said. "Can't weed, can't pick cotton
when the time comes, not in your boiled shirt and monkey
suit. Tomorrow, you'll be out there with everybody else."

"Don't reckon I can keep up too good," Frederick said.
"I'm sore, and I'm stiff like you wouldn't believe."

"Oh, yes, I would. I know what a whipping does," the
overseer said. "I'll cut you some slack at first—for the
whipping, and on account of you don't know what you're
doing and you got soft hands like a girl's. But that's only at
first, mind. You don't want me to get the notion that you're
a lazy nigger. Believe you me, boy, you don't. Understand?"

Boy? Frederick was at least fifteen years older than
Matthew. But slavery succeeded not least by denying that
Negroes and copperskins could ever be men. Unlike his
grandfather, Frederick would never be *Mister*. When his
hair went from gray to white, he would go straight from
boy to *Uncle*.

He still had to answer. "I'm not lazy, sir," he said, showing
none of the useless, hopeless rage that stewed inside him.
Matthew might get his goat, but the overseer would never
realize it. Frederick went on, "If you don't believe me, you
can ask Master Henry."

The overseer's eyes were gray and chilly: chillier than
the weather in these parts ever got. "Master Henry can afford to be soft," Matthew said. "He's the owner, and he can
do what he pleases. Me, I'm just the overseer, so I got to
be rough. And I'm the fella you're dealin' with from here
on out. Not Master Henry, not no more. Me. Have you got
that, boy?"

"Oh, yes, sir," Frederick said at once. "I understand you real good. I'll do everything I can for you." *Till I find out how much I can get away with not doing, anyhow.*

"You better." Matthew nodded to himself. "Yes, sir, you better. 'Cause I got me all kinds of ways to make you sorry if you don't." He said not a word about Helen or about any of the unfortunate things that might happen to her if Frederick left him dissatisfied. He just walked out of the little slave cabin. Like any effective tyrant, he knew the people under his control could form pictures in their own minds far more fearsome than any he could paint for them.

Frederick looked down at his palms. They were paler than the rest of his skin, as any Negro's were: closer to the color his grandfather had been all over. Closer to the color Matthew was all over, too, but Frederick didn't think about that. He had some calluses on those palms—he didn't sit around the big house doing nothing. But his hands weren't as leathery as that chunk of tanned cowhide he'd bitten down on during the whipping. Field hands who used shovels and hoes and rakes year in and year out got palms on which they could stub out a cheroot without even feeling it.

Well, maybe you'll get palms like that, too, Frederick thought gloomily. What he would get beforehand was a bumper crop of blisters. He hoped Helen had some more of the ointment she'd used on his back. His hands would need it, too. And so would hers.

Slowly, almost of their own accord, his hands folded into fists. He made them uncoil. Even here, inside the cabin, such a gesture of defiance could be dangerous. If anyone walking by saw him and told the overseer or Master Henry . . . No, Frederick didn't want that to happen.

"But if I ever get the chance to hit back—" He broke that off short, too, even though he hadn't said it very loud. He'd already told Helen what he'd like to do, and spoken defiance was reckoned worse than a gesture. A slave who talked defiantly could also plot defiantly. The whites feared plots above all else.

Because they feared them, they ruthlessly stamped out every one they found. And, because they were so ruthless, they spawned more plots. Maybe they didn't realize that.

Maybe they did, and accepted it as part of the cost of doing business the way they wanted to. Frederick had hardly been in a position to ask.

"If I ever get me the chance—" He broke it off even shorter this time. But the thought stuck in his mind as a burr might have stuck to his trousers. And, once stuck, it would not be dislodged.

The morning horn sounded like a dying donkey. Up till now, Frederick had always heard it from the house: from a safe distance, in other words. It hadn't had anything to do with him. He'd pitied the poor, sorry field hands who had to get up and go to work under the hot sun—or, sometimes, in the pouring rain.

Never send to know for whom the bell tolls; it tolls for thee. Fancy talk, but fancy talk with a point sharp as a carving knife's. Now that horrible horn brayed for Frederick, and for Helen.

"We got to get up," she said.

"I don't want to," he mumbled. Now that his back was finally letting him sleep, he wanted to make up for all the time he'd spent awake because he'd hurt too much to shut down.

"We got to get up," Helen repeated. "You want Matthew to reckon you're a lazy nigger after all?"

Frederick groaned. He groaned again when he sat up on the edge of the miserable cot. His stripes were better than they had been when he first got them, but they were still plenty sore. He didn't want to put on the shirt Matthew had given him. But what he wanted counted for nothing in the plantation's scheme of things.

Helen wore a wool skirt, a cotton blouse, and a red bandanna on her head. Her shoes were every bit as formidable as Frederick's. All things considered, they were well off. Frederick knew of plenty of plantations where the field hands wore rags and got no shoes at all. That might have made his outfit, and Helen's, a trifle better. It didn't come close to making them good.

They ate cornmeal mush and drank coffee that Helen hastily made. Then they went outside. All the cabins were rapidly emptying. Whoever came out last got in trouble. Frederick had heard that a hundred times. Up till now, it had never mattered to him. It did today. He didn't want the overseer screaming at him, not when he was sore and slow and didn't know what he was doing.

Copperskins and Negroes—men and women—lined up in loose ranks. Seeing their ragged formation, an Atlantean drill sergeant would have wanted to kill them all, or possibly himself. But Matthew didn't complain about that. Slaves weren't supposed to look or act military. If they thought they could fight, that would make them more dangerous to their owners.

A copperskinned couple were the last to try to sneak into the formation. Their furtiveness had a plaintive air to it, as if they knew they'd get caught. And get caught they did. The overseer put his hands on his hips and looked disgusted. "So it's Ed and Wilma this morning, is it? And you're mudfaces! Not even niggers! You sure act as lazy as if you were."

The copperskins hung their heads. Frederick muttered to himself. If the last slaves out had been Negroes, chances were Matthew would have called them savages and asked them if they'd spent the time in their cabin putting on war paint. Something like that, anyhow. Whites played blacks and copperskins off against each other whenever they could. If you didn't trust the slave working next to you, you were less likely to plan together and rise up, more likely to betray each other before your plot ripened into revolt.

"Well, you're here at last." Matthew still sounded as if he hated every last one of them. Frederick wouldn't have been surprised if he did. Overseers might have godlike powers over slaves, but they weren't much in the white man's world. Planters were what mattered there. What woman from a good family would want to marry an overseer? Had Matthew owned slaves of his own ... But he didn't, and he wasn't likely to. He pointed towards a shed. "Come on, God damn the lot of you. Grab your tools and get to work."

With rakes and spades and hoes over their shoulder, they looked something like an army as they trudged out to the cotton fields. Again, though, a drill sergeant would have contemplated murder or suicide. No one tried to stay in step with his neighbors or to hurry. If the slaves had moved any slower, Matthew would have shouted at them—or else whacked them with the long, firm switch he carried in his right hand.

They knew, all of them but Frederick and Helen, how much they could get away with. The two new field hands had to pick it up by watching and listening. One of the first things Frederick noticed was how heavy and clumsy his hoe was. All the tools were like that. Even so, Henry Barford complained about how often they got broken. Frederick hadn't understood that before. He suddenly did. Why should a slave care how he handled tools that belonged to his master? Making those tools extra sturdy helped, but only so much.

The overseer pointed Frederick down a row of cotton plants. "You make God-damned sure you get rid of the weeds, hear?" he said. "But don't you dare hurt the plants any. I'm gonna keep my eye on you, see how you make out."

"Reckoned you would," Frederick said. He bent and assassinated something small and green pushing up through the dirt near the closest cotton plant. His breath hissed out of him as if he were a snake. Moving hurt like blazes. And the heavy iron head on the hoe made it clumsy to swing.

Other slaves advanced up rows to either side of him. To his amazement, he had no trouble keeping up. They weren't getting over a whipping. Why couldn't they move faster? Again, the question was no sooner asked than answered. Why should they? It wasn't as if they'd get anything for themselves if they did more work.

When Matthew was shouting down at the far end of the slave gang, the Negro in the row to Frederick's left paused for a moment and told him, "You don't got to stay even with us, man. He see you workin' like that after a whippin', what's he gonna want from you when you're all right again? 'Sides, he see you workin' like that, what's he gonna want from the rest of us?"

Frederick duly slowed down. If a few weeds got missed, well, how much would that matter in the grand scheme of things? Not enough to get excited about.

He might have slowed down, but he couldn't stop. *Thwock!* Matthew's switch came down on a copperskin's back. "Damn your miserable, shriveled-up honker turd of a soul to hell and gone, Bill, but you got to do *somethin'*!" the overseer shouted. "You stand there with your thumb corkin' your asshole, you reckon I ain't gonna notice?"

Bill didn't say anything. All the same, Frederick wouldn't have wanted any man looking at *him* like that. If Matthew noticed, he affected not to. In his own way, he had nerve. Slowly, the copperskin got back to work.

Sweat ran down Frederick's face. It also ran from the backs of his hands to his palms, and stung the blisters that had swollen and burst there. And it stung the lash tracks on his back; his shirt didn't soak it all up. His shoulders and arms started to ache from the continued unfamiliar motion of swinging the hoe.

A copperskinned boy who couldn't have been more than nine came by with a jug, a tin dipper, and a cup shaped from the dried skin of a gourd. "Want something to drink?" he asked Frederick.

"Lord, do I ever!" the Negro exclaimed.

The boy filled the cup with the dipper. How many other mouths had drunk from that gourd? When was the last time anyone washed it? Frederick wondered about such things . . . afterwards. In the moment, he cared about nothing but the lukewarm water sliding sweetly down his throat. He didn't want to hand back the cup; he thought he could have emptied the jug. But the half-grown copperskin had other people to water. He wouldn't want to go back to the well and fill up the jug again too soon. Reluctantly, Frederick returned the gourd.

"Water?" the boy asked the slave in the next row, the one who'd warned Frederick not to push too hard. The slave made a production out of pausing to drink. Not even Matthew could possibly doubt that he deserved his moment of rest. So his manner proclaimed, anyhow. Frederick had the feeling the overseer could doubt anything he set his mind to doubting. If you were going to be an overseer, doubting was a talent you needed to cultivate.

A couple of pregnant women carried food out to the

work gang when the sun stood at the zenith. The rolls were made from barley, which wouldn't rise like wheat. They were dense and chewy. Frederick didn't mind too much. He thought he was getting more food this way. He hadn't realized how hungry he was till he ate—and discovered that what he was getting wasn't enough to do more than take the edge off his appetite.

Watching the way things worked, he noted the plantation's efficiency. The women with the bulging bellies couldn't weed, but they could fetch and carry. The boy who brought the water jug around again was still too small to swing one of these heavy hoes. That didn't make him too small to work, and work he did.

Had the overseer set up this system? Frederick had known about it before, of course, but he hadn't *known* about it. As a house slave, he hadn't been caught up in it like a grain of wheat between millstones. Had Henry Barford worked it out, or his father before him? Or was it part of the lore all slaveholders knew, the lore they'd put together over hundreds of years? Frederick couldn't have said for sure, but it looked that way to him.

On a harsher plantation, the midday meal might have been smaller, or there might have been none. The break might have been shorter. Henry Barford wasn't cruel for the sake of being cruel, and neither was his overseer. They were cruel simply because you couldn't be anything else, not if you intended to own slaves and to get work out of them.

A handful of free Negroes and copperskins had slaves of their own. From everything Frederick had ever heard, they made sterner masters than most whites. They had to—their animate property was less inclined to take orders from people of their color. They had to use colored overseers, too. That lowered the respect their slaves had for the overseers. But what other choice did such owners have? No white overseer would lower himself to working for someone he thought he should be bossing around. And so ...

"Come on, people!" Matthew shouted. "You done wasted enough time! Get to work, and put your backs into it for a change!"

Whatever Frederick's thought had been, it flickered and blew out like a candle flame in the wind. His joints creaked as he started hoeing again. He wasn't used to this kind of work—no indeed. He didn't know whether he dreaded getting used to it or not getting used to it more.

Was this all he had to look forward to for the rest of his days? A hoe and a row? A shovel? A big sack at harvest time? If it was, wouldn't he be better off dead?

III

*W*hen the horn's bray woke Frederick for his second day as a field hand, he didn't feel a day over ninety-seven. Every part of him ached or stung. Quite a few parts ached *and* stung. As he had the afternoon before, he got about a third of the way toward wishing he were dead.

He'd fallen asleep right after supper. He'd come *that* close to falling asleep in the middle of supper, with his mouth hanging open to show off the cornmeal mush or the chunk of fat sowbelly he'd been chewing when his mainspring ran down. Somehow, he'd kept his eyes open till he and Helen got back to the cabin. But he didn't remember a thing after the two of them lay down.

Beside him, Helen groaned as she sat up. She rubbed her eyes. She had to be as weary as he was. The first words out of her mouth, though, were, "How's your back?"

"Sore," he answered. "Better than it was. Not as good as it's gonna be—or I sure hope not, anyways." He made himself remember he wasn't the only one with troubles. "How *you* doin', sweetheart?"

"Well, I thought I worked hard back in the big house." She shook her head at her own foolishness. "Only goes to show what I knew, don't it?"

She didn't call him twelve different kinds of stupid, clumsy jackass for costing both of them the soft places they'd enjoyed. Why she didn't, Frederick had no idea. If it wasn't because of something very much like love, he couldn't imagine what it would be.

The horn blared out again. This time, Matthew's warning shout followed: "Last one out's gonna catch it!"

Frederick had taken off only his hat and his shoes. Putting the straw hat back on was a matter of a moment. Shoes were a different story. His fingers were stiff and crooked, his hands sore. He had a devil of a time tying the laces.

Then he had to help Helen. Her palms looked even worse than his. "Should've put your ointment on 'em," he scolded.

"I was savin' it for you."

"Well, don't, confound it," he told her. He also kissed her on the cheek, not least because he knew she wouldn't listen to him. Yes, that was love, all right, even if the words the colored preacher'd said over them didn't mean a thing in the rarefied air the Barfords breathed.

They weren't the last ones out. The overseer unbent enough to nod to them as they took their places with the field hands. *With the* other *field hands*—Frederick corrected himself. "Ready for another go?" Matthew asked.

"I'm ready," Frederick said shortly. He resolved to die before admitting to the white man that he was anything less.

"Well, all right." Matthew was taciturn, too. But he could have been much nastier. Maybe he was wondering if Frederick and Helen would go back to the big house before too long. If they did, they would be personages even an overseer had to reckon with. Was he hedging his bets now? Frederick could hope so. That might make life a little easier. And even a little seemed like a lot.

When a Negro couple didn't come out, Matthew went into their cabin after them. The shouting and screeching and carrying on made everybody in the labor gang smile. "I slep' through the blame horn!" the male slave in the cabin wailed.

"You'll sleep in the swamp with a rock tied to your ankle if you don't get moving, you stupid toad!" the overseer said. In less time than it took to tell, both the slave and his woman were out there. If some of her buttons were still undone, if he had to bend down to tie his shoes, Matthew wasn't fussy about such things. They were there. Nothing else mattered.

Frederick wolfed down his breakfast. He wished he could have got twice as much. He wouldn't starve on a field hand's rations. But he would wish—he would always wish—he could get more.

Mosquitoes buzzed around him as he ate. They were worse in the close little cabin at night. So the raised, itchy places on his arms and ankles and the back of his neck insisted, though he didn't remember getting bitten. They were worse, then, yes, but they never went away. He wondered if he could get some mesh or screening for the windows. Or would Matthew think something like that was too good for field hands? Slapping at a bug that landed on his wrist, Frederick thought, *I can find out.*

The overseer glanced at the ascending sun. With a theatrical shake of the head, he shouted at the slaves: "Eat up! You ain't porkers! Master Henry ain't fattening you up. You got work to do."

A Negro pointed to the path that led from the big house to the road to New Marseille. "What's goin' on there?" he said.

"Don't waste my time with your silly games, Lou," Matthew snapped. "You—" He broke off. Lou wasn't playing games, not this morning.

"Dog my cats if them ain't soldiers," another Negro said.

"Cavalry," a copperskin named Lorenzo—a power among the field hands, as Frederick had already seen—added with precision.

It wasn't just that the men were on horseback. Infantry could mount horses when they needed to get from here to there in a hurry. But the soldiers' gray uniforms had yellow piping and chevrons, not the blue foot soldiers would have used. The troopers escorted two supply wagons: smaller versions of the prairie frigates settlers in Terranova used to cross the broad plains there. The copperskins who lived on those plains didn't care for that, but when a folk that had to buy or steal firearms and ammunition bumped up against one that could make such things, the end of the struggle was obvious even if it hadn't arrived yet.

Matthew watched the wagons and their escort come up the path. Absently slapping at a mosquito, he said, "Never seen the like in all my born days. I wonder what the devil they want."

Frederick had never seen the like, either, and he'd lived on the plantation much longer than the overseer. Were he still back at the big house, he would have come out onto the front porch and asked the soldiers what the devil they wanted—though he would have been more polite about it than that. As a field hand with stripes on his back, all he could do was stand there and watch.

Henry Barford came out himself. He was barefoot and wore homespun wool trousers not much better than his slaves', though his linen shirt was white. He hadn't combed his hair; as usual when he hadn't, it went every which way. He looked like a drunken stumblebum. But the unconscious arrogance with which he bore himself declared him the planter here.

"What in tarnation are you doing on my land?" he shouted to the incoming cavalrymen.

Their leader wore two small silver stars on either side of his stand collar: a first lieutenant's rank badges. He gave Barford a crisp salute. "Sorry to trouble you, sir, but we're bound for New Marseille with a cargo of rifle muskets and ammunition." He waved at the wagons behind him. "Much as I hate to say it, three of my men are down with what looks like the yellow jack."

A low murmur ran through the slaves. The morning sun was already hot, but Frederick shivered all the same. He wouldn't have wanted to take men with yellow fever into New Marseille. What would they do to an officer who let a plague like that get loose in a city? Frederick wouldn't have wanted to find out, and evidently the lieutenant didn't, either.

None of which appeased Henry Barford, not even a little bit. He jumped straight up in the air, as if a scorpion had stung him on the ankle. He let out a wordless howl of fury as if he'd been stung, too. Then he did find words: "You mangy son of a bitch! Take your stinking sick soldiers and get the hell off my property! How *dare* you bring the yellow jack here?"

"My apologies, sir, but I can't do that," the officer said stolidly. "The men need bed rest, and we happened to see your place here. Yellow fever doesn't kill everyone who comes down with it—not even close. And I assure you that you will be generously compensated for your time and trouble."

"How can you compensate me when I'm dead and buried—if anybody'd have the nerve to plant me?" Barford said. "Go on, get lost, or I'll grab my shotgun and blow some sense into you!"

The lieutenant nodded to his healthy troopers. In the twinkling of an eye, they all aimed eight-shooters at Henry Barford's head and midsection. "Meaning no disrespect, sir, but don't talk silly talk," the officer said. "We're here, and we're going to stay until my men recover."

"Or until you put *them* six feet under," Barford said. But he made no sudden moves and kept his hands in plain sight. Frederick hadn't thought anyone could make a mistake worse than his in the dining room. If Master Henry made one now, though, he'd never make another. He glumly eyed the revolvers. "Don't look like I can stop you."

"No. It doesn't," the lieutenant agreed. His voice turned brisk. "Now . . . You won't want me to quarter Jenkins and Merridale and Casey in the main residence, will you?"

"In the big house? I hope to spit, I won't!" Maybe Barford said *spit*. "What you ought to do is put 'em in tents way the devil away from anybody."

"No," the lieutenant said in a hard, flat voice. "They're good men. They deserve the best we can give them. I suppose your slave quarters will have to do."

"If my niggers and mudfaces come down sick, I'll take compensation out of your hide," Barford said.

"I understand, sir," the lieutenant said. Of course, if the slaves came down sick, he was liable to do the same thing himself. If he did, he'd be in no condition to compensate Henry Barford.

Barford was also liable to come down sick. The officer didn't say anything more about that. Neither did the planter.

"Matthew!" Barford bawled.

"Yes, Mr. Barford?" the overseer said.

"Put up the sick soldiers in one of the cabins. Make sure they've got themselves a wench to take care of 'em. We'll do the best job we can, but you know as well as I do they're in God's hands now." Barford might be talking to his overseer, but he also aimed his words at the lieutenant. *If your men die, it won't be my fault*, he meant.

"I'll see to it." Matthew turned to the cavalry officer. "Can your men tote 'em into the cabin? They've already been around 'em."

"I'd thought it would be slave work, but.... " The lieutenant nodded grudgingly. "Yes, that does seem reasonable. Let it be as you say." He barked orders at his men. They obeyed more readily—certainly more quickly—than slaves obeyed an overseer. And they were all white men, too! Oh, one of them was swarthy and had a Spanish-sounding name, but he remained on the good side of Atlantis' great social divide.

The sick cavalrymen weren't quite so yellow as the trim on their uniforms, but they weren't far from it. The soldiers who carried them from the wagons to the slave cabins didn't look happy about their work. Frederick wouldn't have been, either. Nobody knew how the yellow jack spread. Come to that, nobody knew how any disease except the pox and the clap spread. Handling someone who already had the sickness seemed as likely a way as any, and more likely than most. The copperskinned woman Matthew chose to care for them wasn't thrilled about the honor, either.

"*Somebody's* got to do it," the overseer said. "Why *not* you, Abigail?"

Abigail had no answer for that. In her place, Frederick didn't suppose he would have himself. He would have looked everywhere he could to find one, though. He was sure of that.

Matthew faced the rest of the slaves. "Well, come on," he said. "Get your tools and head on out to the fields. Or do you *want* to hang around here with the sick soldiers?"

They headed out. The pace left stiff, sore Frederick struggling to keep up. It also left the overseer goggling. Had he ever seen slaves move so fast? Had anybody, since the beginning of the world? If the other choice was sticking close to people down with the yellow jack, even weeding a cotton field under the blazing subtropical sun didn't seem bad at all.

Dragging back as the sun went down, Frederick wearily shook his head. Going out to weed under the subtropical sun might not have seemed so bad. Doing it all day, even at the slowest pace the overseer would let people get away with, was something else again. If it wasn't hell on earth, he didn't know what would be.

The yellow jack, maybe?

One of the troopers died two days later. A copperskin and a Negro dug a grave for him in the plot back of the cabins where they buried their own. Frederick and Helen had lain two small bodies to rest there. The lieutenant—his name was Peter Torrance—borrowed a Bible from Henry Barford and read the Twenty-third Psalm over the man's body. The Barfords and their slaves and the cavalrymen all stood around the grave together, listening to the somberly inspiring words and now and then brushing and slapping at buzzing bugs.

"Wish we could go on to New Marseille," a soldier grumbled after the service broke up.

"Well, we damned well can't," a sergeant answered; angry puffs of smoke rose from his pipe. "We've got to stay put till we're good and sure we ain't gonna make the whole damned town sick."

"Don't want to get sick myself, neither," the soldier said.

"You run off, they'll call it desertion and hang you," the sergeant said. "You ain't like the slaves here—your carcass isn't worth an atlantean while you're still alive." The inflated paper money of the war against England lived on in memory.

"I'm not going anywhere," the soldier assured him.

"God-damned right you're not." The sergeant sounded very sure of himself.

But it was the sergeant who fell sick the next day—and the copperskin who'd dug the dead trooper's grave came down with the yellow jack the day after that. The copperskin rapidly got worse. His kind sickened more readily than whites, who seemed to sicken more readily than Negroes. A copperskin with smallpox was almost sure to die, where a man of some other breed might pull through.

Henry Barford was incensed, as Frederick had known he would be. "You *are* a son of a bitch!" he shouted at Lieutenant Torrance.

Torrance seemed more distracted than offended. "Sorry, Mr. Barford," he managed at last.

That didn't come close to placating the planter. "Sorry? I don't think so!" Barford said. "I'm going to write to my Senator—that's what I'm going to do."

The Atlantean officer looked through him. "Mr. Barford, you may write to the Pope for all I care, and much good may it do you. My back hurts, and so does my head. If I have not got a fever, I should be very much surprised."

Henry Barford stared at him in undisguised horror. "Lord love a duck! You're coming down with it, too!" He edged away from the lieutenant.

If that offended Torrance, he hid it very well: or, more likely, he had other things to worry about. "I fear I am. I hope I am not, but I fear I am." He muttered to himself, then spoke aloud again: "I wish we could have got these rifle muskets to New Marseille. Before long, the garrison there will commence to wondering what has become of them."

Frederick heard that—the two white men were talking outside the big house after the work gang came in for the day. Frederick was healing, and was also beginning to get used to the work. He wasn't collapsing the minute he'd had supper, the way he did the night after his first day in the cotton fields. What Torrance and Barford said didn't fully register, not at the moment, but he took it in so it could spend the time it needed in ripening.

"You could send somebody to let 'em know," Barford said. "Not that far to town—even closer to the nearest place where you could send a telegram." Wires were beginning to crisscross Atlantis. The telegraph was new in the past ten years, so the process wasn't complete yet. But it seemed to pick up speed year by year, because the device was so obviously useful.

Lieutenant Torrance shook his head. "I stopped here to keep from spreading the sickness any farther."

"Oh, and a hell of a job you did, too, my boy!" Barford exclaimed.

As if on cue, his wife's voice floated down from their bedroom. "Henry! Are you out there, Henry?"

"Sure am," he answered. "What's going on?"

"I don't feel well, Henry." By the way Clotilde Barford said it, it could only be her husband's fault.

But that wasn't quite true, was it? It could also be Lieutenant Peter Torrance's fault. If he'd picked a different plantation . . . How much difference would it have made? Maybe not much—when yellow fever spread, it could spread like wildfire. But maybe it wouldn't have come here at all. You never could tell. And if that wasn't enough to drive you crazy, nothing ever would.

Henry Barford absently slapped at a mosquito, then wiped the palm of his hand on his trouser leg. "Don't feel good how?" he asked.

"I've got a headache. My back hurts, too. And I'm warm—I swear I'm warm," Clotilde said. She didn't give her symptoms in the same order as Lieutenant Torrance had, which didn't mean they didn't match.

Frederick realized that right away. Barford took a few seconds longer, and then delivered a double take worthy of the stage. "Oh, you *son* of a bitch!" he snarled at the Atlantean lieutenant. He rushed back into the big house.

Torrance just stood there. He swayed slightly—he looked as if a strong breeze, or even a breeze that wasn't so strong, would blow him away. He caught Frederick's eye. "You. Come here."

"What you need, sir?" Frederick asked as he walked over. He didn't—he couldn't—move very fast.

Chance were it didn't matter. The lieutenant looked through him, too. "I *didn't* mean to bring the sickness here," he said after a long, long pause.

"Who would mean to do something like that, sir?" Frederick said, which seemed safe enough.

The answer seemed to focus the lieutenant's attention on him. Frederick wasn't nearly sure he wanted it. "What's your name?" Torrance asked.

"Frederick," the Negro answered automatically. But, a heartbeat later, something made him add, "Frederick Radcliff."

Most white men would have laughed at him for his pretensions. At a different time or place, in different circumstances, Lieutenant Torrance might well have laughed, too. Now he gave Frederick his full attention. "I can see why you say so," Torrance observed. "You have something of the look of one of the First Consuls to you."

"He was my grandfather," Frederick said.

"Easy enough to claim," the officer answered. But he held up a hand before Frederick could get angry. "It could be so—I already told you you have the look."

"Victor Radcliff's grandson, a field nigger." Frederick didn't bother hiding his bitterness.

"I can't do anything about it," Lieutenant Torrance said. "I can't do anything about anything. If I am alive a week from now, I shall get down on my knees and thank almighty God. If you are alive a week from now . . . " He ran down like a watch that wanted winding.

"What?" Frederick asked.

The lieutenant pressed his palm against his own forehead. Frederick had always found you had a hard time telling whether you had a fever that way, because when you did your palm was also warmer than it should have been. But Torrance's grimace said he didn't like what his own flesh told him. "I am from Croydon," he said, out of the blue—or so it seemed to Frederick.

"Yes?" the Negro said, wondering if Peter Torrance's wits were starting to wander.

"No slaves in Croydon," the lieutenant said, so he had been going somewhere after all. "We don't put up with that kind of thing up there. We haven't, not for a man's lifetime and longer. Doesn't always stop our traders from making money off of what slaves do, but we don't keep 'em ourselves. Some folks think that makes us better. But I'll tell you something, Frederick Radcliff."

"What's that?"

"If folks don't want you to be free, you can still take care of the job. Look what your grandfather did against England."

He made it sound easy. Maybe he thought it would be. Or maybe his wits *were* wandering but he didn't realize it yet. Running off was deadly dangerous and much too likely to fail. Rising up . . . Frederick's mind shied like a frightened horse at the mere idea. Even if slaves did rise up from time to time, they had never yet failed to regret it. And the reprisals vengeful whites took were designed to make the survivors think three times before trying that kind of thing again.

Lieutenant Torrance shrugged. "If you are your grandfather's grandson, you'll find some way to be worthy of his name. And if you aren't . . . " He let that hang, too. After touching one finger to the brim of his black plug hat, he walked back to the tent he'd run up. He wasn't steady on his legs, and it wasn't because he'd had too much to drink.

"What did the white man want?" Helen asked when Frederick came back to her.

"Don't quite know," he answered. "Tell you somethin', though—don't reckon I ever talked with anybody like him before."

"Is that good or bad?"

"Don't quite know," Frederick repeated. He wished he could spend more time ciphering it out. An enormous yawn soon put paid to that notion. He wasn't so exhausted as he had been that first dreadful night, and his stripes didn't pain him so much. But they did still hurt, and he was still weary.

He and Helen headed back to their cabin. He woke up in the night needing to use the chamber pot. As he lay back down, several itchy new mosquito bites reminded him again that he hadn't screened the window. They kept him awake a little while. That was one more mark of progress; the first night, he hadn't even noticed he was getting eaten alive.

*   *   *

No one blew the horn the next morning, not till the sun stood higher in the sky than it should have. And when the horn did sound . . . It always reminded Frederick more of an animal's bellow than of a product of human ingenuity, but this morning it reminded him of an animal in pain.

He soon found out why: Matthew was blowing the horn, and he had no more idea how to do it than Frederick knew how to paint portraits. "What happened to Jonas?" Frederick asked. Several other slaves said the same thing as they came out of their cabins.

"Down sick," Matthew answered economically. He looked toward the newly sprouted tents. "Those miserable, stupid soldiers . . . " Then he sighed, shifted the chaw in his cheek, and spat a brown stream of pipeweed juice. "They're paying for it. But so are we. Mistress Clotilde . . . "

There was no sign of Master Henry, either. Frederick supposed he was tending to his wife. But he might have come down with the yellow jack himself. And Lieutenant Torrance didn't come out of his tent. Only a couple of soldiers did emerge. They cared for the horses with the air of the stunned who'd lived through an annihilating battle.

Worse, there was no guarantee yet that they *had* lived through things, and they were bound to know it.

They went through the day without anyone falling over in the fields. To Frederick, that seemed something worth celebrating. And he might have celebrated if he weren't so stiff and sore and tired, and if he thought the overseer would let him get away with it.

Later, he realized Matthew might have. The white man also seemed delighted to have got through a day's work with no new catastrophes. "Wonder what things'll be like when we get back to the big house," he muttered as the gang shouldered tools and started back for supper.

Things were . . . not so good. Soldiers and house slaves had dug a grave for another of the troopers who'd been sick when the cavalry detachment arrived at the plantation. Had Lieutenant Torrance read the Bible over this dead man, too? Frederick had his doubts. The lieutenant was likely to be too sick to get off his cot or blanket or whatever he was lying on.

Henry Barford came out to watch the slaves return. He hadn't combed his hair or shaved. Frederick thought he had done some drinking, or more than some. "Clotilde's mighty poorly," he announced from the front porch. "Mighty poorly."

Frederick didn't know whether to be sorry or not. He'd spent a lot of years with the Barfords. Most of the time, he'd got along well enough with the mistress of the plantation. But she was the one who'd had him whipped and degraded. She was the one who'd wanted to give him more lashes than he'd got. Why should he sympathize with her now?

Because anything that can happen can happen to you, he answered himself. *Because you could be moaning in a sickbed just like her a day from now. Or, God forbid, so could Helen.*

He ate more supper than usual—not better, but more. Quantity had a quality of its own. No one had thought to tell the cooks to make any less than they would have without sickness tearing through the plantation. They hadn't made any changes on their own. If you waited for slaves to show initiative, you'd spend a long time waiting. So the same amount of food was shared among fewer people. Frederick's belly appreciated the difference.

Another cavalry trooper came down sick not long after supper. The men still on their feet had all kinds of worries. "We got enough men to post a guard on the wagons?" one of them asked.

"Hell with the wagons. Hell with everything in 'em," another soldier replied. "Any of us still gonna be on our feet by the time this God-damned plague gets done with us?"

The first soldier didn't say anything to that. Frederick wouldn't have, either. It was much too good a question.

He glanced over toward the wagons. Sure enough, there they sat—they wouldn't go on to New Marseille any time soon. But so what? The United States of Atlantis were at peace with the world. For the most part, they'd stayed at peace since the war that set them free. No invader was likely to descend on them now. What would the rifle muskets do but gather dust in some armory?

Frederick had been a boy when Atlantis got into a brief second scrape with England. Redcoats had suppressed the Terranovan risings that accompanied Atlantis' revolt against the mother country. The Terranovan settlements rebelled again a generation later when England was distracted by the great war she fought against France. Atlantis covertly aided the Terranovans—but not covertly enough. And so England declared war on her former possession.

Atlantean frigates won their share of glory in what people these days called the War of 1809. But England had the greatest navy the world had ever known, a navy that spanned the seven seas. Despite her endless troubles with France, English ships bombarded Freetown and Pomphret Landing, and English marines burnt the latter town to the ground and slaughtered everyone who didn't run away fast enough. Another force landed south of Avalon, but word of an armistice reached them just as they were about to engage the garrison there. Atlanteans these days sang songs about the Battle That Never Was.

No, New Marseille had no urgent need of those rifle muskets. Frederick had trouble seeing why the soldiers even bothered mounting guard over them.

Were he still a house slave, he probably would have gone on having trouble seeing why. As a field hand—as a field hand with the marks of the overseer's lash still no better than half healed on his back—he suddenly understood. They didn't want the weapons to fall into slaves' hands.

And he understood why, too. Slaves with fancy new rifle muskets could rise against the whites who put stripes on their backs, who lay down with their women whenever they pleased, and who could sell them like so many sacks of beans. No slave rising yet had succeeded. But the chance was always there.

"You awake?" he whispered to Helen when they lay down in the muggy little cabin that night.

"Not me," she answered. "I done went to sleep an hour ago."

Frederick laughed softly. "I been thinkin'," he said.

"You should've gone to sleep an hour ago, too," Helen said, and he couldn't very well tell her she didn't have a point. But she relented enough to ask, "What was you wastin' your time thinkin' about?"

His voice dropped lower still. "Them guns," he said. If those two words reached Henry Barford's ears, it wasn't a lashing matter any more. Frederick would die, quickly if he was lucky but more likely with as much pain and cruelty as his master could mete out. Even talking about uprisings was a capital crime.

Helen's sharp intake of breath said she understood as much. "You out of your mind?" she said. "You pick one of them up, you can't never put it down no more."

"I know," Frederick said. "But do you reckon Victor Radcliff wanted his grandson to be a field nigger?"

"I reckon Victor Radcliff wanted his grandson to be a *live* nigger," Helen said. "Lord Jesus, Frederick, first one of those other field hands you talk to, he's liable to sell you down the river for whatever Master Henry give him. Thirty pieces of silver, I reckon—that's the goin' rate."

"If we're gonna rise up, we'll never find a better time to do it," Frederick said.

"Says who?" Helen retorted. "Way the yellow jack's goin' around, half your army may be dead week after next."

"If it gets us like that, it'll get the white folks we're fightin' the same way," Frederick said, which was true—or he hoped it was, anyhow. He went on, "That's not what I was talkin' about, anyways."

"Well, what *was* you talkin' about, then?" Helen asked pointedly.

"You know that lieutenant, the one who's down sick? He's a Croydon man, from way up north. They don't have slaves up there. He just about told me I had to free myself if I ever wanted to be free," Frederick said.

"Fever must've scrambled his brains," Helen said. "I wish to heaven you would've just dozed off like you should have."

"Most folks from Croydon hate slavery," Frederick went on as if she hadn't spoken. "I hear tell there's even niggers and mudfaces who can vote in the state of Croydon. And

Consul Newton, he's from Croydon, too. Everybody knows he can't stand the notion of one man buying and selling another one."

If he'd hoped to impress his wife—and he had—he failed. "Well, la-de-da!" Helen said. "And Consul Stafford, he's from Cosquer, down here on this side of the slave line. He's a planter his own self. He's got a bigger place than this here one, and he works more slaves'n Master Henry ever dreamt of owning. Gotta have both them fellas on the same side to do us any good." Negroes and copperskins in bondage could no more vote than they could fly, which didn't keep them from paying attention to Atlantean politics.

Frederick grinned, there in the dark. "Most of the time, sure," he said. "The Senate passes a law that says all the slaves are free, Consul Stafford can veto it, and nobody can say boo. But suppose we rise up now. Consul Stafford says, 'The United States of Atlantis got to send soldiers over there and put those slaves down.'"

"An' the soldiers come, an' they start killin' niggers an' mudfaces. It's happened before," Helen agreed.

"It has," Frederick agreed. "But I bet it won't happen this time, on account of all Consul Newton's got to do is, he's got to say, 'I veto it,' and nobody goes anywhere."

"He do that?" Helen didn't sound as if she believed it. And she knew why she didn't: "Even white folks who don't like slavery, that don't mean they do like niggers an' mudfaces. The whites down here start screamin' loud enough ... "

She had a point. Frederick would have been much happier if she didn't, but she did. He paused a while in thought, listening to mosquitoes buzz and to more distant crickets trill and frogs squeak and croak. At last, he answered, "What we got to do is, we got to fight clean, like it's a war, not an uprising. Can't go killing women and children for the fun of it, the way they do in uprisings." *Can't go raping white women for the fun of it, either*, he thought. That happened in every slave revolt. What vengeance was more basic?

"Reckon it'd make any difference?" Helen still sounded dubious.

"Bound to make some," Frederick said.

"Reckon slaves with guns in their hands'll want to let them folks go?" She knew which questions to ask, all right.

"They will if their commanders make 'em," Frederick answered. And then, just before sleep took him at last, he added, "If *I* make 'em." He was ready. Whether anyone else was . . . he'd find out.

IV

*M*atthew blew the horn again the next morning. As Frederick came out to eat breakfast and go on to the fields, he looked at the overseer in a whole new way. He had to be careful not to let it show. Matthew took it for granted that he could hit or whip Frederick, or any other slave, without worrying about reprisal. If he realized Frederick didn't take it for granted, he would do his best to kill him right away. And he could, if he got any kind of chance. He had his switch and a knife with a blade long enough to gut a man like a hog. Frederick didn't think he was a coward, either. Life would have been simpler if he were, but no.

There was plenty to eat. Fewer and fewer field hands came out to work, but the cooks went on making as much as they always had. More than one slave patted his belly and grinned after he finished eating. Frederick was surprised Matthew hadn't noticed what was going on and done something about it, but the overseer hadn't. It wasn't as if he didn't have other things on his mind.

And so did Henry Barford. The planter looked like a man bathing in hellfire when he came out onto the front porch. Eyes wild, he pointed at one of the cavalrymen guarding the precious wagons. "Where's that lieutenant of yours, the God-damned son of a bitch bastard?"

"Sir, Lieutenant Torrance is sick. He's mighty sick," the

trooper answered. "He can't see anybody right now. What's the matter?"

"What's the matter? What's the God-damned *matter*?" Barford howled. "My wife is puking up this horrible black gunk—looks like coffee grounds—and you ask me what's the matter? Your miserable, stinking lieutenant is what's the matter, that's what! Bringing the yellow jack to my plantation! I don't want to see the lousy bugger. I want to horsewhip him!"

"Well, sir, if it makes you feel any better, he's heaving up black stuff, too," the soldier said. "I don't think he's going to pull through."

"Too bad," Barford said, which surprised Frederick till he added, "I wanted to kill him with my own hands. But I reckon the yellow jack'll have to do. Though why a merciful God would take my sweet Clotilde, too . . . " He turned and lurched back into the big house.

Sweet? Frederick shook his head. Mistress Clotilde was about as sweet as vinegar. She was the one who'd wanted to give him more lashes than Master Henry. That was just like her, too. Did her husband really believe what he was saying, or was he trying to make the trooper feel worse?

From inside the house, Barford shouted, "I'll sue the government for every last eagle it's got! You wait and see if I don't!"

The cavalryman only shrugged. He scratched his nose, as if to say it was no skin off that organ. Unless the planter came out shooting—or unless the soldier got yellow fever—it wasn't his worry.

"Come on," Matthew called to the field hands. "Grab your tools. The work doesn't go away. The work never goes away. I know we're shorthanded, but we've got to keep at it. Otherwise, the harvest'll be bad, and then we'll all go hungry."

He wouldn't. Master Henry would yell at him, but that was all. The field hands really might go hungry in a bad year. Or Barford might have to sell some of them, which would be almost as rough. Frederick snorted quietly. He had other things on his own mind besides what the master might do after a bad harvest.

"You ain't said anything to anybody," Helen said as they walked out to the cotton field with tools on their shoulders. Hopefully, she added, "You gone and changed your mind?"

"Nope. Not me," Frederick answered. People said *stubborn as a Radcliff*. By that standard alone, he might have guessed he shared blood with one of the First Consuls. Even Henry Barford had sometimes seemed more proud than annoyed when calling him a hardheaded smoke. But Frederick also had other things than that on his mind. "Sometimes all the talking in the world doesn't do a cent's worth of good. Sometimes you got to show people instead."

Helen clicked her tongue between her teeth. "Oh, Fred, what are you gonna do?"

Burn my bridges, Frederick thought. But that wasn't what she wanted to hear. All he said was, "What I've got to do."

Helen shook her head, but she didn't say anything more, either. Maybe she hoped he would change his mind once they settled down to work. Part of him hoped the same thing: the part that had lived a quiet, pretty easy life all the way up into middle age. Well, his life wasn't quiet or easy any more. By all the signs, it never would be again. And if it wouldn't, why *not* act the way Samson had in the Philistines' temple? What did you have to lose?

He worked for a while, chopping and moving forward, chopping and moving forward. By now he had no trouble keeping up with the slaves working the rows of cotton to either side of him. He methodically weeded till Matthew came along to see how he was doing.

"Going all right, Frederick?" the overseer asked.

Frederick straightened and stretched, though he kept both hands on the hoe handle. "Not too bad, sir."

"Back easing up?"

"A bit." Frederick stretched again.

Matthew nodded, more to himself than to the Negro in front of him. "Told you it would. Whippings are like that."

Yes, he thought of them as nothing more than a rather unpleasant part of plantation routine. And so they were—if you held the whip. If you were on the other end . . . Frederick's hands tightened.

Some of what was going through his mind must have shown on his face at last. "You don't want to look at me that way," Matthew warned. "You *don't* want to look at me that way, by God!" He started to raise the switch, then seemed to realize it wouldn't be enough. He dropped it and grabbed for his knife instead.

Too late. Frederick swung the hoe in a deadly arc, an arc powered by a lifetime's worth of smothered fury. Smothered no more. The heavy blade tore away half the overseer's face. Blood gouted, astoundingly red in the bright sunshine. Matthew let out a gobbling shriek. The knife fell in the dirt as he clapped both hands to the ghastly wound.

He tried to stagger away from Frederick. Frederick hit him again, this time from behind. The heavy hoe blade bit into Matthew's skull. The overseer crumpled. He thrashed on the ground. Frederick hit him one more time. The thrashing slowed, then stopped. The white man's blood soaked into the thirsty soil.

The slaves working to either side of Frederick gaped at him in commingled astonishment, horror, and awe. "Lord Jesus!" one of them burst out. "What did you go and do that for?"

"We're all in trouble now!" the other one added. He stared at Matthew's huddled corpse. "Big trouble, I mean."

"Not if we grab those guns in the wagons," Frederick answered, more calmly than his drumming heart should have let him speak. "Not if we make all the white folks pay for what they've done to us."

Matthew's dying cries made more Negroes and copperskins hurry over to see what was going on. They all eyed the overseer's bloody corpse with the same look of disbelief, as if they'd never dreamt they might see such a thing. And yet how many of them would have wanted to slaughter him themselves?

"They're gonna kill you," a copperskin said. A moment later, he mournfully added, "They're gonna kill all of us."

"They will if we let 'em," Frederick said. "So let's not let 'em. Let's do some killing of our own—as much as it takes till we're free the way we're supposed to be. The United States of Atlantis are so damned proud of their precious

Proclamation of Liberty. But they reckon it stops with white folks. Don't you think mudfaces and niggers deserve their share, too?"

He waited, still clutching the gore-spattered hoe. Their other choice was to kill him now. If they did that, they might convince Henry Barford they hadn't had anything to do with murdering Matthew. They might. Or the planter might decide they *had* had something to do with it, and were using Frederick's death to cover their own guilt.

Or Barford might be down with the yellow jack himself by now. The way things were going, nobody could guess anything he couldn't see.

"Do you *want* to stay slaves the rest of your days?" Frederick asked. "Wouldn't you sooner be free?"

They looked at him. They looked at Matthew's body. Flies with metallic bodies—blue, green, brass—were already buzzing above it. "Don't seem like we got much else we can do," a Negro said slowly. "They gonna kill us any which way. Might as well kill some of them before we's dead."

One by one, the other slaves nodded. It wasn't the grand war cry Frederick had dreamt of, but when did reality ever measure up to dreams? He'd made them move. That much, anyhow, he'd foreseen.

"Let's go," he said. "We got to get those guns."

Leaving the overseer's corpse where it lay (though Frederick took the dead man's knife), they marched on the big house.

Frederick did remember to plunge the hoe blade into the dirt to clean it, and to rub more dirt on the handle to hide the bloodstains. He didn't want to alarm the Atlantean soldiers till the slaves got in among them.

He also didn't want to alarm Henry Barford. He didn't hate his owner. He hadn't even particularly disliked Barford till he got shackled to the whipping post and then sent to the fields. But he saw no way to let the planter live, not in the middle of a slave rebellion. Too bad—but a lot of things that happened were too bad.

"What do we say when they ask us how come we're

comin' back in the middle of the day?" the copperskin called Lorenzo asked.

"We'll tell 'em a snake bit the overseer," Frederick answered—he'd been wondering about that, too. "Tell 'em he's mighty bad off." He chuckled grimly. "An' he damned well is."

The squat red-brown man grinned in admiration. "You think of everything."

"If I'm gonna run this . . . whatever it is, I'd better, don't you reckon?" Frederick said. Lorenzo nodded. Nobody else challenged Frederick's right to lead the uprising. Maybe that meant all the field hands thought they could have no one better at their head. Perhaps more likely, it meant they figured he was the one on whom all the blame would land. And it *would* all land on him. But it would land on them, too. Whites had never shown any mercy to slaves who rose up. In their place, Frederick didn't suppose he would have, either.

There was the big house. There were the wagons with the precious rifle muskets. Without them, the revolt would be stillborn. A couple of troopers dug in the burial plot. If that didn't mean Lieutenant Torrance had died, Frederick would have been very surprised. *Too bad*, he thought, even though the slaves would have had to kill the officer had he pulled through. Torrance might personally disapprove of slavery, but Frederick had no doubt the Croydonite would have done his professional duty against any rising.

A soldier puffed on a pipe in front of one of the wagons. Sure enough, he became curious if not exactly alert when he saw the slaves straggling in from the cotton fields. "What're you doin' here so God-damned early?" he asked—the very question Lorenzo had foretold.

"You know anything about curin' snakebite?" Frederick asked in return. "Coral snake done bit the overseer, an' he's in a bad way."

"Son of a bitch!" the trooper exclaimed. "I bet he's in a bad way. Those bastards'll kill you deader'n shit."

He might be foul-mouthed, but he wasn't wrong. Coral snakes didn't go out of their way to bite people, as some of the bigger poisonous snakes did. But, like a good many frogs in the south of Atlantis, they wore bright colors to warn enemies that trying to make a meal off them wasn't a good idea. If a coral snake did bite you, you were much too likely to die.

"Whiskey or rum'll make his heart stronger," the cavalryman said as the slaves came up to him. "That and praying're about all I know that can help him."

No, he wasn't suspicious—certainly not suspicious enough. He let the slaves surround him; he couldn't believe they meant him any harm. But what you believed didn't always match what was real. Frederick got behind the trooper and stabbed him in the back.

The white man lurched. He groaned. He tried to draw his revolver, but another Negro clamped a hand on his wrist and didn't let him. When he screamed, more blood than noise came out of his mouth. His knees buckled. A sudden foul stench said his bowels had let go. Down he went.

Frederick grabbed his eight-shooter. "Get his knife, too," he said. One way you got to give orders was by coming out and giving them. If people followed them, you could give more, and they'd be more likely to follow those. Lorenzo took possession of the dagger.

"What do we do now?" someone else asked.

"Let's go get the ones who're digging in the graveyard," Frederick answered. "Doesn't look like they noticed anything goin' on here, and that's good." He stuffed the pistol into the waistband of his trousers and let his shirt droop down over it. "We'll try and do with them like we did with this fellow. Shooting's noisy—we don't start till we have to. Lorenzo, reckon you can let the air out of one while I do the other?"

"Turn me loose," the copperskin said confidently.

"All right." Frederick grinned. "But listen, everybody. If they look like they're gonna pull their guns, just jump on 'em any which way. If they start shootin', they can hurt us bad. Got me?" He waited for nods. As soon as he had them, he nodded at the troopers, who weren't digging much faster than slaves would have. "Soon as we bag them, Master Henry next."

That got everybody moving toward the Atlantean cavalrymen. Frederick might not especially dislike Henry Barford, but some of the field hands did.

"Your poor lieutenant die?" Frederick called as he and the slaves with him neared the sweating troopers.

They seemed willing enough to rest on their shovels for a while. "That's right," one of them said, mopping at his red face with a big cotton handkerchief—cotton that, for all Frederick knew, might have come from this plantation. "Once the fever got a grip on him, he went downhill quick. He was pissing blood and puking up black stuff. . . ." His face twisted in disgust. Maybe in fear as well, for he had to know that could happen to him, too.

"It's a shame," Frederick said. "He was a good fellow."

"That he was," the soldier agreed. "Won't catch me saying it real often, not about officers, but it's the truth with Lieutenant Torrance. Was the truth, I mean."

"Hey," the other trooper said suddenly. "What're you, uh, people doing here, anyway? How come you ain't out there workin' like you have been?"

Frederick told the story about the snakebite again. This time, he didn't stumble even a little. Had he heard the tale from his own lips, without question he would have believed it. Some lies—inspired lies—sounded better than truth.

He thought so, anyhow. To his surprise and disappointment, the troopers didn't seem to. "How come you didn't send one fellow back while the rest of you stayed out there?" asked the one who'd wondered why they'd returned. He was the man Frederick was closer to, leaving the other soldier for Lorenzo.

Frederick answered the question as if replying to an idiot: "On account of the snake's still there."

"Huh," the trooper said scornfully. He looked around in alarm. "Why are you people crowdin' around us like this? Watch yourself, Stu! Somethin' funny's goin' on."

Things happened very quickly after that. Lorenzo knifed Stu as neatly as Frederick had killed the sentry by the wagons of guns. Frederick stabbed the other trooper less than a heartbeat later. But the man screamed like a hurt shoat and went for his revolver. One of the slaves tried to stop him, but he shook off the Negro. The pistol cleared the holster.

Another slave grabbed his arm and dragged it down, so he fired a shot into the dirt at his feet.

The noise was horribly loud. And, if one shot had already rung out, two wouldn't make any difference. Frederick held the muzzle of his own pistol against the side of the struggling trooper's head and pulled the trigger.

He'd seen bullet wounds on animals. Henry Barford was proud of his skill as a hunter—and well he might have been, because he helped feed the plantation with it. But Frederick had never seen anything like this. If he was very lucky, he never would again, either. The trooper's head might have been a rotten melon dropped off a roof. It blew apart. Brains and blood and bits of bone splattered Frederick and all the other slaves close by. The Atlantean cavalryman had fought despite a nasty knife wound, but now he dropped like a felled redwood.

Lorenzo already had the other man's pistol. Another copperskin had got his knife. Now a Negro took this trooper's eight-shooter. And Helen pulled the knife off his belt. Frederick smiled at that. It was good that his wife should have a proper weapon. They'd all have them as soon as they unloaded the wagons, but why shouldn't Helen take the lead?

The gunshots brought house slaves running out to see what was going on. To Frederick's heartfelt relief, they didn't bring out any more Atlantean cavalrymen. The rest of the troopers must have been either dead or too sick to care. The house slaves . . . Their eyes went wide with shock. Looking down at himself, Frederick saw why. The cavalryman's blood and brains splashed his shirt and trousers. He looked as if he'd just come from a hard day's work at a slaughterhouse.

"What . . . What happened?" a housemaid quavered, as if she couldn't see for herself.

In case she really couldn't, Frederick answered, "We're free now. We're really free now, and we're gonna stay that way."

"The hell you say!" That furious roar came from Henry Barford. His wife might be dying of yellow fever. For all Frederick knew, Mistress Clotilde might be as dead as Lieutenant Torrance. But the idea of a slave uprising brought the master out onto the back porch, a shotgun cradled in his arms, his over-and-under pistol stuck in his belt. "And hell is where I'll blast the lot of you, too!"

He started to raise the shotgun to his shoulder. House-maids scattered, squealing. Frederick aimed his pistol, too. He knew he would have to be lucky to hit Master Henry at this range, while the master, with that shotgun, wouldn't have to be lucky at all to hit him.

Thunk! Speaking of slaughterhouses, that noise came straight out of one. Davey stood behind the master. The chief cook had buried a cleaver in the back of Henry Barford's head. Barford stood there a long moment, looking absurdly surprised. The shotgun slipped out of his hands. Then his knees buckled and he fell over. His feet drummed on the planking. That wouldn't last long. No one could hope to live with such a terrible wound.

Slowly, Frederick lowered his eight-shooter. "Obliged," he said, wishing his voice weren't so shaky.

Davey sketched a salute. "Any time." He stooped and picked up the shotgun. "Now I got me a piece, too. I know some folks who could use two barrels' worth of double-aught buck, I expect."

"Take Master Henry's pistol if you want, but don't worry about the shotgun," Frederick said. Davey frowned, not following. Frederick pointed to the wagons. "Those're full of guns that'll hit from four or five times as far away as any shotgun ever born, remember? Fancy government muskets, bound for New Marseille."

"That's right." The cook's heavy-featured face cleared. "Reckon we'll need 'em, too."

"Reckon we will," Frederick agreed. "But for now, this here plantation is ours."

What did generals call it when victory had been won but the fighting wasn't quite over? Mopping up—that was what they said. The slaves still had to mop up. Knocking the cav-alrymen down with yellow fever over the head was quick and easy. A couple of them were near death anyway. Fred-erick told himself his people were doing the whites a favor by ending their suffering. He didn't have much trouble making himself believe it.

Clotilde Barford also still clung to life in the upstairs bedroom. Three housemaids got into a catfight about who would have the privilege of holding a pillow over her face till she quit breathing for good. It was a real brawl—their nails drew blood.

"Lord Jesus!" Frederick exclaimed after some of the men separated them—and got clawed in the process. "Let's settle this fair and square."

"How you gonna manage that?" one of the women asked, dabbing at her bleeding cheek with her apron.

Frederick dug out Henry Barford's deck of cards. "Here's how," he said. "You all draw one. High card does the job."

The housemaid who'd asked him won the draw. The other two swore at her as she proudly climbed the stairs to finish the last white person on the plantation. When she came down, she was grinning from ear to ear. "That bitch ain't gonna give nobody grief no more!" she declared.

Everyone cheered. Frederick held up his hands. "Listen to me!" he said. "You got to listen to me!" He wasn't sure they would. Some of them had already got into the master's—the dead master's—barrel-tree rum and whiskey.

"Listen to him, damn it!" That was Lorenzo. He seemed to be the one the copperskins on the plantation heeded most. And he had a fierce bass voice that made people pay attention to him.

Eventually, most of the field hands and house slaves looked in Frederick's direction. "We're free now," he said. Then he couldn't go on, because everybody started cheering again. He held up his hands once more, this time hoping for quiet. After a while, he got something close to it. He continued: "We're free—till the first white man—drummer or preacher or neighbor: doesn't matter which one—decides to pay a call on Master Henry. Then they'll find out what happened here, and they'll try and kill us all."

"Well, fuck 'em!" shouted a housemaid with a whiskey bottle in her hand. "Fuck 'em in the heart, the stinking shit-sacks!" She got a cheer, too.

"Easy to say," Frederick said when he could get a word in edgewise. "Not so easy to do. Way it looks to me is, we got two choices. We can slip away by ones and twos, going every which way. Some of us'll get free if we try that, odds are—some of us, but not everybody."

"We could go off to the woods and the swamps," a copperskin said. Runaway slaves of all colors scratched out livings in places where whites judged pursuit more trouble than it was worth.

"Well, we could try," Frederick said. "When they find out we killed the whites here, though, they'll come after us a lot harder'n they'd chase ordinary runaways. Or does anybody reckon I'm wrong?"

No one said anything. If slaves killed white people, other whites would hunt them down no matter what. Every slave understood that. It was one of the pillars on which slavery rested.

"So slipping away doesn't look so good," Frederick said. "Only other chance I see is, we gotta fight, and we gotta win."

"We got the guns, by God!" Davey's voice was as deep as Lorenzo's.

"Anybody figure there ain't some white folks around these parts who still need killing?" Lorenzo himself added.

No one left alive on the plantation believed that. "And when we liberate a plantation, what happens to the mudfaces and niggers who were slaves on it?" Frederick answered his own question before anyone else could: "I'll tell you what happens to 'em. They join our army—the Liberating Army, that's what we'll call it. And then we go on and we free up the next plantation down the road."

"And the slaves there, they turn into soldiers, too!" That was one of the housemaids who'd lost the draw to kill Mistress Clotilde. By the excited way she said it, the possibility hadn't occurred to her till that very moment. It probably hadn't. Frederick had never thought she was long on brains.

Excitement surged through the assembled slaves—no, through the newborn Liberating Army. They had rifle muskets and ammunition for several plantations' worth of slaves. After that . . . Well, Frederick couldn't imagine any plantation without firearms, both for hunting and for keeping two-legged property in line. Those weapons would arm more Negroes and copperskins.

And what happens when the Liberating Army goes up against the army of the United States of Atlantis? Frederick wondered. *What do we do for cannon? What do we do for grapeshot?*

Well, he didn't have to worry about that, not yet. And, as long as he didn't have to, he didn't intend to. Borrowing trouble never did anybody any good. And, if you were a slave—even more, if you were a slave trying to rise up against white masters—you already had plenty of troubles, and didn't need to borrow any more.

"Where do we go first?" That was Davey: trust the cook to come up with a good, practical question.

Frederick had been chewing that over, too. "Way it looks to me is, first place we ought to set free is Benjamin Barker's," he answered. "It's close, and he doesn't treat his slaves real well, so they'll be ready to swing our way, and—"

"And his wife, that Veronique, she's an even nastier cunt than Mistress Clotilde, an' that's really sayin' somethin'," interrupted the handmaid who'd just snuffed out Clotilde Barford's life.

From everything Frederick had seen and heard, she was right. He made himself nod. "She sure is," he said. "And that's one more reason the slaves on the Barker plantation will see things our way." *They'd better, or this will be one of the shortest uprisings in a history that's seen a lot of short ones.* He looked around. "Anybody got a better idea?"

The people who really counted were Lorenzo and Davey. If either of them thought the Liberating Army should pick a different direction, Frederick would have to listen carefully. He might have to change his mind.

They both paused thoughtfully, considering. At last, almost in unison, their heads went up and down. "Benjamin Barker deserves whatever happens to him," Davey said in the tones of a judge passing sentence.

"He does," Lorenzo agreed. And so it was decided.

*   *   *

They took the rifle muskets out of their crates. Then they had to figure out how to use the percussion caps that came with the cartridges: all of the firearms on the plantation were flintlocks. But several slaves had heard about the percussion system, and had a notion of how to fit the thin copper caps over the nipple on each musket.

Some of the field hands used beat-up old shotguns of their own to kill varmints and hunt small game. The fancy new muskets impressed them enormously. "See, the thing of it is, a flintlock'll misfire maybe one time in five," Lorenzo explained to Frederick. "And even when it doesn't, there's always that wait while the sparks set off the priming powder and the priming powder starts the main charge, so you miss what you were aiming at 'cause it's not there no more."

"Not like that with these guns," Frederick said. His shoulder was sore from a rifle musket's fierce kick. "Soon as you pull the trigger and the hammer comes down—*bang!*" His ears were still ringing, too.

"I hope to shit, it's not like that!" Lorenzo said enthusiastically. "We're gonna kill us a lot of white folks with 'em."

"That's right." Frederick saw the need, but he wasn't so eager. The color of his skin reminded him of the white blood that flowed in his veins. So did the thick beard that rasped under his fingers every time he rubbed his chin.

Lorenzo pressed ahead: "How are we gonna get there? We march down the road with guns on our shoulders, people'll figure out pretty damned quick there's a slave uprising."

"Think so, do you?" Frederick's voice was dry. "Looks to me like they'll figure it out pretty damned quick any which way."

Lorenzo grinned. He had strong white teeth, and his fierce expression made them seem uncommonly sharp. "Looks the same way to me. But do you want to let the whole world know right away, like we're some traveling medicine show?"

"Well . . . " Frederick didn't need long to think that over. "No."

And so they went cross-country—all but the precious rifle muskets they weren't using themselves and the even more precious ammunition. Those rolled down the road, guarded by slaves with eight-shooters taken from dead Atlantean cavalrymen. The Negroes and copperskins slapped paint on the wagons before setting out, so no one who saw them would think of the United States of Atlantis.

One of the slaves who took the lead wagon down the road pulled a black felt hat of Henry Barford's low on his forehead, so the brim was barely above his eyes. It was the perfect touch, especially since he was also smoking one of the dead master's cheroots. If he didn't look like a teamster, Frederick had never seen anybody who did.

"They'll get there ahead of us," Davey said in worried tones as the rest of the Liberating Army started tramping from one big house to the other.

Frederick shook his head. "Don't think so. Hope not, anyways. I told 'em to hold up by the side of the road a couple of times. White folks going by won't think anything of that. You know how they always go on about how lazy niggers and mudfaces are."

"Oh, hell, yes—usually while they're pilin' more work on our heads," Davey said. "Then they get mad on account of we don't finish as fast as they want." He muttered something under his breath; the look in his eyes went as dark as his skin. After a few seconds, though, his face cleared. He set a hand on Frederick's shoulder. "That's good, the way you set it up. Seems like you got a notion of what's likely to happen next. Fellow who's runnin' this show, he better do that."

"Yeah, I know. Right now, main thing I'm tryin' for is not to do anything out-and-out stupid," Frederick answered. Sooner or later, he *would* do something stupid, too. You couldn't help it, any more than you could help needing to piss every so often. He just hoped his mistakes wouldn't be too bad and wouldn't hurt the Liberating Army too much.

He was glad Davey seemed willing to let him lead. The head cook was one of a handful of men who might have wanted to run things himself. Lorenzo was another. He also seemed content with Frederick's leadership.

Well, of course they are, Frederick thought. *Nothing's gone wrong yet, so they can't hang any blame on me.*

A rail fence separated Master Henry's land from Benjamin Barker's. Maybe it was Frederick's imagination, but he thought the crops on the far side of the fence grew taller than they did on this side. Nothing, not even cotton plants, dared give Benjamin Barker a hard time.

He remarked on that as he clambered over the fence and came down on the other side. *Now it's official. Now it's an invasion*, he thought. Helen answered him before anyone else could: "*We're* gonna give Master Benjamin Barker a hard time, by Jesus! And his stuck-up bitch of a wife, too!"

"That's right!" Several Negroes and copperskins said the same thing at the same time. Women's voices were loud in the chorus. Frederick knew nobody liked Veronique Barker very much. Considering what was likely to happen to her, that might be just as well.

"Hey, now! What are you slaves doin' on Barker land?" an officious-sounding Negro demanded. "And"—the fellow's voice suddenly wobbled—"what are you doin' with guns in your hands?"

"This here is the Liberating Army," Frederick answered proudly. "We're here to clean things out, that's what we're here for. Are you with us or against us?"

"Lord Jesus!" the Negro yelped. If he said he was against them, he wouldn't live long. And maybe he didn't need much persuading. "You're gonna do for Master Benjamin?"

"His snooty ol' Veronique, too," Helen said.

"You really are!" Benjamin Barker's slave might have discovered it was Christmas in summertime. "Count me in! You got a spare gun I can shoot?"

"Not yet, but we will pretty quick," Frederick said. If Barker's Negro wanted to think that meant they aimed to plunder the big house, he was welcome to for the time being. Let him prove himself before he got a rifle musket of his own.

"Well, come on, then!" he said now, and he sure seemed enthusiastic. "I'll take you straight to him, I will!"

V

They hadn't gone very far before they came upon a work gang weeding in the fields. Frederick's back and shoulders twinged sympathetically. He'd been doing the same thing himself a couple of days earlier. And making sure the gang actually worked, of course, was Benjamin Barker's overseer.

He was older and tougher-looking than Matthew had been. Matthew had been a man who wanted to rise, the kind who dreamt of owning a plantation himself one day. This fellow was out of dreams. All he wanted was to go on doing what he was doing already. He'd never rise higher than overseer, and he knew it.

Instead of a switch, he carried a lash in his right hand. And, where Matthew had had a knife on his belt, a pistol rode this overseer's right hip.

His hand dropped to that pistol as soon as he saw strange slaves. "All right, you bastards!" he growled. "You've got three shakes of a lamb's tail to tell me what the hell you're doing on Master Barker's land. C'mon! Make it snappy!"

He had to die. Frederick wasn't the only one who realized it. Half a dozen rifle muskets rose as one and trained on the overseer's chest and head. It wasn't anything personal— but, then again, it was. Frederick had trouble imagining a field hand who *didn't* want to shoot an overseer.

"Son of a bitch!" this white man exclaimed. "You lousy,

stupid idiots are trying to rise up!" With startling speed, his pistol cleared the holster.

With startling speed—but not fast enough. Before the overseer could pull the trigger, those rifle muskets spoke together. A couple of the conical bullets the longarms spat might have missed him, but most struck home. A round that caught a man square in the face drastically rearranged his looks, and not for the better. Scarlet flowers blossomed on the overseer's shirtfront, too. He pitched forward and lay facedown in the dirt.

Benjamin Barker's slaves gaped at him, and at the men and women of the Liberating Army. Frederick paid no attention to them for a little while; he was reloading as fast as he could. Only after a new percussion cap sat on the nipple and a new powder charge and bullet were rammed down and firmly seated in the barrel did he start to notice their exclamations.

"What'd you go and do that for?" a mulatto woman asked shrilly, her knuckles pressed against her mouth.

Davey laughed. "You gonna tell me an overseer didn't have it coming? Not likely!"

"But . . . " The woman's gaze traveled to the blood soaking into the ground under the dead white man, then quickly jerked away. "You went and shot him. Just like that, you went and shot him."

Lorenzo laughed at her. "Nothing gets by you, does it, sweetheart?" He'd also reloaded before worrying about anything else. Gunfire might bring Benjamin Barker at the run, intent on finding out what had happened.

"What you gonna do with us?" a copperskinned man asked.

"Set you free. Give you guns," Frederick answered. "Nobody's gonna sell us any more, not ever again. Nobody's gonna horsewhip us any more, neither, not ever again. This here is the Liberating Army. From now on, we're our own people, not anybody else's, not ever again."

The copperskin looked at him as if he'd just declared himself God Almighty. "You're gonna get us all killed, is what you're gonna do." Several of Benjamin Barker's other slaves nodded somber agreement.

Frederick also knew that was possible—and feared it was probable. Even so, he said, "Best thing we can do is whip all the planters around us and make our army bigger. The more people we've got fighting, the better our chances."

"Maybe we can lick some of the planters," a Negro field hand here said. "We ain't never gonna lick the Atlantean army."

Frederick brandished his rifle musket. The long sword bayonet glittered in the sun. "We got these from Atlantean soldiers," he said proudly. He didn't mention that most of them were down with the yellow jack. He also didn't mention that the Liberating Army might have brought the sickness with it. Instead, he added, "Now—who wants to see Master Benjamin dead?"

No matter what Barker's field hands thought about the ultimate fate of the uprising, they did want to see their master dead. "And Mistress Veronique, too!" one of the women said—the one who'd been so horrified when they shot the overseer. Yes, Benjamin Barker's wife had found a way to make herself remembered, all right.

"Well, let's go get 'em," Frederick said, and then, "Scouts forward!" He wasn't going to run into any nasty surprises, not if he could help it.

He could see the big house in the distance. It was larger and fancier than Henry Barford's place. Veronique Barker had always thought herself above Mistress Clotilde. Now Frederick saw why. The Barkers had more money, and with money came status. It was that simple.

No—it had been that simple. Now there was a new game, complete with new rules. One of the new rules was, a white man couldn't get rich off the labor of Negroes and copperskins. Benjamin Barker was about to be taken to school by the Liberating Army. He would remember his lessons for the rest of his life, however long that was.

Here he came toward the fields: a big, sturdy man with streaks of gray in his black hair. He cradled a rifle or shotgun in his arms. Behind him strode his son, who was thinner and not yet graying but otherwise a good copy of the planter. The younger man was also armed.

Seeing strange copperskins and blacks heading his way, Benjamin Barker shouted in a great voice: "What kind of riffraff is this?" He sounded more disbelieving that such people could invade his land than angry.

His son reached out to pluck at his shirtsleeve. Frederick couldn't hear what the younger Barker said. It wasn't meant for him anyhow. But Benjamin's response to it left Frederick in no doubt about what it was.

"Drop those guns this minute, or it'll go even harder for you than it would otherwise!" the planter bellowed.

Frederick almost started to lay down his rifle musket. The habit of obedience to whites—especially to whites who gave orders in a loud voice—was deeply ingrained in him, as it was in all Atlantean slaves. One of Barker's men sent back an answer: "We don't got to listen to you no more! You're gonna git what you deserve!"

"That's what you think, Ivanhoe!" Barker yelled. He raised the longarm he carried to his shoulder. The gun roared. Ivanhoe screeched and fell over, clutching his side.

"Give it to him!" Frederick said urgently. All the slaves turned their rifle muskets on Barker and his son. The guns stuttered out a ragged volley. The younger Barker clapped both hands to his breast, as if he were in a stage melodrama. But the blood on the front of his shirt was real. As the overseer had before him, he fell facedown in the dirt.

Somehow, all the bullets in the volley missed Benjamin Barker, the man at whom they were aimed. He reloaded with almost superhuman speed and fired again. This time, he hit one of his own copperskins. Unlike Ivanhoe, the second slave didn't make a sound. He simply crumpled, shot through the head.

More bullets flew at Benjamin Barker. These didn't bite, either. As slaves went, Frederick wasn't superstitious. He had more education—and more sense—than most bondsmen. But even he wondered if the planter didn't have a snakeskin or a rabbit's foot in his pocket.

Shaking his fist, Barker turned and ran back toward the big house. Another volley pursued him. Yet again, every shot missed. If that wasn't uncanny, Frederick couldn't imagine what would be.

He also couldn't imagine letting the planter get away. That would be ... whatever was worse than a disaster. About as bad, say, as tripping over a floorboard that had come loose. Maybe even worse.

"Come on!" he said. "We've got to do for him!"

"How?" a copperskin asked. "If bullets won't—"

"If bullets won't, we'll burn down the God-damned big house," Frederick said savagely. "I don't want to do that, on account of the smoke'll draw a crowd where we don't need one, but I will if I got to. We ain't gonna let that man get away!"

His determination pulled the rest of the slaves after him. He realized it didn't have to be a white man giving orders in a loud voice. Anyone would do, as long as he sounded sure of himself. Being right plainly wasn't essential, or slaves would have stopped obeying masters hundreds of years ago. Being—or seeming—sure just as plainly was.

Benjamin Barker got inside. He fired at the oncoming Liberating Army, and dropped a second copperskin. A moment later, another gun spoke from upstairs. Veronique Barker didn't aim to sit around and let herself get slaughtered—or suffer the proverbial fate worse than death. Frederick didn't think she hit anybody, but she was making the effort.

"I need five or six men to come into the house with me," Frederick said. "The rest can go on shootin', make the white folks keep their heads down."

"I'm with you," Lorenzo said at once.

"Me, too," Davey said. "Got to finish that fucker."

Frederick soon had his volunteers. As the rest of the Liberating Army banged away, they rushed toward the front door. Benjamin Barker appeared in a window like an angry ghost. He fired and vanished again. The bullet cracked past Frederick's head, much too close for comfort. Involuntarily, he ducked. He hoped that wouldn't make his comrades think him a coward. Whether it did or not, he couldn't help it.

His shoulder hit the door. "Oof!" he said, and bounced off. He might have known it would be locked.

"Here—I'll settle it." Lorenzo fired two shots from a

captured revolver into the lock. Then he rammed it with his shoulder. He fell down as it flew open.

Davey sprang over him and dashed into the big house. He took a shotgun blast full in the chest, and sank without a sound. Benjamin Barker howled laughter. "Thought it would be easy, did you?" He fired again, this time with a pistol. A copperskin beside Frederick screeched and clutched his leg.

Frederick had never thought it would be easy. If slave uprisings were easy, one of them would have succeeded before this. But he thought it might be possible. And one of the things that would make it possible was killing planters who got in the way.

He shot Benjamin Barker in the neck. Barker gobbled like a turkey. He clapped a hand to the bleeding wound. *Why doesn't he fall over?* Frederick wondered. But the answer to that was only too obvious. *Because you only grazed him, that's why.*

He ran forward. Sure as the devil, Barker wasn't badly hurt. He pulled a knife off his belt—no, a razor, the edge glittering even in the dimness inside the big house—and slashed at Frederick.

But a razor in a desperate man's right arm couldn't match the reach of an eighteen-inch bayonet at the end of a five-foot rifle musket. What Frederick had was a spear, and he used it so. He stuck Barker in the chest. The bayonet grated off a rib before sinking deep.

That finishes him, Frederick thought. But it didn't. Benjamin Barker went right on fighting. Killing a man wasn't so easy as it looked: it was a horrible, messy business. Frederick stuck the planter again and again, and still almost got his own throat slashed. Only when Lorenzo brought his pistol up against the back of Barker's head and pulled the trigger did the white man quit struggling.

"Whew!" Frederick said. "That man had no quit in him." Barker was still thrashing on the floor, but he plainly wouldn't get up again.

"Who cares?" Lorenzo answered. "Long as you can make him quit, that's all that counts."

Another shot rang out from upstairs. If Veronique had

fired on the invaders from the landing, she could have done
a lot of harm. Frederick looked around to make sure his
surviving companions were all right. Then he said, "We better find out what that was all about."

Cautiously, they climbed the stairs. The door to the
Barkers' bedroom stood open. Veronique Barker lay on
the bed, the muzzle of a pistol still in her mouth. The back
of her head was a red ruin that soaked into the bedclothes.

Lorenzo grunted when he saw the corpse. "Huh," he
said. "She must've known what she had comin'. I never
stuck it into a white woman before, but I sure would have.
Serve her right, you know—pay her back for all the shit she
done piled on her slaves."

Frederick hadn't wanted the Liberating Army to do
things like that. What would Helen have said had he joined
in the gang rape of the planter's wife? Would she have
screamed at him, or would she also have thought Veronique Barker got what was coming to her? Frederick didn't
know, and he wasn't altogether sorry not to find out.

"One way or the other, she's done for now," he said.
"This whole plantation's done for. Let's drag the bodies
out of the house, let the Barkers' slaves know they're free
for sure."

Veronique Barker's corpse left a trail of gore down the
stairs. Her blood and Benjamin's stained the rugs on the
floor of their front room. Frederick pushed the bodies off
the front porch with his foot. They rolled bonelessly down
the stairs and came to rest in the dirt.

"See?" Frederick said. "They're really and truly dead.
We done killed 'em. They won't ever trouble you any
more."

The Barkers' slaves stared at the corpses with terrible
avidity. Frederick hadn't particularly hated the Barfords—
he'd just hated being anyone's piece of property. Things
were different here: how very different, he didn't realize till
the newly freed Negroes and copperskins surged forward
and took their own vengeance on the bodies.

It wasn't pretty. They kicked them and beat them and
hacked at them with gardening tools. A couple of men
undid their flies and pissed on the bodies. The rest of the

Barkers' slaves—no, the new recruits to the Liberating Army—whooped and cheered. They hung the corpses up by their heels. Veronique Barker's skirts fell down over her head. That drew more whoops, and some lewd jokes.

Moving faster than they would have under an overseer's glare, the copperskins and Negroes piled firewood into a pyre for the Barkers. Someone poured lamp oil on the wood to help it catch. As soon as it was burning well, the newly freed slaves cut down their late masters and threw them on the fire. They cheered again, loud and long, as the stink of charred meat joined the cleaner odor of wood smoke.

"In a way, this is good," Lorenzo said, watching the Barkers' people caper and cavort. "After they do somethin' like this, they can't say they didn't mean it and we made 'em join up with us."

"Who would they say that to?" Frederick asked.

Lorenzo looked at him as if his wits could have worked better. "To the white folks, of course," he answered. Sure enough, he might have been speaking to an idiot child.

He might have been, but he wasn't. Patiently, Frederick said, "Only way the white folks'll get a chance to ask 'em questions like that is if we lose. I don't aim to lose. I been waiting my whole life to get free. White Atlanteans, they take it for granted. They don't know how lucky they are. They've got no idea. But I do, on account of I've seen it from the other side. Nobody's gonna stop me from being free, not any more. How about you?"

By the look on Lorenzo's face, Frederick had startled him. That saddened Frederick, but it didn't much surprise him. "I don't want to go back to being a slave, no," Lorenzo said after a pause, "but I don't know what kind of chance we've got of really winning, either."

"If we don't, they'll kill us all," Frederick said, wishing the copperskin hadn't come out with his own worst fear.

"If we do, we've got to kill them all," Lorenzo said. "Otherwise, they ain't gonna let slaves who rose up live. They never have, and I figure they never will."

Frederick also feared that was much too likely to be true. Even so, he answered, "Main reason white folks didn't is that, when slaves rose up before, they just wanted to murder all the masters they could."

"And you don't?" Lorenzo pointed to the fire consuming the mortal remains of Benjamin and Veronique Barker.

"Got to do some," Frederick admitted. "But the white folks, even the ones without slaves, live pretty damned well in Atlantis. How come we can't live the same way? Proclamation of Liberty set this country free from England. Don't you reckon it's about time Atlantis lived up to all the fancy promises it made itself a long time ago?"

"Don't *I* reckon so? Of course I do," Lorenzo said. "That ain't the question, though. Question is, will the white folks reckon so? I've got to tell you, friend, it looks like long odds to me."

"You'd better run off now, then, on account of that's the only hope we got," Frederick said.

"If it is, we've got no hope at all," Lorenzo said. "But I ain't runnin', neither, 'cause *that's* no hope. Skulking in the woods the rest of my days like a damned honker?" He shook his head. "I don't think so. Shit—who knows? Maybe we can lick the white folks. Maybe." He didn't sound as if he believed it, though.

Frederick didn't believe it, either. Sometimes you had to rise up whether you believed you could possibly win or not. If that wasn't the measure of a slave's damnation, Frederick had no idea what would be.

The Liberating Army had plenty of rifle muskets to arm Benjamin Barker's slaves. Barker's own arsenal would give several more slaves weapons. He'd kept far more guns in his big house than Henry Barford had in *his*. "Why does one man need so much firepower?" Lorenzo asked. "He couldn't shoot 'em all off at the same time."

"Not at the same time, no," one of Barker's men, a Negro, answered. "But if he needed to shoot himself a snake or a hawk or a fox or a deer or one o' them big ol' lizards in a river, he had the right piece for it."

"Or if he needed to shoot himself a nigger or a mudface, he had the right piece for that, too," Frederick said with a shudder.

"Or one of them," the black man agreed. His former owner had put up much too good a fight.

A halloo made Frederick break off the conversation. A warning shout followed the halloo: "Somebody comin' up the path!"

"Oh, good God!" Frederick exclaimed. That was the last thing he wanted to hear. No one had called at the Barford plantation, even before the rebellion broke out. Maybe neighbors knew the yellow jack was loose there. Or maybe it was just that Henry Barford wasn't what you'd call sociable, even if Clotilde was.

Such musings blew out of Frederick's head when Lorenzo asked, "What do we do now?"

That was a fine question. Show the visitor the pyre where Benjamin and Veronique Barker had burned? He'd surely want to see that, wouldn't he? And what about the corpse of the Barkers' son? And the dead overseer? Oh, yes—plenty to show off.

On the other hand, if the slaves chased the caller away, he would ride off and let the outside world know they'd taken over the plantation. If they killed him, more outsiders would come looking for him. That might buy a few hours—maybe even as much as a day—but it would also let the cat out of the bag in short order.

Before Frederick could decide what to do, his sentries went and did it. Two gunshots rang out, one after the other. The first provoked a startled shriek; the second abruptly ended it.

A Negro trotted back to Frederick with a big grin on his face. "We got us a new eight-shooter, jus' like the ones the cavalry soldiers use," he said proudly. "An' that fella was ridin' a mighty fine horse."

"Well, good," Frederick said, hoping it was. By the nature of things, you couldn't keep an uprising secret very long. He made up his mind: "We go after the Menand plantation next. We move out tomorrow morning—*early* tomorrow morning. And, between now and then, we post extra-strong watches all around this place."

Lorenzo nodded. He understood what was going on. Davey would have, too. Frederick worried about how much he'd miss the chief cook in the days ahead. But the field hand who'd brought word of the visitor's demise scratched his head. "How come?"

Frederick sighed quietly. You liked to think the people on your side, the people you were leading into the sunlight of freedom, were all clever and filled with natural nobility. You liked to think so, yes, but they would disappoint you in a hurry if you did. They were people, no better and no worse than any others. For too long, masters had judged them worse than others. That would have to change. But they were no better, either.

And so Frederick had to explain: "Somebody's gonna miss the fellow you shot. Somebody'll come and try to find out what happened to him."

"Oh." The other Negro contemplated that. He didn't need long to find an answer that satisfied him: "Then we plug that son of a bitch, too."

That could work . . . for a little while. "They won't keep coming one at a time, you know," Frederick said gently. "They may not even come one at a time when this poor, sorry bastard doesn't ride home."

"Oh," the field hand said again. He nodded, with luck in wisdom. "Reckon you're right. I didn't think of that."

"Why am I not surprised?" Frederick murmured. Lorenzo's shoulders shook with suppressed mirth. The field hand didn't get it. Frederick wasn't surprised at that, either. A swallowed sigh almost gave him the hiccups.

He gave his orders. One of the new recruits to the Liberating Army, a copperskin from the Barker plantation, said, "I don't want to do no more fighting. Long as I'm rid of the dirty snake who was crackin' the whip on us, I'd just as soon take it easy for a while."

Several others, copperskins and Negroes, made it plain they felt the same way. No, not everybody in the uprising was as bright as he might have been. "Well, you can do that," Frederick said.

"I can? All right!" The new recruit sounded amazed and delighted. He hadn't expected things to be so easy.

And they weren't. "Yeah, you can do that," Frederick repeated. Then he went on, "You can do that if you don't mind the white folks catching you tomorrow—if you're real lucky, maybe the day after. Don't you get it, you God-damned fool? *We've killed masters.* White folks grab us now, they'll kill us as slow and filthy as they know how. Only way we can stay alive is to keep on fightin' and keep on winnin'. *Only* way. You got that through your thick head?"

Were the just-freed slave white himself, would he have turned pale from rage or red with anger? Since he was not much lighter than Frederick, he didn't show what he was feeling that way. His scowl said he was angry. "I got it," he answered. "But who d'you think you are, to play the white man talkin' to me like that?"

"I ain't playin' the white man. I'm playin' the general," Frederick said. "Liberating Army's just like any other kind—it needs somebody in charge. Right now, that's me."

"If I'm in this here army, I'm still a slave, then," the copperskin said.

"If you ain't in this here army, you're a dead man walkin'," Frederick said.

Behind him, Lorenzo cocked his revolver. The click of the hammer going back sounded much louder than it really was. "If you ain't in this here army, you're a dead man—period," he declared.

The man who'd been complaining gave back a sickly grin. "I was just funnin', like," he said. "Can't you take a joke?"

"It's like Frederick said—this here *is* an army. When the general tells you to do somethin', you don't make no shitty jokes," Lorenzo growled. "You do it right away, no matter what the hell it is. Some other stuff you don't know nothin' about may depend on it. And somebody may blow your fuckin' head off if you fart around. Me, for instance. Understand what I'm talkin' about?"

"Uh-huh. Sure do," the younger copperskin said. He took the prospect of getting shot by his own people seriously, anyhow, even if he didn't have the brains to imagine that white folks might do it. Copperskins were supposed to be fierce and savage. Lorenzo used that to his own advantage, even against one of his own kind. And who could say for sure? He might have shot the new recruit as a lesson for the others. Frederick almost asked him, then decided not to. Some things he didn't need to know.

Again, the Liberating Army advanced on a new plantation cross-country. Surprise still mattered, even if it wouldn't for much longer. The rifle muskets and their accouterments all fit in one wagon now. It also went cross-country. If the whites in the neighborhood were alerted to the rising, Frederick didn't want them taking back a big chunk of his weaponry all at once.

Whether the whites were alerted to the rising or not, the slaves on the Menand plantation knew something was up. "You gonna set us free?" they asked eagerly when they met the fighters from the Liberating Army in their cotton fields.

"Not exactly," Frederick answered. Their faces fell till he explained: "You're gonna set yourselves free."

He and Jacques Menand's slaves had been talking in low voices. When they heard that, they let out whoops of delight. Not nearly far enough away, a white man demanded, "What's that stupid commotion all about?"

"Your overseer?" Frederick whispered.

"That's right," answered a man who looked to be of mixed copperskin and Negro blood. "Sooner that God-damned son of a whore gets what's coming to him, happier we'll all be."

"Amen!" added a man who looked like a pure-blooded copperskin.

"I don't reckon you've got long to wait," Frederick said. "Can you lure him here?"

They didn't even need to do that. The overseer came forward of his own accord, to see what was going on. Rifle-musket butts, bayonets, and knives soon finished him off—though perhaps not soon enough to suit him. His screams rose up into the uncaring air. Frederick didn't worry about that. They wouldn't reach the big house, where gunfire might have.

Menand's slaves proved hot to join the Liberating Army. "First we kill this bastard here who's been fucking us," the copperskin said savagely. "Then we kill all the other white bastards, too." The rest of the field hands nodded.

The men who'd got the rifle muskets to the plantation passed them out. By now, they seemed as attached to the guns as any ordnance sergeants in the Atlantean army. "You take care of this piece, keep it clean, or we'll take it away from you and shove it up your ass," one of them warned the wide-eyed copperskin to whom he gave the weapon. "You got that?"

"You bet," the man answered. "I'll do whatever I have to do, long as I get the chance to kill me some white folks."

"Oh, I reckon we can take care of *that*," the Negro said grandly, as if he were personally responsible for it.

Drill sergeants would have despaired at the way the Liberating Army advanced on the Menands' house. The copperskins and Negroes kept no kind of order. *One of these days, we'll have to fight real soldiers*, Frederick thought. *We'd better learn how to do those things, or they'll murder us.* But that day wasn't here yet. At least the men advanced with high spirits. As long as they kept doing that, anything was possible.

No one fired at them from inside the big house. Everything was quiet—too quiet to suit Frederick. "What's wrong with them?" he said. "They must've seen us coming. They reckon we're here for a dance?"

Then one of the house slaves came out. He was wearing a boiled shirt, black jacket, and cravat like the ones Frederick had put on every day for so many years. "Menands done run off," he said. "You ain't gonna catch 'em now."

"How'd they know in time to do that?" Frederick answered his own question: "Somebody came and told them!"

"You're a clever fellow, ain't you?" the house slave said. "A field hand, he came runnin' back here an' palavered with Master Jacques. When they hightailed it, he went with 'em."

"I bet he did!" Frederick said. "Stinking Judas must know what we'd do to him if we got our hands on him. Who was the son of a bitch?"

"His name is Jerome. He's a copperskin." The house slave didn't try to hide his distaste. Frederick understood every bit of it. House slaves always sneered at field hands. And Negroes and copperskins sneered at each other. Masters exploited all those differences. If this uprising was going to get anywhere, Frederick would have to find a way to plaster them over.

"Menands tell you why they were going?" he asked the house slave.

"Master Jacques said he didn't aim to wait around and get killed," the other Negro answered. "He asked if I wanted to go along, but I told him no. I reckoned I'd be safe enough." He brushed two fingers over the back of his other wrist, showing off his own dark skin.

"But they got away," Lorenzo said. "That ain't so good. That ain't even a little bit good."

"Tell me about it," Frederick said. "Word's gonna be out. And that means the white folks'll come after us. No more surprises, not now."

"What are we gonna do?" Lorenzo asked.

"I've said it before—we could try splitting up and disappearing into the woods and the swamps, but you'd best believe they'll come after us," Frederick replied. "Slaves start killin' masters, the white folks don't forget about it. Only other choice—only one—we've got is fighting 'em and whipping 'em."

"We do that?" Three or four anxious slaves, Negroes and copperskins both, said the same thing at the same time.

"Damned right we can." Frederick didn't say they would, only that they could. He hoped they wouldn't notice the distinction. They didn't seem to. "Damned right we can," he repeated, sounding more confident than he felt. "First thing is, we know what happens if we lose."

He waited. Men's and women's heads bobbed up and down. They knew, all right. It wouldn't be pretty. It would be as ugly as vengeful whites could make it. Masters had to be harsh with slaves who rebelled, or they'd face uprisings every day of the week. They understood that as well as the slaves did.

Frederick held up a hand to show he hadn't finished. "Other thing is, with a little luck they won't know we got our hands on these fine guns. They'll come along like we're a bunch of no-accounts. They'll figure they can lick us easy as you please. Are they right?"

"No!" the copperskins and Negroes shouted.

"I can't hear you." Frederick cupped a hand behind his ear, the way he'd seen preachers do when they were riling up their flocks. "Tell me again, people—are they right?"

"*No!*" the men and women of the Liberating Army howled.

"That's right. They're gonna stub their toes. They're gonna fall on their faces. We are free niggers. We are free mudfaces. And we don't aim to let anybody take that away from us, not ever again," Frederick said.

They shouted loud enough to make sure the trees and the rocks heard. Frederick's ears rang. They had the spirit, all right. Whether they would keep it once the white men started shooting at them . . .

"Reckon we can win one fight the way you said—we'll take 'em by surprise, like," Lorenzo said quietly. "But what do we do after that?"

"If we win one fight, we get us more guns and more bullets," Frederick said. "That'll make us stronger. It'll give the white folks somethin' to worry about. And if word of the uprising spreads amongst 'em, it'll spread amongst the slaves, too. What you want to bet this won't be the only hot spot the whites got to pour water on?"

"Hmm." Lorenzo contemplated that. "Well, maybe," he said at last. "It better not be, or we're all as dead as honkers."

"They say some of them big dumb things're still alive, way off in the back country," Frederick said.

"*They say* all kinds of stupid things," Lorenzo replied. "And even if it's true, not enough of 'em are left to do anybody any good—not even themselves."

"Anybody who doesn't want to stay here can run off on his own. I've told folks that before," Frederick said.

"I want to be here. I want to win," Lorenzo said.

"Good," Frederick answered. "So do I."

VI

*T*he Liberating Army could draw on three plantations for livestock and supplies. That went a long way toward making sure the soldiers in that army didn't go hungry right away. Frederick had enough other things to worry about. Adding hunger to the list would have been ... part of what a general was supposed to take care of.

He'd never thought he would be a general. He wondered whether his grandfather had expected the job. He supposed Victor Radcliff must have. The white man had been a prominent officer in the earlier war, the war where English Atlantis and the mother country fought against France. When it came time for Atlantis to rise up against England, who else would the Atlantean Assembly choose to lead its forces? No one else. And who but France would aid Atlantis in her fight against the mother country? Politics could be a crazy business.

Frederick wondered what his grandfather would think of his own rising. Neither Victor Radcliff nor Isaac Fenner, the other First Consul, had done anything against slavery. Maybe they'd thought southern Atlantis would promptly part company with the United States of Atlantis if they tried. Or maybe they hadn't cared—a much more disheartening prospect.

Well, why should they have cared? Frederick thought.

The lash never came down on their backs. It had come down on his. The strokes had healed well enough, but he could still feel them if he twisted the wrong way. He would bear the marks till the day he died. And he would remember the humiliation of being shackled to the whipping post—and the terror of each *snap!—crack!*—till they shoveled dirt over him, too.

If they shoveled dirt over him. If they didn't burn him or chuck him in a river or leave him aboveground as a feast for ravens and vultures and scuttling lizards. Once you raised your hand against the white man, you couldn't expect mercy from him, not even in death.

"You gonna wait for the white folks to come after us, or do you aim to go after them some more before they can?" Lorenzo asked.

"I've been wondering about that." Frederick also wondered if he should admit he wondered. Weren't generals supposed to know everything? Didn't they pull answers out of the air the way a stage magician pulled coins out of people's noses? Maybe white generals did. They got a lot more practice soldiering before they became generals than Frederick ever had. He was reinventing the art from scratch, and had to hope he wouldn't sink the uprising with some silly move a real general would have seen from a mile away. Sighing, he went on, "Looks to me like we ought to move again. If we get used to sitting around on our hunkers, the white folks're liable to just walk right over us once they commence to fight."

"Looks that way to me, too," Lorenzo said. "An' it looks like they'll commence to fight pretty damn quick, too. Longer they wait, more of their slaves'll run off to us."

"Ain't it the truth?" Frederick said. "Mudfaces and niggers're already coming in. Folks want to be free, dammit. And why shouldn't they? Look at what the whites've got. Then look at what they give us. Who wouldn't want to be on the other end of that stick?"

"I want to say nobody wouldn't, but that ain't so," Lorenzo said unhappily. "That son of a bitch of a Jerome who came runnin' in to warn the Menands. And we've had us a couple of fellows who went and disappeared. Don't know where they went, if it wasn't to tell tales on us to the white folks."

"Maybe they just snuck off to hide in the woods," Frederick said. Lorenzo rolled his eyes. Since Frederick didn't believe it, either, he couldn't very well come down on his lieutenant for doubting. He knew how the white folks worked. To stop an uprising, they'd pay spies as much as they had to. They might even reward them with freedom. Frederick didn't think he could stomach freedom bought at the price of betraying other slaves. Some men might not have such a tender conscience, though. Some might not have any conscience at all.

"Which way do you want to go, then?" Lorenzo asked. "Gibsons are off to the east, an' the St. Clairs're north of here. We go after anybody else, we'd have to march back the way we've come."

"Uh-huh." Frederick nodded. "I reckon we better hit the St. Clairs next. If I remember right, their land is on the edge of a good-sized swamp. Things go wrong, that's a good place to hide. White folks won't have an easy time digging us out of it."

"Makes sense," Lorenzo agreed. "Things ain't gone wrong yet, though. Maybe they won't, knock wood." In lieu of wood, he bounced a fist off the side of his own head.

"No, not yet," Frederick said. "But right when you're sure they can't, that's when they do."

Frederick knew that Lucille St. Clair came to Mistress Clotilde's socials, and that she invited Mistress Clotilde to hers. He'd heard that Ebenezer St. Clair was a slow man with an eagle, but not an especially harsh master. The plantation grew cotton and indigo. From everything he'd heard, it made money. Maybe that was Master Ebenezer squeezing every eagle till its eyes popped. Whatever it was, it was something not every plantation could boast.

And it didn't matter an atlantean's worth, not when the Liberating Army was about to call on the place. How would Master Ebenezer record an invasion in his ledgers?

He'd never get the chance, not unless he ran before the slaves who'd freed themselves arrived.

The Negroes and copperskins under Frederick's loose command grumbled when he got them moving. Sure enough, they were happy with what they'd already done. They wanted to sit around and enjoy it for a while.

"You gonna keep sitting when the white folks come and cut your throats?" he asked them. "You gonna wait around for them to do it? You can do that—and I don't reckon you'll need to wait real long. You got to remember, they know we've risen up. Ain't a question that they'll try and smash us. Only question is, when are they gonna come after us?"

His warriors shouldered their rifle muskets. They moved north after him. If they weren't especially enthusiastic, that wasn't the biggest surprise in the world. He didn't think any soldiers could stay enthusiastic about killing—and about laying their own lives on the line. But fighting came with their line of work, and so they did it.

One of the slaves who'd fled to the Liberating Army at the Menands' plantation came from the St. Clairs'. "I think I can get you close to the big house without letting the field hands see you on the way, if that's what you want," he told Frederick as they tramped north.

"That'd be good—let us get at the white folks without anybody warning 'em," Frederick said. He paused, eyeing the Negro he didn't know. "You lead us into an ambush, you may fuck us. All the same, I promise you won't be around to spend whatever the white folks said they'd give you. You understand what I'm talking about?"

"Sure do," the other man answered steadily. "I don't want to fuck you. I want to watch the big house burn, is what I want to do."

"How come? He do somethin' to you in particular?" Frederick asked.

"My woman's gonna have his baby," the Negro said bleakly.

"Oh." Frederick left it right there. That was one of the special miseries black and copperskinned men faced in Atlantis. If a white man set his eyes on their woman, he could take her. Dreadful things happened to slaves who tried to resist. But were you a man at all if you couldn't protect your woman?

Of course, this fellow might be lying, looking for sympathy as he fooled the Liberating Army. If he was, he wouldn't get the chance to profit from it; Frederick had been in deadly earnest about that.

The man led them to a stretch of forest that ran alongside the fields. For a little while, Frederick could imagine himself in the Atlantis that had existed when Edward Radcliffe (his how-many-times-great-grandfather) founded New Hastings. Ferns, barrel trees, a big green cucumber slug clinging to the trunk of a pine, spicy odors in the air, birds chirping . . . No sign that anything had changed, except for the weight of the rifle musket on his back and the pull of the sling against his shoulder.

"Hold up," said the Negro from the St. Clairs' plantation—his name was Andrew. "We're almost there. If you kind of scoot forward, you'll be able to see the big house through the ferns."

Frederick scooted up till the leaves of the ferns started tickling his nose. Sure enough, there was the big house. The columned front porch would have looked incongruous to anyone who didn't take that style of building for granted, but Frederick did, so he saw nothing strange in it.

Chickens pecked in the yard between the big house and the barn. An enormous hog rolled in its wallow. And . . . as Frederick watched, a dozen white men with longarms rode up to the house. Another white, presumably Ebenezer St. Clair, came out to greet them.

"Damnation," Frederick muttered. "They're getting reinforcements." He called Lorenzo forward—he wanted the copperskin to see for himself. When he had, Frederick asked, "Can we take them?"

"If we can't, we'd better go home and let them do what they want with us, because we don't deserve to win," Lorenzo said. "I do wish we would've got here before they went into the house. Killing 'em in there'll be a lot harder. How'd they know to come here, anyways?"

"Maybe one of our runaways went and told them. Or maybe they've sent people to the Gibsons' place, too. Only stands to reason we'd go after one or the other," Frederick said. "Doesn't much matter either way. They're there, and we gotta get 'em. I wish we'd beaten them here, too, but I'm not gonna fret about that now. All I'm gonna do is, I'm gonna make sure we've got our guns loaded."

He passed the word back to his followers. They would vastly outnumber the whites inside the St. Clairs' big house. The defenders would fight from splendid cover, though. And they would be very determined. Frederick was sure of that. How well would his own copperskins and blacks fight? Whites professed to believe slaves *couldn't* fight—and did their damnedest to make sure slaves never got the chance.

Well, they had their chance now. And they were at least as well armed as their enemies. Lieutenant Torrance would be kicking himself if he could know . . . or would he? He was a Croydon man. Maybe he was smiling down from heaven now.

As soon as Frederick had the word that his followers would indeed be fighting with weapons loaded, he said, "Let's go get 'em, then. Use the best cover you can find, and get up as close to the big house as you can. We may have to set it on fire to smoke those white bastards out of there. I'd sooner not, but I won't worry if it comes to that. The secret's out. The white folks know we're in arms against 'em. So now we've got to win. Come on!"

They emerged from the woods and trotted toward the big house. Lorenzo led a smaller party over toward the barn. That would give the Liberating Army cover almost as good as the big house offered the whites.

Bang! A gun barked from the big house. A copperskin howled and clutched at his shoulder. "Get down!" Frederick called to his fighters. "Get flat! Crawl! Get behind things to shoot." Reloading a rifle musket while flat wasn't quite impossible, but it was a long way from easy. On the other hand, getting killed standing up wasn't so good, either.

A bullet cracking past his ear persuaded him to follow his own order. He wriggled forward through the grass. A small yellow-green lizard scooted away from him in horror, or perhaps derision.

"Keep coming!" a white man yelled from the big house. "We'll shoot you down like the mad dogs you are!"

The white didn't believe slaves could fight, not down in his heart he didn't. He stood at an open window to shout defiance at them. Half a dozen rifle muskets spoke in the space of a heartbeat. He clutched at his chest and fell over. If he wasn't dead, he was badly hurt. The Negroes and copperskins raised a cheer.

"Who's next?" Frederick called. Nobody answered him, not the way the first man had reviled the Liberating Army.

Frederick slithered towards a boulder. Once he got behind it, he aimed his longarm at an upstairs window and waited. Sooner or later, somebody would shoot from that spot. Sooner, he judged: it let a marksman look down on targets he wouldn't be able to spot from ground level.

Was that movement there? Sure enough, a gun barrel poked out the window. He pulled the trigger. When the hammer came down on the percussion cap, the cap spat flame into the black powder in the firing chamber. The rifle musket punched his shoulder. Yes, the percussion system beat the devil out of any flintlock ever made. No hang fire, no delay, nothing but instant murder—if your aim was good.

And Frederick's was. The white man up there toppled forward when he was hit, and hung half inside, half outside the window. Several bullets spanged off the boulder after that. The cloud of gunpowder smoke hanging above it might have said *Here I am! Shoot me!*

Off to one side, the pig he'd seen wallowing let out a squeal of agony. *Roast pork after we win*, he thought.

A copperskin came out of the barn with a lantern in his hand. Fire and oil made a deadly combination—if he could chuck the lantern into the big house without getting shot down. He raced toward the white men's shelter. Bullets whipped past him, but he threw the lantern through a window—glass crashed—and then turned to dash for safety. A round caught him then, in the small of the back.

He fell forward and kept on trying to crawl away. More bullets bit him after that. Before long, he stopped moving.

Why didn't the big house explode into flame? Had the white men smothered the fire? Had it gone out? Frederick swore. He didn't want his followers to give up their lives for nothing.

Out of the barn trotted several men carrying a stout pole. Frederick realized at once what they had in mind. A battering ram would knock in the front door . . . if they could get close enough to use it. "Shoot at the front windows, fast as you can!" he shouted to his men. "Everybody with a pistol, now's the time to use it!"

He pulled out his own. The range was long for good shooting from a revolver, but he could keep the defenders ducking. Right now, that counted for more than accuracy.

He and his men banged away at the big house. The copperskins and Negroes with the pole thundered forward. Whites popped up to shoot at them. One of the whites caught a bullet in the face. He slumped back into the big house. A moment later, a copperskin on the pole grabbed his leg and fell. The rest kept coming. Another man was wounded as they climbed the stairs to the porch.

"Come on!" Frederick yelled. "Charge!" If the battering ram broke in, the Liberating Army would win the fight all at once. If it didn't . . . He didn't care to think about that.

He rushed toward the big house. When you were running, not thinking came easier. His fighters were charging the place with him. He would have been mighty lonely had they hung back—but not for long. After that, he would have just been dead.

Thud! After so many gunshots, the noise of the pole slamming into the door didn't seem like much. The door sagged in on its hinges, but didn't open. The men with the battering ram hit it again. One more of them fell, shot from behind the door, but they knocked it in. Then they dropped the pole in the doorway, so the whites inside would have a harder time shoving the door closed again.

Frederick seemed to fly up the stairs. A few men were ahead of him, but not many. A white stood in the doorway with a shotgun. The twin barrels looked wide as a railroad tunnel to Frederick. But one of the slaves shot the white before he could pull the trigger. He fell backward, and sent the charge into—through—the roof of the porch. It blasted a hole big enough to pitch a turkey through. It would have done the same to Frederick's midsection. Yes, not thinking was easier.

Then he was inside the house, blinking as his eyes adjusted to the gloom. That was a mad mêlée. The whites still on their feet swung muskets and shotguns club-fashion— they had no time to reload. One of them smashed a Negro's head with a blow so hard, it broke the stock off his weapon. Another Negro bayoneted him. He squealed like a stuck pig. "Here's another one, you fucker!" the black roared. "And another one! And another one!" A man often needed a lot of sticking before he died. That defender got every bit he needed, and more besides.

Another white man was grappling with a copperskin when Frederick bayoneted him just above the left kidney. He threw his arms out wide and went rigid. It was the pose Frederick imagined a man struck by lightning might take. He didn't hold it long—the copperskin brained him with a hatchet. Something warm and wet splashed Frederick's face. He wiped it away with his sleeve, which showed both red and grayish pink.

His stomach didn't turn over, as it surely would have a couple of weeks before. He was getting hardened to the horrors of fighting.

Quite suddenly, it was over. A couple of whites still writhed on the ground, but the men of the Liberating Army finished them off, one with a bayonet in the throat, the other with a bullet through the head.

"Let's go on upstairs," Lorenzo said as he took the chance to ram a fresh charge of powder and a bullet down the barrel of his rifle musket. "Better make sure nobody's hiding up there."

Frederick nodded. "Do it." A party of copperskins and Negroes hurried up the curving stairway. He didn't think they would find anyone. Whatever else you could say about

the white men who'd tried to defend Eb St. Clair's plantation, they didn't lack for courage.

But he hadn't thought things through. The screams that
rang out there were torn from women's throats. And those
screams went on and on. A few minutes later, Andrew
came downstairs doing up his trousers, a sated smirk on
his face. "Never reckoned I'd get even with the master *that*
way," he said.

"Uh-huh," Frederick said uncomfortably, looking
up from the place where the defenders *had* managed to
smother the fire from the lantern before it took hold. He
hadn't wanted this kind of thing to happen, but he wasn't
surprised it had, even if it wasn't his idea of sport. Whether
all the men had revenge on their minds or nothing more
than a brief good time, he couldn't have said. What he did
say was, "We've got to knock them over the head when
we're through with them. Can't have them telling tales on
us. That'd only make things worse if the white folks catch
some of our people."

Andrew nodded. Then he looked around at the ghastly
aftermath of the fight. "Best thing we can do with this whole
place is burn it down. Then nobody outside will know for
sure what all happened here."

Frederick remembered that he'd said he wanted to
see the St. Clairs' big house burn. He had his reasons for
what he was saying now. That didn't make them bad reasons, though. And Frederick found himself nodding back.
"Yes, we'd better do that. And we'd better make sure we're
ready to fight as soon as we do. The white folks'll figure out
enough of what happened, anyways, and they'll send a real
army against us the next time, not just a little gang like this
here one."

"Always the swamp if things go wrong," Andrew said.

"I know," Frederick answered through the screams that
still rang out from upstairs. "It's there, but how much good
will it do us?"

Andrew took pride in setting the big house alight. Frederick made sure the Liberating Army salvaged all the weap-

ons and bullets and cartridges in the place before firing it. He had more people to arm: Ebenezer St. Clair's slaves were eager to join his force. "We got a lot to pay back, we do," a copperskin said. The rest of the bondsmen and -women nodded agreement.

Even as the big house's pyre rose into the air, Frederick wondered from which direction the white folks would try to hit back. If it was an army, he guessed it would come openly. Like the small contingent that had tried to save the St. Clair plantation, the whites wouldn't really believe their property could fight. They wouldn't sneak through the woods to get close.

"One thing we need," Lorenzo said. "We need to put stuff in front of us to stop bullets and keep the whites from spotting us."

He could have put it more elegantly, which didn't make him wrong. Some kind of barricade would be a lifesaver and a spirit lifter . . . if the Liberating Army put it in the right place. In the wrong place, it would be worse than useless. *Now if only I were sure where the right place is*, Frederick thought. He had his guesses, but that was all they were.

Then he realized he could make those guesses more likely to come true. He talked for a while with one of the young women who'd seemed most zealous about getting her own back against everything and everyone that had conspired to make her a slave. Her name was Jane.

"What happens to me afterwards?" she asked when he got done—also the first question he would have thought of.

"Chance you take," he answered honestly. "Maybe you can find some way to slip off, or maybe they'll reckon you were a poor dumb nigger who didn't know any better. But maybe not, too. I can't make you go tell 'em lies. All I can do is ask."

"I'll do it," Jane said at once. "Don't think I'll ever get a better chance to give 'em one in the teeth."

The story she would tell the local whites was calculated to make them move even faster than they would have anyway. That meant the Liberating Army had to move fast, too. Like Lorenzo, Frederick wanted that barricade so badly he could taste it. The Negroes and copperskins he set to work building it promptly started complaining. "I'm workin' harder here than I did in the cotton fields," one man said.

"Everything you did there went straight into your master's pocket," Frederick told him. "Everything you're doin' here sets the white folks up for a kick in the balls. Which one you like better?"

"Huh," the fellow said, and went back to work.

Slaves from all over the countryside kept coming into the Liberating Army's encampment. "You got the white folks jumpin' like fleas on a hot griddle," one of them said. "They're bellowin' like bulls. Everybody's speechifyin', goin' on about what a mess they'll make out o' you."

"Well, they can try," Frederick answered. It was what he wanted to hear, which didn't mean he trusted it. If he could send lies out to the white folks, nothing stopped them from sending lies in to him.

When he explained that to Helen, her eyes widened. "It's a wonder you trust a living soul," she said.

"I trust you. I trust Lorenzo. I'd trust Davey, if he didn't stop that shotgun charge with his chest," he said. "Past that . . . Past that, I make sure I cut the cards. Twice. Wouldn't you?"

He had no reason to doubt that the local militia had been called up. The only reason the militia existed was to crush slave uprisings. If the whites *didn't* call it up, they were fools.

And then word came that they were moving on the St. Clairs' plantation. Frederick imagined a straggling file of men singing marching songs left over from the war where their grandfathers—and his own—beat the English. Maybe it wasn't really like that, but that was how he saw it.

His own men—and the occasional woman who carried a rifle musket or one of the old-style guns the Liberating Army had taken from the plantations they'd overrun—started to grumble about staying close to the barricade. "You didn't want to build it, and now you don't want to use it?" he said. "Where's the sense in that?"

And then, early the next morning, a big cloud of dust rising from the road that went by the St. Clairs' place warned that the white militiamen were getting close. After that,

Frederick had no more trouble getting his fighters to take their places. He wondered if any of them would leg it for the friendly swamp. He didn't catch anybody doing that, anyhow.

He could see the militiamen pretty soon. They were coming the way he wanted them to. Maybe they would have anyhow, or maybe they'd listened to brave Jane. Some of them wore gray uniforms like Atlantean regular soldiers. Others had on ordinary farm and town clothes. They showed no better order than his own followers—worse, if anything. But he gulped when he saw them manhandling along a small fieldpiece. He didn't have anything that could answer a cannon.

"Let them start shooting first," he told his troops. "They think they can scare us away." He hoped the whites were wrong. If they were as overconfident as he thought, they would get too close before they opened up. That would make them easier targets. "And . . . " He told off a handful of his best marksmen. "Shoot the fellows serving that cannon. The faster you kill 'em, the less harm it'll do."

"Right," one of them said tightly. They were nervous. Well, so was he, but he had to do his best not to show it.

A white man with a flag of truce stepped out in front of the militia's ragged battle line. "You slaves better give up now!" he bawled. "You do, and we'll let some of you live— the ones who ain't leaders or anything. You fight, though, and there'll be no quarter for you."

The Negroes and copperskins crouched behind their barricade looked toward Frederick. If answering was up to him, he'd make things as plain as he could. "Go fuck your-self!" he shouted back.

"All right, nigger," the militiamen's herald said in a voice like iron. "If that's how you want it, that's how it'll be." He turned on his heel and walked back to his men. He evidently trusted his foes not to violate a flag of truce, anyhow. Frederick wondered why. The white man pointed toward the barricade. "Fire!" he roared.

His men delivered a rippling volley. The cannon thundered. The men tending it plainly had little expertise. The ball flew high over the barricade and smashed into the St.

Clairs' barn on the fly. A few musket balls struck people who'd been peering over the barricade at the militiamen. Howls of pain rose into the humid air. The Liberating Army had no surgeons. They would have to learn battle-field medicine on the fly or do without.

The militiamen stood there in the open while they re-loaded. Were they begging to get killed? If they were, Frederick was happy to oblige them. "Fire!" he yelled, and drew a bead on the enemy commander, whose coat was splendid with gold epaulets and buttons.

He missed. The man stayed on his feet, waving and shouting orders. What those orders were soon grew plain: he wanted his troops to charge the slaves' barricade. Did he really believe the sight of white men advancing on them— most of the militiamen didn't even have bayonets—would make the copperskins and Negroes crouching there break and run? If he did, he was too stupid to live, even if Frederick hadn't knocked him down at the first try.

Boom! The cannon fired again. This time, the ball flew just over the heads of the Liberating Army. The men at the piece could be deadly dangerous if they got the chance to figure out what they were doing. But Frederick's sharp-shooters were making sure they wouldn't last long enough. In the whites' wrath and inexperience, they'd pushed the gun too far forward—it sat within easy rifle-musket range. One after another, the artillerymen went down. Wounded or dead hardly mattered here. As long as they couldn't aim and fire the field gun, one would do as well as the other.

Frederick looked for the enemy commander again. He didn't see him—somebody else must have shot him. The whites advancing on the barricade leaned forward, as if into a heavy rainstorm. But rain wasn't hitting them; bullets were. Most of their foes had longarms better than the ones they carried themselves. The copperskins and Negroes weren't great shots, but they didn't have to be to do what they were doing.

A white man in a gray uniform tunic and wool home-spun pants stopped to shake his fist at the rough wall from which fire and death spat. "You shitasses don't fight fair!" he cried, as if the Liberating Army's fighters were supposed to. No one stood up to answer him, which might have proved his point. He gathered himself and kept coming.

He got shot a few paces closer to the barricade. Maybe *that* proved his point. Frederick didn't care one way or the other. Fighting fair wasn't his biggest worry. Fighting to win was.

A couple of militiamen who seemed to know what they were up to remained at the cannon. The men who tried to help them plainly had no idea what they were supposed to do. The experienced artillerists shouted and gestured, which made them more obvious targets for Frederick's marksmen. They went down one after the other. The cannon kept firing after that, but wildly.

Some of the whites actually reached the barricade. It did them less good than they'd thought it would. The Negroes and copperskins on the other side didn't run away. They went right on shooting. At close quarters, they used the bayonet. As Frederick had seen inside Ebenezer St. Clair's house, it gave them a big reach advantage on men trying to fight with clubbed muskets.

"Godalmightydamn!" That was Lorenzo's joyful shout. "We really can lick these sorry sons of bitches!" Some wonder was mixed with the delight. Had he doubted it before? Frederick sure had, though it would have taken hot pincers to tear the admission from him.

The whites—those of them still on their feet—took longer to reach the same conclusion. When they did, it seemed to suck the spirit out of them. Fear swallowed fury. They turned and ran back the way they had come. Some of them threw away their muskets and shotguns to run faster.

None of them, Frederick noted, tried to surrender. That was just as well. He had no idea how he would have tended to prisoners of war. His men were as happy to shoot their enemies in the back as they had been to shoot them in the chest. Happier: now the whites weren't shooting back.

A few militiamen escaped. It took a lot of bullets to hit a man, especially in the heat of battle, when fighters weren't aiming so carefully as they might have. But only a few got away. "Lord Jesus!" Frederick said in wondering tones. "We just shot down most of the white men for miles around."

"Serves 'em right," Lorenzo said. "They weren't gonna worry about how many of us they shot."

"I know," Frederick said. "But what'll they do now? What *can* they do now?"

"They can leave us the hell alone, that's what," the copperskin said. "What else do we want, except to stay free and live in peace?"

"Ain't gonna happen," Frederick said sorrowfully. "They can't afford to let us do that. They'd have uprisings all over the slave states, and slaves runnin' off to come live with us instead of the white folks they belong to."

"Good." Lorenzo's voice was savage.

"Good for us, sure. Not so good for the white folks," Frederick said. "They aren't stupid. They'll see that for themselves. They'll see they've got to finish us off no matter what."

"You should have thought of that before you rearranged Matthew's face," Lorenzo said.

"Oh, I did," Frederick answered. "Not a lot of hope here, but no hope at all livin' the way I was livin'."

"Speaking of finishing off, that's what we'd better tend to with all the wounded whites on the ground," Lorenzo said.

Frederick didn't need to give orders for that. The men and women of the Liberating Army were tending to it on their own. They climbed over the barricade and started looting the corpses—and making sure the bodies they looted *were* corpses. Bayonets were more useful for that than clubbed muskets would have been, too.

They didn't just take weapons and money, though those delighted them. But they also harvested shoes and clothes—many of which would have to be soaked in cold water before anyone could wear them again—as well as pocket knives and other such small prizes. By slavery's modest standards, the fighters were newly rich.

They didn't want to bury the bodies. Frederick had to cajole them into digging a long, shallow trench into which they tossed them. Otherwise, the stink and, probably, the disease would soon have become unbearable. Yellow fever hadn't followed them from the Barfords' plantation, for which he thanked heaven. He didn't want other plagues coming down on their heads.

"Gonna be a while before the white folks try and mess with us again," Lorenzo said proudly. "We learned 'em a real lesson, by God."

"We did. We really did." Frederick sounded almost as surprised as Lorenzo had before him. For now, he was master of all he surveyed.

For now.

BOOK II

VII

New Hastings in August could be hot and muggy, as if it belonged with the states much farther south. Or, at the same season, it could be the kind of place where you needed an extra blanket on your bed. It all depended on which way the wind blew.

And that was also a good enough description of how politics worked in the United States of Atlantis. Senators shouted and shook their fists at one another. Some of them brandished canes. No one had yet pulled an eight-shooter on the Senate floor, but it was probably only a matter of time.

Up on the dais, Consul Leland Newton and Consul Jeremiah Stafford eyed each other with perfect mutual loathing. The quarrel on the floor was about slavery. The Senators quarreled about other things, too, but slavery lay at the bottom of most of them.

Consul Newton reached for his gavel at last. He rapped loudly. "Order!" he said. "There will be order!"

"King Canute commanded the tides, and look how much good it did him," Consul Stafford said scornfully.

Bang! Bang! Newton rapped again, even louder this time. "There will be order! The Sergeant at Arms has the authority to impose order on the Conscript Fathers, and he will!"

The Sergeant at Arms sat at the foot of the dais. His person was inviolable; any man who presumed to strike at him would be banished from the Senate floor. That gave him a certain prestige no other government official enjoyed. All the same, he didn't look eager to perform his duties.

And he didn't have to. "I forbid it," Stafford said, which was all it took. The Sergeant at Arms relaxed. Both Consuls had to agree before anything happened.

Back when the victors in the war against England framed the Atlantean Charter, they'd arranged this system to make sure no one exercised too much power. They'd assumed both Consuls would pull in harness most of the time, and that one would veto the other's actions only in rare and extraordinary circumstances. So it proved, too—for about a generation. After that . . .

They didn't see how the two halves of the country would pull apart, Leland Newton thought bitterly. He was a small, sharp-nosed man in his mid-fifties, with very blue eyes. He had Radcliffe blood on his mother's side, but so what? Most politicians did, on one side of the family tree or the other. Consul Stafford did, too. They might be cousins, but they weren't kissing cousins.

"Consuls! Consuls! Let an honest man address the honorable Consuls!" cried Senator Bainbridge of New Marseille.

Oh? Do you know one? went through Newton's mind. Justinian Bainbridge was as slippery as a sleet-coated sidewalk, and everybody knew it. But he had followed the rituals of the Senate—no mean feat in these turbulent times. "You may speak," Newton said. Jeremiah Stafford did not forbid it. Why should he, when Bainbridge belonged to his faction?

"I thank the honorable Consul," the Senator said. "I rise to protest the government's impotence in the face of the vicious and cruel slave insurrection convulsing my state at this very moment."

That touched off the match under the powder barrel. Everybody in the chamber started yelling at everybody else. Somebody swung a cane. Someone else blocked it with his own. The noise, like a gunshot—much too much like a gunshot—cut through the rest of the furious racket. It seemed to sober the Senators, at least for a little while.

Consul Newton turned to Consul Stafford. "May I speak to that?"

His colleague's gaze was full of contempt. "You may as well, yes. Since you are the main reason the government remains impotent, putting yourself on the record would make a pleasant novelty."

"I thank you." Newton, as was his habit, met contempt with irony. He looked out at Justinian Bainbridge. "Are you not the man who commonly trumpets loudest when the Atlantean government proposes to do anything that infringes upon what you style state sovereignty?"

"I am," Bainbridge answered proudly; he wouldn't have recognized irony had it tiptoed up to him and piddled in his boot. "But the circumstances differ this time."

"If you say that in English, doesn't it mean, *This time, my ox is being gored*?" Newton's manner was pleasant, his words and expression anything but.

"My ox *is* being gored, God damn it to hell!" Yes, Senator Bainbridge was irony-proof. "These miserable niggers and mudfaces running around loose as if they're as good as white men, killing, stealing—!" He broke off, spluttering in indignation.

"Yes, white men have proved remarkably good at killing and stealing," Newton agreed in his politest tones. "It must be surprising to see our colored brethren imitate us so well."

Jeremiah Stafford favored him with a glance that could have curdled milk. Stafford and Bainbridge believed the same things. Bainbridge believed them because he believed them—for the same reason he accepted the mysteries of his faith. Stafford had carefully examined slavery and what it did for his section of the United States of Atlantis. Having examined it, he'd found it good. And he knew all the reasons he found it good, and could—and did—argue most cogently from them.

To Newton, that he could find it good to begin with was incomprehensible. But the depth of the other Consul's knowledge of the subject made him formidable in debate. So did his native cleverness. People didn't call him the Greased Snake for nothing.

"May I ask my fellow Consul a question?" Stafford inquired in his politest, and most dangerous, tones.

"By all means, sir." Leland Newton could also be formidably ironic. He gestured in invitation. "You see? I refuse you nothing."

"Why refuse when you can veto?" Consul Stafford shook his head. "Never mind. That was not the question I intended. This is: imagine, sir, if you will, that an insurrection has broken out in the sovereign state of New Marseille, an insurrection marked by murder and arson and all manner of lesser crimes."

"He doesn't need to imagine it!" Justinian Bainbridge howled. "It's happening right this minute!"

"Bear with me, Senator," Stafford said easily. He turned back to Consul Newton. "Now imagine that this insurrection is the product of white ruffians and robbers, with not a single mudface or nigger attached to it. If New Marseille appealed to the Senate of the United States of Atlantis for aid under those circumstances, would you prevent that aid from coming?"

Howls and whoops rose from the slaveholding states' Senators. Porfirio Cardenas of Gernika roared so loud, he suffered a coughing fit. One of his colleagues had to pound him on the back. Newton muttered under his breath. He supposed it had been necessary to incorporate what once was Spanish Atlantis into the USA. Now the red-crested eagle flew over the whole mid-Atlantic land mass. But adding the new state gave weight to the pro-slavery side, and the Spaniards had a name for being harsh masters. So did the Atlanteans from farther north who'd flocked into the new state to try to get rich quick.

Newton had waited too long. Stafford called him on it: "You see? Against white rebels, dragoons and artillery would already be on the way."

"Not necessarily," Newton said, buying himself time to think.

"Oh? How not?" Stafford returned with ominous calm.

"If white men rebelled because they were dreadfully

mistreated, because they could suffer any sort of punishment at their masters' hands without due process of law, because they were not allowed to take wives, and because the women with whom they cohabited could be forced into a master's arms at his whim, would we not applaud them? Would we not send *them* dragoons and artillery to aid their fight against injustice?" Consul Newton took a deep breath.

He got the same tumultuous cheers for his answer as Stafford had for his question, but not from the same men. The Senators from north of the Stour (the Erdre, southern men still sometimes called the river, preserving the French name) clapped their hands and shouted. Those who favored slavery tried to drown them out with hoots and catcalls, but couldn't quite.

When something close to order returned, Jeremiah Stafford said, "There is a difference, you know."

"Oh? And that would be . . . ?" Newton asked.

"Simply that white men are of our own kind, our equals by nature. Niggers and mudfaces are not, and never can be."

"Such an assertion would be all the better for proof," Newton remarked.

"I have a great plenty of it, and should be delighted to give you as much as you require," Consul Stafford said.

"Move we adjourn!" shouted Harris Mitchell of Freetown. His state bordered the Stour on the north. Slavery had lasted longer there than elsewhere in the north of Atlantis. Freetown wasn't neutral ground, but came closer than any other state.

And a motion to adjourn was always in order. Half a dozen Senators roared seconds. The motion passed overwhelmingly. Everyone seemed relieved to stream out of the Senate chamber. One more day without blood on the floor . . . One more day, yes, but it had been a damned near-run thing.

When Jeremiah Stafford talked with officers in the Ministry of War, he was exceeding his authority under the Atlantean Charter. Consuls commanded an army in the field on alternate days—if an army *was* in the field. If not, they were supposed to fight shy of matters military.

You had to know where a man came from. More than anything else, that told you where he stood. Oh, there were exceptions. Some northern officers despised Negroes and copperskins enough to lean toward keeping them in bondage. Rather fewer southerners thought slavery morally wrong. On the whole, though, geography and politics walked hand in hand.

Major Sam Duncan was from Cosquer. Consul Stafford had known him for years. Duncan had Radcliffe blood, too, which made them kinsmen of sorts. Stafford passed his latest news on to the officer: "Do you know what the nigger leading the rising is claiming? He says he's Victor Radcliff's grandson."

"Likely tell!" Duncan said. He was a solidly built man in his early forties, with bushy muttonchop whiskers that didn't suit the shape of his face. "One of my brother's copperskins said he was descended from the Holy Ghost. A good dose of the lash changed his mind in a hurry."

"I expect it would," Stafford agreed.

"When are we going to be able to send our soldiers over there and clean out those coons, sir?" Duncan asked. "The longer the government shilly-shallies, the more trouble they'll kick up. Liable to be insurrections all the way from the Hesperian Gulf to the Atlantic coast."

"You understand that, Major, and I understand it, and most men of sense do as well," the Consul said. "Too many people, though, don't appreciate the difficulties inherent in the situation."

"Damn fools, if you care what I think," Duncan said.

"Oh, I agree with you," Stafford answered. "But our founders, in their wisdom—if that's what it was—made it possible for determined folk, wise or not, to hamstring the government. Consul Newton remains opposed to the national government's movement against the insurrectionists. This being so, nothing official may be done."

He waited. He'd always thought Sam Duncan politically astute. That was one of the reasons he'd cultivated the man. But, if the major didn't hear what he was saying, he might have to change his mind.

Duncan tugged at one of his muttonchops. He didn't

smoke; the side whiskers gave him something to do with his hands while he thought. His eyes, always heavy-lidded, narrowed further. "Nothing official, you say?"

Jeremiah Stafford smiled—inside himself, where it didn't show. He hadn't been wrong after all. Major Duncan *did* have ears to hear. "Unfortunately, that is correct," Stafford said, sounding grave as a doctor delivering a gloomy prognosis.

"Some unofficial things might be done, though?" Duncan, by contrast, spoke in musing tones. "Give some fellows leave to return home, say? Or transfer weapons to state militias without worrying too much about paperwork? Things like that?"

"If they're done unofficially, I don't need to know about them," Stafford answered. "No one needs to know about them, not officially."

"All right, Consul. I get you." Duncan laid a finger by the side of his nose. "Nobody will find out. We'll do—"

Stafford held up a hand. "This discussion has been purely hypothetical, you understand. I would prefer that it stay that way. What I have not heard, I am not in the least responsible for."

"I get you." Major Duncan nodded. "I wouldn't be surprised if something like that happened."

"Well, it might be interesting if something like that did." Now Jeremiah Stafford let the outside of his physiognomy show amusement. He felt muscles creaking under his skin; he didn't smile all that often. "I wager the mudfaces and niggers would think it was pretty interesting, too."

"That's the idea, isn't it?" Duncan sketched a salute. "A pleasure talking hypothetically with you, your Excellency."

"Always glad to visit with someone from the old stand." Stafford meant that. To him, New Hastings was another world. People here didn't see things with the same simple certainties they used down in Cosquer. They had their own convictions. Those often struck Stafford as lunatic if not wicked, but the locals clung to them all the same.

The Consul left the Ministry of War: an impressive neoclassical marble pile with an even more impressive statue of Mars (done by a Frenchman who'd ended up quarreling about his fee) in front of it. In the streets around the Ministry stood a number of eateries and other shops that catered to the soldiers and civilian employees who worked there. If Stafford ever needed a cavalry saber or a waterproof oilskin cape, he knew where to get one.

A gray-uniformed sentry came to attention as Stafford loosed his horse's reins from the hitching rail and swung up onto the animal. Then, gravely nodding in return, he rode back toward the center of town. As the horse walked along, Stafford felt the weight of history pressing down on him. Despite the New in its name, New Hastings was the oldest town in Atlantis—four centuries old now. Everyone learned the jingle "In fourteen hundred and fifty-two, Ed Radcliffe sailed the ocean blue."

Not everyone remembered that François Kersauzon, a Breton fisherman, showed Edward Radcliffe the way to Atlantis. Cosquer, Consul Stafford's hometown, was a Breton foundation. But it dated from after New Hastings. The Radcliffes and Radcliffs always seemed to be half a step ahead of the Kersauzons—always when it mattered most, anyhow.

And, while Cosquer grew, it never thrived the way New Hastings did. Only a few years after the first settlement, people from New Hastings had founded Bredestown, miles up the river from the coast. They'd kept pushing west ever since, too.

The great redwood church still dominated the center of New Hastings. Built before the Reformation, it had begun as a Catholic cathedral. It stayed Catholic for some years after England went Protestant but eventually conformed to the Anglican rite. The Atlantean Assembly had met there to plan the war against England ... till the redcoats ran the Conscript Fathers out, after which they carried on as best they could from the hamlet of Honker's Mill. Once victory was won—rather to the Atlantean Assembly's surprise, unless Stafford missed his guess—the country's leading lights returned to hammer out the Charter that bedeviled Atlantis to this day.

Stafford muttered under his breath. Maybe things would have gone differently, gone better, had the Senate chosen to build a new capital away from everything instead of settling down in a northern city already opposed to slavery. There was talk of it, but it had seemed too expensive to a country bedeviled by debt from the war for liberty.

He muttered again. The black grandson of Victor Radcliff demanding liberty for bondsmen? Jeremiah Stafford knew it was possible. The First Consul would have been no more immune to the lusts of the flesh than any other man. Possible or not, though, it had to be denied. If true—no, if believed true—it gave the rising too much prestige.

A constable held up a white-gloved hand. Stafford halted his horse. So did the other riders and drivers on his street. The constable turned and waved, letting cross traffic through. After a while, he held up his hand to stop it, and Stafford's forward progress resumed. Not all of New Hastings' notions were ancient. The Consul quite liked the traffic-control scheme.

By contrast, he could have lived without the railroad station. It resembled nothing so much as an enormous, soot-stained brick barn. The rumble from arriving and departing trains frightened horses, and the smoke their engines belched fouled the air. Yes, they made travel much faster than it had ever been before. Yes, they could haul far more people and goods than horse-drawn coaches and wagons. But they were filthy. That was the only word that fit.

He wasn't sure he liked gas lamps, either. They threw more light than candles and lanterns, true. But they were also more dangerous. When a gas line broke and caught fire . . . Several square blocks had burned in Hanover two years before, or was it three now?

Telegraph wires crowded the sky. They had their uses. News that would have needed days, maybe weeks, to cross the country now raced at the speed of lightning. The government could have taken advantage of that to help put down this insurrection quickly. It could have, but it hadn't. That made the wires seem even uglier to Consul Stafford than they would have otherwise. His lips moved as he silently damned Leland Newton.

Well, no matter what the other Consul thought, there

were ways around things even if there weren't ways straight through them. He'd started using some of those ways. Now he had to hope his machinations would let the local whites do the job that needed doing.

A moment later, he found his own way straight through to the Senate House and adjoining Consular residences blocked. A wagon had lost a wheel, spilling barrels and clogging the street. The pungent smell of beer hung in the air. A teamster cursed in a sonorous brogue. People milled about, trying to escape the jam.

The way around, Jeremiah Stafford thought. He turned his own horse back the way he'd come. First to find the way out. Then to find the side streets that would, eventually, get him where he wanted to go.

Consul Newton gave a newsboy a cent for a copy of the new day's *New Hastings Strand.* "Here you are, sir," the boy said, handing him the paper.

"Thank you kindly." Newton held it out almost at arm's length. The print was small, and his eyes seemed to have more trouble with it every month. He had a pair of reading glasses, but didn't like them. They turned the more distant world to a fuzzy blur.

By wire from New Marseille, a story boasted. It told of people fleeing to the West Coast city from plantations and smaller towns to the east. *The rampage of the colored desperadoes only continues and intensifies!* the reporter in New Marseille wrote. *Local authorities seem powerless to quell their depredations, while the national government does nothing.*

Anyone could guess where his affiliations on the question of slavery lay. But the *Strand* wasn't a pro-slavery paper. There weren't many of those north of the Stour. Maybe it printed this story because the choice lay between printing it and going without news. Or maybe the *Strand* had decided the uprising needed quashing even if mistreated slaves—a redundancy if ever there was one—had finally had more than they could stand.

The governor of New Marseille had proclaimed a state of emergency, the piece went on. He was drafting all able-bodied men into the state militia. He wasn't quite begging the Atlantean soldiers in New Marseille to desert and sign up with the militia, but he was quoted as saying, "We're looking for men experienced in handling weapons."

Governor Donovan was also appealing for aid from other states "that share our institutions and our dangers." Reading the rest of the front page, Consul Newton doubted whether Donovan would get as much help as he wanted. Insurrections were breaking out in the states of Cosquer and Gernika and Nouveau Redon: like forest fires in a lightning storm after a long drought. The slaveholding states east of the Green Ridge Mountains might be too busy closer to home to send men or guns off to the west.

A man in a plug hat came up to Newton and demanded, "What are you going to do about the niggers, Consul?"

No one would have spoken to Queen Victoria that way. No one would have addressed her Prime Minister like that, either. Atlanteans were convinced they were as good—and as smart—as their magistrates. The United States of Atlantis rested on that presumption of equality . . . for white men. The idea that men of other breeds might crave the same presumption hadn't sunk in, not south of the Stour it hadn't.

With a sigh, Newton answered, "Right now, friend, I believe I'm going to wait and see what happens next. A lot of the time, you only make things worse when you move too fast."

"How could things *get* any worse than they are?" the man inquired.

"I don't know, and I don't want to find out by experiment, either," Newton said. "One thing I'm sure of: the distance between bad and worse is a lot bigger than the difference between good and better."

"Huh," said the man in the plug hat. "How about the difference between bad and good? Isn't that what we're talking about here?"

"I don't know. Is it?" the Consul answered. "What is good, and how would you make what you don't think good better?"

"You're trying to confuse things." The man strode off

in disgust. Asking questions like that hadn't done Socrates much good, either.

If Leland Newton's foes got sick enough of him, they wouldn't trump up charges against him and make him drink hemlock. They were much more likely to ignore him, to do what they wanted despite justice and Atlantean legality. The Consul opened the paper to see what was on the inside pages. One of the first things that caught his eye was a gunsmith's advertisement. That made him pause for a moment. Back in Socrates' day, no one had carried an eight-shooter. Assassination was easier now than it had been then.

Newton shook his head, annoyed at himself. If you let the hobgoblins of modern life get to you, what could you do but spend your time hiding under the bed and quivering? The hobgoblins were there. They weren't going to go away. You just had to keep on as if they weren't.

And sometimes they even worked for you. When Newton went to his office in the Senate House, his secretary handed him a sheaf of telegrams and letters. "What are these, Isaac?" he asked.

Isaac Ricardo paused a moment, organizing his thoughts. He was at least as clever and capable as his principal. Newton often though he might make at least as good a Consul, too, if not for the impediment of his religion. Consul's secretary was as high as a Jew was likely to rise in Atlantis.

"Some of them are from the southern states, calling you a hound and a swine and a snake in the ferns," Ricardo said. "More come from the north, telling you what a stout fellow you are. After you get through those lots, the rest are the usual sort that want something from you."

"Nothing much out of the ordinary, then," Newton said. His mail had divided into those three categories even before this slave insurrection broke out. From what Jeremiah Stafford said, so had the other Consul's. The only difference was that people from north of the Stour swore at Stafford, while those from his own side of the river praised him to the skies. Newton presumed the people who wanted something from Stafford could come from anywhere.

"Not *too* much out of the ordinary." Ricardo was also

relentlessly precise. "The tone of the political letters—not the begging ones and the scheming ones—seems much more impassioned than it did since the latest unpleasantness commenced."

"Can't say I'm surprised. Well, I'll have a look at them." Consul Newton shook his head ever so slightly as he went into his inner office. On second thought, his secretary, no matter how clever, no matter how capable, probably didn't have what it took to try to lead the United States of Atlantis. *The latest unpleasantness?* Isaac Ricardo would have to become more impassioned himself if he aspired to be a political man.

Newton snorted. So far as he knew, Ricardo harbored no such aspirations. Odds were his secretary was too sensible for it. There were times—more and more of them lately, too—when Leland Newton wished he'd been sensible enough to stay away from politics himself.

He went through the stack of correspondence from the slaveholding states first. He already knew what the people who agreed with him thought: the same as he did. The people who disagreed did so in different ways.

Some of them quoted Scripture to prove he was an idiot. Others simply loaded up their pens with grapeshot and scrap metal and commenced firing. No printer would have dared put several of the day's letters into type, not unless he wanted to spend time behind bars for obscenity. A few of the missives seemed drooled onto the page. Ricardo's *impassioned* didn't begin to cover it, either.

One of the less incandescent letters read, *White men are superior. Black men and copperskinned men are inferior. This being so, white men have the natural right to rule over the other races. Any lover of truth can see as much.* The author, one Zebulon James, appended <u>*A true*</u> *Christian gentleman* to his signature.

"Well, Mr. James, any lover of truth can see you're assuming what you wish to prove," Newton murmured. But if he wrote that back to the true Christian gentleman, would said gentleman understand it? The odds seemed depressingly slim.

A wicked grin spread across the Consul's face. He inked

a pen. *Dear Mr. James*, he wrote, *I am in receipt of yours of the seventeenth* ultimo, *for which I thank you. Before I can act on it, I find that I require more information. Would you be good enough to tell me whether you yourself are a white man, a black man, or a copperskinned man? In any of those cases, I fear your opinion may be imperfectly objective. If perhaps you are a yellow man or a green man, you may have a more dispassionate view of the situation. Do let me know. Kind regards, Leland Newton, Consul, United States of Atlantis.*

If that didn't infuriate Zebulon James, the man was even denser than Newton gave him credit for. The Consul supposed Mr. James could be, but it wouldn't be easy.

Newton also supposed his secretary would disapprove of sending out a letter like that. Well, too bad. If you couldn't have a little fun with your work every now and again, what point to doing it?

"Here is the latest outrage perpetrated by the colored insurrectionists," Jeremiah Stafford growled in the Senate chamber. "They derailed a train bringing volunteers from Nouveau Redon to the state of New Marseille, then set the overturned cars on fire. Many white men were killed, many others badly burnt or otherwise injured. How much longer must this vileness persist before the national government is permitted to take arms against it?" He aimed the question at his fellow Consul.

Senators from the south cheered him. Senators from the north for the most part sat impassive, though several of them looked troubled. Plenty of men who disapproved of slavery remained convinced that white men were better than their copperskinned and black brethren.

If Consul Newton was one of those men, however, he concealed it very well. "May I ask my distinguished colleague a question?" he said mildly.

"How can I refuse you, when we both know you're going to do it regardless?" Stafford returned.

"How right you are," Newton said. "My question is this: what do you suppose those white volunteers would have

visited upon the colored insurrectionists had they reached
New Marseille?"

"What they deserved, by God!" Consul Stafford exclaimed.

"Why does it matter so much to you that these men
have white skins and those men have darker ones?" Newton asked. "Are they not all men, regardless?"

By the angry rumble rolling up from the Conscript Fathers, Consul Stafford knew a great many of them did not
believe a man was a man regardless of the color of his skin.
Stafford didn't believe it, either. "White men made the
United States of Atlantis," he said proudly. "Niggers didn't,
nor did mudfaces. In the wild, they're all savages. And I will
tell you something else, sir, since you seem to have forgotten it: white men's *ideas* made the United States of Atlantis,
too. Thanks to the Greeks and Romans, we are a republic,
and a republic of laws rather than men. No feathered chief-
tain rules us, his every utterance the same as the word of
God."

"Hear, hear!" "Bravo!" "Well said!" The cries of approval and the applause that went with them made Stafford smile. Not all of that came from southern men, not by
any means. Stafford's eyes slid over to his fellow Consul.
He wanted to see how Leland Newton enjoyed this.

If it fazed Newton, he didn't show it. "Wouldn't you
agree, sir," he said, "that one of the so-called white men's
ideas we've built upon is the notion that white men are better than any other sort?"

"I would," Stafford said proudly, "for that claim is the
truth. White men *are* better than any other sort. The proof
of which may be seen in the way that white men conquer
and prevail all over the world." More applause echoed
from the ceiling.

Consul Newton merely steepled his fingertips. "A few
hundred years ago, Marco Polo visited Cathay. His book
tells of all sorts of wonders the people there had, of which
white men knew nothing. The cities in Cathay were bigger
and cleaner and grander than any in Europe. The people
used printing and paper money—not always a blessing, but

they devised it first. Even the lowly noodle comes from Cathay. Would not any reasonable man in those days have said that the yellow folk there were far superior to the barbarous white Europeans?"

"You twist things!" Stafford didn't like to let Newton know his barbs stung, but couldn't stop himself this time.

"Do I? I think not. What looks to you like natural superiority seems to me more like picking the present in place of the past and a bit of luck besides. What does Ecclesiastes say? 'I returned, and saw under the sun, that the race is not to the swift, nor the battle to the strong, neither yet bread to the wise, nor yet riches to men of understanding, nor yet favour to men of skill; but time and chance happeneth to them all.' Or will you tell me you reckon the Good Book mistaken?"

"I will tell you that the Good Book has as much to do with Cathay as chalk has to do with cream cheese," Stafford snarled. "And I will tell you it has even less to do with mudfaces and damned niggers!"

"'I am black, but comely, O ye daughters of Jerusalem, as the tents of Kedar, as the curtains of Solomon.'" Like the Devil, Consul Newton could quote Scripture to his purpose. As far as Jeremiah Stafford was concerned, the resemblance didn't end there.

He looked out onto the floor of the Senate chamber. Some of the Conscript Fathers looked as furious as he felt. Others seemed more thoughtful than usual. Not all the men who did were northerners, which alarmed him.

He said, "I suppose you will next tell me, sir, that the Bible condemns slavery. It does not, and you must know it does not, neither in the Old Testament nor in the New."

"True enough." But Newton spoiled what should have been a telling admission by adding, "It does, however, mitigate the conditions a slave is forced to endure, and liberates him during the jubilee. The institution as practiced in Atlantis does none of these things. I suppose *you* will next tell *me* that it does."

Consul Stafford growled, down deep in his throat. His colleague was the slipperiest thing this side of a greased eel. "In Biblical times, men enslaved others much like them," he said. "Our system, being different from theirs and based on the inferiority of those enslaved, naturally has different requirements. Aristotle noted that some men are slaves by nature, which we see proved here."

"Aristotle said all sorts of things," Newton answered easily. "Quite a few of 'em have turned out not to be so. Maybe this one is true, maybe it isn't. But it sure isn't true just because Aristotle says so. And the only thing the slave system in Atlantis proves is that white men here have the guns and the dogs and the whips, and the colored men don't. The Bible talks about sowing the wind and reaping the whirlwind, too. You might do well to remember that."

"You are helping the insurrection!" Stafford howled.

"Me? I'm just sitting here," Newton said.

"When you should be moving! When we should be!" But Stafford couldn't make the other man see.

VIII

℮nterprising restaurateurs in New Hastings brought fat frogs and big flapjack turtles up from the southern part of Atlantis and served them in stews and soups to men from that part of the country: men who'd grown up on such fare. Leland Newton hadn't. Oh, Croydon had its share of frogs and pond turtles, too. But they hardly ever got bigger than the palm of a man's hand. There wasn't enough meat in them to bother with, especially since they spent the cold seasons sleeping in the mud at the bottom of streams and puddles.

He'd had flapjack-turtle stew a few times since coming to New Hastings, when he was eating with southern men. It was fine . . . if you'd grown up eating it. These days, as pro- and antislavery forces found themselves ever more often at loggerheads (a different kind of turtle altogether), he felt less inclined to make such gestures. When he ate at Kingsley's Chop House, he ate mutton chops. Whoever wanted to gorge on turtles and frogs was welcome to his share.

A mutton chop with mint jelly, some fried potatoes, a glass of beer or burgundy or perhaps a tawny port . . . That was a civilized way to make a midday meal. If you had to eat something that swam, salmon and cod were tasty enough.

Which didn't mean the Consul ignored gentlemen who had other cravings. He was enjoying Master Kingsley's art-

istry with the mint jelly when a party of southern men took
the table next to his. He sat more turned away from them
than not, or they might have recognized him. They were
talking a blue streak when they got there, and they went
right on doing it.

His ear identified them as southerners even before they
ordered. Like Jeremiah Stafford, they kept the faintest
trace of a French accent—the ghost of a French accent, really. He wouldn't have been surprised if they were all of
English stock. Even so, the tones of the first settlers lingered. Irishmen who knew not a word of Erse spoke English with a brogue.

"Can you believe the nerve of those niggers and mudfaces?" one of them said. Before his friends could answer, a
waiter came up to see what they wanted. Their orders also
showed they'd grown up on the far side of the Stour. After
the waiter went away, the fellow who'd spoken before resumed: "A Free Republic of Atlantis for their own kind?
Sweet Jesus, don't make me laugh!"

"Likely tell!" one of his friends scoffed. "It's all talk to
make the northern states keep putting the screws to us. But
we know how things really work, we do." He sounded more
silly than worldly wise.

Consul Newton thought so, anyhow. The man's friends
didn't. "I should hope we know. That damned nigger will
keep telling them what to do, and they'll keep doing it."

"That devil!" The first man had an uncommonly raspy
voice. "The nerve, to call himself Victor Radcliff's grandson!"

"Yes. The nerve!" his comrades echoed. Did their voices
sound a little hollow? Newton thought so. He knew his
would have in their place. Where did all the griffes and
mulattos and quadroons and their copperskinned equiva-
lents come from if white men didn't lie down with colored
women? No one south of the Stour would let colored men
lie down with white women: that was certain sure.

And hadn't Victor Radcliff been a man like other men?
No matter what the schoolbooks said, Consul Newton figured the man who gave Atlantis liberty had sometimes
needed to squat behind a bush and clean himself with a

handful of leaves. He'd probably needed to get his ashes hauled now and again, too. He might well have left a by-blow behind.

The waiter came back with beer for the men at the next table. "Your stew will be along soon," he assured them.

"Not slow as a turtle, eh?" one of them said. They all thought that was funny, which made Newton wonder how much they'd drunk before they got to Master Kingsley's establishment.

"Not even," the waiter answered, and went away.

One of the men said, "I don't care if that nigger says Alexander the Great is his grandfather. Ain't gonna do him any good any which way."

"Well, it wouldn't," another one answered. "We could squash him like a katydid if the government didn't act like a honker with its head stuffed up its—"

"It doesn't matter, not in the long run," the raspy-voiced man broke in.

"Devil it doesn't!" said the fellow he'd interrupted. "Tell that to all the decent white folks who've had to run for their lives. Tell it to the ones who didn't get away, too. Some of those poor ladies . . . Jesus God!"

"Doesn't matter," Raspy Voice repeated. "Doesn't matter what the damnfool Consul from damnfool Croydon says, either, not a cent's worth."

The aforesaid damnfool Consul pricked up his ears. Leland Newton was of the opinion that his opinion mattered. If these fellows weren't, he wanted to know why.

And one of them obligingly spelled it out for him: "Army's going to get New Marseille what it needs to whip the slaves no matter what. If they don't have to talk about it, who's going to know the difference?"

Isn't that interesting? Newton thought. He felt like thumping himself in the head. The only reason he didn't was that it might have made the mouthy men at the next table notice him. But he knew he should have realized the southerners might try such a ploy. Since he was an uncommonly upright man himself, the idea of dealing from the bottom of the deck hadn't sprung into his mind right away.

But he could see the possibility once someone else pointed it out to him.

The waiter brought the southern men their flapjack-turtle stew. The heavy smell of the spices—and of the turtle meat—reminded the Consul of his efforts to accommodate other southerners by eating as they ate. It hadn't worked; he knew that. He had tried, though. He didn't want to accommodate them any more. He wanted to hamper their every move.

And they wanted to hamper him, too. If they couldn't get their way through the legal channels the Atlantean government afforded them, they'd do it any way they could. Yes, he should have seen that that might—would—happen.

A barrister named Ezra Pilkington came up to his table. Pilkington was a Croydon man, too; they'd known each other since they went to Radcliffe College together. Tipping his hat, the lawyer said, "Eating by yourself, your Excellency? Mind if I join you?"

He ignored Newton's frantic but subdued shushing motions. They must have been too subdued to do any good. Resignedly, Newton glanced over to the next table. All the men sitting there were staring at him in dismay altogether unfeigned. How much had he heard? Too much; that was plain. Even more resignedly, the Consul said, "Not at all, Ezra. Sit right down."

"Don't mind if I do." Pilkington didn't notice anything amiss in Leland Newton's voice, either. Or, if he did, he had the skill to dissemble. Waving to draw the waiter's attention, he said, "What *are* the United States of Atlantis going to do about that damned slave insurrection?"

Now the men at the other table listened attentively to Consul Newton. He said as little as he could. Some of the things *he* was going to do, he couldn't do officially. But, if he was going to start bending the rules, he didn't aim to let anyone else know about it beforehand.

Meeting by night in a dive in one of New Hastings' dingier quarters, Jeremiah Stafford felt like a conspirator. And with reason: he was. He sat in a dark corner nursing a shot of popskull and waiting impatiently for his fellow plotter to show up. A woman as good as you paid her to be sidled up to him. She must have seen a lot in her time, and little of it good, but the look he gave her sent her reeling away.

"You could just say no!" she shrilled.

"No," he said. She glared, but she left him alone after that.

When Major Duncan appeared at last, Stafford had all he could do to keep from laughing. The Atlantean officer had swathed himself in a great black cape that covered everything from the eyes down. A broad-brimmed black hat covered everything from the eyes up. He looked like a woodcut in a lurid novel translated from the French.

A man larger than he was planted himself in his path. "What are you supposed to be?" the fellow demanded.

Duncan's voice came from behind the black cape as if from beyond the grave: "Get the hell out of my way, shit-heel, or you'll find out."

The man let out a roar of rage and swung on him. A moment later, the fellow was on the floor. It happened so fast, Stafford couldn't see what the major did. Whatever it was, Duncan had proved himself a man of parts. For good measure, he kicked the bigger man behind the right ear to make sure he didn't get up for a while.

Then he looked around. "Anyone else?" he inquired.

Stafford wondered when the dive had last been so quiet. Into that silence, the ring of the silver tenth Sam Duncan tossed onto the bar seemed double sweet. Duncan took his barrel-tree rum and strolled back to the table where Stafford was sitting. Slowly, slowly, the tavern came back to life. People stepped over or around the man the major had decked. After several minutes, the fellow stirred and groaned, clutching the back of his head. He stayed flat. The dazed look in his eye said he didn't remember what had happened to him: only that he hadn't enjoyed it.

"That was nicely done," Stafford remarked.

"Thanks," Major Duncan said.

"All the same," the Consul continued, "why didn't you paint yourself blue and come in juggling flaming torches?"

"I didn't want anybody to know what I looked like." Duncan sounded aggrieved.

"But the idea is to make sure no one wonders about you," Stafford said. "They're not the same."

The Major looked almost comically astonished. He'd lowered the cloak to reveal his face—and to be able to drink. After pouring down his rum, the officer gave his attention back to Stafford. "Be damned," he said. "You're right. Fry me for an oil thrush if you're not. Have to remember that." He waved for a refill.

"Do," Stafford urged. "*Cloak and dagger* doesn't mean literally."

"I haven't got a dagger, by God," Duncan said. "I've got an eight-shooter in my belt, and a double-barreled derringer with a charge of shot in the bottom barrel, too. If that bastard gave me even a little trouble, I would have ventilated his spleen for him."

"You don't need to worry about that," Stafford said. The tavern tough still lay where he'd gone down. He'd barely wiggled; he wouldn't be getting up any time soon. Someone bent over him, perhaps to minister to him, perhaps to pick his pocket.

The barmaid brought the major a new shot of rum. She seemed to have to remind herself to linger long enough to get paid. Then she disappeared again.

Consul Stafford still had whiskey in his glass. He raised it. "Your health," he said, and they both drank. Then he asked, "What's gone wrong? Something must have, or you wouldn't have come to meet me" *dressed like a damned fool.* But the last handful of words Stafford kept to himself.

"Newton knows what we're up to." Duncan delivered the bad news as straightforwardly as he would have reported a reverse on the battlefield.

But Leland Newton, damn his black heart, wouldn't let the Atlantean army take the field against the colored insurrectionists. If he was going to try to snuff out covert aid to the southern states as well ... "How did he find out?" Stafford asked.

"My best guess is, somebody blabbed." Duncan spoke in tones of resigned anger. "I have a notion who, too:

some clerks from the Ministry of War. They all looked like they wanted to hide when people came around asking questions."

"Did they give straight answers?" Stafford asked. "That could be inconvenient." He was proud of himself. Duncan would have to go some to outdo his understatement.

Instead of attempting it, the major drained his glass, then held it up and waved for another refill. Stafford finished the whiskey, too. He also waved for a fresh one. Maybe the first would have numbed his tongue enough to keep him from tasting the second so much. And his brain needed more numbing than it had got yet.

Only after Major Duncan got halfway down his third glass of rum did he say, "I can't tell you for certain, Consul. The snoops made sure they questioned each man alone. In their boots, I would have done the same thing. Doesn't make life any easier for us, though."

"No. It doesn't," Stafford said. He'd never denied Newton's competence—he'd only regretted the other Consul's adherence to the vile cause of equality for niggers and mudfaces. "Have you got any notion how much they know?"

"More than they ought to. That's all I can tell you for sure," Duncan answered. "Knowing anything at all is too damned much."

"So it is. Well, I did need to know that myself, and I thank you for bringing me word," Jeremiah Stafford said. "We should leave separately." It might help less than Stafford wished it would. Anyone who saw the major wouldn't forget him in a hurry, and might also remember his companion too well.

"I was last in. I should be first out," Sam Duncan said. Why that followed eluded Stafford, but he didn't argue. Life was too short. And so Duncan gulped what was left of the rum, stood up, and draped himself in his cape once more. He couldn't have been more conspicuous had he caught fire.

The man he'd decked was just starting to sit up when he swept by. Stafford wondered whether Duncan would flatten him again—for the sport of it, you might say. But the officer just walked into the night.

"Who was that crazy son of a bitch?" someone asked.

"Beats me," someone else answered. "He may look dumber'n a honker, but he's nobody you'd want to mess around with—that's for damned sure. Ain't it, Scrap Iron?"

Scrap Iron proved to be Major Duncan's victim. He rubbed the side of his head again, then winced and thought better of it. "He better hope I never see him again," he said, but his voice lacked conviction.

And well it might. The fellow who'd addressed him laughed and said, "*You* better hope you never see him again." Thus do the heroes fall. Scrap Iron got to his feet. He needed three tries, but he made it. When he set money on the bar, the man behind it poured him a restorative.

Consul Stafford slid out of the tavern. He had a pistol on his belt, too. In this part of town, you might need one. Better to have and not need than to need and not have. Gas lamps lit the streets and sidewalks in richer quarters of New Hastings. Hereabouts, the only warning a passerby gave was the glowing coal on the end of his cigar. And if he didn't smoke a cigar, he gave no warning at all—which was just what footpads had in mind.

Stafford didn't quite sigh with relief when he reached a lighted street. A less disciplined man surely would have, though. He made his way back to his residence. A couple of sentries stood outside the door. One puffed on a stogie—all of it visible under a hissing gas lamp—while the other sent up smoke signals from a pipe.

The cigar smoker's rifle musket screaked on its sling as he shifted weight. How many longarms just like that did the insurrectionists have? One would have been too many, and they had far more than one.

"Out late tonight, sir," the sentry said.

"Some business I needed to attend to," Stafford answered.

"Yes, sir," the sentry said. But his eyes slid toward his comrade's. Did they think his business had to do with someone perfumed and softly curved? As a matter of fact, Stafford did not care one broad copper cent for what they thought. His wife's opinion was another matter. Was Annabelle sitting up in there, waiting for him to come back? A man might take a mistress, but flaunting one was bad form.

Here, though, Stafford had done no such thing. And all he smelled of were whiskey and pipeweed—no perfume. Annabelle ought to notice that—if she was in a mood to notice anything.

She was waiting for him, darning socks by the light of a lantern. She was small and dark and sad-looking, as any mother who'd buried three babies would have been. Jeremiah Stafford feared he might be the last of his line. Annabelle put down the sock she was working on (she was shortsighted, which helped her with the needle if not with the wider world) and blinked up at him. Like the sentry, she said, "You were out late."

"Business," he said, as he had before. But he would explain to his wife, where he wouldn't for a no-account soldier: "Sam Duncan."

"Ah. Your . . . friend." She knew the name if not the man. Her voice didn't say whether she believed him.

He described Duncan's disguise and the way it concealed and proclaimed at the same time. He also described how the major had rusted Scrap Iron. Annabelle smiled faintly. "Quite a man," she said.

"Yes—almost as much as he thinks he is. If only he had more common sense to go with his courage and strength. That costume! Good Lord!" Stafford rolled his eyes.

"And why did you have to meet him in some low dive? Why wouldn't a walk around the Senate House do as well?" Annabelle asked.

"Because if anyone connected to northern Senators or to my esteemed fellow Consul"—Stafford's tone turned the praise into a filthy lie—"saw us walking together, he would understand *why* we were talking together, whereupon trouble would immediately follow. You know we are quietly doing what we can to aid the states against the servile insurrection?"

"Well, of course." His wife had been born in the state of Cosquer, too, down close to the border with Gernika. She came from a slaveholding family, as he did. In fact, the threat of uprisings always seemed worse in that part of the country. Gernika had still been Spanish Atlantis when she was a girl, and Spanish Atlantis always sizzled and sometimes exploded. The dons squeezed all they could from their copperskins and blacks, and squeezed out hatred along with everything else.

"You see," Stafford said. "Duncan's news was that Consul Newton has found out about our quiet efforts. Having learned of them, he is doubtless doing everything in his power to thwart them."

"How wicked of him! No wonder you went out, then, Jeremiah," Annabelle said, and something behind Stafford's breastbone unknotted. Whatever she had thought, she believed him now. She went on, "What can you do to stop him from disrupting things?"

That question cut to the quick. "I don't know yet," Consul Stafford admitted. "But knowing we have a problem is bound to give us our best chance of keeping it from getting worse."

Before his wife could answer, a clock that had been quietly ticking on a side table chimed the hour: two in the morning. Annabelle yawned. "Come to bed," she said. "Whatever your best chance may be, you can't do anything about it till the sun comes up."

Stafford feared the nighttime might prove better. Some of the deeds that wanted doing would be dark. She was right about tonight, though—and her yawn was contagious. "Sleep," he said longingly.

Things looked less bleary in the morning, if not necessarily better. Stafford primed his pump with several cups of strong, sugared coffee. Men from north of the Stour were more likely to drink tea. Leland Newton did, as Stafford had seen. The Consul from Cosquer thought he got the edge on his colleague in the morning.

Whether he could keep it might be another story. Consul Newton was up and doing ahead of him. Instead of ignoring him, as Newton often did, the other Consul made a point of buttonholing him. "I have a question for you, sir: one concerning the safety of the nation," Newton said.

"I have had a good many questions of that sort for you lately, sir," Stafford answered. "You seem less than less than willing to answer them, however. But let it be as you wish for now—how can I say no?"

"If you've ever had any trouble with the word, you hide it marvelously well." Newton shook his head. "I will steer clear of gibes, as I do hope for a serious answer from you. My question is this: if so many capable officers and men leave the Atlantean army, how shall we defend ourselves against some foreign foe?"

"Does foreign war loom on the horizon? If so, against whom?" Stafford asked, adding, "I must confess, the portents have escaped my notice."

"You are being deliberately difficult." Newton sounded severe.

"You are being deliberately hypothetical," Stafford retorted.

"Am I? It could be, but I think not," Newton said. "The army depends on professional soldiers of large experience. If a number of them suddenly leave and must be replaced with less seasoned men, how can it fail to suffer a loss of efficiency—to say nothing of effectiveness?"

"You will not allow the army to be used to reestablish order in the southern states," Stafford said. "This being so, how can it surprise you that soldiers would sooner do what they see as their duty even without army auspices than sit idly by with the blessings of the Ministry of War?"

"Their conception of duty is defective," Newton said.

"I do not for a moment agree with you. But even supposing you are right, so what?" Stafford said.

Leland Newton frowned—scowled, in fact. "I did beg you for the courtesy of a serious response."

"Serious? Sir, I am serious to the point of solemnity," Stafford said. "You must bear something in mind: that your opponents are as much in earnest as you yourself. Their sense of duty may seem defective to you, but it does not seem so to them. They hold to it with as much devotion as you cling to the deluded idea of nigger equality. I know you believe in that, but I am damned if I know how."

He wondered whether Newton would laugh in his face. The other Consul had a firm faith in his own beliefs, and faith every bit as firm that his foes' beliefs were only delusions. After hearing Stafford out, he looked almost comically surprised. "Well, well!" he said, and then, "Upon my soul!"

"Meaning what exactly?" Stafford's voice was dry.

"You really mean what you say," the other Consul blurted.

"I should hope so. I am in the habit of it. Anyone looking at my career would be hard-pressed to doubt it. If you do, I hope I may take the liberty of asking why," Stafford said.

He was surprised in turn when his colleague actually blushed. "I always assumed you were in the habit of saying what your constituents wanted to hear, as most politicians are," Newton said. "That any man of sense could believe some of the things you have said . . . "

"I am going to say something now that you had best believe: I find your views every bit as repugnant as you find mine. Note, however, that I do not do you the discourtesy of thinking you hypocritical," Stafford said. "I think you are every bit as misguided as you declare yourself to be."

"Thank you . . . I suppose," Newton said. "Since you then prefer to be judged a knave rather than a fool—"

"No," Stafford broke in sharply. "Someone who thinks you are wrong is not a knave on account of that. He is only someone who thinks you are wrong. Recognizing the difference—not necessarily liking it, but recognizing it—is important."

"Will you tell me you do not think me a knave?" Newton demanded.

Jeremiah Stafford hesitated before answering, which he seldom did. "Personally? No. You have the courage of your convictions," he said at last. "In what you are doing to my section of Atlantis, the effect, intentional or not, is knavish."

"This is my view of your effect on Atlantis as a whole," Consul Newton said.

"Why not say, of slavery's effect? That is what you mean, eh?"

"No. Slavery is altogether knavish, while you are not. Yet you support the infamy nonetheless. Can you not see that this makes you worse, not better?"

Stafford started to tell him he did not find slavery infamous. To Stafford, true infamy was the idea that Negroes and copperskins could presume to be equals. But Consul Newton didn't wait for explanation. Like a banderillero in a bullfight down in Gernika (something Consul Stafford did find infamous, but also something he lacked the power to root out), Leland Newton planted a barb and walked away before his victim could gore him on account of it.

Senator Hiram Radcliffe came from the state of Penzance, north of Croydon. As the English Penzance, its namesake, lay close by Land's End, so the Atlantean town that gave the state its name wasn't far from North Cape, where ocean finally won the battle against land. Penzance held hardly any copperskins or Negroes. Penzance didn't hold all that many whites, and the ones it did hold were of an uncommonly independent streak. To say they didn't approve of chattel slavery would have been putting it mildly.

And so Consul Newton thought he would be glad to see Senator Radcliffe. He had no idea from which branch of the founding clan the Senator sprang; only a genealogist could keep them all straight. That didn't matter, anyway.

Whichever branch Hiram Radcliffe sprang from, he looked nothing like the most famous modern member. Where Victor Radcliff had been tall and lean, his distant cousin had a short, well-upholstered frame and some of the most ornate whiskers the Consul had ever seen: his muttonchops grew into his mustache, but he shaved his chin—or rather, chins.

"Consul, what do you propose to do about the slave rising?" Senator Radcliffe asked, at the same time sending up clouds of pungent smoke from his pipe.

"Why, just what I have been doing," Newton answered. "I propose to keep the Atlantean government from pulling the southern states' chestnuts out of the fire for them." The image had traveled across the sea from England. The only chestnuts growing in Atlantis were a few ornamentals, likewise imported. The land had none native to it, nor any other broad-leafed trees.

More smoke came up from Radcliffe's pipe. "That's

what I thought," he said, and then, amplifying, "That's what I was afraid of."

"Afraid of?" Leland Newton didn't dig a finger into his ear to try to make it work better, but he caught himself barely in time to stop the motion. "Why do you say that?"

"On account of it's true," Radcliffe answered. "Yes, the slaves have their grievances. Lord knows I understand that. But it's still a damned uprising, Consul. They're burning and ravishing and killing. New Marseille doesn't seem able to put 'em down, and brushfires are breaking out in some of the other southern states."

"That is the point of the business, is it not?" Newton said. "The rebels are being as moderate as their circumstances permit. Even accounts from their foes—the only accounts we have, remember—admit as much. They seem to aim to set up a colored republic of their own."

"And what will they do with the white folks caught inside it?" Radcliffe asked. "Treat them the way they've been treated themselves, for all these years? That's how it looks right now."

"What if it is?" Consul Newton returned. "Can you deny the justice in such a turn of fate?"

"You can't make your own cause just by murdering or tormenting folks on the other side."

"Even when they've been doing the same to you since time out of mind?"

"Even then," Hiram Radcliffe said stubbornly. "One reason I want a national army down there is to get between the rebels and the militias trying to do unto them. If the uprising stops, maybe we can get around to talking sensibly about what made it start in the first place."

"Good luck! Meaning no disrespect, sir, but you will need it," Newton said. "Expecting a southern white to talk sensibly about slavery is like expecting the sun to rise in the west. You may if you so desire, but you will be doomed to disappointment."

"D'you suppose the copperskins and Negroes are any more likely to?" Radcliffe said. "Seems to me they're just the other side of the same coin."

"Would you not say they have two or three hundred years' worth of pent-up spleen to vent?" Newton asked.

"I would. I would indeed. But if they keep venting it, they will make the white southerners decide the only way to stop them is to kill them all. And if they set about it, how do you propose to stop 'em?"

"They would do no such monstrous thing!" Newton exclaimed. But then he remembered his conversation with Consul Stafford. How monstrous would disposing of Negroes and copperskins seem to a man like that? Monstrous enough to keep him from trying it? Newton wished he could think so.

His face must have shown what was going through his mind, because Senator Radcliffe said, "Now you see what I'm driving at."

"Well, maybe I do," Newton said. "But keeping an army like that on anything close to an even keel won't be easy. You know the law as well as I do: one Consul commands one day, the other the next. Against a foreign foe, this is no great disadvantage, since both men would naturally work toward the same end. But where one aims to push while the other wants to pull . . . "

"Consul, if a Croydon man can't slicker some poor slob from Cosquer, he isn't worth the paper he's printed on," Hiram Radcliffe declared.

"Your confidence flatters me," Newton said dryly.

"It had better, your Excellency, on account of that's what I had in mind," the Senator from Penzance replied, not a bit abashed. "But you need to think about this whole business some more, and I'm not the only one who figures you do."

"I . . . see. And how large is your cabal?" Leland Newton's tone remained dry, which didn't mean he didn't mean the question. What kind of plotting had been going on behind his back?

"Large enough, by God," Radcliffe said, which conveyed strength without informing: no doubt exactly the effect he had in mind. He coughed a couple of times. "Large enough so that, if we have to vote with the southerners to get an army sent down there, the size of the majority on the resolution will make your eyes pop."

"It can be as big as a honker, for all I care," Consul Newton answered, doing his best not to show how much the warning—the threat?—shook him. Hiram Radcliffe was, or had been, on his side. Still trying to seem unconcerned, he went on, "The resolution can be unanimous, for all I care. If I disagree with it, it will not pass."

"You know what the history books say about Consuls who forbid measures just for the sake of forbidding," Radcliffe warned.

Newton did know. There had been a couple of Consuls like that in the early days of the United States of Atlantis. The horrible bad example they offered dissuaded later Atlantean leaders from imitating them. All the same, Newton said, "Let history judge me. I will do what I think is right."

"What's wrong with being able to ride down a road without worrying about whether you'll get robbed or murdered before you get where you're going?" Radcliffe asked.

"If since time out of mind you have been robbing and murdering the people who have finally risen in arms against you, maybe you deserve to worry," Newton said.

"Maybe." By the way Hiram Radcliffe said the word, he didn't believe it for a minute. He took the pipe out of his mouth to lick his lips. "I hate to say it, Consul, but you'd better worry that people don't finally rise in arms against you."

Newton had been in politics for many years. He didn't miss much. And he didn't miss the key phrase here. "In arms?" he echoed quietly.

Senator Radcliffe looked unhappy—he looked most unhappy—but he nodded. "In arms," he repeated.

"Well." Leland Newton made a steeple of his fingertips. "I never looked to be threatened with assassination— never so politely, anyhow." In the hurly-burly of the Senate chamber, anything could happen. But this wasn't like that. This spoke of dangers in a back alley in the middle of the night, or maybe of poisonous mushrooms garnishing a plate of boiled pork.

"I am not threatening you, Consul. I am trying to warn you," the Senator from Penzance said. "If you keep on with it, more and more people will want to put you out of the way. Surely you can see that?" He sounded as if he was pleading.

"I might have expected something like this from Senator Bainbridge or some other froth-at-the-mouth southerner," Newton said bitterly. "But ... *Et tu, Hiram?*"

"*Et ego*," Radcliffe answered, proving he remembered at least some of the Latin he'd had drilled into him as a schoolboy. "Sometimes you need to have your friends tell you, because you don't take your foes seriously enough. We've got to do *something* down there, Leland. Doing nothing isn't enough any more."

"So you say."

Hiram Radcliffe nodded. "So I say." He heaved his bulk up from the chair in front of Newton's desk. "And now I won't take up any more of your time."

"Does Consul Stafford know you came here?" Newton asked.

"Not yet," Radcliffe said. "I hope I don't have to tell him. And if you publish abroad what's personal, private business I will damn you as a liar from here to Avalon."

"I assumed that," Newton said. Photographers had started capturing light. If only there were some way to capture sound as well!

"Figured you did, but even so ... Good day to you, your Excellency." Radcliffe lumbered out of the office. Newton fought down the impulse to speed him on his way with a good kick in the breeches.

IX

"*W*ait." Sitting up there on the dais in front of the Conscript Fathers of Atlantis, Consul Jeremiah Stafford had trouble believing what his colleague had just said. "Repeat that, if you would be so kind."

He wasn't the only one to doubt his hearing, either. Half the Senators were staring at Leland Newton as if he'd just disappeared an elephant right before their eyes. One fellow dropped his glasses. Jaws dropped on both sides of the aisle in the Senate House, but especially among the men who came from south of the Stour.

Consul Newton turned to Stafford with an ironic smile. "You heard me correctly, sir," he said. "I spoke, and I shall continue to speak, in favor of using an Atlantean army to interpose itself between the insurrectionists and the New Marseille militia—and, if necessary, between the insurrectionists and the militias belonging to the other southern states."

A burst of applause echoed from the ceiling of the Senate House. Some of it, again, came from southern men. But others—firebrands like Radcliffe of Penzance—also joined in the cheering. That they did roused Stafford's ever-vigilant suspicions.

"Wait," he said again. "What precisely do you mean

when you say you want to interpose an Atlantean army down there?"

"I mean what I say: neither more no less," Newton answered blandly. "As you do, sir, I consider that an admirable habit. In my opinion, we would be better off if more persons in political positions followed our example."

"We would also be better off if fewer persons in political positions were as exasperating as you make a point of being," Stafford said.

His colleague gave him a seated bow. "I am your servant, sir."

Stafford ignored that. It wasn't easy, but he managed. "In a game of chess, for instance, you may interpose a bishop between your king and your opponent's castle."

Newton beamed at him. "Just so! You see? You understand perfectly! So why were you so troubled a moment ago?"

"Why? I'll tell you why," Stafford answered. "Because an interposed piece does not necessarily capture the one that is causing the difficulty."

Leland Newton stopped beaming. Consul Stafford got the idea that his colleague hadn't expected him to realize that quite so fast. Croydon men commonly thought no one was clever except their own kind. Comprehension took longer to dawn out on the Senate floor than it did inside Stafford's mind—which might have meant that Consul Newton had a point.

In case any of the Conscript Fathers missed anything, Stafford made it—he hoped—unmistakably clear: "You want to put the national army between the niggers and the honest white men now fighting them. You have not said one word about using the national army to fight them, however. Why is that, if I may enquire?"

"Separating the opposing forces seems to me an excellent first step toward peace," Newton answered.

"Wait a minute!" Senator Bainbridge shouted from the Senate floor. "You just wait one damned minute! An excellent first step toward peace is stringing up all the slaves who rose up against their rightful masters. That's what a first step toward peace is!"

He got thunderous cheers from his southern friends. This time, though, Senator Radcliffe and the other northern firebrands sat on their hands. That told Stafford as much as he needed to know about the kind of game Newton and his cohorts were playing.

But there were games, and then again there were games. "I am willing to support Consul Newton's resolution," Stafford said. Jaws dropped again. Eyes popped—among them, those of Leland Newton. No, Newton wouldn't be able to call Stafford names for rejecting the resolution out of hand, even if it came with a poison pill. Stafford went on, "The usual command arrangements will of course apply."

"Of course," Newton said. "I am not trying to change the way the United States of Atlantis work."

"No, indeed." Sarcasm dripped from Stafford's tongue. "Freeing the mudfaces and niggers would do nothing of the sort."

"As a matter of fact, sir, it wouldn't," Newton said. "It would only extend citizenship to men and women who are now but residents."

"And it would ruin an entire class of white men who have contributed greatly to making Atlantis strong," Consul Stafford pointed out.

"Some form of compensation might be arranged," Newton said.

"How generous!" Stafford fleered. "Tell me: what compensates for murder?"

"Killing in war is not murder," Newton replied.

"Killing in an uprising is," Stafford said. "And inflicting a fate worse than death upon helpless women is a foul crime in war or peace."

"I would agree with you," his colleague said. "So, no doubt, would countless black and copperskinned women compelled to be the vessels of their masters' lusts."

"It's not the same thing," Stafford insisted uncomfortably, recalling the mulatto woman who'd initiated him into the rites of loving.

"No, eh?" Newton said. "It all depends on who is doing what to whom, I suppose."

"You make that into a joke, and a nasty one, at that,"

Stafford said. "But you are quite right. A chattel has no say over his person—"

"Or over hers," the other Consul broke in.

"Or over hers," Stafford agreed. "But when a slave callously violates a free white woman—"

"He only imitates what white men have done to the women he is not permitted to call wives."

"That is not what I was going to say."

"Really? Why am I not surprised?"

Once the bickering ended, the resolution passed. *And we'll see who ends up outsmarting whom*, Jeremiah Stafford thought. His guess was that, once an army full of white men bumped up against the insurrectionists, it would go after them full bore whether Consul Newton wanted it to or not. And even if by some mischance it didn't, he could still use his alternate days in command to steer it in the direction he wanted it to go. He looked forward to it.

Politicians in Atlantis won votes by railing at bureaucrats. Leland Newton had done it himself. If you listened to politicians, bureaucrats were miserable old slowcoaches. The fist-sized snails in the southern states could move faster than they did. And cucumber slugs had more in the way of brains (to say nothing of less in the way of slime).

If you made a speech like that, you commonly believed it, at least while you were giving it. Newton knew he sometimes exaggerated for effect, but even so. . . . He expected the Ministry of War would need weeks to gather together the soldiers and munitions and other supplies an army required if it proposed campaigning against the rebels west of the Green Ridge Mountains.

The army was ready to move four days later. The Minister of War told Newton that Colonel Balthasar Sinapis, the senior officer who would accompany the Consuls into the field, had already apologized for taking so long. "I hope you will not be hard on him because of the delay," the functionary added.

"Well, I may possibly forgive him this once," Newton said.

"He does promise to do better in any future emergency," the Minister of War said.

"Good," was the only answer Newton could find.

Colonel Sinapis was a swarthy professional soldier who spoke with some sort of guttural accent. He'd come to Atlantis in the wake of the upheavals following the recent failed revolutions in Europe. Consul Newton thought of him as a human rifle musket: aim him at whatever you pleased, and he would knock it over for you.

What the colonel thought of the Consuls was something that hadn't occurred to Newton till Sinapis sat down in the leading railroad car of the leading train that would take the army into action against the rebels. Sinapis had an axe-blade of a face, a shaggy gray mustache under a scimitar nose, and the fierce, unblinking stare of a peregrine falcon.

"You gentlemen will have a plan of campaign for the days ahead?" he asked. When he spoke, his accent and his ferocious manner gave him the aspect of a talking wolf. The only wolves Newton had ever seen paced an iron-barred cage back in Croydon. Had one of those wolves worn a gray uniform instead of coarse gray fur, it might have been Balthasar Sinapis' brother-in-law.

However lupine Colonel Sinapis' manner, his question was only too cogent. Newton glanced over at Jeremiah Stafford. He was anything but surprised to find the other Consul looking back at him. "Well . . . " they both said slowly. Neither seemed to want to tell the colonel how much they disagreed about what ought to happen after the army encountered the insurrectionists.

A flash of scorn in Sinapis' dark eyes warned that he already knew they couldn't even agree to disagree. "Some thought now would spare us much trouble later," he said, as if to squabbling children.

His accent might remain strong, but his English was grammatically perfect. Newton had already noticed as much. The colonel might have said, *Some thought now* will *save us much trouble later*. He might have, but he hadn't. Which meant . . . what? That he expected no such planning; he just wistfully hoped for it.

Consul Stafford's expression said he was making the same calculation, and liking it no better than Newton did. "We'll do what we can to obtain a satisfactory result," he said at last.

"Certainly, your Excellency," Colonel Sinapis said. "And how do you propose to define success?"

"When we find it, we'll know it," Newton said.

"Yes, I suppose we will," Stafford . . . agreed?

Colonel Sinapis sighed like a wolf that had failed to outrun a deer. *So many images in our language of animals not native here*, Newton thought. The colonel said, "What you mean is, you have not got the faintest idea of what you want the army to do. Or perhaps each of you has an idea, but you have not got the same idea. Is this true? Am I right or am I wrong?"

The two Consuls looked at each other. They both sighed, too, at the same time and on the same note. "You may be right—for now," Newton said. "I think we both hope we will have the answer once the army goes into action."

Sinapis' brows came down over his eyes like battlements protecting a keep. The lines on his cheeks deepened like entrenchments in a siege. "Meaning no disrespect to you gentlemen," he said, a phrase that always meant disrespect to its targets, "but an army without a plan is like a drunkard on a stroll. If you have no notion where you are going, how will you know when you get there? Or if you get there?"

"Let's get there first," Consul Newton said. "Once we do, I expect we'll sort things out."

"I hope we'll sort things out," Consul Stafford said. That wasn't exactly agreement, but it wasn't exactly disagreement, either. Newton decided he would take it.

By the way Balthasar Sinapis whuffled out air through his mustache, he was less satisfied. "Politics," he said disdainfully. "*Gamemeno* politics."

That sounded like a participle derived from *gameo*, the classical Greek verb meaning *to marry*. Leland Newton was mildly surprised and pleased that he recognized the form, and that he remembered what the verb meant . . . or had meant. *Marrying politics* made no sense. Perhaps the word had changed meaning in the centuries since Plato and Xenophon used it.

Before he could ask, the emigré officer went on, "All you think of are your *gamemeno* political points." There it was again, just as incomprehensible as before. "What I think of, gentlemen—and you had better keep it in mind—is the blood of my soldiers. It is what you intend to spend to make your political points, and I do not believe you care a cent for it."

Newton started to deny that indignantly. He stopped with the words unspoken. It wasn't that he didn't care what happened to the Atlantean soldiers rattling along behind him. Sinapis had that wrong, but Newton hadn't thought at all about what might befall the gray-uniformed men. If he admitted as much, the colonel would be within his rights to call him on it.

"I have been thinking more of what our army will do to the insurrectionists," Consul Stafford said.

"Of course you have—you are a politician, too." No, Sinapis didn't bother hiding his dislike for the men who outranked him. "You leave it to a soldier to worry about the other, don't you?"

Stafford seemed to have no comeback for that. Newton knew too well he didn't. Except for the dull, metallic rumble of iron wheels on iron rails, silence filled the compartment.

Wheee-oooo! The locomotive whistle screamed as the train crossed the railroad bridge from the state of Freetown to the state of Cosquer. The land on the south side of the Stour looked no different from that on the northern side. All the same, Jeremiah Stafford let out a long sigh of relief. At last, he was back in God's country—or at least in a country with civilized laws.

Before long, the train stopped in a sleepy little town called Pontivy. A gang of black and copperskinned slaves lugged fresh lumber to the tender. A swag-bellied white man in overalls had a pistol on his belt, but Stafford would have bet he hadn't had to draw it for years. *Thump! Thump!* The sawed lengths of wood replaced what the locomotive had devoured since the last stop.

Another slave went down the train, oiling the wheels. The lazy black devil didn't bother lifting the spout of his oil can between one set of wheels and the next. He just let the expensive oil spill out onto the dirt. Why should he worry? He wasn't paying for it.

Seeing that kind of thing made Stafford grind his teeth. The overseer either didn't notice or didn't care—he wasn't paying for the oil, either. Somebody was, though, dammit: the railroad company's supply department, or the shareholders, or, on this journey, the Atlantean government.

Stafford hated waste. He knew slaves generated more of it than he would have liked. Because things weren't their own, they didn't care about them. That was why, for instance, planters had to give their field hands those heavy, clumsy tools. They would have broken the better ones white farmers used, and in short order, too.

"We have to do something about that," he muttered. Atlantean slaveholders had been saying the same thing since the seventeenth century. The only answer anyone had come up with was making the slaves afraid to be careless with their tools—their owners' tools. And that worked only up to a point. Press a nigger or a mudface too hard and he'd either try to murder you or he'd run off. Both were more expensive than broken tools.

Consul Newton had also got off the train to watch the refueling and to stretch his legs. He didn't seem to notice the Negro wasting oil, which relieved Stafford. But he did notice Stafford mumbling to himself, and asked, "What was that?"

"I wish we would make our workers more efficient and considerate," Stafford said.

"Why don't you try paying them?" Newton asked, his tone not in the least ironic. "Nothing makes a man a careful worker like the fear of getting docked."

"The whole point of our system is to keep from enslaving workers to money," Stafford said.

His fellow Consul raised an eyebrow. "So you enslave them to their masters instead? A dubious improvement, I fear. And I have never yet heard of a slaveowner who broke out in hives when some cash came his way. No, the owners only worry when their slaves see a coin once in a blue moon."

"Slaves don't need money," Stafford said. "Remember, their masters feed and clothe and shelter them."

"None too well, more often than not," Newton said.

"They live better than factory hands in Hanover—or in Croydon, come to that," Stafford retorted. "Who said that the first freedom was the freedom to starve? Whoever he was, he knew what he was talking about."

"I don't see white factory hands swimming across the Stour to work on your plantations," Newton said tartly.

"We would not enslave them if they did, and you know it perfectly well," Stafford said.

"Fine. Have it however you please. I don't see free Negroes and copperskins volunteering to go back under the lash, either."

"It has happened," Stafford said. "I recall one such case just a couple of years ago. The copperskin couldn't make a go of it in Freetown, so he decided to come south. He knew he wouldn't starve here, and his children wouldn't, either."

"It must not happen very often, by God, or you would not be able to call particular instances to mind," his colleague said.

Since that was true, Stafford maintained a discreet silence. The train whistle blared again. It was even louder when heard out in the open than from inside a railroad car. The windows, commonly closed against soot and cinders, muffled some of the ferocious squeal.

"All aboard!" the locomotive driver bawled from the back of his iron chariot. He might have been piloting a ferry boat, not the most modern conveyance in the world. "All aboard!" The whistle shrilled once more.

Colonel Sinapis nodded coolly to the Consuls when they joined him in the compartment they shared. He hadn't got off the train. Reading glasses perched on that curved blade of a nose, he pored over maps of the southwest. Regardless of whether the Consuls were ready for whatever might happen when the army got where it was going, he intended to be.

What he wasn't ready for, any more than they were,

was their train derailing just outside of Pontivy. The only thing that saved them from worse misfortune was that they hadn't got going very fast yet. There was a jolt and a crash. The next thing Stafford knew, the locomotive and tender had flipped over onto their sides—and so had the car he was riding in. He had time for one startled exclamation before he landed on what had been the side of the car and Colonel Sinapis landed on him.

"Oof!" Stafford said, which summed up exactly how he felt about the situation. The colonel had a more detailed opinion, which he expressed in English and what sounded like several other languages. Stafford didn't understand them all, but admired the effects, especially the one that sounded like ripping canvas.

Leland Newton had also fetched up against the side of the car. He, however, was not festooned with a colonel, so his remarks were less impassioned. "Are you all right, Jeremiah?" he asked.

It was, as far as Stafford could remember, the first time his colleague had used his Christian name. "I seem to be, Leland," he said, returning the courtesy, "or I will be, if the good Colonel Sinapis would remove his elbow from the vicinity of my navel."

The good colonel did move the pointed part in question, and the Consul did gain considerable relief as a result. Sinapis scrambled to his feet. He stepped on Stafford once more in the process, but without malice. "We must help the injured—and there will be some," he said.

Stafford only grunted, because Sinapis was bound to be right. Derailments were lamentably common, and produced more than their fair share of lost limbs and broken bones. The colonel wrestled the door open. It didn't want to open sideways, but he made it obey. He scrambled out. Stafford and Newton followed.

Sinapis' prophecy was confirmed at once. A couple of the stokers lay on the fern-splashed ground. One was clutching his leg and groaning. The leg had a bend in a place where it shouldn't.

Consul Stafford's stomach did a slow lurch. He looked away in a hurry. If an injury like this threatened to sicken him, how would he do on a battlefield with bullets and cannonballs ripping flesh? He hadn't thought about that when he set out from New Hastings. Maybe he should have.

The engine driver limped out of the capsized locomotive. He was not only hurt but incandescently furious. "A rock!" he screamed. "Some God-damned fucking son of a bitch put a fucking boulder on the fucking tracks!" He started to hop up and down in his rage, but his ankle made him think better of it. "That shit-eating bastard, whoever the devil he was, he went and derailed us on purpose! I hope he rots in hell and Old Scratch uses his short ribs for toothpicks!"

Slow, cold certainty formed inside Jeremiah Stafford's mind. "That shit-eating bastard, whoever the devil he was, was a mudface or a nigger." He sounded as sure of himself as any Biblical prophet.

"Yes. Very likely." Colonel Sinapis nodded. "Those people are the ones with the most reason to slow us down or stop us."

Rounding on his colleague, Stafford said, "You don't say anything, sir."

Consul Newton spread his hands. "What would you have me say? I agree: most likely a slave did place a rock there to derail us. I have never claimed slaves loved us. The most I have ever said is that they may well have good reason not to love us."

"Bah!" Stafford turned away from him in disgust. That let him look down the track. Half a dozen cars after the one in which he'd been riding had also overturned. Some of the soldiers inside them were bound to be hurt, too. The cars farther back had managed to stay on the rails. Had the train been moving faster, more of them would have gone off.

Those slaves were fools, the Consul thought. *They would have done better to plant their boulder farther from town, so we would have built up more speed. Or maybe they didn't know we would stop in Pontivy.*

A horrible shriek derailed his train of thought. The phrase had quickly become a commonplace after railroad lines began crisscrossing Atlantis. Now Stafford was reminded of the reality that had given rise to it.

Colonel Sinapis crouched beside the stoker with the broken leg. Among other things, the colonel knew how to set fractures, even if the process was painful. Stafford hoped the army surgeons had laid in a good supply of nitrous oxide and ether. The newfangled medicines seemed sovereign against even the worst agony.

"Hold still," Sinapis told the stoker. His strong hands made sure the man obeyed. The officer nodded to the other stoker, who hovered nearby. "Draw my sword. Cut a couple of saplings. Cut strips of cloth, too, so I can splint this leg. Don't just stand there, man! *Move!*"

Move the other stoker did, and smartly, too. When Balthasar Sinapis told you to do something, you did it first and worried about why later. He would have made a marvelous overseer. Consul Stafford chuckled softly. What was a colonel but an overseer who used a uniform and army regulations instead of a bullwhip to get his way?

Stafford stared this way and that. No slaves in sight now. He'd wondered if they would stick around to enjoy the chaos they'd caused, but no such luck. Even stupid slaves knew better. Too bad.

And the army was going to be later than it had expected getting to the insurrection. That was also too damned bad.

The train derailed once more before it got to Nouveau Redon. This time, people—no doubt colored people—had set logs on the rails. The train was going faster when it hit them. Leland Newton ended up with a knot on the side of his head and a left wrist sprained so badly, he had to wear it in a sling.

One of the army surgeons gave him a tiny bottle of laudanum for the pain. The potent mixture of brandy and opium pushed it off to one side, anyhow. The opium also settled his bowels, which had been flighty on a traveling diet of hardtack and salt pork: army rations.

"Slaves don't love you, either," Consul Stafford pointed out to him. "No matter how splendid you think they are, they'll kill you if they get the chance."

Worst of it was, Newton's colleague wasn't wrong. Newton hadn't let that enter his calculations when he left with the army. He wondered what else he hadn't thought about that he should have. He hoped he didn't find out the hard way.

When he remarked on that, Colonel Sinapis said, "Plan ahead. Always plan ahead. It will not be perfect, but it will help."

The latest dose of laudanum had worn off, leaving Newton sore and irritable. He wiggled his arm in the sling the surgeon had put on him. That only hurt more. "How do you propose to plan against what happens in a derailment?" he snapped.

To his amazement, the colonel had a sensible answer for him: "Belts across the seats would hold the passengers in place and not let them fly about promiscuously in an accident. That would save many casualties."

"Damned if it wouldn't," Newton said in surprise, his pique evaporating. "I wonder why we don't do it now."

"Because the railroad companies say it would cost money to put all these belts into place. Because, they say, some people do not care to be closed in with a belt. Because, they say, feminine costume would be inconvenienced. And so people break limbs and sometimes break their heads, but a few cents are saved! Hallelujah!" Sinapis did not so much as raise his voice, which only made the irony more cutting.

Gingerly feeling the side of his own head, Newton could sympathize with that irony. He turned to Jeremiah Stafford, who'd come through the latest derailment unscathed. "Here is something about which the government should have its say, don't you think?"

"Not quite so urgent as a servile insurrection," Stafford remarked. But that wasn't necessarily a veto, for he went on, "Bound to be easier to gain consensus on account of that."

"One would hope so, yes." Consul Newton was not about to let anyone display more sangfroid than he did.

"A plan," Colonel Sinapis said again. "Have you gentlemen yet devised one?" He was relentless as a hurricane.

"How can we?" Newton did *his* best to sound reasonable. "We won't fully know the situation till we arrive. Many telegraph lines are down—"

"Slaves' doing," Stafford broke in.

Newton shrugged. "As may be. But what comes over the surviving wires is the most amazing twaddle. If you tell me the slaves are responsible for that, I shall be most surprised."

"No, no," the other Consul said impatiently. "Do you expect calm and good judgment in the middle of an uprising, though?"

"Perhaps not. Occasional accuracy, however, would be welcome," Newton said.

"Do we fight the colored rebels? Do we fight the people fighting the colored rebels?" Sinapis persisted. "Do we try to keep them from fighting? What do we do if they don't feel like stopping?"

Those were all good questions. Newton had answers to none of them. Well, that wasn't strictly true. He had his own answers. Unfortunately, Consul Stafford also had *his* own answers, which weren't the same . . . which were, in fact, as different as coal and kohlrabi.

At least Stafford also didn't try to tell Colonel Sinapis exactly what would happen when the army got off the train in the state of New Marseille. He knew Newton had different answers, too.

Sinapis looked from one Consul to the other and back again. He might have been examining two insects with revolting habits. His voice suggested that he was: "Or will the army try to do one thing one day and something else the next, depending on who is in command? I tell you, gentlemen, this army is not a toy to be pulled back and forth between you as if you were a couple of spoiled children who needed spanking. You will cost me soldiers if you try to do things that way, and I remind you that soldiers are not toys."

"The innocent white men and women being despoiled by the insurrectionists are not toys, either," Stafford said.

"Neither are the slaves who have been despoiled for centuries by these so-called innocents," Newton returned. He stared steadily back at Balthasar Sinapis. "What is your personal view of slavery, Colonel?"

"It is my personal view, sir, and I prefer to keep it that way," Sinapis said. "Whatever it is, it is less important than my view that throwing away an army on account of lack of foresight and cooperation will do Atlantis more harm than good."

"We are all three of us men of strong opinions." Stafford sounded—amused? Yes, amused: Newton was sure of it. The other Consul went on, "Now, if only any two of us shared some of those opinions."

"We are what the country has," Newton said. "If from among us we can't piece together a course that will do the country good, then Lord have mercy on the USA."

"Yes. *Kyrie eleison*," Sinapis said, which meant the same thing but sounded much more elegant.

In the eastern foothills of the Green Ridge Mountains, the insurrection really caught up with the army. Like his colleague, Jeremiah Stafford was discovering that a diet of salt pork and hardtack left a lot to be desired to start with, and went downhill in a hurry from there. When the train stopped in the evening, some soldiers pounded their hardtack crackers into crumbs and fried them in pork fat. Stafford tried that himself—once. He found that different and better meant two widely separate things.

He also found he hardly needed pipeweed. The inside of the car in which he and Newton and Colonel Sinapis traveled was smoky enough without pipes or cigars. The derailments had broken several windows. He supposed they were lucky all of them hadn't broken. Even as things were, he feared he looked like the end man in a minstrel show. The soot on his white shirtfront told him how much he was likely to have on his face. The rasping coughs he let out every so often certainly warned him how much he had in his lungs.

Iron squealed on iron and sparks flew up from the wheels as the locomotive driver braked as hard as he could. "What the deuce?" Stafford said.

"I wonder if some of our not-quite-friends put something new on the tracks." Leland Newton sounded pleased with his own cleverness.

Colonel Sinapis, by contrast, sniffed scornfully. "If they had any tactical sense, they would have put the boulder or log or whatever it was around a bend in the track," he said. "Then the driver would not have been able to see it until he had no chance to stop."

But the insurrectionists did have tactical sense, even if not of the sort Balthasar Sinapis had looked for. As the train slowed, they started shooting at it from the pines and redwoods to either side of the roadbed.

For a moment, those bangs meant nothing to Stafford. But when a bullet punched through the side wall of the car and cracked past his head before drilling out the far side, he figured things out in a hurry. "They're firing at us!" he exclaimed, more angry than frightened.

"What do we do?" Newton added.

"For the sake of the country and for the sake of your own skins, I suggest you get low and flat—*now*," Colonel Sinapis said.

He couldn't give the two Consuls orders; they outranked him. But his "suggestion" had the snap of what would have been a command. It also seemed a very good idea. No sooner had Stafford got down than another bullet smashed through the space where he had been.

Sinapis did not get down. He drew his eight-shooter and started banging away through one of the broken windows. The reports only a few feet from Stafford's head stunned his ears. Lying beside him on the none-too-clean planks, Leland Newton grimaced every time the colonel fired. "This is most undignified," Newton said.

"Among other things," Stafford agreed.

He wondered what would happen if they both got killed here. He knew what the Atlantean Charter prescribed. If both Consuls died or abandoned their office for other reason, the Senate had to choose an interrex to serve as the chief executive till the next Consular elections were held. It had to choose him by a two-thirds majority, too. The way the Senate was divided these days, Stafford doubted whether Jesus Christ Himself could win a two-thirds majority of the Conscript Fathers.

Which meant that, if they both perished, chaos would descend on the United States of Atlantis. *Worse chaos*,

Stafford amended as another bullet snarled by not nearly far enough above his prostrate frame.

If only one of them died here, the other Consul would serve alone till the next election. Stafford eyed Newton, and found his colleague eyeing him right back. "Isn't it nice that we're friends?" Newton said.

"Wonderful," Stafford said in distinctly hollow tones. His colleague laughed.

That the USA did not suffer a Charter crisis lay to the credit of the army's junior officers and sergeants. The cars in which they rode farther back were getting peppered with bullets, too. They rushed their gray-uniformed soldiers out with fixed bayonets to drive the insurrectionists away. A few of the soldiers went down as soon as they jumped from their cars. The rest, stolidly professional, advanced into the woods regardless, shouting as they went.

The firing kept on, but it wasn't aimed at the train any more. The rebels were shooting at the soldiers, and vice versa. Stafford and Newton got up again to watch. Colonel Sinapis grunted. "That ought to shift them," he said.

And it did. When the soldiers came back, some of them dragged rebel corpses by the feet. One rebel they caught wasn't a corpse—and then, quite suddenly, he was. They brought out their own casualties, too. The surgeons attended to them as best they could. Consul Stafford watched with great—if slightly nauseated—interest. His colleague might admire the rebels, but these men sent to put them down would probably feel differently.

X

$\mathcal{D}$own the west side of the Green Ridge Mountains the train chugged ... slowly. Coughing a little, Leland Newton peered out through the swirling smoke that belched from the locomotive's stack. "Well," he said, "I did think we would get to New Marseille faster than a horse can walk."

"So did I," Consul Stafford said fretfully.

Balthasar Sinapis coughed, too: a cough of correction, Newton judged, not one caused by smoke. "As a matter of fact," he said, "we are going at the speed a horse can trot."

So they were. Atlantean dragoons in their tall black felt hats trotted along to either side of the railroad track. They had eight-shooters, shotguns, and carbines. Their job was to keep the Negroes and copperskins who'd risen in these parts from attacking the train. The foot soldiers inside the cars carried loaded weapons. Sinapis had made it plain he didn't like doing that, but he recognized the need.

The dragoons had done their job up till now. No more bullet holes marred the battered railroad cars. No more screams rose as surgeons probed for musket balls. Newton missed them not at all.

But if the copperskins and Negroes thought of themselves as the army's enemies, as they seemed to, wouldn't the soldiers in the army think of those Negroes and copperskins the same way? If that wasn't what Consul Stafford expected, Consul Newton would have been astonished.

Setting out from New Hastings, Newton would have called Stafford's expectations so much foolishness. The Consul from Croydon wasn't so sure now. If a man was willing to lay his life on the line to try to kill you, you weren't going to love him on account of it. No: you were going to want to keep him away, or else to do unto him before he could do unto you.

And if the soldiers got off the train with the notion that they needed to kill any slave who looked at them sideways firmly fixed in their heads, they wouldn't be interested in interposing themselves between the rebels and the whites they were rebelling against. No: they'd want to join the local whites in slaughtering every insurrectionist they could catch.

Stafford had clearly seen that from the beginning. *Why didn't I?* Newton wondered. Like a lot of northern foes of slavery, he'd tended to romanticize the men and women who were the victims of the institution. It was much harder to romanticize someone who was trying to blow your head off. You were much more likely to make someone like that into a demon, there in the fortress of your mind.

Maybe that was why Stafford had foreseen so clearly what was coming. He didn't suddenly need to turn the uprisen slaves to demons inside his head. As far as he was concerned, slaves who rose against their masters demonized themselves.

Muttering to himself, Newton looked out through the swirling smoke again. He could imagine that it was the veil of time, and that he was looking back into the past. The tall trees, some of them with moss hanging from their branches, the understory of squat barrel trees, the ferns growing in green profusion below them . . . The only signs of modernity were the railroad line—and the dragoons.

"We might see a honker pulling up leaves somewhere," he remarked.

"I wonder if any honkers are left alive," Stafford said.

"A few years ago, that artist fellow set out from Avalon to find some, remember? And he did, too, in some hidden mountain valley." Newton scratched his head. "What was his name, anyhow?"

"Audubon." That wasn't Consul Stafford—it was Colonel Sinapis. "A very fine artist indeed."

"You know him?" Newton asked in surprise. Imagining the fierce and dour Sinapis with any interests beyond those of his sanguinary trade wasn't easy.

But he sighed now as he shook his head. "Alas, I did not have that privilege—he died last year. No one could match his paintings of viviparous quadrupeds and especially of birds for their accurate vivacity. No one came close. Even if honkers are no more, they will still live for us in his portrayal of them."

"I had not thought you such a friend of nature," Stafford said, so the colonel had surprised him, too.

"Time often hangs heavy in the Ministry of War," Sinapis answered. "Having a hobbyhorse to ride helps make the hours pass. One of my colleagues translates chronicles from the medieval Latin. Another has become an expert on the history of mining iron. Several drink or play cards. Me, I prefer nature."

A career soldier's life in Atlantis: one more thing Newton hadn't thought through. The country had no serious foreign threats. Lying where it did, how could it? And the navy, not the army, would deal first with any threats that did appear. In his time in Europe, Colonel Sinapis would have been used to adventure and upheaval. Sitting around gathering dust in the Ministry of War couldn't have been easy for him. No wonder he'd found something besides soldiering to interest him.

Well, Atlantis had its own share of adventure and upheaval now. The navy couldn't do much about it, either, not unless the rebels came close enough to the water's edge to be bombarded by sea. If any part of the national government was going to restore order, it would have to be the small, sleepy, much-maligned army.

"*Can* our soldiers do the job required of them?" Consul Newton asked the colonel.

"If you and Consul Stafford tell me what the job is and stick with it, they will do it, whatever it may be," Sinapis answered. "They do not have much experience fighting, but they are well-disciplined men. You can rely on them—if I know, and they know, what they must do. If the two of you cannot make up your minds, or if you change them more often than you change your drawers, we shall have trouble."

He looked melancholy, but then he usually looked melancholy. He sounded melancholy, too: as if he expected they would have troubles. But it was a peculiar kind of melancholy, because he also sounded as if he was looking forward to whatever troubles they found.

Leland Newton had been looking forward to whatever troubles they found when he set out from New Hastings. He wasn't so sure anymore.

Jeremiah Stafford had always been a man of the Atlantic coast. In that, he was like most of his countrymen. Atlantis had been settled from the east, and remained most densely populated on the coast facing England and the European mainland. Only one real city—Avalon—lay on the Hesperian Gulf and looked toward Terranova. New Marseille gave itself airs, but wasn't in the same league.

During the fight for freedom, Victor Radcliff had marched an Atlantean army through western Atlantis to face the redcoats in New Marseille. The country on this side of the mountains had been a howling wilderness then. Now, a lifetime later, the pursuit of profits from cotton had turned much of it into an imitation of the plantations farther east. Much of it, but not all.

Here and there, the wilderness still howled. In stretches between plantations, only the railroad line proved that anyone had come this way before. Ferns and barrel trees and conifers got dull in a hurry. Like Consul Newton—and, no doubt, like Colonel Sinapis—Stafford wondered if he would see a honker, but he didn't.

Even market towns were fewer and farther between on this side of the mountains than in the longer-settled east. But people turned out to cheer the soldiers whenever the train stopped for fuel and water. Stafford couldn't resist pointing that out to his colleague in the Consulship.

"Well, some people do," Leland Newton allowed. "But

I don't see any blacks or copperskins dancing in the streets and singing hosannas because we've come."

"Good God in heaven! Who cares about them?" Stafford said. "White people made Atlantis."

"They did indeed: on the backs of the colored people they fetched here to do the hard, dirty work they didn't care to do themselves," Newton answered.

"You're spewing that rubbish again," Stafford said. "If you think white people don't work in this country, you've been walking around with your eyes closed. Without white men and their work and their capital, slaves would have nothing to do."

"This part of Atlantis would be better off if it had been settled by small freeholders, the way the lands farther north were," Newton said.

"Better off how, pray?" Stafford retorted. "Would you rather come to this climate in a wool shirt, and sweat and itch nine months of the year? If you would, by God, you're welcome to it. But I see you are wearing cotton instead, the same as I am. Try growing cotton on one of your precious small freeholds. It takes too much labor to make that possible."

"I could wear linen in a pinch," Newton said in musing tones. "Linen is tolerably cool, or better than tolerably."

"And it wrinkles if you give it a hard look, and it costs far more than cotton does—all of which, I have no doubt, you understand perfectly well," Stafford said. "You are being difficult for the sake of being difficult."

"I have no idea what you're talking about," Newton said. Stafford only snorted. He'd come to politics from the practice of the law, just as his colleague had. He knew a denial that wasn't a denial when he heard one.

While he and Newton bickered, Colonel Sinapis looked out the window. The Atlantean officer suddenly pointed. "There," he said. "This is part of the trouble of the countryside."

This was a rude encampment alongside the railroad tracks. Tents and lean-tos sheltered white people who were dirty and wore ragged clothes. A few of them waved to the train. More just sat or sprawled where they were, too apathetic to salute the men who had come to rescue them.

"You see." Stafford rounded on Newton and made the words an accusation. "This is what the insurrection does. These poor innocents got away with their necks, nothing more. All they worked for through their lives is gone now."

"Yes, it's very sad," the other Consul said. But that was at best a barbed agreement, for Newton went on, "They seem to have it as hard as the slaves did before the uprising."

The monstrous unfairness of that almost choked Jeremiah Stafford with rage. "Every time you open your mouth, all you prove is that you don't know what you're talking about. Any master who housed his slaves like that would get a quick talking-to from his neighbors, or maybe a horsewhipping. Putting mudfaces and niggers in such miserable quarters would be begging for an insurrection."

"I see," Newton said, nodding wisely. "You house your slaves better than this for the sake of your own safety, not on account of their comfort."

He doubtless thought that would make Stafford angrier. If so, he was doomed to disappointment. Stafford only laughed at him. "And I suppose the factory owners in Croydon pay their workers even one cent more than the least they could give while still keeping the workers alive. We were talking about freedom and the freedom to starve not long ago, if I recall rightly."

By Leland Newton's sour expression, the other Consul did. "We are not perfect paragons, either," Newton said. "But we hire our workers' labor. We don't buy it and sell it. Our workers are free to—"

"Starve in a different job if they don't like the one they have," Stafford interrupted. That probably wasn't what Newton had been about to say, which didn't mean it wasn't true.

"To change jobs as they please," Newton went on, as if the other Consul hadn't spoken. "They can move about as they please. They can marry as they please, and raise their own legitimate children."

"They can watch them starve, too, you mean, or waste

away from consumption," Stafford shot back. "And who gives a damn whether mudfaces and niggers have legitimate children?"

"They do," Newton said. "Do you suppose they enjoy it when the father is sold to one plantation, the mother to another, and the children, maybe, to a third?"

Jeremiah Stafford's snort was full of exasperation. "You have been reading sensational novels again. That rarely happens, and is always condemned when it does."

"But the law allows it, which is the point," Newton said.

"Only if you make it the point," Stafford replied. "And how often do women in Croydon have to sell themselves on the streets to survive? How often are the children they bear *legitimate*?" He laced the word with scorn.

By the way his colleague grimaced, that happened more often than Newton would have wanted. Before the other Consul could answer, Colonel Sinapis said, "Whether these slaves are legitimate or not, we are going to have to try to deal with them. The two of you are in command here." That plainly disgusted him, but he couldn't change it. He continued, "You had better figure out a way to work together, because you will get my men killed, and pretty likely yourselves with them, if you go on like this."

"You know what we need to do, Colonel," Stafford said. "I know what we need to do. I think even Consul Newton knows what we need to do. The question is, is he willing to do it?"

Newton didn't say anything. He did look like a man who knew what needed doing. But whether what he knew was the same as what Stafford knew was liable to be a different question.

Leland Newton eyed Crocodile Flats with distaste. It was bigger than a village, smaller than a town. It had got carved out of the primeval Atlantean wilderness on the banks of the Little Muddy River, a name that struck Newton as perfectly accurate. Once upon a time, crocodiles had laid their eggs there—hence the name. Now the crocodiles were gone. A more deadly species raised its broods in Crocodile Flats.

A militia captain in homespun, a broad-brimmed, floppy hat all but covering his eyes, told Colonel Sinapis, "You can't go no further by railroad. It's all niggers and mudfaces from here on out."

"They have spread this far?" Sinapis muttered to himself. "This is not what we were told when we left New Hastings."

"Yeah, well, it's so anyways," the captain said.

"Can we force our way through the rebel pickets to get to the heart of the insurrection?" Sinapis asked.

"Not by train, you can't," the militia captain answered. He paused to spit a stream of pipeweed juice into the dust, shifted a chaw to the other cheek, and went on, "Bastards have torn up as much track as they could."

"God damn them to hell!" That wasn't Colonel Sinapis—it was Jeremiah Stafford. The news made his temper burst like a mortar bomb. "Have they got any notion how much money they're costing the USA? Why, without a railroad connection New Marseille will wither on the vine!"

Newton wasn't sure whether he meant the state or the town that gave it its name. The town still had all its sea commerce, of course. The colored rebels weren't likely to turn pirate and harry that. A couple of hundred years before, Avalon had been a famous pirates' roost, but times were different now. Newton looked to Sinapis and asked, "What do you recommend, Colonel?"

"That we disembark and advance," Sinapis answered. "High time we discover what we are up against."

"I couldn't agree more!" Consul Stafford declared.

Whether he agreed didn't matter . . . today, because it was Newton's turn to command. But tomorrow the southern man would lead. Unless Newton marched east, away from the Little Muddy, they would go into action then in any case. Newton saw little point to putting things off a day. "Very well," he said. "Prepare the advance as you think best, Colonel."

Balthasar Sinapis saluted crisply. "Just as you say, your Excellency."

He turned away to start giving orders to his subordinates. Before he could, the militia captain tugged at his sleeve. "You'll want our men to go along, won't you? We know the countryside like you know the shape of your wife's . . . Well, hell, you know what I mean."

"They may come." If the prospect pleased Sinapis, he hid it very well. "But if they do, they will find themselves under the command and under the discipline of the army of the United States of Atlantis."

The captain shifted the wad of pipeweed from cheek to cheek again. "What does that mean exactly?" he asked.

"To give you a basic example, if they kill prisoners or torture them for the sport of it, I shall hang them from the closest strong tree branch," Sinapis answered calmly. "Is that plain enough, or do you need further illustration?"

"But—" The captain broke off. He might have said several different things, but he wasn't stupid enough to imagine that any of them would have done him any good. "All right, Colonel. Have it your way. We'll play along."

We'll play along till we don't think you'll catch us. So Newton judged his meaning, anyhow. Did Sinapis judge it the same way? Newton expected he did. The colonel might be a good many things, but he was neither foolish nor naive.

The bridge across the Little Muddy remained in the militia's hands. They had pickets on the west side of the river. Those men seemed mighty glad to see regular Atlantean troops come join them.

"Now we get down to business," Stafford said, ferocious anticipation in his voice, as Newton and he crossed the plank bridge together.

"So we do—whatever the business turns out to be," Newton said. His shoes and Stafford's thudded on the timbers. So did those of the soldiers they led. The men broke step as they crossed, lest rhythmic vibrations from marching in unison shake the bridge down. It wasn't likely, but it could happen. They took no chances.

Colonel Sinapis sent pickets—some militiamen, others regulars—out ahead of his main force and into the woods west of the river. Newton waited a little queasily for the sound of gunfire. Consul Stafford looked to be waiting for the same thing, and to be looking forward to it. The more the army fought the insurrectionists, the less inclined it would be merely to keep the peace.

A corporal came back to Colonel Sinapis. "There's a copperskin up ahead carrying a flag of truce, sir," he said. "What do we do about him?"

Sinapis looked a question to Newton. "Honor it," Newton said at once. "Let's find out what they have to say." Stafford made a disgusted noise, but he couldn't do anything about it—not today he couldn't, anyhow. The colonel told the corporal what to do. The two-striper saluted and went off to do it.

He came back fifteen or twenty minutes later with a strong, stocky copperskin who still carried his white flag. Newton had expected the rebels' emissary to be wearing stolen white men's finery, but he still had on homespun wool trousers and an undyed, unbleached cotton shirt: slave clothes.

"My name is Lorenzo," the fellow said. "I speak for Frederick Radcliff, the Tribune of the Free Republic of Atlantis."

"There is no such place!" Consul Stafford exploded. "There is no such title! And slaves haven't got the right to last names!"

"There is such a place, because that's where I come from. Frederick Radcliff *is* the Tribune there," Lorenzo answered calmly. "And he's not a slave—he's a free man. And so am I. Wouldn't be much point to talking if we weren't, would there?"

"What do you want? What do you expect from us?" Leland Newton asked.

"Leave us alone, and we'll do the same for you," the copperskin said. "The Free Republic of Atlantis is a place where anyone can live in peace. A lot of whites have run away from us, but they didn't need to. As long as they don't try to make anybody into a slave any more, we won't give them any trouble."

"Likely tell!" Stafford jeered.

"You've already killed a lot of people and done a lot of damage," Newton said. "Why shouldn't we treat you as so many rebels and criminals?"

"Because this is a war, and wars mean fighting, and fighting means killing," Lorenzo replied—the same answer Newton had given to Stafford back in New Hastings. "And because Frederick Radcliff is fighting for the same thing his grandfather fought for a long time ago—the chance to be free."

"Mudfaces and niggers have no business being free!" Stafford shouted, his face purpling with fury.

"Easy, Jeremiah, easy," Newton said. He turned back to the rebels' emissary. "You are not going to be allowed to form a nation apart from the United States of Atlantis. If you think that can happen, you are only fooling yourselves. Your commander is only fooling himself."

"By God, that's the first sensible thing I've heard you say all day," Stafford told him.

Newton ignored him. If Lorenzo was fazed, he didn't let on. Nodding to the Consul, he said, "Give us our rights inside the United States of Atlantis, then, and we'll be happy enough to stay."

"You have no more rights than a cow," Stafford said. "You have no more rights than a *chair*, damn you!"

"What rights do you have in mind?" Newton asked the emissary. Ignoring his colleague seemed best.

"The same rights white folks have," Lorenzo answered. "The right to be free. The right to a last name. The right to marry and raise a family. The right to buy and sell things. The right to learn reading and ciphering. Frederick, he can do that, but not many slaves can. The right to vote, even."

"You want to become citizens." Consul Newton summed it up in a handful of words.

Lorenzo nodded gratefully. "Yes, sir. That is just what we want."

"Will you let the whites who have run away return to their land?"

"As long as they don't try to buy us or sell us or order us around," the copperskin said. "Some of us want land of our own, too, so we can farm. If the white folks take everything back, nothing's left for us."

Stafford clapped a hand to his forehead. "They're as

Red as the crazy radicals in Paris! They probably preach
free love, too."

"You weren't listening," Newton said. "He told you one
of the things they wanted was the right to get married."

"Yes, he said that," Stafford answered. "Why do you believe him? They're full of savage animal lust."

Lorenzo stretched out his arm and looked at his hand.
Then his eyes went to Stafford's hand. "My skin is darker
than yours," he said, "but it is lighter than Frederick Radcliff's. Past that, I do not see much difference between us."

"No, eh? Well, you will," Stafford said.

"Tell your principal that, if you put down your guns and
petition peaceably for the redress of grievances, something
may come of it," Newton said. "It is hard for Atlantis to talk
with men in arms against us."

This time, the copperskin looked Stafford in the face.
He shook his head. "If we put down our guns, you will
slaughter us," he said. Stafford didn't waste time denying it.
Lorenzo went on, "Better we should fight."

"If you do, we will slaughter you anyway," Newton
warned.

"Well, you can try," Lorenzo said.

The corporal took him back past the pickets then. "You
tried it your way. See what it got you," Stafford said to
Newton.

"You didn't help," Newton said.

"Let me understand," Colonel Sinapis said. "It is to be
war now?"

"For the moment, yes," Newton answered regretfully.

War against slaves who'd risen against their masters! Jeremiah Stafford could imagine no more noble cause. He must
have done something right, or God wouldn't have been so
generous to him.

But it wasn't the kind of war he'd had in mind when he
set out from New Hastings with the army. The gray-clad
soldiers owned the ground where they marched, but not
another square foot of soil in the so-called Free Republic
of Atlantis. Any man who left the line—say, to go behind

some ferns and answer nature's call—was liable not to come back again. A Negro with a dagger or a copperskin with a bayonet might cut his throat and sneak off with his rifle musket and boots.

Any time the soldiers came within a quarter-mile of trees or ferns or fences or buildings, they were in danger. Enemies would pop out or pop up, fire, and then run off as fast as they could. The Atlanteans would shoot back, but it took uncommon marksmanship and uncommon luck to hit a single man at that range, even if he didn't disappear. Firing at large masses of soldiers, the mudfaces and niggers had much better luck.

No, it wasn't the way Stafford had imagined it. In his mind's eye, he'd seen dramatic pitched battles, like the ones Victor Radcliff had fought against the redcoats. Paintings of those—or woodcuts, sometimes colored, copied from paintings of those—hung in every government building from the Senate House down to the lowliest village post office. He didn't suppose the actual battles were just like the paintings, but the art gave him his most vivid notions of what war was like.

Colonel Sinapis didn't seem surprised at how things were going. "In charge of raw men like that, I would fight the same way," he said as the army encamped two evenings after crossing the Little Muddy. "Why should they risk a big battle? All the advantage would lie with us."

"What better reason?" Stafford said.

Sinapis gave him a crooked smile. "And do you also look for your chicken to climb up onto your plate already fried, your Excellency?"

"Well . . . no," the Consul admitted.

"Then do not expect the enemy to do what is convenient for you," Sinapis said.

Reluctantly, Stafford nodded. "All right. I can see the sense in that. How do we go about forcing the damned insurrectionists to fight on our terms, then?"

"That is a better question." Balthasar Sinapis plucked at his shaggy mustache. "In Europe, I would say the way to do this is to attack some place the enemy feels obliged to defend."

"In Europe? Why not here?" Stafford said.

"Because I see no place in these parts that the enemy would feel he had to hold," the colonel replied. "Where is the capital of the so-called Free Republic of Atlantis? Wherever Frederick Radcliff happens to be, unless my guess is wrong. Where are the rebels' manufactories? As far as I know, they have none. This being so, what position must they hold to the death?"

He waited. By all the signs, he really wanted an answer. Stafford opened his mouth, then closed it again when he realized he had no good one to give.

"You see the difficulty," Sinapis said. Even more reluctantly, Stafford nodded again. The Atlantean officer continued. "Do you intend that we should kill every Negro and copperskin within the area the rebels claim?"

"If that is what it takes to put down the insurrection, yes!" Stafford said.

"Those who own these persons under current Atlantean law would not thank you for destroying their property," Sinapis warned. "And what better reason to give the rebels still in the field to keep fighting instead of yielding?"

He might be nothing but a damned foreigner, but he was a shrewd damned foreigner. Slaveholders *didn't* want their human property destroyed; they wanted it restored to them. As far as Stafford was concerned, they hadn't thought things through. "How far will they be able to rely on slaves experienced in rebellion?" he asked. "Would you trust such a man to shave your face, Colonel?"

"Me? Not a bit of it," Sinapis answered. "But if a man can get no use from this form of property, what point to having it?"

It wasn't so simple. House slaves had to be trusted. They gave personal service and cooked; if you couldn't be sure they wouldn't turn on you, you couldn't keep them around. Field hands were different. All you needed from them was work, and even before the uprising overseers had had to watch their backs. Plantations could stay profitable after the insurrection. But even if they did, white planters' lives on them would have to change. Colonel Sinapis saw that clearly. So did Stafford.

"We shall burn that bridge when we come to it," the Consul said after what he hoped wasn't too awkward a pause. "First we have to win this war one way or another. If we lose it, nothing else matters any more. Or do you disagree?"

"No, your Excellency," Sinapis answered. "As you say, winning comes first. Maybe not even winning, though, will solve all our troubles here. What do we do in that case?"

"Worry about it after we win," Stafford said at once. "If we don't win, we'll have a pile of other things to worry about. Will you tell me I'm wrong?"

"About that? No," Sinapis said.

He does think I'm wrong about other things, Stafford realized angrily. *About what? About slavery? Well, the Devil take him if he does.*

By the map, the Gunston plantation lay only a couple of days' march to the west. Leland Newton had studied maps till he was sick of them. What difference did they make if the enemy wouldn't stand and fight? He didn't like thinking of the insurrectionists as enemies, but he couldn't think of people who'd shot at him as friends.

This stretch of countryside had belonged to the rebels till the Atlantean army marched in to reclaim it. Signs of that were everywhere. Big houses stood empty. Doors gaping open and smashed windows said they'd been plundered. Every so often, the army would march past one that had burnt to the ground.

Fields went untended. Ripening maize and wheat stood forgotten. So did acres and acres of cotton and pipeweed. No livestock was in sight. Even if surviving white plantation owners reclaimed this land, they would have lost a fortune. Consul Stafford couldn't open his mouth without going on about that.

Consul Newton didn't need long to get sick of listening to his colleague. "You didn't care while whites were taking everything away from blacks and copperskins," he pointed out. "Why do you bellow so loud when the shoe is on the other foot?"

"Because I *am* a white man, damn it," Stafford snapped.

"And so are you, if you take the time to remember it. The United States of Atlantis are a white man's country, in case you hadn't noticed."

"I thought we were a free man's country," Newton said mildly.

"Same thing," Stafford insisted.

"Come to Croydon and you'll see how wrong you are," Newton said.

"If I came to Croydon, I would see all kinds of things I don't care to see: free niggers and mudfaces, screeching bluestockings, trade unionists, free lovers, and every other sort of crackpot under the sun," Stafford said. "Since I already know as much, I have the sense to stay away."

Before Newton could come up with the retort that would leave the other Consul gasping for air, a brisk racket of gunfire broke out ahead. "I wonder what that's in aid of," he said.

"It's a demonstration of patriotism," Stafford said. "What else would it be?"

"I'm sure the people shooting at our men would agree with you," Newton said. "I own myself surprised, though, that you of all people would say such a thing." Sometimes the worst thing you could do to sarcasm was take it literally.

This skirmish seemed sharper than the Atlantean army was used to fighting. Maybe the insurrectionists held no vital strongpoints. Maybe they could melt off into the woods whenever they chose. But they could also fight whenever they chose, and they seemed to have chosen to fight here.

Newton rode forward to get a better look at what was going on. That made him a target: something he didn't realize till he came close to the fighting. When he did belatedly figure it out, he wasn't sorry to dismount and hand the horse's reins to an ordinary soldier. He continued on foot.

As they usually did, the rebels fought from the edge of a stretch of forest. If things went wrong, they could melt away in a hurry. Not only that, but they'd dug themselves holes and trenches from which to shoot. They made much smaller targets than they would have had they stood up and volleyed the way the Atlantean regulars did.

A grizzled sergeant near Newton knew exactly what he

thought of that. "Yellow dogs!" he growled, the stub of a stogie shifting in his mouth as he spoke. "Well, we can shift 'em even if they want to play silly games."

Soldiers went forward in neat lines. Every so often, one would fall. Sometimes he would get up and stagger toward the rear on his own. Sometimes medical orderlies would carry him to the rear. Sometimes, ominously, he would lie where he fell, not to rise again till Judgment Day.

Those neat lines did not wash over the dug-in rebels. They couldn't get close, not in the face of that galling musketry. Some men fell back. Others lay down themselves and returned fire. Then a flanking column went in off to one side of the insurrectionists' line.

That shifted them where the frontal attack couldn't. The Negroes and copperskins saw they were about to get enfiladed. They didn't wait around to let it happen, but slid away into the woods. And they kept on sniping at the men who came up to look at their trenches and the handful of bodies in them.

"Well, we licked 'em," an Atlantean soldier said. It was true, Newton thought—but only if you didn't count the cost.

XI

Rain on a cobblestoned road was a nuisance. If you rode a horse, you wore a broad-brimmed hat and an oilskin slicker to stay as dry as you could. Many of the roads east of the Green Ridge Mountains were cobblestoned. Some were even macadamized. Traffic moved on them the year around.

Jeremiah Stafford was discovering that cobblestones and macadam were sadly scarce on the far side of the mountains. One day, no doubt, they would come, but that day was not yet.

And rain on a dirt road was not a nuisance. Rain on a dirt road—especially the hard, driving semitropical rain that pelted down now—was a catastrophe. What had been a perfectly ordinary, perfectly decent, perfectly respectable road turned into a long strip of something with a consistency between soup and glue. Foot soldiers swore as mud sucked boots off their feet. Cannon and limbers and supply wagons bogged down. The foot soldiers had to shove them through the muck by brute force. Not surprisingly, that made the men swear more.

On horseback, Consul Stafford had it easier than most of the men in the Atlantean army. His mount struggled to move forward, but it was doing the struggling. He wasn't. Colonel Sinapis, also on horseback, said something to him.

Whatever it was, Stafford couldn't make it out. The rain was coming down too hard. "Eh?" The Consul cupped a hand behind his ear.

"When I was a subaltern, we could not fight in weather like this," Sinapis said, louder this time.

"Why not? What makes the difference?" Stafford asked.

"Percussion caps," the Atlantean officer answered. "A wet flintlock is nothing but a fancy club—maybe a spear if you have a bayonet on the end of it. But a percussion cap will still go off in the rain."

"Interesting how a mechanical device can change the way we wage war," said Stafford, who hadn't dwelt on the idea before.

"This always happens." For Sinapis, such things fell within his area of professional competence. "If you doubt it, ask the Terranovan natives how much they have enjoyed opposing muskets with bows and arrows."

"Mm—no doubt. The next question is, how well supplied with percussion caps are the damned insurrectionists?" Stafford said.

"Better than I would have thought," Colonel Sinapis said, which was not what Stafford wanted to hear. Sinapis continued, "They showed every sign of having plenty at the skirmish yesterday. They fought quite well, in fact. Their steadiness impressed me."

That was something else Stafford didn't want to hear. "They're nothing but lousy mudfaces and niggers," he growled.

"No man with a rifle musket in his hand is 'nothing but' anything, your Excellency," the officer warned. "No man who holds his ground till he sees himself outflanked and then draws back in good order is 'nothing but,' either . . . sir. You will get us in trouble if you think of the rebels as 'nothing but.'"

"I want to get *them* in trouble," Stafford said angrily. "We haven't had much luck with that, have we?"

Balthasar Sinapis looked up into the heavens. A raindrop splashed on the end of his long nose. "If you can persuade God to ease this downpour, your Excellency, you will have shown me something I did not know before."

"Even when the weather was good, we didn't have much luck shifting the black bastards." Yes, Consul Stafford was in a fine fury.

If that impressed Sinapis, the colonel's face didn't know it. "This campaign is just beginning, sir," he said. "We will do some splendid things—I am sure of it. And we will have some terrible things done to us, and to the rebels those will seem splendid. Such is war."

"It shouldn't be war, not against these—these damned ragamuffins," Stafford protested. "It should be like, oh, cleaning up broken crockery."

"Never judge a soldier by the kind of uniform he wears, or by whether he wears a uniform at all," Colonel Sinapis said. "Some of the most dangerous men I saw in Europe looked like farmers. They *were* farmers, till they picked up the guns they'd hidden in barns and sties and pigeon coops. After that, you would have thought they were devils straight out of hell."

"What happened to them?" Stafford asked, intrigued in spite of himself.

"My men hunted them down and killed them," the foreigner replied dispassionately. "We did, perhaps, too good a job. That was one of the reasons I . . . left that service and pledged my sword to Atlantis."

Too good a job? What kind of howling wilderness had Sinapis' men left behind? Stafford didn't much care. As long as the insurrectionists got what was coming to them, nothing else mattered.

The rain came down harder. Stafford hadn't been sure it could. With a little luck, it would wash Frederick Radcliff and the rest of the insurrectionists out to sea. But that was bound to be too much to hope for. The Consul began to hope the downpour wouldn't wash him and the Atlantean army out to sea.

Every once in a while, a great storm would slam into southern Atlantis. Savage winds would tear off roofs and sometimes blow down buildings. The cyclones would roar inland till they finally weakened and petered out. This wasn't one of those. It wasn't blowing very hard at all. It was just raining and raining and raining.

Forty days and forty nights went through Stafford's mind. For hundreds of years, theologically inclined writers had wondered how Noah had put Atlantis' peculiar natural productions aboard the Ark, and how those productions had ended up here and nowhere else. That sort of writing seemed to have tapered off in recent times. The consensus was that nobody knew, except possibly God.

A junior officer came back to Colonel Sinapis from the vanguard. Stafford admired him. Moving against the tide had to be even harder than going with it. The officer spoke to Sinapis. Whatever he said—again, the drumming rain muffled it for the Consul—made Sinapis gnaw at his mustache. Stafford thought that a disgusting habit.

After gnawing, the colonel dipped his head. He might have been Zeus in the *Iliad*, which Stafford remembered from his college days. He said something to the junior officer, who looked relieved and sloshed forward again.

At last, Sinapis condescended to explain: "We stop here. We can't go forward any more. We will start killing animals if we do."

"Soldiers will start drowning, too," Stafford said.

"Well, so they will." Colonel Sinapis cared about losing his men when they faced the rebels. When it came to a downpour, he seemed to worry more about his horses and mules. Stafford almost called him on it. But the rain also drowned his urge for a brand new row.

Even making camp wasn't easy. Tent pegs didn't want to stick in the soggy ground. Once up, the tents leaked like billy-be-damned. All soldiers were supposed to have oil-skin groundsheets so they could sleep dry. Some had never been issued them. Some had thrown theirs away. And even the ones who had them weren't happy, because muck slopped over the edges.

Cooking hot food—even boiling coffee—was impossible. Soggy hardtack made an uninspiring supper. Salt pork was next to indestructible, but in weather like this it was liable to start getting moldy, too.

Stafford's tent was bigger than the ones the soldiers used, but no drier. He sat inside glumly, wondering what would happen if the insurrectionists chose this moment to attack. Colonel Sinapis had posted sentries all around, but so what? How much could they see, and who would hear them if they yelled a warning? Then Stafford thought, *If the rebels do attack now, they'll go over their heads in goo, and good riddance to them.* He felt—a little—better.

Someone tugged at the tent flap. "Leland Newton. May I come in?" the other Consul asked.

"Why not? Everything else has gone wrong," Stafford said.

"Heh." Newton ducked inside and let the tent flap fall behind him with a wet, dismal splat. "You should take your comic turn on the stage. You'd make more than Atlantis pays us."

"Comic turn? Did you think I was joking? I am not glad to see you," Stafford said.

"Nor am I enamored of you, believe me. But we are in harness together, like it or not," Newton said. "And, one day soon, evidence to the contrary notwithstanding, this army will start moving forward again."

"Evidence to the contrary notwithstanding, indeed," Stafford muttered.

Newton pulled out a flask. "Here. Have a knock of this. It may improve your outlook. Something ought to."

"Maybe I'm glad to see you after all." Stafford swigged. Barrel-tree rum kicked him in the teeth and flamed down his throat. "By God, maybe I am!"

"Are you glad enough to answer a question for me?" Newton asked.

"I don't know. Let's see." Stafford almost drank again, but handed the flask back instead.

"Suppose the rebels decline pitched battles. Suppose they keep sniping and raiding and skirmishing, as they have been doing. Are you ready to post thousands of soldiers in little garrisons all through these parts for the next twenty or thirty years to try to hold down the countryside?"

"If that is what it takes, why not?" Stafford said. "The Terranovans do it on their frontiers, to keep the copper-skins from sneaking in and detaching people's hair."

"It will cost us dear," Newton warned.

"What do you suppose *not* stopping the insurrectionists will cost us?" Stafford asked icily.

"Something," Newton said, which surprised Stafford—he hadn't expected the other Consul to admit even that much. Newton went on, "Change always costs something. But don't you see? We have to change either way. I fear trying to hold down slaves in southern Atlantis for the next generation will cost us our souls."

"I think we'd be fighting for them—and for our backbones," Stafford said.

"Maybe you're right, your Excellency. Maybe, but I wouldn't care to bet on it." Newton ducked back out into the rain, leaving Stafford alone, the taste of barrel-tree rum still on his lips.

Balthasar Sinapis pointed up into the sky. "Do you see that small, bright, yellow ball there?"

Squinting, Consul Newton nodded. "I do, Colonel. What of it?"

"If I remember rightly, in the old country we used to call that 'the sun.'"

The craggy colonel *did* have a sense of humor. Leland Newton wouldn't have bet a cent on it. Smiling to show he appreciated the joke, he said, "How long do you think the roads will take to dry out enough to let us travel on them?"

"They probably should be good enough for us to use just before it starts raining again," Sinapis answered. Newton started to smile again. Then he realized the colonel wasn't joking this time—merely expressing his faith in the innate perversity of nature. Since Newton had seen plenty of that perversity himself, he decided he couldn't very well disagree.

All around them, the encampment steamed. That hot sun drew vapor up from the drenched canvas of the tents. The grass and weeds and ferns on which those tents were pitched steamed. So did horses' backs. And so did soldiers' clothes. Every time Newton inhaled, he felt as if he were breathing soup.

As if picking that thought from his mind, Colonel Sinapis remarked, "No one would say the state of New Marseille has a Mediterranean climate."

"Avalon, farther north, is said to be quite pleasant the year around," Newton replied.

Sinapis only sniffed. "It would not be the same. Are you familiar with the notion of dry heat, your Excellency?"

"Only by reading of it." Leland Newton spread his hands. "Atlantis is surrounded by the sea, after all. And I believe it is a positive good that she is. Her position has gone far toward making her rich."

"No doubt," Sinapis said. "It has also gone far toward giving every citizen of this country rheumatism and lumbago. Or do your bones not creak when you get up of a morning? Till I came here, mine never did."

He was talking about New Hastings, where he'd spent the bulk of his Atlantean military career. The capital had a good climate—or Consul Newton had always found it so. It was certainly a better climate than chilly Croydon's. But Sinapis had different standards of comparison.

The colonel stuck a stogie in the corner of his mouth. Then he tried to strike a lucifer on the sole of his boot. The boot sole was wet, and the match wouldn't catch. Muttering an unpleasantry that wasn't in English, Sinapis pulled a small piece of shagreen from a tunic pocket. He scraped the lucifer against that. The rough sharkskin gave enough friction to touch off the match. Sinapis lit his cigar and puffed out pungent smoke to flavor the prevailing steam.

"You are ready for anything," Newton said as the colonel put the shagreen back in his pocket.

"I try to be," Sinapis answered. "If I may speak frankly, though, your Excellency, I was not ready for a war intended to be waged along political lines. I do not see how any army or any officer could be ready for such a thing."

"All wars are political, wouldn't you say?" Newton parried.

"In their goals, yes," Colonel Sinapis said. "A clever modern German called war the extension of politics by other means. I agree with this. Anyone who thinks about it is bound to agree, I believe. But when political affairs interfere with the way the war is fought, it becomes less likely to have a happy result. I believe anyone who thinks about it is also bound to agree with this."

Newton didn't need to think much about it to decide it seemed quite likely. All the same, he said, "When the war touches slavery in the USA, political affairs are bound to interfere. Half the country takes the institution for granted, while the other half hates it. We should count ourselves lucky not to have flown at one another's throats."

"Do you expect this fight to solve your problems for you?" Sinapis didn't sound as if he thought any fight could solve any problem.

"I hope so. *Expect* may be too strong a word." Newton remained an optimist.

"Oh, well." By the way Sinapis sounded, he didn't. What had he seen, what had he done, in Europe to leave his attitude so curdled? Consul Newton realized he didn't know the details of the colonel's career before Sinapis got to Atlantis. He hadn't cared enough to find out. That might have been a mistake. But asking now would seem awkward, so he didn't.

In his own way, Consul Stafford was an optimist, too. Most Atlanteans—most white Atlanteans, anyhow—were. What were the United States of Atlantis if not a place where a man could build on his hopes? But Stafford's hopes were different from Newton's. The sun's return prompted only one thought in him. "Now we can go after the insurrectionists and finish them off!" he declared.

Maybe the sun's return prompted some thoughts among Frederick Radcliff's Negroes and copperskins, too. They weren't an army, or weren't exactly an army. They could, and did, move around by ones and twos and small bands, where Colonel Sinapis' men wouldn't have felt happy or safe doing any such thing. And they popped up here and there and started sniping at the Atlantean soldiers.

One bullet snarled through the air between Newton and Stafford. Both Consuls automatically ducked. They exchanged sheepish looks. Almost everybody ducked. It didn't mean a thing.

"We ought to hang every black bastard we catch sneaking around with a musket!" Stafford said after he straightened up.

"That will really make the rebels want to give up," Newton observed.

"I don't care whether they want to give up or not," Stafford said. "I want them dead. I want the ones who are left alive to be afraid to lift their hands against their masters for the rest of their days. I want the United States of Atlantis to be safe for decent, God-fearing white people again."

"You want things to go back to the way they were before the uprising started," Newton said.

"Yes. That is what I want," the other Consul agreed.

"How do you propose to get it, though?" Newton asked. "We've been over this ground before. Can you unscramble an egg? Can you make all the rain we've just had fall up into the sky?"

"The sun can dry out the rain," Stafford said stubbornly. "That makes it as if it had never been. The sun of justice can dry out the insurrection, too, enough to let us get by."

He meant it. He meant every word of it. Realizing as much alarmed Leland Newton, but he knew it was so. "When Pilate asked 'What is truth?' he didn't wait for an answer," Newton said. "Now I ask you, sir, what is justice? I will wait as long as need be for your reply."

"Justice is giving people what they deserve for what they have done." Jeremiah Stafford sounded as stern and certain as the Old Testament prophet whose name he bore.

Newton nodded. "We can take that for a beginning place. What do people who have held other people in bondage for centuries deserve? What do people—?"

"They deserve thanks and congratulations." Stafford still sounded certain. He had the courage of his convictions. "Compare the lot of those bondsmen here with that of their savage cousins in Terranova and Africa and you will see that I speak the truth."

"I had not finished," Newton said. "What do people who buy and sell other human beings at a whim, who take the fruits of others' labor, who violate their bondswomen whenever it strikes their fancy—what do those people deserve?"

"What do people who Christianize the heathen, who

build a thriving country out of empty wilderness, who make the United States of Atlantis into the earthly paradise—what do those people deserve?" Stafford returned. "We are talking about the same people, you know. What justice is depends in some measure on the angle from which you view it."

"Well, I would agree with you there," Newton said. "You have a perspective different from mine about the planter class."

"I know them. You don't," Stafford said.

"Let it be as you say," Newton told him. Stafford raised an eyebrow; he hadn't expected even so much of a concession. Consul Newton went on, "What you will not see is that we also have a differing perspective on the rebels. You think of them as murderous, bloodthirsty wild beasts—"

"Which they are," Stafford broke in.

"To you, perhaps," Newton replied. "To me, they look more like men and women who, having been treated intolerably for generations, seek liberty so these abuses cannot go on. They seem very much like proper Atlantean patriots, in other words, even if their skins be dusky."

"That is a madman's perspective," the other Consul exclaimed.

"Oh, piffle! You know better. Do I caper? Do I gibber?" Newton said.

"You do not, as you must know. But you are more dangerous, not less, because you do not," Stafford answered. "An obvious lunatic ends up in jail or an asylum, where he can do others no harm. A lunatic who is not so obvious will deceive many others and persuade them to follow him. What is the name of that maniac minister?"

"Which one?" Newton asked. Atlantis permitted all faiths, which meant strange ones sometimes sprang up in the backwoods like weeds. Most flourished for a while and faded, but some seemed likely to last longer.

"The fellow who founded the—what do they call it?—the House of Universal Devotion," Stafford said. "I know there are others, but he's the one I had in mind."

"Oh. Him. Well, we have agreed twice in a few minutes—how strange. I think he's a maniac, too," Newton said. The

House of Universal Devotion was indeed a backwoods sect, one with an unsavory reputation. People who didn't belong to it claimed that far too much of the devotion went to the founder, far too little to the Lord. Members kept to themselves as much as they could. There were rumors some of the rites were licentious, even lewd. Newton didn't know if those rumors were true, but he wouldn't have been surprised. Something else he didn't know . . . "I can't tell you what his name is. He goes by the Reverend or the Preacher."

"If I came out with nonsense like that, I wouldn't want my real name associated with it, either," Stafford said.

"People listen to him," Newton said. "He doesn't seem to do much harm." That was as far as he would go to praise the House of Universal Devotion.

It was too far to suit Jeremiah Stafford. "The devil!" the other Consul snapped. "The only reason you say that is, he rants against slavery along with his other ravings. That he does should make you ashamed to hold the same views."

"Even a broken clock is right twice a day," Newton said.

"That clock ought to be smashed, not broken," Stafford said.

"If the sect provably violates the laws, or if we find good reason to set aside the Charter, no doubt it will be," Newton said. "Until and unless that happens, tolerance seems the better policy."

"You will tolerate a tumor on the Atlantean body politic, which wants only growth before it can extinguish the Charter. But an institution long sanctioned by our laws? That, you oppose." Stafford sounded bitter as wormwood.

Consul Newton hadn't thought of things in such a light. Uncomfortably, he said, "The Reverend and his followers do not harm others—"

"Not where they get caught," Stafford retorted.

"Slavery does," Newton went on as if his colleague had not spoken. "That is why I oppose it, and why so many in the north do."

"Servile insurrection must be checked!"

Newton waved to the soldiers all around. "Well, here we are. What are we doing, if not trying to check it?" They were doing more along those lines than he'd had in mind when they set out from New Hastings.

"Whatever we're doing, it's not enough." Stafford plucked at his whiskers. "I wonder if we have any weak-minded House of Universal Devotion men in this army. If we do, I shouldn't be surprised to hear that they were discovering our plans to the niggers and mudfaces."

That hadn't occurred to Newton. He wanted to say the other Consul would be hearing voices next. He wanted to, but discovered he couldn't. What Stafford had suggested might be unlikely, but it was far from impossible. What did come out of his mouth was, "We shall have to find out about that."

"Yes. We shall." Even the soft answer failed to satisfy Stafford. "We should have done it a long time ago."

"Maybe we would have, had you suggested it then," Newton said. "If you bring it to Colonel Sinapis' attention, I am sure he will handle it."

"He does not favor slavery," Stafford said darkly. Newton wondered why that surprised the other Consul—few immigrants did. Stafford scowled. But then he unbent enough to add, "He will not care for the House of Universal Devotion, either: it is destructive of good discipline."

"Something else on which we agree," Leland Newton said. "We may have more in common than either of us would have believed."

"So we may. But so what?" Stafford had no more give to him than the rocks of North Cape. "We also know where we disagree, and we know which carries the greater weight."

"I am not your enemy," Newton said. "You mistake me if you judge me so."

"You are the enemy of things I hold dear, however," Stafford replied. "You oppose me there, and I will oppose you to see those things strengthened and protected. I do not see how we can make a friendship of that."

Neither did Consul Newton, however much he might have liked to.

Jeremiah Stafford scowled at Lorenzo. The copperskinned emissary from the Free Republic of Atlantis stared back impassively. Whatever Lorenzo was thinking, he didn't tell his face about it: a useful quality in an envoy. Only the flag of truce he carried kept Stafford from ordering him seized and hanged from the closest tree. The Consul was tempted to do it despite the white flag.

"Here I am again. Now you start to see you can't hope to beat us," Lorenzo said. Even his voice grated on Stafford's nerves. He talked like what he was: a slave, and likely a field hand at that. A pig in an archbishop's robes would have made a more unlikely diplomat than Lorenzo, but only a little.

"We haven't seen anything of the kind," Stafford growled. "If your precious Frederick Radcliff is such a wonderful general, why doesn't he come out and fight instead of skulking around like a coward?"

Lorenzo still didn't change expression, though something might have flickered in his eyes. "If you are such a wonderful general, Consul Stafford, why don't you make him come out and fight when he doesn't want to?"

Beside Stafford, Leland Newton snickered, then tried to pretend he hadn't. Colonel Sinapis coughed, which might have been even more embarrassing. Stafford's ears felt ready to burst into flame. He couldn't even show his fury, lest he hand Lorenzo another point. "That," he ground out, "can be arranged."

"So you say, your Excellency." By his tone, Lorenzo didn't believe a word of it.

"I also say you deserve lashes for your insolence," Stafford told him.

Lorenzo only shrugged. "If you want, I will take off my shirt and show you my stripes. I have tasted the lash before. Have you?"

"No, and I have not deserved it, either," Stafford said.

"Oh? Deserved!" Lorenzo's face might not show much, but he had an expressive voice. "Well, I did not deserve my whippings, either. But that did not stop the overseer. And many of the people in the Free Republic's army will tell you the same story. That is why we keep fighting. That is why you will never make us give up, no matter what."

"In a pinch, killing the lot of you will do," Stafford said.

The copperskin started to laugh. Then he took another look at Stafford's face and thought twice. He hadn't realized Stafford might mean it. After a considerable pause, he said, "Well, you can try. Giving us the freedom we want, the freedom we deserve, would come cheaper, though."

"You don't think you have earned punishment for your insurrection? Punishment for your treason?" Stafford asked.

"Your Excellency, any man with stripes on his back who does not rise up against the folk who gave them to him deserves punishment for not having any balls," Lorenzo said. "That is how it seems to me, and I have tasted the lash. Let us be free men and citizens, and we will trouble you no more. Say we have no right to that, and we will fight you forever."

"Go fight, then, because we will do just that," Stafford said.

"You say so now. Will you say so in five years' time, or ten, or fifteen?" Without waiting for an answer, Lorenzo raised his flag of truce and strode away from the white men who led the army opposing him.

"You should know you were speaking for yourself there," Consul Newton told Stafford. "Certainly not for me, and I would say not for the Atlantean government, either."

"Well, so what?" Stafford said. "Today is my day in command. You let that Lorenzo get above himself when it was your turn. High time the insurrectionists understand that we will not put up with their insolence. And, whether I speak for the government of Atlantis or not, you may rest assured that I do speak for the government of every state with a servile population. This kind of thing cannot be allowed to spread, or it will consume us all." He turned to Colonel Sinapis. "We ought to shadow that rogue of a Lorenzo, see where he goes. With any luck at all, he will lead us straight to Frederick Radcliff. If we take off the insurrection's head, the body ought to die."

"Interesting you should say so, your Excellency," Sinapis answered. "I tried it the last time he called. I lost two men and gained nothing. The rebels may be many different things, but naive they are not."

"Oh," Stafford said on a deflated note. "Too bad."

"It would not have worked in Europe," Sinapis said. "Here, I thought, perhaps the enemy is not so clever, so I might learn something worthwhile. But no." He spread his hands, as if to say, *What can you do?*

What Stafford wanted to do was dispose of every slave who had risen. He still wasn't convinced it was impossible. The will was there—or it would be, if it wouldn't cost the slaveowners so dear. The means were the harder part.

He found out just how hard it might be a couple of days later. To his surprise, and even more to his dismay, he found out not from Consul Newton or Colonel Sinapis—men he'd come to see as obstacles in his own path—but from a messenger who galloped in out of the east.

The news the man brought was particularly unwelcome. The slave uprising had broken out in earnest behind the army. The railroad line over the Green Ridge Mountains was cut. No supplies would get through any time soon.

Balthasar Sinapis' long face got even longer when he heard that. He said several choice things in English, then several more that sounded even juicier in what seemed like three or four other languages. Once the thunder and lightning stopped crashing down, he said, "This presents us with a serious problem. Two serious problems, in fact: food and munitions."

"If the God-damned insurrectionists can live off the countryside, so can we," Consul Stafford declared.

"But they have already been living off *this* countryside for some little while," Sinapis said. "That makes it more difficult for us to do the same."

"Hard to get more meat off bones the vultures have already picked clean," Consul Newton agreed.

"*Vultures* is right," Stafford snapped. "That's just what they are, and high time you admitted it, too." Having put the Consul from Croydon in his place—or so it seemed to him—he gave his attention back to the colonel. "We have enough ammunition to keep fighting, don't we?"

"For a while," Sinapis answered dubiously. "If we should run dry without getting any more . . . In that case, our troubles get worse."

"Translated into English, that means we get massacred shortly thereafter, doesn't it?" Newton asked. Put in his place he might be, but he refused to stay there.

Colonel Sinapis didn't tell him he was wrong, either. Of course, that was because Consul Stafford beat him to the punch: "Oh, rubbish. The insurrectionists are bound to run dry before we do. And if we aren't better men with bayonets in our hands, then something is dreadfully wrong with the way the drillmasters train our soldiers." He turned back to Sinapis again—no, he rounded on him this time. "Or will you tell me I'm wrong?" *You'd better not*, his voice warned.

And Colonel Sinapis didn't. "No, both those points hold considerable truth," he said.

"Then why were you panicking a moment ago?" Stafford asked.

"I was not," the officer replied with dignity. "I would be remiss in my duty if I did not point out difficulties."

He was right, which didn't make Stafford love him any better. Growling deep in his throat, the Consul said, "Well, sir, things being as they are, what do you recommend we do?"

"March for the town of New Marseille," Colonel Sinapis answered at once. "We establish a secure base, and we secure a supply route by sea—all the more important now that the land route has failed. We also prevent the insurrectionists from seizing the place, which would be a disaster for us."

He was right again. Leland Newton promptly nodded. Even Stafford could find nothing to quarrel at, not this time. He nodded, too. "Very well," he said. "And we should do that as quickly as we can, before the niggers and mudfaces hereabouts find out what's happened farther east and try to steal a march on us."

"Assuming they don't already know," Newton said.

"Yes. Assuming." Stafford contrived to make the innocent word sound more than a little obscene.

"All right, your Excellencies. For once, we find ourselves in complete accord. If only we did not require misfortune to cause it," Sinapis said. He waved to his junior officers, who stood in a knot off to one side, waiting to learn what had happened.

After their commander explained, they seemed no happier—which was putting it mildly. "Sweet suffering Jesus!" one of them exclaimed. "We're supposed to push the savages around. They aren't supposed to push us!"

"War is not about what is supposed to happen, Captain," Colonel Sinapis replied in tones so wintry, they should have frozen the subtropical landscape all around. "War is about what does happen, and about responding to it as best one can."

"Er—yes, sir," the captain said. That was one answer that was never out of place.

Not even Consul Stafford could complain about the way Sinapis and his officer corps got the men moving. The soldiers grumbled and swore, but soldiers always grumbled and swore. They marched along the muddy roads, which was what mattered. And the insurrectionists did not seem inclined to do more than harry them. Maybe that meant Frederick Radcliff didn't aim to attack New Marseille himself. Stafford hoped so, anyhow.

XII

*M*ore hard rain further slowed the army's march to New Marseille. Even after the soldiers got there, Leland Newton reminded himself, New Hastings would be a while learning of their misfortune. A ship or a land traveler would have to carry the news. The rebels had proved much too good at cutting telegraph lines. All the southern ones seemed to be out. Maybe a working line still ran from New Marseille up to Avalon. Even if one did, it wouldn't help much. There'd been talk of stringing wires from New Hastings to Avalon, but it hadn't happened yet.

Frederick Radcliff's irregulars kept sniping at the Atlantean soldiers, rain or no rain. "The reports said the damned insurrectionists somehow got their hands on proper percussion pieces," Jeremiah Stafford grumbled. "Why couldn't they have been wrong for once?"

"It could be worse," Newton said.

"Of course it could," the other Consul said. "They could have got their hands on a couple of batteries of field guns, too? Wouldn't that be delightful?"

Newton thought how he'd like to be on the receiving end of a cannonade. "Now that you mention it, no," he answered. He might sympathize with the downtrodden Negroes and copperskins, but not enough to lay his life on the altar in expiation for generations of white men's sins.

And then, just as he'd said it could, it proceeded to get worse. First one soldier and then several more came down with yellow fever. That did nothing to improve the morale of the men who managed to escape it. A good number of them were down with a bloody flux of the bowels. It was less dramatic than the yellow jack, which didn't mean it was a sickness anyone would want.

A few men trickled away. Colonel Sinapis responded by setting out even more sentries than he was already posting. Desertions slowed, though they didn't quite stop. Newton suspected more soldiers would have tried skedaddling had they not feared what might happen if the rebels caught them.

"God in heaven!" Stafford said. "The way things are going, I wonder whether we deserve to win."

"I've wondered all along," Newton said, drawing an irate glare from his colleague.

Colonel Sinapis looked at things from a different angle. "You must remember, your Excellency—these are green troops," he told Stafford. "Many of them have been in the army for years and years, but they are green anyhow, because whom has Atlantis fought in all that time?"

Instead of reacting to the obvious justice of the comment, Stafford only muttered, "Whom," as if he were a grammatical owl.

"Accusative case, is it not?" Sinapis said. "English is not my native tongue, but I do not care to make mistakes using it."

"You were accurate," Newton assured him. "You were more accurate than many people who grew up speaking English would have been."

"Oh. One of those," Colonel Sinapis said. "Every language has them, I suppose. They are like ambushes, set in place to trap the unwary."

A breeze from off the Hesperian Gulf blew the rain clouds to the east. It brought with it the scent of the sea. Newton was familiar with that sharp salt tang, of course; he couldn't very well not be, not when he'd spent most of his life in Croydon and New Hastings. But he thought the Hesperian Gulf smelled fresher than the ocean off the east

coast of Atlantis. It probably was no coincidence that less
sewage went into the Gulf than into the ocean off the East
Coast.

A sentry rode back to the army and said, "Looks like
there's a bunch of spooks and coppers laying for us up
ahead."

"Can we give them a surprise for a change?" Consul
Stafford asked.

"*I* command today," Newton said pointedly.

"Do you *not* wish to surprise the enemy?" Colonel Sinapis asked him.

Part of him wanted to say yes. If he did, he could get
away with it—for the day. Sooner or later, though, the news
would get back to New Hastings. Odds were it would get
back in whatever distorted form Stafford chose to use. And
Newton had discovered he liked getting shot at no better
than any other human being.

Not without reluctance, he replied, "Proceed as you
think best, Colonel."

"Maybe you are smarter than you look," Stafford said.

After a salute that might have come from a clockwork
mechanism, Sinapis conferred with the scout. Then he sent
a cavalry screen forward to keep the insurrectionists from
getting a good view of anything else he was doing. With
luck, the flanking party that hurried off to the right would
do unto the enemy what he wanted to do unto the Atlantean army.

With luck . . . The thought brought Newton up short.
The soldiers hadn't had much, not so far in this campaign.

He didn't need to wait long for another lesson on the
dubious joys of being the target of flying lead. The rebels
lurking among the ferns at the edge of a stand of hemlocks
opened up on the Atlanteans from cleverly concealed
positions.

Those positions didn't stay concealed for long, of course.
When a rifle musket went off, it spat a long tongue of fire.
And a cloud of black-powder smoke rose above the man
who'd fired. If anyone ever invented gunpowder that didn't
smoke, he'd make a fortune. Nobody'd come close to doing
it yet.

"Return fire!" Colonel Sinapis shouted.

Quite a few of his men had already started shooting back without orders. They marched with loaded weapons, something they wouldn't do in anything but the most dangerous country. Two or three Atlantean soldiers fell. Screams rang out. One man, though, went down like a dropped rag doll. Shot through the head, he'd never get up again.

As they had more than once before, the Atlanteans in gray advanced on the ragged Negroes and copperskins harrying them. Before long, the rebels would slide back into the woods and disappear. Then the whole miserable process would start over a few miles farther down the road.

That was what the rebels thought, anyway. It was how things had worked out the last time they tried this stunt, and the time before that. It wasn't how things worked out today. As the copperskins and blacks started their withdrawal, the flanking column hit them. A great thunder of musketry from their left—the Atlantean army's right—announced the collision.

"That'll shift them!" Colonel Stafford yelled. "The biter bit—and let's see how the sons of bitches like being on the receiving end!"

By all the signs, the rebels liked it not a bit. That didn't surprise Leland Newton. In war more than perhaps in anything else, it was better to give than to receive.

Now that the rebels had to fight the flanking party, they couldn't simply fade away. The main body of the Atlantean army got into the scrap at close quarters. The soldiers had a lot of pent-up rage to vent.

Thinking about that, Newton turned to Balthasar Sinapis. "Colonel, don't you think you ought to order your men to take prisoners?" he said.

"Why?" Stafford yelped, as if he'd proposed requiring the soldiers to start practicing some unnatural vice.

Newton looked at him. "If you have learned the art of interrogating corpses, your Excellency, I hope you will be good enough to acquaint the rest of us with it."

"You mock me, sir." By the way Stafford said it, his seconds would confer with Newton's at any moment to arrange the terms and time of the duel. The *code duello* wasn't dead south of the Stour, so maybe that was exactly what he had in mind.

Whether he did or not, Newton didn't. "Don't be a bigger blockhead than you can help," he said, which made Stafford gape. He went on, "You've been mocking me since before we left New Hastings. Have you seen me take offense?"

"Some people are more sensitive to slights than others," Stafford said, but his heart didn't seem to be in the quarrel any more.

Newton looked back to Colonel Sinapis. "Prisoners," he prompted.

"Yes, yes. The point is well taken." Sinapis gave orders to a captain, and sent the junior officer forward to convey them to the troops. Then he sighed. "I hope they will heed him."

That hadn't occurred to Newton. When he thought of an order, he thought of its being obeyed without fail. But men and all their works were imperfect. What ever happened without fail?

Some captured rebels might have got shot or bayoneted, there in the woods with no one but angry Atlantean soldiers to see the job done. This was one of those places where asking too many questions didn't look like the best idea in the world. All the same, the soldiers did lead out more than a dozen disgruntled rebels, most with their hands tied behind them, a few with nooses already around their necks.

"We ought to smoke them over a slow fire," Stafford said. "That would give us what we need to know, and in a hurry, too."

"In my experience, torturing prisoners is usually more trouble than it is worth," Colonel Sinapis said. "Not always, and not in all circumstances, but usually. A better way is to question them separately, telling each man his answers will be compared to those of the others. Anyone whose answers do not match his friends' will know he is to be singled out for punishment. This has proved a good way to get at the truth."

It struck Consul Newton as a good way to get at the truth, too. "Let's do that, then," he said eagerly. *Too ea-*

gerly? he wondered. Maybe so, but he had no stomach for tormenting captives.

And even Jeremiah Stafford gave a grudging nod. "We can try it," he said. "First."

Sinapis carefully instructed the men he told off to question the captives. Chances were he didn't think they'd be gentle without careful instruction. Chances were he was right, too.

"Do we keep moving toward New Marseille?" Newton asked him. "Or do we wait to see what we find out? If we can strike at the heart of the uprising . . . " Had he just said that? Damned if he hadn't.

Stafford neither sneered at him nor clapped him on the back. That other Consul left him to stew in his own juices. That was liable to mean Stafford was cleverer than Newton had given him credit for: one more worrisome thought among so many others.

"I don't know, your Excellency. You are the commander . . . today." Colonel Sinapis' long face showed what he thought of Atlantean practice. It certainly had some flaws the framers of the Charter hadn't thought of. The colonel continued, "I am here, as I understand my position, to put your orders and those of Consul Stafford into effect. As long as I am doing that, I may legitimately give orders of my own. Otherwise, those orders lie outside my region of responsibility." His fleshy nostrils quivered. No, he didn't like Atlantean arrangements even a cent's worth.

"I am not asking you for orders, Colonel," Newton said, as diplomatically as he could. "I am asking for your opinion, for your professional judgment."

"Ah. My opinion. That, I am certain, is worth its weight in gold." Sinapis could be formidably sardonic in a language not his own. "My opinion, your Excellency, is that it is better to put out a fire while it is still small, because dousing one after you let it get bigger will be much harder."

Newton glanced over at Jeremiah Stafford. Again, his colleague failed to rise to the bait. Newton wondered whether something was wrong with him. He had the perfect chance to tax Newton for not letting the army move sooner—and didn't use it. Such restraint seemed out of character.

Or maybe Stafford was letting events bludgeon Newton. Even if in the abstract you admired someone's cause, it was much harder to feel loving-kindness toward him after he'd almost killed you. Newton had had that thought before. It came home to roost again.

He deliberately turned his back on the other Consul. Stafford's soft chuckle said he had much too good an idea of what Newton was thinking. Ignoring it, Newton addressed Colonel Sinapis: "You want to go after Frederick Radcliff, then, if we find the chance?"

"I do." Sinapis dipped his head, which he seemed to do more often than not in place of nodding. Newton thought again of Zeus in the *Iliad*. Sinapis made a mournful, bedraggled excuse for a Greek god. Well, what these days was so fine as it had been once upon a time? The officer's figure of speech wasn't Greek at all: "Maybe we can put the genie back into the bottle after all. Do they tell that story in Atlantis?"

Newton had heard it or read it, though he couldn't remember where or when. Stafford did. "'Ali Baba and the Forty Thieves,'" he said, and Colonel Sinapis dipped his head again. The other Consul added, "Ali Baba may be stuck in *The Arabian Nights*, but, believe me, the thieves made the crossing here ahead of you."

"It would not surprise me," Sinapis said. "I have never found a place where thieves did not make the crossing. Perhaps heaven is such a place. Perhaps not, too . . . " A long pause. "We shall pursue Frederick Radcliff, then, given that chance?"

"We shall," Newton and Stafford said together. They eyed each other suspiciously. Newton couldn't guess which of them that agreement bothered more.

Colonel Sinapis looked most dubious as he peered up from the ground at Jeremiah Stafford on horseback. "Are you sure you must ride with them, your Excellency?" he asked in tones that couldn't have meant anything but *Are you out of your mind, your Excellency?*

But Stafford nodded. "You'd best believe I am, Colonel. If they—if we—catch the rebel, I can make sure he gets what's coming to him on the spot."

"A written order carried by the commander of the raiding party would accomplish the same thing," Sinapis said.

"No doubt. But I would not see it happen," Stafford said.

The colonel sighed. "Have it your way, then. You will anyhow. I cannot give you orders—only suggestions. Still, if you slow down the men with whom you ride, you will make them less likely to do what you most want done."

Flicked on his vanity, Stafford said, "I won't slow them down."

He hadn't been riding long before he wondered if he'd told Sinapis the truth. The raiders were mostly young, bandy-legged, and small. They spoke in gleeful obscenities. And they seemed to think the presence of an Atlantean Consul was the funniest thing they'd ever run into.

"If I was back in the real world," one of them said to him, "I'd think holding slaves was the wickedest thing a man could do." The trooper's accent proclaimed him a northern man, from Hanover or possibly Croydon.

"The real world?" Stafford waved. The ferns and grass and hemlocks and barrel trees all around seemed real enough to him and then some. "What do you call this?"

"This here?" The cavalryman thought the question was pretty funny, too. "Your Excellency, this here is fucking Nowhere with a capital N." His friends on horseback nodded. They thought it was fucking Nowhere, too.

And they had a point. The only work of man in sight, besides the narrow road that might have started its career as a honker track, was a ruined, tumbledown shack. Stafford didn't think the insurrection was the reason it was empty. By the look of it, nobody'd lived in it for the past twenty years.

"How do you feel about slaves rising up and killing their lawful masters?" Stafford asked. "How do you like it when they try to kill you and your friends?"

"On account of something's lawful, that don't make it right," the young soldier answered. "But the other part of that there . . . You'll have to wait a while before you find the next fella who tells you he's only happy when some God-damned son of a bitch is shooting at him."

Again, the other cavalrymen nodded. Consul Stafford would have been hard-pressed to tell the northern man he was mistaken. The captain leading the detachment glanced down at something in his hand—a sketch map, Stafford supposed. But for the gold braid on his hat and the three stars on each side of his collar, he looked little different from his men: not much older than they were, either.

"We swing in here," he said, pointing down an even nar-rower track toward the dark woods ahead. "Lousy rebels are in there. We pitch into 'em from the flank, drive 'em off, and snatch the shitheel who tells 'em what to do." Staf-ford couldn't place him by the way he talked. Maybe he'd come from England or Ireland when he was young. He didn't seem hesitant about what they were doing, anyhow. That was good. An officer who didn't believe in the cause for which he was fighting could easily contrive to botch his mission while making the failure look like an accident.

As soon as they got to the edge of the woods, the captain told off horse-holders to tend to the other men's mounts. He didn't choose very many, which pleased Stafford: he wanted to get as many soldiers as he could into the fight.

They plunged into the woods. Some of the cavalrymen carried carbines. Others had eight-shooters at the ready. Stafford had a revolver himself. A carbine or a rifle musket could easily outrange it. In a forest where you couldn't see past pistol range, though, so what? And, with eight bullets in the cylinder, he could put a lot of lead in the air in a hurry if he had to.

Would the insurrectionists even bother posting sentries on their flanks? Copperskins and Negroes were notoriously lazy and shiftless, so Stafford wouldn't have been surprised if they didn't. But that thought had hardly crossed his mind before somebody let out a startled, "Who's there?"

"The Atlantean army and the Lord Jehovah!" the cap-tain answered, stealing a line one of Victor Radcliff's of-ficers had used a lifetime earlier.

"Well, shit!" the enemy lookout exclaimed. If the red-coats had said anything like that in response to the Atlanteans long ago, it hadn't got into the history books. It probably wouldn't get into the history books now. The shooting started a couple of seconds later. Shooting would make the books. Shooting always did.

Bullets cracked past people. They slammed into tree trunks. They whispered through the undergrowth, cutting leaves and fronds as they went. And a few of them smacked into soft flesh. Shrieks rose up along with the shots and the fireworks smell of gunpowder smoke.

Something up ahead moved. Jeremiah Stafford thought it did, anyway. He squeezed the trigger. The revolver bucked and roared in his hand. Maybe he drilled a vicious Negro right between the eyes and dropped him to the forest floor before he could even blink. Or maybe he'd wasted a bullet on ferns stirred by a vagrant breeze. Unless he tripped over a corpse on his way forward, he'd never know.

On the Terranovan mainland, they called something like this a copperskin fight. Both sides hid behind trees and shot at each other as they tried to move. The savages on the western mainland used bows and arrows, too: silent, unnerving weapons. The copperskins here banged away like their black brethren.

So did the Atlantean cavalrymen. They still had the advantage of surprise, and tried to make the most of it. Frederick Radcliff was in there somewhere. The faster they could grab him, the better.

When Stafford ran forward, his shoes sank into the ground. His feet felt wet—water was leaking in. Almost without his noticing, the hemlocks and pines were giving way to moss-draped cypresses. A flapjack turtle stared at him out of cold yellow eyes from a puddle—one of too many puddles that suddenly seemed to appear out of nowhere.

"Sweet suffering Jesus!" he exclaimed. "We're in a swamp!"

The cavalrymen had made the same unwelcome discovery at about the same time. Their complaints were even more heartfelt, and much more profane. Stafford started swearing, too, though he was an amateur alongside virtuosos. It might have been funny if it weren't so revolting. This whole mission had been predicated on speed and surprise. Surprise was gone, shot dead by an alert sentry. As for speed . . . How could you do anything in a hurry with mud trying to suck the shoes off your feet, and maybe trying to suck you down into it?

Another maybe crossed Stafford's mind. Maybe the insurrectionists' leader wasn't so foolish to base himself in a place like this. Maybe he wasn't so foolish, period. That might have made the Consul wonder whether Negroes and copperskins generally were as foolish as he'd always thought. It might have, but it didn't. Instead, it made him decide that Frederick Radcliff had his grandfather's blood in him, all right.

"Those lying, poxed—!" The captain's furious voice broke off, as if he couldn't find anything bad enough to say about the people he had in mind, whoever they were. That came a moment later, when he tried again: "Nobody said anything about this being a God-damned mudhole!"

Back in the Atlantean camp, the captured insurrectionists would no doubt claim their captors hadn't asked them the right questions. Technically, Stafford supposed they'd be telling the truth. All the same, he couldn't help wondering what would have happened had the soldiers hurt them a little, or more than a little, to make sure they weren't withholding.

It couldn't very well have turned out *worse*.

"Snake!" a trooper wailed on a rising note of horror. "Lousy snake just bit me!" That gave Stafford one more thing to worry about: not what he needed at such a crowded moment.

"Frederick Radcliff!" the captain shouted. "Come out and surrender, Frederick Radcliff!"

A chorus of voices told him what he could do with his surrender. Their curses showed more ingenuity than Consul Stafford would have expected from such a pack of colored riffraff. "Go after them!" Stafford called. "The more noise, the more insurrectionists, and the more likely we are to catch our man."

He wondered whether they would know their man even if they caught him. What exactly did Frederick Radcliff look like? Who would bother painting a slave's portrait? Nobody—no money in it. And the leader of the uprising wasn't likely to have sat stock-still for a newfangled photograph, either. Stafford pictured Frederick Radcliff as looking like his famous grandfather, only with dark skin and kinky hair. That might be right, or it might not. He wasn't sure within twenty years how old the jumped-up slave was. That might make things harder, too.

But much harder? Stafford didn't think so. Some Judas among the insurrectionists would give their leader away if he saw him. Maybe the copperskin or black wouldn't do it on purpose. An involuntary gasp of surprise would serve well enough, though. And then Frederick Radcliff would dance on air or face a firing squad or suffer whatever other lethal fate his captors decided upon.

And then . . . what? Would the insurrection quietly fold up and fail because the man who started it got what was coming to him? Stafford hoped so. That was why the raiding party had come here, after all.

But what would happen if someone else—that damned arrogant Lorenzo, say—kept things going even after Frederick Radcliff was dead and gone? What would happen farther east, where slaves were rising up even though chances were they'd barely heard of Frederick Radcliff?

Stafford muttered under his breath. It wasn't a happy kind of muttering. The closer he looked at the insurrection, the worse it seemed. Back in New Hastings, he'd thought everything was simple. Sally forth, slaughter the insurrectionists, and march home in triumph.

He hadn't imagined the uprising was like the Hydra, sprouting two heads for each one you chopped off. But just because he hadn't imagined it back in New Hastings, that didn't mean it wasn't so.

To make matters worse, the enemy must have heard his well-intentioned advice to the cavalrymen. The Negroes and copperskins started making a racket first here, then there, then somewhere else. Anyone who tried following the trail of noise would be chasing a will-o'-the-wisp.

Panting, his heart pounding, Stafford thought, *Sinapis was right, damn him. I am too old for this.* He pushed through the ferns anyhow. Maybe he would stumble over Frederick Radcliff. Maybe—a bigger unlikelihood, however little he cared to admit it to himself—he would recognize the rebel leader if he did stumble over him. Or maybe something else worthwhile would happen.

Something else did happen, worthwhile or not. The green curtain in front of him parted. A Negro carrying a musket he must have stolen off a planter's wall was also hurrying forward. They stared at each other in mutual shock and horror for a split second, the dapper, middle-aged white man and the young black in filthy, ragged clothes. Then, after simultaneous gasps, they both raised their guns and fired.

And they both missed.

They couldn't have been ten feet apart, but they missed anyhow. The twin shots and the crack of the insurrectionist's bullet darting much too close past Stafford's ear all but stunned the Consul. The Negro looked as desperately unhappy as Stafford felt. But they were in different situations. It would take the insurrectionist at least half a minute to reload and fire another round. All Jeremiah Stafford had to do was pull the trigger.

The black man figured that out in an instant. Had he been the natural-born coward Stafford assumed him to be because he was a Negro, he would have thrown himself down in the thick undergrowth or tried to run away. Instead, he clubbed his musket and rushed at the Consul.

Stafford did fire again. He didn't miss this time. The bullet caught the insurrectionist just to the left of the middle of his chest. Stafford couldn't have placed it any better aiming at a target with all the time in the world to shoot.

When you shot somebody—especially when you hit him right where you wanted to—you expected him to fall over. Stafford had done enough hunting to know that deer didn't always fall over as soon as you shot them. He'd thought it would be different with people, though. For one thing, no deer ever born had tried to smash in his skull with a reversed musket.

He ducked the stroke that would have scrambled his brains. Then he fired yet again—and hit the Negro yet again. The man still didn't fall over, though he did grunt in surprise and pain when the bullet bit into him. He also dropped the musket, but only to try to snatch the eight-shooter out of Stafford's hand.

"Why don't you die, damn you?" Stafford groaned.

"Fuck your mother, you white devil," the Negro said. He opened his mouth to add another unpleasantry, but blood poured out between his lips and from his nostrils. For a heartbeat or so, he looked astonished. Then—at last!—his eyes rolled up in his head and he slowly crumpled to the forest floor. A sudden nasty stench amid the forest's green odors said his bowels had let go.

He twitched a few times, but now he was plainly dying fast. Stafford stared down at him. He smelled the man's sweat and his blood as well as his shit. He'd never dreamt killing could be so dreadfully intimate—the Negro was the first man he'd ever known he'd slain. All at once, he doubled over and was sick. Some of his vomit splashed the black man, but it seemed more tribute than defilement.

"You all right, Consul?" a rough voice asked. A sergeant with grizzled side whiskers stood there. He jerked a thumb at the corpse. "Never done for anybody before, have you?"

"No," Stafford choked out. "Have you got anything I can rinse my mouth with?"

"Here you go." The sergeant handed him a tin canteen with a cloth cover.

"Thanks." Stafford undid the cover and gulped. He'd expected water. He got barrel-tree rum. He almost puked again, as much from surprise as for any other reason. Then he spat out some of it.

The sergeant nodded. "That's the way, friend. Gets rid of the taste better'n water would, doesn't it?"

"It does," Stafford agreed, a different kind of surprise in his voice. He took another swig, and swallowed this time. Then he handed back the canteen.

After putting it on his belt again, the sergeant said, "I don't think we're going to catch the son of a bitch."

"Neither do I, I'm afraid," Stafford said. "But even if we don't, we're making him run away. We're making the insurrectionists dance to our tune for a change." Potent excitement and even more potent rum were hitting him the way the Negro's musket ball would have had it connected. "That's got to be worth something, doesn't it?"

"Well, we can hope so, anyways," the veteran answered, and with such doubtful assurance Stafford had to be content.

Leland Newton nodded to himself when the cavalry column came back without the rebel leader. Then he noticed that his fellow Consul was splashed with blood and distinctly green around the gills. "Are you all right, Jeremiah?" he asked, more real concern in his voice than he'd expected.

He watched as Stafford looked down at himself and noticed the blood for what seemed likely to be the first time. "Oh," Stafford said, and then, as if explaining everything in three words, "It isn't mine."

"Well, good," Newton said. "Ah, whose is it, then?"

"This nigger and I saw each other in the woods at the same time," Stafford answered. "I ended up shooting him."

Newton would have thought the Consul from Cosquer would sound proud of himself after doing something like that. Instead, Stafford seemed unwontedly subdued. Colonel Sinapis understood that before Newton did. "Your first time, your Excellency?" the officer asked.

"That's right." Stafford nodded jerkily. "You aren't the first one to ask me, either. It must stick out on me like spines. Is that the mark Cain wore?" He sounded altogether in earnest. Newton hadn't killed. He had no idea what it would be like, and wasn't anxious to find out. Whatever Stafford had learned about himself, it seemed to have come closer to shattering him than bucking him up.

Sinapis' gaze swung to the captain who'd commanded the raiders. "You did not capture the rebel chief. Did you kill him?"

"No, sir, not that I know of," the captain said. "My guess is that he *was* there, or somewhere close by. There were plenty of insurrectionists in those parts, and I can see no reason why there would have been if they weren't guarding something or someone important to them." He paused for a moment. "I wish we would have had a better description of the scalawag, and I wish someone would have told me we'd be squelching through a bog after him."

"Were you?" Sinapis said, his eyebrows leaping. The captain nodded—unhappily, if Newton was any judge. "We did not learn that from the prisoners who told us where Frederick Radcliff would be hiding?"

"We sure didn't, sir," the captain said. "Maybe they were holding out on us, or maybe we just didn't find the right questions to ask. Any which way, we got into something we weren't prepared for. The troops performed bravely. Not catching our man wasn't their fault. They did everything they could. They might have done better if they'd known what they'd be getting into."

"It must be the fault of the questioning," Colonel Sinapis said. "Had we asked the question we needed, we would have got the right answer. A bog? *Malakas!*" He didn't bother to translate that. He sounded splendidly disgusted. With the bog? With the questioner? With the captives, for not volunteering more? With the whole campaign? That last seemed most likely to Newton.

He put the best face he could on things: "On to New Marseille, then?"

Sinapis dipped his head. "On to New Marseille, your Excellency. We shall make sure the rebels cannot steal the place. "That would be"—he paused to look for words—"unfortunate. Yes, unfortunate. To say nothing of embarrassing." The ones he found seemed to fit altogether too well.

They roused Stafford from his sorrowful lethargy, too. "New Marseille already has a garrison! It has cannon!" he said.

"It has cannon," Sinapis agreed. "Most of them point out to sea, to protect the harbor from enemy bombardment. It has a garrison: a small one. So far as I know, it has not been reinforced by sea. These people we are fighting have already done several things I had not imagined they could do while I was still in New Hastings. If they should surprise us again, it would not surprise me."

Newton tried to parse that last sentence. Logically, it made no sense. Logic or no, he understood what Sinapis was talking about. So did his colleague. "Well, we'd better get there ahead of them, then," Stafford said. "Or, if we can't manage that, we'd better drive them out once we do get there."

"Indeed," Colonel Sinapis said. "I should not care to be remembered as the man who lost the city." His mouth tightened. He must have been remembered for some failures back in Europe; he'd made glancing allusion to at least one of them. Plenty of people came to Atlantis to try to redeem failure elsewhere. Some succeeded. They were the ones who wrote their names in life's book in large letters. Others went right on failing. Most of those, by the nature of things, were soon forgotten. But a soldier who failed might end up better remembered than one who triumphed.

The same, Newton realized uneasily, held true for a Consul who failed. Newton had understood from the start that either he or Stafford wouldn't get what he wanted from this campaign. Now he realized *neither* of them might get what he wanted. And what would come of *that*?

BOOK III

XIII

They were gone. The last gunshots petered out at the edge of the wooded swamp adjoining the St. Clair plantation. Frederick Radcliff allowed himself the luxury of a long, heartfelt sigh of relief. He'd known the Atlantean soldiers were dangerous fighting men. He hadn't dreamt how dangerous they were till they almost snatched him from his redoubt here.

He wouldn't even be able to stay here any more. The soldiers were liable to come back without warning. If they did, his own men might not be so lucky holding them off.

How had the white Atlanteans learned where he made his headquarters? Only one answer occurred to him: they must have squeezed it out of a captive. What had they done to the men they took? All sorts of unpleasant possibilities occurred to Frederick. With the scars of the lash on his own back, he wouldn't have put anything past the enemy.

But he was still in the fight. That was the most important thing. The Free Republic of Atlantis remained a going concern. And it remained an inspiration for slaves all over the southern half of the USA. Not all the uprisings that had broken out from the Hesperian Gulf to the Atlantic were under his control. That had worried him at first. It didn't any more. They all had the same goal: to give Negroes and copperskins the freedom they deserved simply by virtue of being men and women.

Some of those distant uprisings had ended in massacre, either of whites by furious slaves or of slaves by victorious and vengeful whites. That kind of slaughter would make it harder for the two sides to come back together when peace finally returned, if it ever did. Frederick urged his followers and everyone who rose with him to limit killing whenever they could. And he hoped his urging did some good. He hoped, yes, but he wouldn't have staked more than ten cents on it.

His scouts still kept a close eye on the Consular army. The main body didn't seem to be coming after him. As far as the watchers could tell, it was heading for New Marseille.

Lorenzo clicked his tongue between his teeth when he got that news. "I told you we should have grabbed the town when we had the chance," the copperskin said. "Ain't gonna get it again."

"We might not even have taken it. We couldn't have held it," Frederick said, as he had a good many times before.

As Lorenzo had before, he responded, "But think of the newspapers yelling 'Rebel army takes New Marseille!' Headlines like that, they're worth money to us."

"Getting run out and shot up isn't," Frederick said. "Do you reckon we could keep those soldiers from running us out?"

"Well . . . no," Lorenzo admitted.

"There you are, then." Frederick would have boxed Lorenzo's ears if the copperskin had tried to tell him anything different.

"Here I am, all right," Lorenzo said mournfully. "Here I am, trying to cipher out what we do next."

"We hang on, that's what," Frederick answered. "Long as we hang on, sooner or later we're gonna win. They have to squash us flat to lick us. And even if they do, we'll just pop up again somewhere else."

"All right. I hope it's all right, anyway," Lorenzo said. "We ain't got killed yet, and when we started out I sure thought we would have by now. Reckon that puts us ahead of the game."

Frederick thought that put them ahead of the game, too. Had their cause failed, they wouldn't just have been killed. They would have been put to death with as much pain and ingenuity as their white captors could come up with.

A brightly colored little bird fluttered from branch to branch above Frederick's head. Every so often, it would peck at a bug. He pointed to it. The motion was enough to send it flying away. A lot of Atlantean creatures had no fear of man. As far as Frederick could see, the little warblers were afraid of everything.

He knew how they felt.

Lorenzo saw the bird, too. His thoughts went down a different track: "Not much meat on those, but they're tasty baked in a pie. Dunno why the rhyme talks about blackbirds. They ain't half as good."

Off in the distance, more gunshots erupted. Frederick frowned, but that seemed to be the last flurry. "If you're sure you don't want to have anything to do with New Marseille, maybe we'd better head north, up towards Avalon," Lorenzo said. "Plenty of plantations up that way. Plenty of mudfaces and niggers who'd be glad to see us, and plenty of white folks who wouldn't."

He commonly put his own kind first. Frederick commonly thought of Negroes first. That wouldn't matter unless the two groups paused in their fight against oppression and went after each other instead of the whites who held them both down. Some of the whites had tried to provoke them into doing just that. So far, it hadn't worked. Frederick wanted to make sure it wouldn't.

"We've got to remember: the white folks are the ones we've all got to go after," he said. "Blacks don't fight copperskins. Copperskins don't fight black folks, either."

"Well, sure," Lorenzo agreed. "We'd have to be pretty damned stupid to pull a harebrained stunt like that."

"Plenty of people are stupid. Doesn't matter what color they are. Fools all over the place," Frederick said. "What we've got to do is, we've got to make sure the fools don't drag everybody else into the chamber pot with 'em."

"That sounds good to me," Lorenzo said. "We've got

enough trouble taking on the white folks, looks like to me. We fight our own little war while we're trying to do that, they'll lick all of us."

Frederick Radcliff nodded. "Looks the same way to me." He was glad he and Lorenzo both saw it like that. To Negroes, copperskins, even enslaved copperskins, had more touchy pride than they really needed. They were always ready for trouble, and would sometimes start it themselves if they couldn't find it any other way.

"That's how come you can go on running things, far as I'm concerned," Lorenzo added. "Maybe I wouldn't mind being on top. But I won't do anything that'd mess up the war against the whites. So help me God, Fred—I won't." He held up his right hand, as if taking an oath . . . not that slaves were allowed to take legally binding oaths in the United States of Atlantis.

"That's big of you, Lorenzo. Matter of fact, that's downright white of you." Frederick grinned crookedly. The copperskin groaned. Frederick went on, "Plenty of time to worry about all kinds of things once we win. Till we do, we better keep going like we've been going."

"We ought to go toward New Marseille instead of north, though. We really should." Lorenzo kept gnawing like a termite. If he chewed long enough, he figured whatever he was chewing at would fall over. "Maybe we don't attack— all right. But we should be in place to attack if we see the chance."

"Well, all right. We can do that," Frederick said. Lorenzo's jaw dropped. Smiling, Frederick went on, "Just because I don't think we ought to attack it right now, that doesn't mean it won't be a good idea later on, maybe. We should be ready to grab the chance if we can."

The former field hand's face lit up. "Well, hell, Frederick, why didn't you tell me that sooner?" Lorenzo said. "For a little while there, I thought you were softer than you ought to be, but I see it ain't so."

"Not me," Frederick said. "We've come this far. We'll go as much farther as we have to."

"Now you're talking!" Lorenzo's grin got wider yet.

*   *   *

Jeremiah Stafford had thought New Marseille would be very much like Cosquer. Why not? They were both seaside, slaveholding cities in the United States of Atlantis, weren't they? So they were, but they were no more identical than barrel trees and barrels.

Over on the east side of Atlantis, Cosquer had real seasons. Oh, they were milder than New Hastings'—and much milder than Hanover's or Croydon's—but they were there. Once in a while, it even snowed in Cosquer. Washed by the warm current of the Bay Stream, New Marseille seemed to bask in an eternal June. It was always warm. It was always humid—not muggy, the way it got in Cosquer in the summertime, but moist.

And Cosquer was an old place, the second oldest city in Atlantis: four hundred years old now, or as close as made no difference, only a year or two younger than New Hastings. The Bretons, after all, had found Atlantis even before the English fisherfolk. But the Radcliffes had seen right away that the new land needed settling, while the Kersauzons were slower on the uptake.

Well, the Kersauzons paid for it, the way slowcoaches commonly did.

New Marseille, by contrast, *was* new, as new as a freshly minted gold eagle. It hadn't been much more than a fort and a trading post back in Victor Radcliff's day. The best harbor south of Avalon on the West Coast, but so what? When it was hundreds of miles from the settled regions of Atlantis, that hardly mattered.

Once the railroad and then the telegraph connected New Marseille to the rest of the world, it mattered a lot. Over the past twenty years, New Marseille had seen a growth spurt the likes of which the world had never seen the likes of, as one local boaster put it. He wasn't so far wrong, either.

There was one other big difference, too. Right this minute, all the white people in New Marseille were scared out of their wits. Many of them—most of the more prosperous ones—owned slaves. And it was impossible to look at a slave without wondering if he wanted to wring your neck as if you were a chicken, or to accept a cup of coffee from a house slave without fearing she'd slipped rat poison into it.

(Even worse was the idea that New Marseille might *not* be so different from Cosquer. Had servile insurrection raised its ugly head back there, too? Did whites look askance at Negroes and copperskins there, too? The cut telegraph wires made it impossible to know for sure. But they let Stafford's imagination run wild, and he could imagine things far worse than reality was likely to be. Or maybe, in the present disordered state of affairs, he couldn't—and that was a genuinely terrifying thought.)

Every so often, somebody in an upstairs window would fire at somebody down in the street. The somebody in the street—the target—was invariably white. The somebody in the window almost invariably got away. Jeremiah Stafford would have been willing to bet the shooter was bound to be colored.

He would have been willing to bet, yes, but he couldn't find anyone who would put up money against him. Not even Consul Newton was that big a sucker.

Towns in eastern Atlantis had broad cleared belts around them. New Marseille didn't. Insurrectionists lurked in the woods right outside the city limits. Sometimes they sneaked in to stir up the slaves in town. Colonel Sinapis' soldiers tried to seal off the perimeter. There was too much of it, and there were not enough of them.

The garrison that had held New Marseille was pathetically grateful for reinforcements. "Don't know what we would've done if those devils got in here first," was something Consul Stafford heard again and again.

Stafford had a pretty good notion of what the garrison and the white populace would have done had New Marseille been forcibly incorporated into the Free Republic of Atlantis. They would have died: that was what.

Big guns bore on the stretch of the Hesperian Gulf in front of New Marseille. They crouched in casemates of brick and iron and earth and cement. No naval cannon could smash them, except by luck. But they pointed only out to sea. Their giant iron cannonballs and bursting shells wouldn't cover the landward side of the city. When engineers laid out New Marseille's works, they never imagined anyone would attack from that direction.

Well, life was full of surprises. Aside from small arms, the only pieces that would bear on the insurrectionists were three- and six- and twelve-pounders like the ones Colonel Sinapis had brought from New Hastings. Field guns were better than nothing—and they frightened the copperskins and Negroes in a way that rifle muskets didn't—but Consul Stafford couldn't help longing for all the massive firepower that pointed the wrong way.

"Can we get those big guns out of their works and turn them around so they give the niggers and mudfaces a dose of what for?" he asked Sinapis.

"It might be possible," the colonel said slowly, and Stafford's hopes leaped. But then Sinapis went on, "Even if it is, it would not be easy or quick or cheap. If you seek my professional opinion, your Excellency, the project would not be worth the trouble it causes them."

Stafford did want Sinapis' professional opinion. He wanted that opinion to match his own. When it didn't, his temper frayed. "What would some of the other soldiers here say if I asked them the same question?" he inquired, his voice holding a certain edge.

Balthasar Sinapis looked him over. Stafford got the feeling he reminded the Atlantean officer of something nasty squashed on the bottom of his boot. After a moment, Sinapis answered, "Well, that is your prerogative, your Excellency. If you find someone who asserts that this is a practicable step, perhaps the army would be better served with a new commander."

If you don't care for my judgment, I resign. That was what he meant, in plain English. Stafford might not have been sorry to see Sinapis go, had he had someone in mind to replace him. But accepting his resignation would no doubt cause a flaming row with Leland Newton. The Senate would wonder whether either one of them had the faintest idea of what he was doing. And the Senate might have good reason to wonder, too.

Colonel Sinapis stood there calmly, waiting to hear what Stafford chose. Sinapis had the courage of his convictions.

Stafford was uncomfortably aware that on this issue he lacked the courage of his own. "Well, I expect you know what you're talking about," he said gruffly.

"One always wonders," Sinapis said. "At the beginning, we thought this would be an easy campaign. . . . "

He was generous to say *we*, not *you*. Stafford *had* thought it would be easy. The insurrectionists were more in earnest than he'd dreamt they could be. They also showed more in the way of courage and discipline than he'd dreamt they could. He associated those traits with white men, not with what he thought of as the dusky races. But Frederick Radcliff's fighters had them.

Stafford didn't want to admit that, even to himself. He especially didn't want to admit it any place where Leland Newton might hear. He knew what would happen then. Newton would start yapping about full freedom for natives of Africa and Terranova. Well, he could yap all he pleased. He wasn't going to convince Stafford.

That Stafford might convince himself was one more possibility he hadn't imagined before he set out from New Hastings.

While he was woolgathering, Sinapis said something he missed entirely. "I'm sorry, Colonel?" he said in faint embarrassment.

"I said that we are lucky we made it here. We would have had to live off the already bare countryside or else commenced to starve if we had not," Sinapis repeated. "If the insurrectionists were a little more energetic, they would have done everything they could to block our progress."

"Could they really have managed that?" Stafford asked.

"I do not know, your Excellency," the colonel replied. "But I tell you this: I am not altogether disappointed that we did not find out."

"Now that we have a sea connection to keep us supplied, how soon can we move against the enemy again?" Stafford asked.

"Whenever you and your colleague agree that we should, we can," Sinapis said. "Sooner or later, also, the roads and railroad line from the east will become passable again. They had better, anyhow, or this uprising is far more severe than we imagined, and certainly far more severe than any that came before it."

It was already the worst insurrection in Atlantean history. Stafford had no doubt of that. And it was worse than it might have been because the other Consul and the northern Senators had kept the national government from doing anything about it till almost too late.

And now Stafford had to persuade his colleague that the army needed to go over to the offensive again. If the soldiers weren't going to fight, why had they come at all?

Leland Newton nodded. "Yes, I think we should move out, too," he said. "We didn't come west to defend New Marseille."

"I couldn't have put that better myself." Stafford sounded astonished.

"We did not come to massacre Negroes and copperskins, either," Newton warned. "We came to establish peace by whatever means prove necessary."

"If they are dead, they are likely to be peaceable," Stafford said. "It's the ones who haven't gone to their eternal reward that you've got to watch out for. Sending them up before the celestial Judge strikes me as a good way to make sure they trouble Atlantis no more."

"Killing every Negro and copperskin in Atlantis might make Tacitus' peace, but it would change the country forever," Newton said. "It would also leave our good name a stench in the nostrils of every other nation in the world."

"Oh, nonsense. The Grand Turk massacres Armenians for the sport of it. The Czar murders Jews instead," Stafford returned. Newton was about to ask him how he liked lumping the USA with the Ottoman Empire and Russia. But before he could, the other Consul continued, "Over in Terranova, they aren't fussy about disposing of their copperskins whenever they need to. And England kills off as many people in India as it has to to keep the nabobs from causing trouble. Stafford paused, then murmured in Latin: "*Ubi solitudinem faciunt, pacem appellant.*"

"'Where they make a desert, they call it peace,'" Newton agreed. That was the Roman historian's line, all right.

He and Stafford might—did—disagree on a great many important things, but they came from the same educational tradition and argued from the same assumptions. Even disagreeing, they talked to each other, not past each other.

"If we can't get rid of the mudfaces and niggers, we might ship the lot of them back to Terranova and Africa," Stafford said. "That would solve our problem, too."

"In your dreams, it would." Newton ticked off points on his fingers: "Item—the Terranovans, as you pointed out yourself, have more copperskins than they want, and they don't want ours. Item—shipping these people away would cost millions of eagles: money we haven't got. Item—even if we had the money, we haven't got the shipping. And item—these people are here in such numbers, they can breed faster than we can send them out of the country. This kind of talk you're spouting has been going round for years. Nothing's ever come of it, and nothing is likely to."

He waited for Stafford to get angry at him. Instead, the other Consul cocked an eyebrow and said, "Well, Leland, if you're going to complain about every little thing . . . "

Taken by surprise, Newton started to laugh. He wagged a finger at his colleague. "You got me that time, but I'll pay you back."

"Oh, I have no doubt of that," Stafford said. "In the meantime, though, what do you say we snuff out this insurrection if we can?"

"If we can," Newton agreed. "But if that should prove impracticable, we had better try something else."

"Such as?"

"I don't know yet," Newton said. "Something—anything—designed to hold the United States of Atlantis together."

"I can imagine circumstances where it might be better if Atlantis came apart." Before Newton could respond to that, his colleague held up a hand. "Let it be as you say: crush the insurrection first, and worry about everything else afterwards."

Newton didn't think he'd said precisely that. On the other hand, he and Stafford rarely came so close to sharing the same view of anything. His glance slid toward the woods where the rebels lurked. Maybe the Atlantean army could smash them once for all. Maybe. Then why did he have so much trouble believing it?

Yet another messenger found Frederick Radcliff. He was scratching a mosquito bite, which was one of the things you did when you made your headquarters deep in a swamp. He hadn't been deep enough when the Atlanteans assailed him before, which meant they'd almost caught him. The obvious solution was to move where they would have a harder time getting at him. The trouble with the obvious solution was that it meant getting eaten alive.

All of the messengers brought the same news: "They're coming out!" It wasn't what Frederick wanted to hear. He'd hoped the white Atlanteans would hole up in New Marseille and stop taking the war seriously.

No matter what he'd hoped, that wouldn't happen. He sighed. He might have known it wouldn't. Come to that, he *had* known it wouldn't. As soon as he touched off the uprising, his greatest fear was that the whites would put everything they had into crushing it. From their point of view, ruthlessness made perfect sense. Anything less than a crushed insurrection, and slavery was dead.

What hadn't occurred to him then was that slavery might be dead even if the whites crushed the insurrection. The men and women who fought under him—and the others, all over southern Atlantis, who'd flared into rebellion in his name even if not under his command—could be beaten, but so what? From this day forth, how could any master rely on his two-legged property to stay quiet? And if you couldn't rely on your slaves to stay quiet, how were you going to get any work out of them?

"What are we gonna do?" the messenger asked, bringing him back to the here and now.

"Which road are they using?" Frederick asked.

"Looks like they're marching by the northeast one," the other Negro said.

Frederick swore under his breath. If the Atlantean soldiers had headed straight east again—if they'd started back along the same road they'd used to get to New Marseille—he still could have imagined they were giving up the fight and heading off to the Green Ridge Mountains again. But no. They intended to keep on with their campaign, all right. In fact . . .

"Ain't that where we got us most of our fighters?" the messenger said.

"Yes," Frederick said, and left it right there. He'd wanted to spread the insurrection towards Avalon. The more of the southwest that fell under the influence of the Free Republic of Atlantis, the better, as far as he was concerned.

None of the whites needed to be Julius Caesar—or, for that matter, Victor Radcliff—to see as much. And they would have taken prisoners, and squeezed them hard. Frederick had to assume they knew as much about his plans as any of his ordinary soldiers.

He thought of something else: "Did they bring everybody out of New Marseille, or did they leave a garrison behind?"

"More soldiers in there now than there was before the white folks marched in," the messenger answered.

That made Frederick swear again. He knew it would make Lorenzo swear even more ferociously. But now he could truthfully tell the copperskin that he'd thought about trying to take the town, and he'd had good reason to decide it wouldn't work.

He got to tell Lorenzo exactly that a couple of hours later. Lorenzo only nodded. "Too damned many snowballs stayed behind," he said. If whites had rude names for their colored bondsmen, it was only natural that the folk who sprang from Terranova and Africa would return the disfavor.

"That's right," Frederick said, wondering how Lorenzo had got the news. Messengers were supposed to bring it straight to Frederick himself, not to anyone else. Well, that was a worry for another day. The worry for today was all those white soldiers on the move.

Lorenzo had to be thinking the same thing. "We can bushwhack 'em," he said.

"We can, and we'd better," Frederick said. "If they go

wherever they want and we don't try to stop them, we've lost."

"I won't try and tell you you're wrong," Lorenzo said.

Frederick wasn't sorry to leave his swampy fastness. The state of New Marseille was warm and sticky and bug-ridden from one end to the other. Having lived there for so many years, Frederick knew that all too well. But things weren't quite so bad when he came out into drier country.

He carried a revolver taken from a dead Atlantean cavalry trooper. That gave him seven bullets to fire at the enemy—and one for himself if everything went wrong. After the raid, he'd decided the whites wouldn't take him alive. One pull of the trigger got everything over with in a hurry. They wouldn't be able to torment him, and they wouldn't be able to use him to scare other slaves who'd rebelled.

Most of the whites had fled this part of the country. A couple of big houses bristled with warning signs and had sentries parading outside of them. They might as well have been forts. Frederick thought his men could overrun them at need, but he didn't see the need. The whites holed up in them wouldn't come out to attack his fighters, which was all that really mattered. If the army went away or lost, the holdouts wouldn't count for beans. And if the army won . . .

If the army won, Frederick would be dead. He wouldn't care what happened later on.

The Negroes and copperfaces were eating what they scavenged from the countryside, and from granaries taken when plantations fell. Most whites lacked the presence of mind to set fire to barns or to pour water into storage pits before fleeing. A good thing, too, or the rebels would have had a—literally—thinner time of it.

Soldiers, from what he'd heard, often turned up their noses at frogs and turtles and the big flightless katydids that were more common than mice in the woods. Slaves couldn't afford to be so choosy. Nothing wrong with turtle stew, not if you'd been eating it since you were little and took it for granted.

Of course, the soldiers didn't have to worry about such

things now. They had a baggage train, a luxury the rebels did without. The soldiers could ship hardtack and salt pork and bully beef into New Marseille and bring it along with them when they marched. No, they wouldn't go hungry.

Along with the other slaves, Frederick had sampled captured hardtack and bully beef. You could eat the stuff if you had to: no doubt of that. Given a choice, Frederick preferred turtle stew and frogs' legs and whatever flatbread his cooks could bake on griddles or hot stones.

Scouts—both blacks and copperskins—shadowed the Atlantean column. The gray-clad soldiers were moving into the country where Frederick wanted to spread the insurrection. If he could keep them out, uprisings against the local planters would stand a better chance.

But he knew he would have to win a stand-up fight against them to keep them from penetrating the country between New Marseille and Avalon. Shooting at them from behind fences and out of the woods wouldn't do it. The soldiers shrugged off those losses and kept marching. Their scouts also hurt the rebels. The whites were no stronger, not man for man. They were no better in the woods. But they were better shots, and they were better at supporting one another. They were professional soldiers, in other words, not the amateurs he led.

"*Can* we stop 'em in a regular battle?" he asked Lorenzo.

The copperskin shrugged broad shoulders. "Damned if I know," he said. "Time to try, though, don't you think?"

"Part of me does," Frederick said. "Then I start wondering how many of us get shot if we try it and it doesn't work."

Lorenzo only shrugged again. "It's a war. We hope we hurt the other bastards worse than they hurt us, that's all."

Frederick's other fear was that the insurrection would fall to pieces after a lost battle. That worried him less than it had in the early days, though. The Negroes and copperskins who fought alongside him had shown their resilience. Chances were a loss wouldn't scuttle everything.

And they might win. He would have had trouble believing that when the rebellion started, but they really might.

"Let's try it," he said. "You know a place where we can hold 'em up—and where we can fall back from if we've got to?" He didn't want his optimism running away with him.

"Not me." Lorenzo shook his head. "I ain't from around these parts, either. We've got some folks who are, though. Best thing we can do is find out from them. Bound to be somebody who'll know of one."

And a bald, long-faced Negro named Custis said, "Reckon I know a place. Got to slow the white soldiers down some, or they're liable to get to it 'fore we does."

Skirmishing with the column of white Atlanteans was easy. Making sure the skirmishes didn't get too costly proved less so. The soldiers seemed much more eager to mix it up with the bushwhackers than they had on their march to New Marseille. They usually had the better of it at close quarters, too. Like any other art, bayonet fighting took practice. The soldiers had more than the rebels did.

But the series of little fights did slow down the men in gray. And Custis' promised spot proved as good as he claimed. A stone fence near the top of a low rise gave cover against musketry. A stream to one side and woods to the other made the fence hard to outflank. The road ran just in front of the woods. Putting a barricade across it was easy. The rebels behind the fence could rake the soldiers with gunfire if they tried to decline battle.

"If we can beat 'em anywhere, this here is the place," Frederick said.

"I think so, too," Lorenzo agreed. "It's like the places where the white Atlanteans fought the redcoats way back when."

"It is!" Frederick nodded eagerly. He hadn't thought of that, but he could tell it was true as soon as Lorenzo said it. The Atlanteans under his grandfather had needed to fight in places like this. Less steady, less disciplined, than their English foes, they needed all the help the ground could give them. His own colored rebels needed that kind of help today.

He put men in the woods to keep the Atlanteans from outflanking his position by surprise. He posted men behind the barricade, too. Why let the enemy have an easy time tearing it down?

He knew when the soldiers drew near. They raised a column of reddish dust that hung in the dusty air. The Barfords had always complained about road dust when they visited friends and relations. Clotilde Barford said—over and over—the problem would go away if the government (sometimes it was the state government, sometimes the national) only macadamized or cobbled the highways. She wanted the government (whichever government it was on any given day) to start with the one that ran next to the Barford plantation.

Frederick might have been a slave, but he could see the trouble with that. He'd never set eyes on a macadamized road, or even a cobbled one, but he knew what they were and what making them entailed: lots of rocks (whether crushed or fist-sized), lots of labor, and lots of money. The government might not have to pay slaves in work gangs, but it would have to feed them and water them and doctor them, and it would have to pay their owners for their services and for their time away from the fields. Where would the government get money like that, especially since white folks squealed like hurt hogs about every cent they grudgingly coughed up in taxes?

People who liked paved roads talked about other advantages besides their being dust-free. The most important was that you could use them in any weather. Rain didn't turn them to muck.

But horses' hooves did better on dirt than on cobblestones or macadam. And dirt roads didn't have to be expensively rebuilt. They didn't have the added cost of maintenance, either. They were just . . . there. And odds were they would go right on being there for many years to come.

Frederick examined his preparations one more time. He turned to Lorenzo. "Are we ready?" he asked. "Did we forget anything?"

The copperskin started to answer. Then he caught himself and took another long look at things himself. Frederick liked that. The more you checked, the less you took for granted, the better off you were likely to be. At last, Lorenzo said, "Only thing I wish we had are some cannon of our own."

"Me, too," Frederick said. "Don't know what we can do about that, though, except maybe grab some from the white folks."

"If we'd taken New Marseille—" Lorenzo began.

Frederick cut him off with a sharp chopping motion of his right hand. "Too late to worry about that now, 'specially since we might *not*'ve taken it."

"Still looks to me like we could've," Lorenzo said stubbornly.

They might have gone on arguing—it was nothing they hadn't done before—but several Atlantean cavalrymen rode out from under their army's dust cloud and trotted forward to look over the rebels' dispositions. "Hold fire!" Frederick yelled to his men. The clouds of powder smoke would tell the white horsemen just where their foes waited.

For a wonder, the men under his command did as he asked. The cavalrymen stared at the rise and the barricaded road and the woods off to the side. Then they rode back to report to their own superiors. Frederick's stomach knotted. It wouldn't be long now.

XIV

*J*eremiah Stafford peered at the insurrectionists' position through a spyglass. He couldn't judge how many men they had behind that stone wall. Enough to let them think they could challenge the Atlantean army, anyhow. They couldn't possibly be right ... could they?

By the way Colonel Sinapis lined up his men with fussy precision, and by the way the corners of his mouth turned down, he wasn't so sure. Instead of sending the foot soldiers forward to sweep aside the riffraff of Negroes and copperskins, Sinapis advanced his field guns till they weren't far out of musket range. "Hit the wall with everything you have," he told the artillerymen.

"What good will that do?" Stafford asked him.

Patiently, the Atlantean officer answered, "A stone wall will protect the men behind it from musketry. If they think they are safe from cannonballs ... Inexperienced troops often make that mistake." He turned back to the men with the red chevrons and piping on their uniforms. "Now!" he commanded.

The field guns belched fire and smoke. They scooted backward from the recoil; a few artillerymen had to step smartly to keep the carriages from running over them. As soon as the recoil stopped, the gun crews wrestled their pieces back into position, swabbed the guns' iron and brass throats, and started reloading them.

Several roundshot smacked into the fence that protected the insurrectionists. From the way Colonel Sinapis had talked, Stafford thought the guns would smash down the wall all at once. They didn't. But through the spyglass he saw turmoil among the men on the far side. *Something* was going on, sure enough.

When he asked about it, Sinapis answered, "The balls break the stones they hit. You stand behind a stone wall that gets cannonaded, it is like standing up under shotgun fire. Those little bits of stone can kill you and will hurt you if they do not kill."

"Ah," Stafford said, enlightened. The cannon went on thundering. The commotion on the far side of the stone wall got worse. Here and there, roundshot bit chunks out of the wall. Even when they didn't, the copperskins and Negroes stirred like bees when their hive was kicked.

"So we shall see how they like that for a while, and then we shall see how steady they are after a cannonading," Colonel Sinapis said. "Artillery is what inexperienced troops commonly fear most. If it unsettles the—what do you call them?—the insurrectionists, yes, they will be easy enough for our infantry to handle."

"I expect they will be," Stafford said. "It's not as if they were white men, after all." He wondered how he would like to face artillery fire from behind a stone wall that offered less protection than he'd expected. Chances were he wouldn't like it much, but he didn't dwell on that.

Something gleamed in Colonel Sinapis' dark eyes. But the colonel didn't call him on it. The fieldpieces thundered again and again, hurling cannonballs up the slope. The *whack!*s the roundshot made when they hit the fence were shorter and sharper than the blasts that flung them forth.

Sinapis waved. The cannon fell silent. The officer turned to the bugler beside him. "Blow *Forward*," he said.

"Yes, sir," the man replied, and raised his battered brass bugle to his lips. Under the subtropical sun, it gleamed like gold. The imperious notes rang out.

"Hurrah!" the soldiers shouted as they started toward the enemy. They advanced with fixed bayonets. The sunshine also glittered from the sharp steel. Bayonets were another thing that made raw soldiers' knees knock. Somehow, it was easier to put up with the notion of taking a bullet than to imagine yourself screaming your life away, pierced by a foe who'd come all that way to stick you and who had within himself not a drop of the milk of human kindness.

While the main force advanced on the fence, a smaller group of soldiers moved against the barricade blocking the road. Copperskins and Negroes popped up from behind the fallen trees and fired at the oncoming men in gray. And plenty of insurrectionists in back of the fence blasted away at the Atlanteans moving toward them.

"They have nerve," Sinapis said.

"They have their nerve!" Jeremiah Stafford exclaimed, which meant something altogether different.

"I had hoped we could get in among them without needing to fire," Sinapis said. "That does not seem likely now."

Sure enough, the Atlantean infantrymen began shooting back at the foes behind the fence. Then they had to reload under fire from the enemy, which nobody in his right mind could have been enthusiastic about. Some of them got shot ramrod in hand—as ignominious a way to go out of the fight as any Stafford could think of.

Artillerymen wrestled some of the cannon around half a turn, so they bore on the logs across the road. Twelve pounds of high-speed iron smacking an obstacle like that did much more visible damage than the roundshot did to the stone fence. Logs tumbled like jackstraws. Consul Stafford hoped they squashed some of the fighters behind them when they fell over.

"This is good," Sinapis said in somber satisfaction—the only kind he seemed to show. "That is very good. If the flanking party gets through there, the frontal assault matters less."

Stafford hadn't thought the flanking party would matter. He'd assumed the frontal assault would overwhelm the insurrectionists in back of the fence. They proved steadier than he'd ever imagined they could. Despite the bombardment from the field guns, they kept pouring a galling fire into the Atlantean soldiers assailing their position. Dead and wounded men in gray uniforms dotted the slope, more of them every minute. There was a limit to what flesh and blood could bear. The Negroes and copperskins firing as if their lives depended on it—and they did, they did—forced the soldiers right to the edge of that limit.

And the attack on the barricade didn't go as well as either the colonel or the Consul wanted. Some of the men behind the logs might have got squashed. The rest kept on shooting. And insurrectionists hiding in the woods banged away at the flanking party from the flank—an irony Stafford failed to appreciate.

"Make them stop that!" he shouted to Sinapis.

The colonel looked at him without expression. "If you have any practical suggestion as to how I am to accomplish that end, I should be delighted to hear it." He didn't add *If you don't, shut up and quit joggling my elbow*—not out loud, he didn't. Stafford heard the suggestion whether it was there or not. He knew too well he didn't have any practical suggestions along those lines. He could see what was wrong, but not how to fix it.

Leland Newton pointed to the slope and the wall. "They're getting up to it," he said, and then, diminishing that, "Some of them are, anyhow." Yes, a lot of bodies dotted the slope.

"Once they get over it and in amongst the damned insurrectionists, the fight is as good as won," Stafford said.

"You hope," the other Consul said.

"Yes. I do," Stafford agreed. "And if you do not, I should like to know why."

"Oh, no—I won't fall into that trap. Now that we are in the field, you will not be able to accuse me of failing to support our soldiers in every way," Newton said.

"I suppose you also wish to pretend you did not do everything in your power to keep them from taking the field," Stafford growled.

"My dear fellow, had I done everything in my power to prevent it, the army never would have left New Hastings," Newton replied easily. *My dear fellow*, here, had to mean something like *You silly son of a bitch*. He wasn't wrong, either. But he certainly had delayed the army's departure.

Stafford might have pointed that out. Instead, he peered toward the fight at the stone fence. Some of the Atlantean soldiers were scrambling over it. Through the spyglass, he could see soldiers and insurrectionists stabbing at one another with bayonets. The copperskins and blacks weren't giving much ground. Were they giving any ground at all? He had trouble being sure.

Over on the wing, the flanking party had reached the barricade. Not many white men had got past it, though. The gunfire from the woods alongside the road was too intense to let the flankers ignore it. They had to turn and respond, which meant they had trouble going forward.

"The insurrectionists planned this battle well," Colonel Sinapis remarked. "I do not think I could have improved on their dispositions."

Hearing that did nothing to improve Stafford's disposition. "We can beat them?" he asked anxiously.

"Yes, we can beat them," Sinapis said. "But they can also beat us, which I had not counted on before we set out."

If enough Atlanteans got over the wall, they would win. But the enemy had more men, and more determined men, back there than Stafford had dreamt possible. Colored fighters, savages, couldn't be that brave ... could they?

Sinapis' spyglass also surveyed the front. Under it, his mustache-framed mouth twisted. He lowered the telescope. "I am very sorry, your Excellency. I do not think we shall succeed this day."

"Dear God in heaven!" Stafford cried. "Can that—that rabble beat our finest soldiers?"

"It would seem so, yes," the colonel answered impassively.

"They must not!" Stafford said. "Do you hear me? They *must* not!"

"It is war," Sinapis said. "There are no *must*s in war. There are only *are*s."

Consul Stafford almost hit him. One thing alone made the Consul hesitate: the likelihood that he would lie dead on the ground a moment after he did such an unwise thing.

He groaned instead, watching everything he held dear crumbling before his eyes.

Eight shots in one weapon were wonderful. Reloading the pistol after firing eight shots at the Atlantean infantry was a son of a bitch bastard, as Frederick Radcliff discovered to his sorrow. Put a bullet in each chamber. Measure a charge of black powder and stuff each charge into a chamber without spilling it. Fix a percussion cap for each chamber. Do all that while your hands trembled because you'd just come as near as dammit to getting killed.

Doing it seemed to take about a year. But Frederick methodically went on. He couldn't afford to stay unarmed. Seven more bullets for the white men—some of them would probably hit, anyhow. One more bullet for himself, just in case.

They'd got over the wall. He hadn't dreamt they could do that. He'd also assumed that, if the white soldiers did get over the wall, the battle was as good as lost. But it turned out not to be. The Negroes and copperskins he led didn't flinch, even from the soldiers' most savage bayonet work. They rushed toward the white men in gray, not away from them. They might be less skilled with the bayonet themselves, but they were every bit as plucky.

And they turned the wall to an advantage. They pinned the soldiers who'd got over against it and started killing them there. It was madness. It was mayhem. Neither side asked for quarter, and neither side offered it. For longer than Frederick thought possible, neither side gave ground, either.

A white man's voice, furious and astonished, rose above the din of shrieks and gunfire: "You nigger assholes can't do this!"

"Hell we can't!" Frederick shouted back. He had no idea whether the soldier heard him. He'd finally got that damned eight-shooter reloaded. As he raised it, he breathed a small prayer that it wouldn't explode in his hand. If you didn't do a good enough job cleaning off excess powder, more than one chamber would fire when you pulled the trigger. Only one bullet could get out, of course. The rest . . . the rest would probably blow off the hand that held the revolver.

More whites scrambled up over the wall to try to help their comrades. Frederick fired at one of them. The man clutched his ribs and tumbled back on the far side of the stone fence. Only after that did Frederick realize the gun had hurt the enemy, not him.

Then—and the thought within him warred between *all at once* and *at last!*—more Atlantean soldiers were climbing over the fence to get away than to come to their friends' rescue. "We licked 'em!" Lorenzo cried exultantly. He asked, "Shall we go after 'em?"

"If we do, their cannon will murder us." Frederick unbent enough to follow that with a question of his own: "Or do you think I'm wrong?"

"Nooo." The way Lorenzo stretched the word showed his reluctance. But he didn't try to talk Frederick out of the decision. He might not like it, but he saw it was right. A moment later, he brightened: "When word of what we done here gets around, every copper man and black man in these parts is going to come running to join our army."

"Expect you're right." Frederick hoped he sounded more enthusiastic than he felt. That would bring his army more men—men he mostly didn't have weapons for, and men he would have trouble feeding.

Lorenzo went on, "Planters around here'll have to light out for the tall timber, too, unless they want to get their big houses burned down while they're layin' in bed asleep."

"That's a fact." Now Frederick could sound happy without reservation. "The Free Republic of Atlantis just got bigger."

"Damned right it did," Lorenzo agreed. "Those white sons of bitches'll run back to New Marseille with their tails between their legs. Everything outside the city limits, I reckon that's ours from now on."

Half an hour later, a Negro who'd been a butler before the uprising and served as the rebels' quartermaster these days came up to him. "You know where we can get more percussion caps, boss?" he asked. "We're mighty low on 'em, mighty low. We're short on powder and bullets, too, but we can come up with some of those, anyways. Percussion caps, though ... You know how to make 'em?"

"Not me." Frederick shook his head. "They got mercury in 'em—I know that. Mercury fulmisomethin'."

"Know where we can get our hands on some this mercury whatever-the-devil-you-called-it?" the quartermaster persisted. "Can you dig it out of the ground?"

"Don't think so. I think you've got to make it some way, like they make sugar out of sugar cane," Frederick answered.

"But you don't know how." It wasn't a question. But, by the way the other Negro said it, Frederick should have known how. The quartermaster set his hands on his hips. "How are we supposed to keep fighting if we can't get no more percussion caps?"

"I never said we couldn't do that," Frederick replied. "I just said we couldn't make 'em ourselves. But we can steal 'em from the Atlantean soldiers. We're getting more from the men we killed at the wall, right?"

"Some more," the quartermaster said grudgingly. "Not hardly enough to fight another battle with, though."

"Well, we'll get lots." Frederick soothed him as best he could. "Some of the white folks in these parts'll have percussion muskets, too. We'll grab us more caps once we kill them or run them off."

"A few more," the quartermaster said. "But if the white soldiers just keep on picking fights with us, we're licked, on account of before long we won't have nothin' to shoot back with. What do you propose to do about that, Mr. Frederick Radcliff?"

Frederick wondered whether his grandfather had ever had the family name flung in his face like that. Probably— the Radcliffs and Radcliffes had been prominent in Atlantis for so long, the surname made a handy curse.

And, even if the quartermaster was a snotty nigger (yes, Frederick knew that was how Master Barford would have thought of the fellow, but it fit too well to let him pretend it didn't), the question needed answering. "They just got whipped, remember," he said. "They won't be hot to jump on us again right away. And I figure we'll get our hands on more percussion caps by the time they do."

"How you gonna do that?" the other man challenged.

"I'll manage." Frederick actually had an idea. He was damned if he'd tell it to anybody who talked like that.

Stafford wanted to try to hit the insurrectionists again. To Leland Newton's surprise, Colonel Sinapis was thinking about it, too. "Are you both out of your minds?" Newton said. "We'll just bang our heads on the stone wall again." He pointed to the fence where the Negroes and copperskins had taken such a toll of Atlantean soldiers two days earlier.

"They can't do that twice," the other Consul declared.

"You didn't think they could do it once," Newton reminded him.

"This is the only reason I pause now," Colonel Sinapis said. "I was surprised once. If I must take these people more seriously, then I must, that is all. If we were in touch with New Hastings by telegraph, I could ask for reinforcements. Without them, I fear we could not defend a perimeter after another misfortune."

"Plenty of New Marseille militiamen to draw on," Stafford said. "They're a lot closer than any regulars except the garrison in New Marseille city. And they'd be up for fighting slaves who've risen up—Lord knows that's so."

"How well they would do it is, I fear, a different question," Colonel Sinapis told him. "They have no experience in the field, they have little experience in drill, they are unaccustomed to following orders—as what Atlantean is not?—and they would be armed with flintlock muskets no better than the ones their great-grandfathers used against the English."

"But they want to fight," Stafford said. "That counts, too."

"No doubt," the colonel replied: one of the more devastating agreements Newton had ever heard. Sinapis went on, "In any case, we are lower on ammunition than I would like. After the next supply column comes in, we will be in a better position to try the enemy again."

"That makes sense," said Newton, who didn't want to fight again any time soon.

"That does make sense," Stafford agreed. "When we fight again—and we'd better do it pretty quick—we ought to make damned sure we win." Differing motives led the two Consuls to the same conclusion now.

But that conclusion turned out not to be worth a cent, or even an atlantean. The next supply column didn't bring more bullets and powder and percussion caps and hardtack and salt pork and coffee to the Atlantean army. The next supply column never arrived. A handful of harried soldiers did. The tale they told wasn't pretty.

"Bushwhacked!" one of them said, his eyes wide and staring. "We were going through the woods, and all of a sudden, like, there were these trees across the road, and wild men shooting at us from both sides. Wagons couldn't turn around. Hell, we couldn't do anything. I'm a good Christian man, and it's God's own miracle I'm here to give you the word. You'll see me in church a-praying every Sunday from here on out."

Another survivor nodded sorrowfully. "They came on us screamin' and yellin' and leapin' and carryin' on," he said. "Some of 'em had bayonets, and some of 'em had hatchets, and. . . . Dear Lord, I don't want to remember some of the things I seen when they jumped us."

How soon did these fellows quit fighting and run away? Newton wondered. Were they the ones who'd fled first and fastest? Or had they played dead till the insurrectionists weren't interested in them any more? Either way, they hadn't covered themselves with glory.

Balthasar Sinapis had more immediate worries. "What became of the wagon train?" he demanded. "Where are our munitions and victuals?"

"Damned niggers grabbed all that shit," answered the soldier who'd promised to go to church every Sunday from now on. "Reckon they'll send us more from New Marseille sooner or later."

"If we get it later but the insurrectionists have it now . . . " By the way Jeremiah Stafford looked around, he expected fighters in slave clothes to start popping out of the ground like skinks. (So Newton thought, anyway; a man from Europe or Terranova would have been more likely to compare them to moles.)

"This is not good," Colonel Sinapis said, and Newton would have had a hard time quarreling with him. "This is not even slightly good. The loss of the munitions . . . The bullets and powder are bad enough, but the percussion caps are worse. The rebels had not a prayer of making their own percussion caps."

"Can we recapture them?" Newton asked.

"The wagons, perhaps," Sinapis said. "What they held? I would doubt that. Can you not see the Negroes and copperskins in your mind's eye, each with a crate in his arms or on his back?"

Unhappily, Newton nodded. He could picture that only too well, the men singing the same songs they would have used at harvest time as they carried away their precious booty. Consul Stafford would know from experience what songs those were. Newton didn't, but his imagination seemed to serve well enough.

"Maybe we *should* attack now," Stafford said, "before they bring the loot up to their position."

"Your colleague has the command today," the colonel reminded him.

"Tomorrow is bound to be too late," Stafford said. *You'll get the blame if we sit here*, he meant. "Well, we can try," Newton said. He did not mind if papers south of the Stour screamed at him. If newspapers in his own section did the same, that wouldn't be good. He could be only so dilatory before they started. If he wanted another term as Consul, which he did . . . "Yes, we can try."

It was almost noon by then. The soldiers didn't expect to attack the rebels' position that day. Getting orders to the junior officers and forming the men up for the assault took longer than Leland Newton thought it should. The soldiers went forward willingly enough, but with no great enthusiasm.

And it soon became plain that Sinapis had waited too long to give the order. (Newton didn't think about his own role in the troops' late start.) Either the insurrectionists had

had enough percussion caps and ammunition all along or the copperskins and Negroes lugging those stolen crates had got to their position before the Atlantean attack went in. A rippling wave of fire from behind the stone wall greeted the white men in gray who advanced on it.

The soldiers didn't press the assault the way they had before. None of them reached the wall, let alone got over it. They returned the insurrectionists' fire for a while, then fell back toward their encampment once more, bringing their dead and wounded with them. Newton had a hard time getting angry at them for their performance. They could see they had no chance to break the position before them. What sensible professional would let himself get killed with so little chance to realize a return on the investment of his life?

But their failure left another question hanging in the muggy air. Newton asked it: "Well, gentlemen, what do we do now?"

Setting out from New Hastings, Jeremiah Stafford had thought everything was obvious. They would close with the insurrectionists. They would smash their gimcrack army and hang or shoot or burn Frederick Radcliff and as many other leaders as they could catch. They would return the copperskins and Negroes to the servitude for which they were fit by nature. And then they would go back to the capital in triumph.

Right now, getting back to New Hastings in one piece would have looked like triumph to Stafford. More things had gone wrong than he would have imagined possible before the army set out. And the uprising had proved much worse than he'd dreamt it could in his worst nightmares.

"What are we going to do?" he demanded of Colonel Sinapis. "If we don't put down the insurrectionists—" He held his head in both hands, as if the enormity of the idea made it want to explode. And that wasn't so far from true, either.

"We need more munitions. We need more soldiers," Sinapis said. "I do not believe any troops will be forthcoming from the national government for some time—if ever. The state militiamen you have mentioned are less desirable, but.... " He shrugged.

"A drowning man doesn't care a cent what kind of spar he grabs," Stafford said. "Send out the call, Colonel, by all means. If we have twice as many men under arms here, we can do ... more than we can now, anyway. Will you tell me I'm mistaken?" *You'd better not*, his voice warned.

And Sinapis didn't. "Yes, I think the time to do that is here, if we are serious about quelling the insurrection."

"What else would we be?" Stafford yelped.

Colonel Sinapis shrugged again. "I am not a political man, your Excellency. I am a soldier. You and your colleague decide the policies here. Once you have done that, I shall carry out to the best of my ability any part of them involving soldiers."

Stafford muttered darkly. Agreeing on anything with Consul Newton seemed to require a special miracle every time it happened. But Newton didn't try to dissuade Sinapis from summoning the New Marseille militia, though he did say, "I worry that they may prove oversavage when they encounter armed Negroes and copperskins."

"The enemy is not gentle himself," Stafford pointed out.

"No doubt he has his reasons for harshness," Newton said.

"No doubt the militiamen do, too," Stafford snapped. "Some of them were forced to flee their homes. Some had their wives ravished, or their sisters, or their daughters."

"Ravished, perhaps, by mulattos or halfbreed copperskins," Newton said.

"What is that supposed to mean?" Stafford asked coldly.

"What it says," the other Consul answered. "You are not a naive man, your Excellency. You know slaveholders have been going in unto their bondswomen for as long as Negroes and copperskins have been in Atlantis."

"That's different," Stafford said.

"I believe you believe it is," Newton said. "Whether the slaves believe the same thing may be open to doubt."

"Be damned to the slaves!"

"Are they not saying, 'Be damned to the masters!'? In their place, would you not say the same thing?"

"I am not in their place. They want to place me there, though," Stafford said. "If they win, we shall have colored masters whipping white slaves and forcing white women to go on ministering to their filthy lusts. Is that what you have in mind?"

"Of course not. And, if you listen to the insurrectionists, it is not what they have in mind," Newton replied. "They claim the Free Republic of Atlantis is to have equality for every man of every color."

"Likely tell!" Jeremiah Stafford rolled his eyes. "They will claim anything to keep on fighting. You believe them, do you? And I suppose you will also believe that mothers find babies under cabbage leaves."

He had the satisfaction of watching Newton turn red. "I know where babies come from," the other Consul said tightly. "I am merely trying to point out to you that the rebels have more reasons for rising than Satanic wickedness. In fact, that is how they judge the system that brought their ancestors here and turned them into property."

"As if I care how they judge it!" Stafford fleered. "Their cousins in squalid so-called freedom live worse, more benighted lives than they do. They have learned our language here. They have learned of our God here, the one true God. They are part of a . . . a great country."

Newton was very quick. He heard the small hesitation and knew it for what it was. "You started to say 'a free country,' didn't you? What does it profit a slave to be part of a free country? It profits only his master."

"Maybe one day the mudfaces and niggers may be advanced enough to deserve freedom," Stafford said. "But that day is not here."

"And you are doing your best to make sure it never comes," Newton said. "If you do not give a boiler a safety valve, it will explode when you keep the fire too hot for too long. We are watching one of those explosions now." He walked away before Stafford could answer.

The Consul from Cosquer was much happier when militiamen started coming into camp. He could have been happier yet, for they seemed less like soldiers and more like braggarts and blowhards and ruffians. Little by little, he realized the Atlantean regulars had spoiled him. They were hard-bitten men, too, but they had discipline. Anyone among them who got out of line promptly suffered for it.

By contrast, the militiamen did as they pleased . . . till regular sergeants and corporals started knocking sense into them. One underofficer died in the process. So did six or eight militiamen, most of them quite suddenly. That did not count the fellow who'd knifed the regular corporal. His company commander didn't want to turn him over for punishment, and his friends seemed ready to defend him.

They soon changed their minds. Staring into the muzzles of a dozen fieldpieces double-shotted with canister would have changed Jeremiah Stafford's mind, too. Stafford judged it would have changed anybody's mind. The militiaman got a drumhead court-martial. Then he was hanged from a stout bough sticking out from a pine. The drop wasn't enough to break his neck and kill him quickly. He writhed his life away over the next several minutes.

After he finally stilled forever, Colonel Sinapis looked out at the wide-eyed amateur soldiers who'd watched the execution. "Follow orders from your officers and from our officers and underofficers, and nothing like this will happen to you," he said. "We all face the same enemies, after all. If you work with us, we can beat them together. And if you work against us, I promise you will discover we are more frightful than any Negro or copperskin ever born." He paused, then added one word more: "Dismissed."

The militiamen couldn't have disappeared any faster if he'd called down thunder and lightning on their heads. A couple of dozen of them disappeared for good during the night. Sinapis took that in stride. "We shall be better off without them than we would have been with them," he said.

"Technically, they're deserters. If you catch them, you can hang them, too," Consul Newton said.

"No, the colonel's right," Stafford said—words that didn't come out of his mouth every day. "If they can't stand the heat, they shouldn't go near the fire. Let them run. Not everyone is a hero, even if he can fool himself into thinking he is for a little while."

"Well, maybe." Newton was even less eager to agree with Stafford than Stafford was to agree with Sinapis.

With the army reinforced, the colonel was able to send a good-sized force down to New Marseille to protect the next wagon train. The wagons reached the army without much trouble. The insurrectionists must have known they were well protected, because they did no more than snipe at them from the woods.

Hardtack and salt pork weren't inspiring—Stafford had already discovered how inspiring army rations weren't. But having enough of them was better than not. And having enough munitions was literally a matter of life and death. Unfortunately, that also held true for the insurrectionists. What they'd hijacked would keep them fighting for some time to come.

And what they'd hijacked would also let them—did also let them—expand the insurrection. More white refugees began streaming out of the north, most of them with nothing but the clothes on their backs and perhaps a musket or an eight-shooter clenched in one fist. The stories they told made Stafford's blood boil.

"How can you stand to listen to these people without your heart's going out to them?" he demanded of Leland Newton.

"I'm not saying it doesn't," his colleague answered. "But my heart also goes out to the Negroes and copperskins these same people have been mistreating for generations, while yours is hard as a stone toward them."

Stafford only stared. "How anyone could care about those savages . . . How anyone could say they are mistreated when they gain the benefits of Atlantean civilization . . . "

"The lash, the shackles, the ball and chain, the auction block, the unwelcome summons to the master's bedchamber," Newton said dryly.

"You have entirely the wrong attitude," Stafford said.

"If I do, then so does most of Atlantis north of the Stour," the other Consul replied. "And so does almost all of Europe. The font of what you call Atlantean civilization thinks little of what has sprung from it."

"I care nothing for what Europe thinks. We needed to get free of Europe, by God. Or would you rather we still flew the Union Jack and bowed down to Queen Victoria?" Stafford said.

"You must know I would not," Newton said, which was true enough. "But I would also rather that we did not bow down to injustice here."

"Nor do we," Stafford declared.

His colleague sighed. "More and more people—of all colors—think we do."

XV

A couple of dozen white men had holed up on a plantation. They held the big house and the nearby barn. Frederick Radcliff decided they showed enough determination to make a rush more expensive than he cared for. He approached the big house holding as large a flag of truce as he could carry.

He'd barely got to hailing distance before a white man inside the house yelled, "Hold it right there, nigger! Flag or no flag, ought to shoot you down like the mad dog you are."

"Go ahead," Frederick answered. "See what happens afterwards." He feared that what would happen was that the uprising would fall apart. But that wasn't what he wanted the white man to think about. And he hadn't named himself, so the desperate whites couldn't know they had the leading insurrectionist in their sights.

"Well, say your say, then," the white man told him grudgingly. "We'll see how much manure you pack into it."

"Got no manure," Frederick said. "What we got is, we got enough men to kill the lot of you. You think we won't use 'em, you're crazy." He didn't want to use them. How many eight-shooters did the white defenders carry? Those were the guns that made a difference when things came to close quarters.

Their spokesman jeered at him: "Likely tell, black boy!

You're tryin' to scare us out on account of you ain't got the balls to drive us out. Probably another dozen skulkers back there behind you, and that's it."

"Think so, do you? You'll see." Frederick had looked for some such response from the whites. Because he'd looked for it, he'd got his own men ready for it ahead of time. When he turned and waved, they knew what to do.

Black men and copperskins with shouldered, bayoneted rifle muskets marched out of the woods to one side and into the trees on the other side. Frederick's force *did* greatly outnumber the fortified whites. He made it seem even larger by having the men hurry through the trees where the whites couldn't see them and then march out into the open again.

He finally waved again, this time for the parade to stop. "Well?" he called. "Have we got the men we need, or what?"

No one answered him for some little while. He could guess what that meant: the defenders were arguing among themselves. Some had to think they couldn't hold off the rebels, while others would be more hopeful. At last, the leather-lunged spokesman bawled, "Well, if you don't want to fight, what do you want?"

"Come out. You can keep your guns, but come out," Frederick answered. "You don't want to stay in the Free Republic of Atlantis, you can march away. Long as you don't shoot at us, we won't shoot at you. You do start shootin', you're all dead. You stay in there, you're all dead, too. That'd hurt us some, but it sure wouldn't do you any good."

Another pause. Then the white man asked, "How do we know we can trust you? We come out, you got us where you want us."

"You're in deep water any which way, and you know it," Frederick said. "Have you ever heard of the Free Republic of Atlantis makin' a deal like this and then going back on it?"

"No, but if you murder everybody who comes out we wouldn't've heard about it, would we?" The white man had his reasons for being suspicious. Frederick made himself remember that. The fellow was dicing for his life with enemies he hated.

"Killing everybody ain't that easy. Somebody plays pigsnake or something," Frederick said. Everyone in southern Atlantis knew about pigsnakes. They weren't poisonous. When they got into danger, they puffed themselves up and hissed and snapped—and then they rolled onto their backs and played dead. Frederick went on, " 'Sides, some of us'd brag if we did that kind of thing. People run their mouths, no matter what color they are, and that's a fact."

He waited again. He didn't know what the white men would decide. He didn't know what he would have done himself in a mess like that. He was glad he wasn't the one who had to figure it out.

"Time's a-wasting," he called, hoping to speed things up.

He didn't, though, or not very much. He stood there in the hot sun till the front door to the big house finally opened. "All right," the spokesman shouted. "We're coming out. You lied to us, we'll kill as many of you bastards as we can."

Some of the whites carried muskets, others pistols. They all looked wide-eyed and jumpy, as if they were dealing with so many ferocious wild animals. Like as not, they thought they were. And they seemed to get even jumpier as they moved away from the cover of the house and barn.

Frederick waved encouragingly. "Go on. Nothing's gonna happen, not unless you start it."

They came up to him. "You got nerve, nigger," the spokesman said.

"Maybe you got nerve, too, trustin' me," Frederick answered. He almost said *trustin' a nigger*, but he couldn't make himself call himself by that name to a white man, even if he sometimes used it among his own people.

The white studied him with disconcertingly keen gray eyes. "You're a smart fellow, ain't you?"

Frederick shrugged. "Anybody who brags on bein' smart really ain't."

Ignoring that, the white went on, "I wouldn't tell you this if you didn't already know, but I reckon you do. We get out of here, we'll join up with the soldiers first chance we find."

"I suppose so," Frederick said. "You reckon that, just as soon as your bunch comes in, they'll have enough people to whip us up one side and down the other?"

"I—" The white man paused and sent him another sharp stare. "You *are* a smart fellow. No, I don't figure we'll make the difference all by our lonesome."

"In that case, we may as well let you go, long as you don't kick up trouble," Frederick said.

As the white man walked on with his comrades, he got off one last verbal shot: "Some smart fellows, they come to grief on account of they ain't as smart as they think they are."

That was bound to be true. Frederick hoped it wouldn't turn him upside down. But how could you know you were outsmarting yourself till you'd actually gone and done it?

Those white men would have found they'd outsmarted themselves if they opened fire on the insurrectionists. At least half of Frederick thought they would. Whites had trouble taking blacks and copperskins seriously as fighting men. Maybe the sight of all those bayonets had made these whites more thoughtful than usual. Bayonets didn't have to kill to be useful weapons. They only had to intimidate, and they were splendid for that.

"You sure you should have let them go?" Lorenzo asked.

"No," Frederick answered, which made the copperskin blink. He added, "But if we break a bargain once we make it, we give the whites an excuse to do the same thing."

"Like they need one," Lorenzo said scornfully.

"Army hasn't fought dirty," Frederick said. "They'd be worse if *we* did. Why give ourselves more trouble? Don't you reckon we got enough?"

"Well, it's pretty bad, way things are now," Lorenzo allowed. "I don't like getting shot at, and that's the Lord's truth. But I know what's worse."

"What's that?" Frederick asked.

"Way things were before," the copperskin answered. "I was gonna be a field hand the rest of my days—till I got too old and feeble to go out to the harvest, anyhow. Then I'd sit in my damn cabin till I got sick and died, or else Master Barford'd knock me over the head on account of I cost too much to feed. If I'm gonna go out, I'd sooner go out fightin'."

Frederick pondered that, but not for long. "Me, too," he said.

White militiamen coming up from the south were one thing. White militiamen coming down from the north were something else again. Their leader, a bushy-bearded ruffian named Collins or Conlin or something like that, spread his battered hands and told Leland Newton, "I'm damned glad to be here, your Honor. I'm damned glad to be anywhere right now, and that's a fact."

"They let you get away, I heard," Newton said.

"They did," Collins or Conlin agreed. "They could have killed the lot of us, but they made terms and they kept them." He might have been a man announcing a minor miracle.

"We would have done our best to avenge you," Newton said.

"I expect so." The militiaman nodded. "Wouldn't've done us a hell of a lot of good, though, would it?"

Newton didn't know what he could say to that, so he didn't say anything. Instead, he asked, "Who made the arrangement with you? Were you sure he could get his friends to keep it?"

"We weren't sure of *nothin'*." Collins or Conlin spat a stream of pipeweed juice to emphasize that. "We damn near—*damn* near—started shootin' at each other before we decided we didn't have no choice. We was trapped where we was at. Fellow who dickered with us was a nigger. That's all I know about him for sure. Later on, some people told us he was Fred Radcliff hisself, but I can't say for sure he was and I can't say for sure he wasn't."

"What would you have done if you'd known he was?"

"Good question." The ruffian spat again, expertly. "If we'd plugged him then, they would've massacreed us for sure."

He massacreed the pronunciation of the word, but Newton didn't correct him. Instead, the Consul asked, "So the rebels observed the usages of war, then?"

"Observed the what?" Plainly, the militiaman knew no more of the usages of war than a honker knew about history. After a pause for thought, the fellow said, "They told us they wouldn't kill us if we came out peaceable-like, and they didn't. So if you mean, did they play square, well, I reckon they did."

"That will do," Newton said, nodding.

"But what difference does it make?" The militiaman sounded honestly puzzled. "They're still a bunch of mud-faces and niggers. They're still slaves in arms against their masters, too." He might not know anything about the usages of war, but he was sure what such folk deserved.

At the time, Consul Newton had no idea whether that would matter. It turned out to, and the very next day. Atlantean soldiers brought in four rebels they'd captured spying on the camp: a Negro and three copperskins. It was the first success the gray-uniformed men had had for a while. Their friends whooped and hollered. "String 'em up!" somebody shouted, and in an instant everyone was baying out the same cry.

Jeremiah Stafford nodded like an Old Testament prophet. "Just what the renegades deserve," he said.

He had the command that day. If he ordered the captives hanged, hanged they would be. All the same, Newton said, "I think we ought to treat them as prisoners of war."

The other Consul stared at him as if he'd taken leave of his senses. "You've come out with a lot of crazy things, but that may take the cake," Stafford said. "Why on earth should we act like a pack of fools? I mean, look at those villains!"

Newton did. Copperskins were said to be impassive. One red-brown prisoner was trying to put up a strong front. The other two, and the Negro, seemed frankly terrified. Even so, Newton answered, "They didn't kill that pack of militiamen, and they could have. Besides, if we hang these fellows, what will the insurrectionists do when they get their hands on some of our men? After the last two fights, chances are they already hold white prisoners."

He made Stafford grunt, which was more of a response than he'd thought he would get. "Why on earth do you imagine they would respect anything we do?" Stafford returned.

"*Because* they've kept terms after agreeing to them," Newton said. "War is bad enough when both sides stick by the common rules. It only gets worse when they throw them over the side."

Stafford grunted again. "The insurrectionists threw them over the side when they began their rising."

"Will you talk to Colonel Sinapis before you go looking for the closest tree with a thick branch?" Newton asked. "Why not see what a professional soldier thinks of the whole business?"

"He's soft on the insurrectionists, too," Stafford muttered, but he didn't say no. With Newton following in his wake, he hunted up the colonel.

Balthasar Sinapis gnawed thoughtfully at his mustache. "There are times when you *do* hang prisoners," he said. "When the other side has committed some atrocity, you want them to know they have not put you in fear, and that you can repay them in their own coin. Here, though . . . In battle, the rebels have not acted like savages. Do we want to give them the excuse to start?"

"If they weren't savages, they wouldn't have risen against their masters," Stafford insisted.

"No doubt the English papers said the same thing about the Atlantean Assembly's army a lifetime ago," Newton said.

"It's not the same thing, damn it," Stafford said.

"It never is when the shoe goes on the other foot," Colonel Sinapis put in. Stafford scowled at him. Sinapis went on, "Is it different enough to make us fierce for the sake of fierceness? History argues that if you make a war against slaves a war to the knife, a war to the knife it shall be."

"True," Stafford said. "How many tens of thousands of them did the Romans crucify after they beat Spartacus?"

"How many Romans did those slaves kill before the legions beat them?" Newton said.

One more grunt from his colleague. Stafford threw his

hands in the air. "All right, let them keep breathing for now. If their friends give us cause, we can always hang the wretches later."

"That seems fair," Newton allowed—it was more than he'd expected to win from his fellow Consul.

"So it does," Colonel Sinapis said, and that seemed to settle that.

Jeremiah Stafford felt like a man struggling in quicksand. It wasn't just that he'd let Leland Newton talk him into treating captured blacks and copperskins as prisoners of war. That was bad enough, but there was worse. The servile insurrection sizzled everywhere but the places where Atlantean soldiers actually stood.

A man who went off into the woods to ease himself might not come out again. If he didn't, his friends were all too likely to find him with his throat cut or his skull smashed in. They weren't likely to find the skulkers who'd murdered him.

"Is this what you call fighting in accordance with the usages of war?" Stafford asked Newton after three ambushes in two days.

"It may not be sporting, but I wouldn't say it breaks international law," the other Consul answered. "If Colonel Sinapis feels otherwise, I'm sure he'll let us know."

"Bah," Stafford said. The colonel didn't agree with him often enough to suit him. As far as he was concerned, Sinapis had a soft spot in his heart for the insurrectionists. Stafford wondered why. Hadn't the colonel been a loyal—maybe even an overloyal—servant of the status quo back in Europe? Did he have a guilty conscience he was trying to salve years too late?

More and more whites fled the territory north and east of the city of New Marseille. Some of them took service with the militiamen fighting alongside the Atlantean regulars. Others seemed more inclined to moan about their sea of troubles than to take arms against them.

"Why haven't you people killed all those raggedy-ass bastards by now?" an unhappy planter demanded of Stafford.

"I wish it were as easy as you make it sound," the Consul answered.

"Well, why ain't it?" the planter said. "Nothin' there but a pack of slaves. You should take the lash to 'em. They'd run miles, dog my cats if they wouldn't."

Something inside Stafford jangled. Someone in ancient days was supposed to have put down a slave uprising like that. He tried and failed to remember who it was. He suspected the failure was a sign the ancient historian who told the story was talking through his hat.

He also suspected the planter was doing the same thing. "Did you try scaring them off with a whip?" he asked.

"Well, no," the fellow admitted. "They woulda shot me if I had."

"Then why do you think things are any different for us?" Stafford inquired.

"On account of you're the government," the planter said.

By the way he said it, that gave the army everything but power from On High. *If only it were true*, Stafford thought. Aloud, he said, "Don't you see that the insurrectionists have rejected government along with everything else?"

"But they've got no business doing that!" the man exclaimed.

How often had he rejected government when it tried to do something he didn't fancy? Raise his taxes, for instance? No doubt he'd done it without thinking twice. Now he needed what government could give him, and so he was crying out for it. Listening to him made Stafford very tired.

"We shall do what we can for you, sir," the Consul said. "If you will pick up a musket and do something for yourself, that will also help your country's cause."

"Maybe I will," the planter said, which meant he wanted nothing to do with a notion that might endanger his precious carcass. Seeing as much, Stafford went off to talk with another refugee, hoping that fellow would show more sense. Just because a man hoped for such things didn't mean he got them.

"I wish we knew more about what's going on in the rest

of the country," Stafford said to Consul Newton the next day.

"That we don't probably isn't the best sign," his opposite number replied. "The rebels are doing too well at cutting the telegraph wires. They control the countryside, and I don't know what we can do about that."

"We ought to do more than we have been," Stafford said fretfully. "We are not aggressive enough—not nearly. And that is not least your fault: you want the insurrectionists to prevail."

"I want justice to prevail and peace to return," Newton said.

"What you call justice is a southern man's nightmare," Stafford said.

"A southern white man's, maybe," Newton answered. "To a southern colored man, the way he lived up until the rebellion was the nightmare. If we could find some way not to leave anyone of any blood too dissatisfied—"

"Wish for the moon while you're at it," Stafford said. "And, if anyone is to be satisfied, I intend it shall be the white man. Believe me, your Excellency, that is my first concern."

"Oh, I believe you," Newton said. "That is a large part of the problem." He walked away, leaving Stafford obscurely punctured.

"Here they come!" a copperskin called, hurrying back toward the position the rebellious slaves held. Frederick Radcliff grimaced. He didn't want to fight the white men. He wished they would leave the Free Republic of Atlantis alone. Too much to hope for, of course. Whites hated the idea that Negroes and copperskins might be able to take care of themselves. They hated the idea that Negroes and copperskins ought to be free even more. And so another battle was coming.

Another chance for things to go wrong, Frederick thought. The Free Republic's fighters had done better than he'd ever dreamt they could. But if things went wrong—no, when they did—he had to hope his makeshift army wouldn't fall to pieces. They weren't professional soldiers. Could they deal with defeat?

Militiamen had finally let the Atlantean army flank its way past the strong position Frederick's men held for so long. This new one the Free Republic occupied wasn't nearly so good. It was the best the colored fighters could do, though. If they let the white men in gray march wherever they pleased, the Free Republic of Atlantis was only a sham. If land was really yours, you had to fight to keep it.

Frederick wasn't about to let his men stand there and trade volleys with the soldiers. That was asking to get the fighters chewed to pieces. The white professionals were trained to fight that way. His men weren't. They would sweep the open area in front of the woods where they crouched with musketry. If the whites wanted to try advancing through it, they were welcome to.

But counting on the enemy's foolishness turned out to be a bad idea. Atlantean soldiers in their gray and militiamen in blue or brown or green or colorless homespun did attack across the field in front of the forest. There were enough of them to keep Frederick's men busy: enough to make him think there were more.

A man who knew how to do card tricks or seem to pull coins from someone else's ear or nose had learned the art of misdirection. He made the audience look away from the important part of what he was up to so it wouldn't catch on till the trick was done. The soldier commanding the Atlantean army had picked up the same knack.

Frederick was pleased with how well his men were fighting ... till somebody ran in from the left shouting, "We is fucked! We is fucked all to hell an' gone!"

"What do you mean?" Frederick asked, but the ice in his belly said it knew before his brain did.

Sure as the devil, the scout pointed back the way he'd come, towards a swell of ground that hid the view to the southeast—hid it much too well, as things turned out. "They movin' up behind that!" the Negro said. "They gonna cornhole us like nobody's business!"

"Son of a bitch!" Frederick said, and then, more sensibly, "We've got to get out of here before they can do it."

"Before who can do what?" Lorenzo, who'd come over from the shooters at the edge of the woods, plainly hadn't heard about this scout's news. As if to prove as much, he added, "We're giving the white men hell. They're pretty damned stupid, to keep coming at us like that."

"I only wish to God they were," Frederick said. As the scout had before him, he pointed to the southeast. "They got themselves a column movin' up on us over there. We better pull back quick, or else they'll ..."

He didn't go on, or think he needed to. Lorenzo showed he was right—the copperskin swore in English, French, and Spanish. Lorenzo wasted no time arguing. He just ran back into the woods, shouting for the Negroes and copperskins who had been holding off the Atlantean regulars and militiamen to stop what they were doing and fall back to the north. Only a rear guard of sharpshooters would hold off the whites coming straight at them. The rest of the fighting slaves had more important things to worry about. Lorenzo was soldier enough to see as much right away. If only he'd been soldier enough to see the possibilities of that flanking move.

If only he'd *been?* Frederick asked himself. *If only* I'd *been. Who's the Tribune of the Free Republic of Atlantis, anyway? Who started this damned uprising?* But it wasn't so simple. Frederick knew he was inventing his generalship as he went along. So was Lorenzo, of course. But Lorenzo showed a talent for that side of things Frederick knew he himself couldn't match.

Now he had to hope his rapidly retreating army wouldn't fall apart because it was retreating rapidly. He also had to hope the Atlanteans wouldn't knock his army to pieces. A bullet from some white man's rifle musket cracked past his head, close enough to make him hunch his shoulders and duck before he could catch himself. Another bullet snarled past, this one a little farther off. They reminded him that, like his army, he'd stayed here too long.

Fall back, then. It wasn't what he wanted to do, which had nothing to do with anything. If he and his fighters didn't fall back, the white Atlanteans would have them at their mercy ... if the soldiers knew the meaning of the word, which struck Frederick as unlikely.

They got out barely in time. A volley from the flanking column raked them as they retreated, but only one, and from fairly long range. The soldiers in gray hadn't yet unlimbered their field artillery. That could have cost Frederick's men far more than musketry did, and it was something to which the Negroes and copperskins could not reply. Frederick hated and feared cannon and the men who served them.

His rear guard did what it was supposed to do. It held off the white men in gray whose frontal attack had done such a good job of blinding the insurrectionists to the flanking column's movement. The fighters in the rear guard fell back from tree to thicket to barrel tree. Quite a few of them didn't make it out of the woods they'd defended. That was the price you paid for joining the rear guard.

The Negroes and copperskins volleyed back at the whites in the flanking column. Frederick was delighted to watch several soldiers in the enemy's firing line fall over. "That'll show 'em we haven't quit," he said to Lorenzo.

"Damned right it will," the copperskin agreed. "They beat us, but they didn't lick us—know what I mean?"

"Yes!" Frederick had been thinking the same thing, though not so precisely. "We can stand up to them, no matter what."

"We really can," Lorenzo said. "It's taken us a while to figure that out, and it's taking them even longer, but that's a fact. They march smarter than we do, and they've got those blasted fieldpieces. Forget about those, and there ain't much difference between them and us."

"If we'd seen that a hundred years ago ... " Frederick shook his head in frustration. "Almost like it's our own fault we didn't get free."

"Wouldn't be so easy without the rifles and muskets we got from the soldiers who came down sick," Lorenzo said. Frederick nodded; the copperskin had a point. Lorenzo went on, "And they always did their best to keep us from learning the secret."

"That's a fact," Frederick said. Whites genuinely believed they were better than copperskins and blacks. Because they did, they made the people they enslaved believe it, too. Frederick knew his own life would have been entirely different had his grandmother been white. *I might've been one of the Consuls fighting the insurrection*, he thought in surprise.

Of course, he also might *not* have. He might have been anything at all as a white man. The one thing he surely would not have been was the Frederick Radcliff he was now. Changing the color of his skin would have changed everything else that had happened to him since he was born. It wasn't the color itself so much that mattered. It was how everybody else treated you because of the color.

Right now, all these white men in gray uniforms wanted to kill him because he was trying to change how much color counted. And if that didn't go miles and miles toward proving his point, he was damned if he knew what would.

Lorenzo pointed north. "After we get over that rise, there's a stream with thick woods on the north side. If we can't stop those white bastards there, we can't stop them anywhere."

"We'd better try, then," Frederick said. Maybe they couldn't stop the white soldiers anywhere. He'd feared that after the insurrection started. He didn't fear it so much any more. But it was still possible. All kinds of things were still possible. One thing wasn't: a black man wouldn't become a Consul of the United States of Atlantis any time soon. And if that wasn't all of what the insurrection was about, it sure was a big part of things.

"Well," Colonel Sinapis said philosophically, "we almost had them there."

Jeremiah Stafford fumed. To say he was not inclined toward philosophy was putting it mildly. "God damn it to hell, we *should* have had them there!" the Consul exclaimed.

"One of the things you must understand, your Excellency, is that war is not like a steam engine or a threshing machine," Sinapis said. "The manufacturer cannot promise it will perform in such-and-such a way for such-and-such a time."

"War!" Stafford loaded as much scorn into the word as he could. "Putting down uprisen niggers and mudfaces shouldn't be dignified with the name! What are we doing but whipping curs back to their kennels?"

"When you whip dogs back to the kennels, the dogs do not pick up whips and try to whip you away," the colonel replied. "Making this a smaller business than it truly is will do us no good."

He was right. Stafford knew it, which only made him angrier. He said, "The point is, it should not be a grand business. These damned insurrectionists should not have the power to make it into a grand business."

"Well, I cannot say anything about what they should be able to do and what they should not. That is God's business, not mine." Sinapis made the sign of the cross, not quite as a Roman Catholic would have done it. Then he thrust a twig into a campfire and used the small flame he got to light a cigar. After a couple of meditative puffs, he went on, "All I can speak to, all I can deal with, is what is. And what is, here, is a serious rebellion, your Excellency. It seems only to be getting worse, too. The enemy soldiers have learned a great deal from facing our men several times. This happens more often than governments trying to put down rebellions wish it would. Before long, the enemy soldiers who live are troops as good as our own."

"These are not enemy soldiers, damn it!" Stafford thundered. "They are nothing but a pack of stinking insurrectionists!"

Balthasar Sinapis only shrugged. "You may call them whatever you please, of course. But it makes no difference in the end. The only thing that makes a difference is whether they perform as soldiers. Unquestionably, they do. That retreat they brought off ... I quite admire them for it. No raw rebels could have come close to doing anything like that."

"Bah!" Stafford stomped away from the fire. He did not care to hear what Colonel Sinapis was telling him. Even if it was the truth—no, especially if it was the truth—he didn't care to hear it. If copperskins and blacks could fight well enough to make an experienced officer admire them, everything white Atlanteans had always believed about their social system was a pack of rubbish, no more.

Stafford couldn't believe that. He wouldn't believe it.

Frederick Radcliff was nothing but a nigger. He was a nigger in arms against the USA. That meant he had to be put down like any other sheep-killing dog.

He was, of course, also a Radcliff. He was a grandson to one of the First Consuls. No doubt at all that his grandfather had been a very able man. Little doubt he was a very able man himself—he wouldn't have caused so much trouble if he weren't. Again, that made things worse, not better. Frederick Radcliff was a slave by blood and a slave by nature. If you started bending that principle, where would you end up?

You'd end up as Leland Newton, that was where. You'd end up with nigger equality. They had it up in Croydon, or something close to it. They even let niggers and mudfaces vote up there! Stafford shook his head. He did not care to let such a tragedy befall his own state.

Out in the woods, crickets and katydids chirped. Nighthawks and bats swooped low over the fires to seize the bugs the flames had lured. Soldiers' shadows lurched here and there as the men walked in front of their tents. Other soldiers, out farther from the campfires, watched to make sure the insurrectionists didn't sneak in and kick up trouble.

Those sentries, these days, were every one of them experienced woodsmen. Ordinary Atlantean troopers on night sentry had shown a lamentable tendency to get their throats slit or otherwise to perish silently. That made night attacks all the easier. Dead men seldom gave timely alarms. There, at least, Colonel Sinapis did seem to have solved a problem.

"A little one," Stafford muttered discontentedly. "A tiny one." The real problem wasn't keeping insurrectionists from sneaking into camp and raising Cain. The real problem was that there still were insurrectionists.

He spat in disgust. The wind sprang up. It was heavy with rain, as it often was in these parts. It was also heavy with the stink of the encampment's latrine trenches. Stafford wrinkled his nose, though the stench was anything but unfamiliar. Anyone who lived in a city got to know it well—indeed, often got to the point where he took it for granted.

Right now, it made Stafford think of all the trouble the insurrectionists were causing. Did Atlantis have to take that for granted, too? Even if this uprising was crushed, would another as bad or worse break out in a few years' time? How could the country hope to hold together if slave revolts tore into it the way cyclones did?

Stafford spat again. He saw only two ways to keep that from happening. Either you had to cede equality to the slaves or you had to make them too afraid even to think of rising. Maybe you'd have to kill a lot of them to make sure the rest got the message.

He shrugged. If that was what it took, that was what it took. Who except for the whites who'd lose money when their niggers and mudfaces died would waste grief on them? And the owners could be compensated. Things might work out. They just might.

XVI

A supply column that came northeast from New Marseille brought fairly recent papers from the West Coast city and older ones from New Hastings. Leland Newton wasn't delighted at the headlines, but he also wasn't much surprised. No one anywhere seemed happy with the army's progress—or rather, lack of progress—against the insurrectionists.

New Marseille reporters and editors found a simple explanation for the failure: as far as they were concerned, the army was a bunch of bunglers led by idiots. The *New Hastings Chronicle*—the one daily in the capital that took a pro-slavery line—had a similar opinion. The other papers from the capital took a different tack, one Consul Newton enjoyed more.

"Here. Listen to this," he said to Jeremiah Stafford, holding a month-old *New Hastings Daily War Whoop* out at arm's length so he could read it without his spectacles. "'The way the blacks and copperskins in southern Atlantis have succeeded in resisting government forces for so long proves the point Atlanteans from the north have been making for many years: men are men regardless of color. Courage is not the exclusive property of whites. The sooner this is recognized by all, of every hue, the sooner peace will return to our republic.'"

"I'm glad they sent it," Stafford said. Before Newton could show his surprise at such a sentiment, his colleague explained, "It will wipe my backside better than a handful of old leaves."

Patiently, Newton said, "You can use the paper however you please. That doesn't make what's printed on it any less true."

"Lies! All lies! Every single word!" Stafford's voice was too loud, and sounded like a cracked bell. Little drops of spittle flew from his lips as he spoke. One of them landed on Newton's sleeve.

Newton eyed it with distaste, distaste leavened by alarm. "Jeremiah, I mean no offense, but you are talking like a fool, or maybe like a madman. You may not care for everything the papers say, but much of it is true whether you care for it or not. This rebellion *is* more difficult and intractable than you dreamt it would be when the campaign against it began. And the rebels *are* different from what you thought they would be. Can you blame the papers for noticing what you must have seen, too?"

"Yes!" Stafford said, which was not what Newton hoped to hear. "If things are the way they say they are—if they are the way you say they are—then dickering with the insurrectionists becomes the only practicable course. I tell you frankly, sir, I should rather die a thousand deaths."

Leland Newton believed that, believed it beyond a fragment of a doubt. His own voice gentled as he replied, "Would you rather Atlantis died a thousand deaths? What else lies ahead on the track you have chosen for the country?"

"I want the insurrectionists to die a thousand deaths," Stafford said savagely. "That might begin to repay them for their atrocities. It might."

"It might also be beyond our power to arrange," Newton said. "If that is not the lesson of the past few weeks, they have none."

"We have not done what we wish we would have. It does not follow that we cannot do it," Stafford said.

"How?" Newton asked.

For the first time since seeing the newspapers, some

of the other Consul's dreadful certainty leached out of him. He no longer looked as if he were going to give the Preacher a run for his money. His mouth sagged unhappily. So did his shoulders. His answer came in a much smaller voice: "I don't know."

"Well, we are on the same trail there, anyway, because I don't know how to do that, either," Newton said.

"But we must!" Pain filled Stafford's words.

"What do we name someone who insists we must do something that cannot be done?" Newton answered his own question: "If he is lucky enough to be young, we name him a child. Otherwise, we call him a fool. If he keeps on insisting . . . we have asylums for such people."

Stafford turned the color of a sunset. But before he could come out with whatever he'd been about to say, musketry started up off to the north. The encampment boiled like coffee in a tin pot. Soldiers ran this way and that. Before long, quite a few of them purposefully trotted north.

"We have another chance now to do what we came here for," Stafford did say at last.

"What do you think the chances are that this next battle will settle the insurrection once for all?" Newton asked.

"I don't know," the other Consul said, "but I do know they're better if we win than if we lose."

"Are they what a man might call betting odds?" Newton persisted.

"I don't know that, either." Stafford sounded as if he wanted to change the subject, or else drop the whole conversation. Which he did, for he went on, "I am going up to the front, to see what our brave soldiers and militiamen *can* do. You are welcome to accompany me, if you care to."

If you aren't yellow, he meant. Stung, Newton said, "There is not a place on this campaign where you have gone and I have not." If the other Consul tried to quarrel with that, Newton was ready to box his ears.

But Stafford said only, "Come on, then," and hurried off toward the sound of the firing. He drew his eight-shooter as he went.

Sighing, so did Newton. The idea of shooting insurrectionists did not delight him, as it did his colleague. All the same, he could not believe the copperskins and Negroes would spare him for the sake of his belief in individual liberty. So many bullets flew almost at random; no one could do anything about those. If someone at close quarters aimed at him in particular, he intended to fire first. He might favor individual liberty, yes, but not at the price of his own survival.

That thought made him miss a step and almost stumble. The insurrectionists *were* risking their lives for individual liberty. No wonder they made such difficult foes!

By the time he and Stafford got to the scene of the firing, it was already dying away. They'd passed a couple of parties of stretcher-bearers taking wounded men back to the surgeons, and one foul-mouthed corporal going back under his own power cradling a bleeding wrist in the crook of his other arm.

"Only a skirmish, your Excellencies," said the middle-aged first lieutenant who seemed to be in command of the Atlantean soldiers thereabouts. "They probed to see if we were ready to receive 'em, they found out we were, and then they faded off into the woods again."

"Didn't much care for the reception, eh?" Stafford said, still holding his revolver at the ready.

"No, sir." The lieutenant scratched at his graying side whiskers. Was this the kind of glorious action he'd imagined when he joined the Atlantean army in the flower of his youth? Leland Newton had trouble believing it. But then, the difference between what you imagined and what you got was one of the yardsticks by which you measured your passage into adulthood.

Out in the ferns and barrel trees from which the insurrectionists had opened up, a wounded man screamed his guts out. One thing Newton had noticed: all badly hurt men sounded the same. Maybe that said something in favor of the basic equality of the races. Hoping so, Newton proposed it to Stafford.

His colleague snorted. "Huzzah," he said sourly. "If I shoot this horse here, it'll make pretty much the same noises, too. Shall we pick it for Consul next term, the way Caligula did with Incitatus?"

"Well . . . no," Newton said. Stafford was just the kind of man who would remember the name of the mad Roman Emperor's cherished charger and trot it out when it did him the most good.

"All right, then. Don't waste my time with foolishness," he snapped, and turned away. Had the injured Negro or copperskin lain out in the open, Stafford probably would have tried to finish him off, or to hit the fellows who came out to pick him up and do what they could for him. Newton didn't think that was a sporting way to make war. He also didn't think Stafford cared a cent's worth for sport.

Something in Colonel Sinapis' long, sad face told Jeremiah Stafford the army's senior officer didn't want to listen to him. *Too damned bad, Colonel*, Stafford thought. A colonel who didn't listen to a Consul wouldn't stay the army's senior officer for long.

"We need a decisive victory over the insurrectionists," Stafford declared. "We need to break their fighting force, and we need to break their spirit."

"Such a victory would be desirable—yes, your Excellency." Was that resignation in Sinapis' voice? *It had better not be*, Stafford thought.

"We need to go after that kind of victory more aggressively," he said.

"I shall certainly be as aggressive as seems advisable," Colonel Sinapis said.

"Be more aggressive than that," Stafford told him.

One of the colonel's shaggy eyebrows rose. "Do you want me to lead the army into a trap, sir?"

"No, damn it! I want you to trap the insurrectionists—trap them and smash them," Stafford said.

"If you smash a glob of quicksilver, all you have are smaller globs here, there, and everywhere," Sinapis said.

"Fine," Stafford said. The Atlantean officer gave him a look—that wasn't the answer Sinapis had expected. Consul Stafford went on, "After we smash the big glob, we can destroy the smaller bits one by one at our leisure."

"Ah." Sinapis relaxed fractionally. *He hasn't gone round*

the bend after all. The colonel didn't say that, but Stafford saw it in his eyes. A beat slower than Sinapis might have, he resumed: "That may be possible. I hope it is, but I would be lying if I said I was sure."

"If we don't make the effort, Colonel, why the devil did we ever leave New Hastings?" Stafford asked, and answered his own question: "We came to fight the insurrectionists. We came to beat them. Let's do that, then."

Balthasar Sinapis sketched a salute. "Very well, your Excellency."

Stafford had learned that *Very well, your Excellency* could mean anything—or nothing. When Colonel Sinapis got an order he didn't fancy, he saluted, promised to obey, and then sat on his hands. Stafford didn't aim to let him do that this time. Sinapis' fingers wouldn't be warm under his behind—they'd be flaming in the fire.

But Stafford didn't have to hold Sinapis' hands to the fire this time. The colonel sent his men against the insurrectionists with what struck the Consul as almost a devil-take-the-hindmost enthusiasm. Sinapis might have been thumbing his nose at Stafford, in effect saying, *Well, this was your idea. If it goes wrong, blame yourself, because it's not my fault.*

If it went wrong, Stafford supposed he would have to do that. If he didn't blame himself, Leland Newton damned well *would* blame him . . . and would make sure all the papers back in the more civilized parts of Atlantis blamed him, too. He could see headlines in his mind's eye. They would scream about his recklessness—and about his fecklessness, too. They would ask why he overrode a professional soldier's judgment. That would make a painfully good question, too.

No one was happier than he, then, when it didn't go wrong. The Atlantean soldiers fell upon and routed a good-sized force of copperskins and blacks. The insurrectionists hardly formed a line of battle. They fired a few shots and fled. The soldiers killed over a hundred of them, and captured close to a hundred more. Casualties among the whites were seven dead and seventeen wounded.

"You see?" Stafford said exultantly, eyeing the unhappy

prisoners. "We really can do this. We just have to push hard."

"It worked this time," Sinapis said, and not another word.

The Consul jerked a thumb toward the captives. "We ought to hang the lot of them, is what we ought to do."

"You agreed we would not, your Excellency," Colonel Sinapis reminded him. "Harming prisoners is a game both sides can play. Nor would your colleague approve of breaking the agreement."

Stafford backtracked: "I didn't say we would. I said we ought to. And I still believe that. After this war is won, there will be a great reckoning. Slaves have to learn they cannot rise against their masters."

"What comes afterwards is politics." As Sinapis was in the habit of doing, he spoke the word as if it tasted bad. "That is your province. I have nothing to say about it. While the fight goes on . . . there, I am obliged to tell you what I think."

"Yes, yes." Jeremiah Stafford made himself nod. Sinapis could croak as much as he pleased. If he wanted to think he was obliged to imitate a chorus of frogs, he could do that, too. But, if he thought Stafford was obliged to listen to him, he needed to think again. Stafford did some more talking of his own: "Keep on pressing them, I tell you. It is our best hope of victory."

"You are one of the men in a position to give me orders." By the way Sinapis said that, he didn't care for it, either. Even his salute, though technically perfect, felt somehow reproachful. "Of course I shall obey them . . . and then, your Excellency, we will see what comes of that."

Frederick Radcliff didn't like falling back before the white soldiers. During his life, though, he'd had to do any number of things he didn't like. He couldn't imagine a slave who hadn't. And so he retreated, and retreated again. The Atlantean regulars and the militiamen who reminded him of hyenas skulking along next to lions came after his men.

Lorenzo fancied retreating no more than he did. "We've got to pin their ears back," the copperskin said.

"That would be good," Frederick agreed. "But how do we make sure they don't pin ours back instead?"

"Ambush 'em," Lorenzo answered at once. "Only way to teach 'em respect. Only way to make 'em keep their distance, too. Bastards have been eating pepper—they're right on our heels."

"If we can, I want to give them a jolt," Frederick said. "My only worry is that they'll slide around our flank the way they did before."

"We need to find a place where the ground won't let 'em," Lorenzo said. "Plenty of people carrying guns on our side who'll know about places like that."

"If there are any places like that," Frederick said.

"Bound to be some," the copperskin insisted. "Let me ask around—I'll see what I can come up with."

Frederick didn't tell him no. He didn't want the Atlantean army hounding his rebels, either. And, before long, Lorenzo found a mulatto (or maybe he was a quadroon—he was nearer yellow than brown) who said he knew about a place where the main road ran through a valley wooded on both sides. "They go in there, a bunch of 'em don't come out the other side," the man said.

"That sounds good," Frederick replied. "Next question is, can we get there without hanging out a sign telling the white folks why we're heading that way?"

Lorenzo sent him an admiring glance. "That's the kind of thing you wouldn't've worried about when we started. Neither would I, chances are."

"Long as you live, you better learn somethin' from it," Frederick said. "Only wasting your time if you don't."

"Got that right," Lorenzo said. He put his head together with the light-skinned Negro. When the two men separated, Lorenzo was smiling. The white men leading the Atlantean army would not have rejoiced to see that smile. To top it off, Lorenzo nodded. "I think we can do it without making the buckra suspicious."

That made Frederick smile in turn. Every slave used the word *buckra* from time to time to refer to white men. Every Negro slave Frederick had known insisted it came from an African language. No copperskin he'd ever heard of claimed it sprang from Terranova, but that didn't stop copperskins from coming out with it.

And Lorenzo and the high-yellow local slave turned out to know what they were talking about. The valley—Happy Valley, the local man called it—was the perfect place for an ambush. Frederick's fighters retreated toward the northeast and passed through the valley. They seemed to, at any rate. A lot of them melted away to either side instead. After the white Atlanteans charged forward, the insurrectionists would make them pay.

Only one thing went wrong: the Atlantean soldiers didn't charge forward. They paused at the southern end of Happy Valley and sent patrols forward to see what was going on in there.

At Frederick's orders, and Lorenzo's, no one fired at the white scouts except what appeared to be the retreating rebel army's rear guard. The idea was to make the white soldiers and militiamen believe the insurrectionists hadn't posted men in the woods to ravage them when they stormed after the withdrawing Negroes and copperskins.

It was a good idea. Frederick remained convinced of that even afterwards. So did Lorenzo—but then, of course, he would have, because it was his. The one trouble was, it didn't work.

The white scouts seemed to know something smelled like rotting crayfish right away. Instead of pressing on after the tail of the withdrawing rebel army (a tail now much stronger than the body of which it had been a part), the white men studied the trees and ferns to either side of the dirt road. They scratched their heads and rubbed their chins and generally acted like men who didn't like what they were seeing.

Come on in! The water's fine! Frederick thought at them, as loudly as he could. By the intent expression on Lorenzo's face, the copperskin was also doing his best to will the white men forward. Which only went to show that willing someone forward was a hell of a lot easier to talk about than to do.

Little by little, the Atlantean army advanced till it was close to the edge of the woods. The field artillery unlimbered and sprayed as much of the forest as the guns could reach with cannon balls and canister. Frederick hoped his fighters had had the sense to scoot back when they saw the cannon taking aim at them. If they hadn't, it would be too late for some of them.

"How many of those white bastards can you see?" Lorenzo asked. "Are they screening us so they can go around to our right or our left before we cipher out what they're up to?"

Frederick wanted to say no. He couldn't, not when the Atlantean army had repeatedly done that before. He peered through a purloined spyglass, then passed it to Lorenzo. "Doesn't seem like they are," he said. "Or does it look different to you?"

After a long stare of his own, Lorenzo said, "I don't *think* they are. Harder to be sure, though, now that they've got all those God-damned militiamen alongside the regulars. I hate those sons of bitches."

"Well, Jesus Christ! Who in his right mind doesn't?" Frederick said. "The soldiers are just ... soldiers. They've got a job to do, and they do it. But most of the militiamen are the shitheels who bought and sold us. They want to keep on doing it, too."

"And killing us. And fucking us," Lorenzo added.

"Yes. And those," Frederick said heavily. "Are we going to let that keep on happening?"

"Maybe they can still kill me. We've already killed a lot of them, but nowhere near enough. The rest ... " Lorenzo shook his head. A lock of his straight black hair flopped down over his eyes. He brushed it back with the palm of his hand. "No one's gonna *own* me any more, not ever again."

He was bound to be right about that. If he and Frederick were unlucky enough to be captured, they wouldn't be returned to slavery, as some of the men and women who followed them might. No, they would die whatever lingering, instructive death the ingenuity of the whites who'd taken them might devise.

Frederick had always known such things were possible, even likely. That was why he always kept a last bullet for himself in his eight-shooter. What slave didn't have such knowledge? Fear of consequences, fear of failing, kept insurrections rare—but made them all the more desperate when they did break out. Right now, Frederick didn't care to dwell on all the things that might happen to him and his followers if they failed. He aimed to keep from failing if he possibly could.

Because he did, he went back to dwelling on what the white Atlantean soldiers and militiamen were up to. "We've taught 'em respect," he said slowly. "They've learned they'd better not just rush up like a herd of cows. We carve 'em into steaks when they try."

"Too bad they've figured that out," Lorenzo said. "They were easier to fight when they played the fool."

The white Atlanteans had taught Frederick a lesson, too: not to keep his own scouts too close to the main body of his army. When the whites did try another flanking maneuver, he found out about it in time to shift part of his own force and delay the enemy. That let the rest of his men take new positions at their leisure. Seeing that the flanking move was doomed to fail, the white men broke it off early.

Both armies held their positions for a while. Frederick sent out raiders to try to wreck the enemy's supply columns. His own men foraged from the countryside; he thought the whites would have more trouble doing that. To his disappointment, he turned out to be wrong. When the whites got hungry, they didn't stop at chickens and ducks and geese. They ate turtles and frogs and snails, the same as his men did. Maybe they drew the line at katydids, but so what?

"Only proves what we already knew," Lorenzo said. "They're nothing but a bunch of thieves."

"What does that make us, then?" Frederick asked in wry amusement.

"Folks with sense," the copperskin answered. "Don't know about you, but I'd sooner eat frog stew and fiddlehead ferns any day of the week, not their rancid salt pork"—he made a face— "and—what do they call them?—desecrated vegetables."

"Desiccated," Frederick said.

"What's the difference?" Lorenzo asked.

Frederick only shrugged. He knew he had the word right, though. When you soaked the dried vegetables in water, they regained a faint resemblance to what they'd been once upon a time. You could eat them, even if Frederick, like Lorenzo, had trouble seeing why anyone would want to.

Lorenzo waved the question aside and came back to more important things: "What are we going to do to stop the white devils? Sure doesn't look like we can starve them back to New Marseille."

"No. It doesn't," Frederick admitted glumly.

"Well, then?" Lorenzo's voice seemed sharper than a serpent's tooth. The comparison came from the Bible, though Frederick couldn't remember exactly where.

But he did have an answer for his copperskinned marshal, even if Lorenzo hadn't expected him to: "As long as we don't lose, we win. As long as we keep on fighting, keep on making trouble, we win. Sooner or later, the United States of Atlantis'll decide we cost more than we're worth—too much money, too much time, too much blood. That's when they decide they better start talkin' instead of fightin'."

"You sound sure, anyway." By the way Lorenzo said it, he was far from sure himself. He did unbend enough to ask, "How come you sound so sure?"

"On account of that's the way my grandfather licked the redcoats," Frederick answered. "He hung around and he hung around and he hung around, till finally they got sick of the whole business. That's why there are the United States of Atlantis today."

"And a fat lot of good they do us, too," Lorenzo said.

"Oh, things could be worse," Frederick said. "Some of the islands south of here—the ones the Spaniards still hold—the way they treat slaves makes Atlantis seem like a kiss on the cheek. And the Empire of Huy-Braseal, in southern Terranova, that's supposed to be just as bad, or maybe even worse."

"But I ain't in any one of those places. I'm here," Lorenzo said pointedly. "If they catch me, they'll kill me. How does it get any worse than that?"

Frederick had had a similar thought not long before. "Don't suppose it does," he replied. "Thing is, then, not to let 'em catch us, right?"

"Right." Lorenzo's head bobbed up and down. "First sensible thing you've said in quite a while—you know that?"

"Well, I try," Frederick said. They both laughed. Why not? They were—for the moment, for as long as their followers could hold off the white soldiers, or until the Atlantean government got sick of what looked like an endless, hopeless war—free men. Despite all the qualifications, this tenuous freedom was as much as Frederick had ever had. While he had it, he aimed to make the most of it.

Jeremiah Stafford fixed Colonel Sinapis with a glare that would have reduced any government functionary back in New Hastings to a quivering pile of gelatin. "We aren't pressing them anywhere near so hard as we might," Stafford said. He could have made the statement sound no more ominous had he demanded *Have you stopped beating your wife?* Whatever Sinapis answered would be wrong.

Or so Stafford thought. The officer, however, declined to turn gelatinous. "You wanted us to rush into that Happy Valley, too, your Excellency," Sinapis said. "How many casualties do you suppose that would have cost us? It would have been the worst disaster since Austerlitz, or maybe since Arminius massacred the Romans in the Teutoberg Forest in the year 9."

Quinctilius Varus! Give me back my legions! Stafford remembered the Emperor Augustus' anguished cry from his own slog through Suetonius in his university days. *Consul Stafford! Give me back my soldiers!* just didn't have the same ring. But would it have come to that? He didn't think so.

"We could have whipped those savages," he said.

"I'm sure Varus thought the same thing," Colonel Sinapis replied. "Sometimes, your Excellency, you have to know when *not* to fight."

That was bound to be true, in war as in a barroom argument. All the same, Stafford said, "It sometimes seems to me that you abuse the privilege of not fighting, Colonel."

"Isn't that interesting?" Colonel Sinapis said. Then he turned on his heel and walked away.

Stafford gaped. He'd been a Senator before he was chosen Consul, and a prominent man before he was elected Senator. How could it be otherwise? *Only* prominent men reached the Senate; one measure of an Atlantean's prominence was whether he reached the Senate. No one had had the nerve to be openly rude to him for many years.

"Come back here, you!" he snapped, as if Sinapis were an uppity house slave.

The colonel stopped, but did not return. "No," he said calmly, and made as if to walk off again.

Before he could, Stafford's voice went deadly cold: "Have you a friend with whom my friends may discuss this matter further?" Dueling might be illegal in every state of the USA, but that did not make it extinct. Men from the south, especially, were still apt to defend their honor with pistols.

As calmly as before, Colonel Sinapis said "No" again. That made Stafford gape once more. The colonel continued, "Your military regulations wisely forbid officers from dueling. Otherwise, your Excellency, please believe me when I say that I should take no small pleasure from killing you. Good day." Sketching a salute, he ambled off as if he had not a care in the world.

What had been in his eyes as he responded? If it wasn't a pure, wolfish pleasure at the idea of bloodshed, Stafford had never seen any such thing. He reflected that he didn't know what kind of fighting man Sinapis was; army commanders seldom got to display their mettle in the front line. Maybe he was lucky not to find out the hard way.

Maybe, just maybe, he was very lucky indeed.

I was not afraid, he told himself. He wondered how much that mattered, or if it mattered at all. A man might not fear an earthquake or a flood or a wildfire—which wouldn't keep a natural disaster from killing him. Something told Stafford that Balthasar Sinapis held about as much compassion as fire or flood or temblor.

How exactly *had* Sinapis come to Atlantis? What were the circumstances under which he'd lost his position in Europe? Was it because some prominent man—a government minister, say, or a prince—got ventilated in a quarrel or a formal duel? Stafford hadn't thought so, but. . . .

His encounter with Sinapis didn't stay quiet. By the nature of things, encounters like that never did. Everybody was talking about it the next day. Not much of what people said was true, but when did that ever stop anyone?

"I hear the good colonel wanted to load you into a cannon and fire you at the insurrectionists," Consul Newton remarked.

"No such thing!" Stafford said, which was true—not that truth had ever outrun a rumor. With such dignity as he could muster, the Consul went on, "I keep trying to spur him to more activity against them."

"From what folks are saying, you keep trying to get yourself killed," his colleague observed.

"If you wade through everything folks are saying, you'll need to hold your nose and take a bath before you reach down to the truth," Stafford said. "The smell will tell you what you're wading in, too."

"You didn't challenge him to a duel, then?"

"What? Yes, of course I did. I might have won, too."

Newton's raised eyebrows said everything that needed saying about how likely he thought that was. And chances were he had a point, too; Colonel Sinapis was bound to get more pistol practice than Stafford did, and to have got more for many years. If Stafford was to win the duel, he would need luck on his side. Sinapis would need only routine competence. That, he had.

"The idea, you know, is to work *with* the colonel," Newton said. "If you make him hate you, you won't have much luck with that."

"He's a soldier. Soldiers do what you tell them to do," Stafford growled. But he knew you caught more flies with honey than with vinegar. There was a difference between obeying orders from a sense of duty and obeying them because you really wanted to. The latter got good results. The former . . .

Again, the other Consul needed no words to let Stafford know what he was thinking. "We *are* gaining ground against the insurrectionists, you know," Newton said, turning the subject.

"We're in deeper, anyhow," Stafford answered. "I'm not so sure about gaining ground. What they do to the wagon trains coming up from New Marseille . . . " He angrily shook his head. "They have no business doing such things, God damn them to the blackest pits of hell."

Leland Newton smiled thinly. "I never thought I'd learn how tasty frog-and-snail stew could be," he said.

"I never thought I would have to find out," Stafford said. "We were guarding the wagon trains well for a while, but things have slipped again."

"If you put everything you have into going forward, doing anything else with your soldiers is going to slip," Newton pointed out. "Even with the militiamen along, we're stretched too thin for that not to happen."

Stafford grunted and turned away, almost as rudely as Colonel Sinapis had turned away from him. Doing anything else would have meant admitting some of the army's failures were his own fault, and he was damned if he would. Newton didn't challenge him to a duel, although no regulations (except the laws of the United States of Atlantis, which a gentleman could ignore if he chose) prevented one Consul from meeting the other on the field of honor.

Newton's voice pursued him: "Don't you think we'd be better off talking with the insurrectionists and seeing if there isn't some way we might all live together peacefully? This is the only home any of us have, you know."

That made Stafford turn back. "We had been living together peacefully for many years, under a system that assigned everyone his proper place—"

"From a white man's perspective," Newton broke in. "From a Negro's or a copperskin's, maybe not. Easier to be impressed, I daresay, if you're doing the buying and selling than if you're bought and sold."

"You sound like *you're* selling nigger equality, Newton," Stafford said. "You may huckster as much as you please, but I'm here to tell you I'm not buying."

"Oh, I can see that," the other Consul answered. "Better to let Atlantis tear itself to pieces than to change one iota of the way we do things. Iota . . . That goes all the way back to the theological controversies of the fourth century, you know: the difference between *homo-ousios*, of the same nature, and *homoi-ousios*, of like nature. One little letter, and plenty of blood spilled over it. A few hundred years from now, will our quarrels seem as foolish?"

"No," Stafford said, and then, "It would, no doubt, be pointless to remind you that our Lord accepted the idea of slavery."

By Newton's face, it would indeed. He credited the parts of the Bible that pleased him and ignored the rest. Stafford didn't pause to wonder whether he did the same thing himself.

XVII

$\mathcal{N}$one of the fifteen or so prisoners Atlantean troops had taken in their latest skirmish with the insurrectionists seemed happy with his fate. The blacks and copperskins were alive, but hardly convinced they would stay that way for long. Maybe they'd heard the white soldiers weren't hanging captured enemy fighters, but they plainly had trouble believing it.

Surveying them, Leland Newton saw three who looked even more miserable than the rest. Two were copperskins, the other a Negro. Only one of them wore a skirt; the other two had on baggy homespun trousers like their menfolk. But, no matter what they wore, they were all of them women.

"Taken in arms with the men?" Newton asked the sergeant in charge of the soldiers guarding the prisoners.

"Sure as hell were, uh, your Excellency." The underofficer pointed to the black woman. "That there bitch damn near—*damn* near—blew me a new asshole before Paddy Molloy jumped on her while she was reloading. She fought him, too, till he clouted her a good one."

"May I talk to her?"

One of the sergeant's gingery eyebrows jumped. "You're the Consul, sir. Seems to me you can do any old God-damned thing you please."

Only proves you've never been Consul, Newton thought. But he didn't waste time explaining to the man with three stripes on the sleeve of his sweat-stained gray tunic. Instead, Newton stepped past him and walked up to the captured insurrectionist. "What's your name?" he asked her.

By the way she looked at him—looked through him, really—he might have been calling to her from a mile beyond the moon. When she answered, "Elizabeth," her voice seemed to come from at least that far away.

Newton pushed ahead anyhow: "Is it true, what the sergeant said? Did you fight against our soldiers, the same way a man would have?"

"Reckon I did." She regained a little spirit as she added, "Might still be doin' it, too, 'cept the fuckin' mick who grabbed me was too damn' big to whup." She couldn't have stood more than five feet two. A knot on the side of her jaw said Paddy Molloy *had* clouted her a good one.

"Have they treated you the same as the men they took?" Newton asked.

Elizabeth's first startled glance went to the two female copperskins who'd been captured with her. Then her eyes swung back to Consul Newton. He couldn't have said why, but her gaze made him feel like an idiot. That must have been what she thought, too, because she said, "You ain't the brightest candle in the box, is you?"

"What do you mean?" Newton didn't think he'd risen to the highest rank in Atlantis by being stupid.

Elizabeth did, though. As if to a half-wit, she explained, "They don't throw the men down on the ground and hold their legs apart and screw 'em eight or ten or twenty times. You may be white devils, but I don't reckon you's cornholin' devils."

"They did *that* to you? To all three of you? Molested you? Violated you?" The Consul heard his own horror.

Matter-of-factly, the captured female fighter nodded. "Chance I took. I knew that when I asked the menfolk to learn me to shoot. Didn't reckon I'd get caught, though." Her grimace declared she wished she hadn't. " 'Sides, they liable to give me the clap or the pox."

Newton hardly noticed that. He stormed back to the

white sergeant. "Did you and your troops take unfair advantage of those women?" he thundered, as full of righteous wrath as Jehovah watching the Children of Israel bow down before the Golden Calf.

"Unfair? Don't look that way to me, sir." The sergeant seemed to think Newton was an idiot, too. Like Elizabeth, he wasn't shy about telling him why: "Jesus Christ, they were doing their damnedest to murder the lot of us! Were we supposed to kiss 'em on the cheek and invite 'em to a waltz, like?"

"No, but you weren't supposed to, to rape them, either!" Newton had to fight to get the dreadful word out.

"Chance they take if they fire at us." The underofficer and Elizabeth used the same brutal logic.

Seeing he would get no satisfaction—under the circumstances, perhaps not the perfect word—there, Newton stormed off to talk to a captain. The young officer only shrugged. "What do you expect from men who find women in arms against them, your Excellency?"

"Civilized behavior?" Newton suggested.

Sarcasm rolled off the captain's back. "War is not a civilized business," he said.

"It has its rules and customs. On the whole, the insurrectionists have lived up to them."

"Well, what do you want me to do about it? Put 'em up on charges?" the captain asked. That was exactly what Newton wanted, but the younger man's laughter told him he wouldn't get it—not here, anyhow.

Fuming, he stomped away to talk to Colonel Sinapis. The colonel had given Consul Stafford a hard time, so Newton assumed *he* would find him reasonable. He didn't. Sinapis said, "The soldiers took the women after the women fought against them?"

"That's right," Newton said. "It's disgraceful. It's barbaric. It's—"

"It is to be expected," Sinapis interrupted. "Officers may be gentlemen. Your regulations say they are. So do the ones in most of the kingdoms of Europe. Perhaps that makes it so. But soldiers? My dear fellow! The Duke of Wellington, a very fine commander even if he is an Englishman, calls them the scum of the earth. Believe me, your Excellency, he knows what he is talking about, too."

"All the more reason to punish them harshly when they do something this outrageous!" Newton exclaimed.

"Outrageous?" Sinapis tossed his head, as he often did where a native Atlantean would have shaken it. "I think not. This is revenge. What would *you* do if a woman tried to shoot you?"

"Not that, I hope," Newton answered.

Sinapis studied him. The colonel's eyes lingered—insultingly long?—on his crotch. At last, Sinapis said, "It could be that you would not. But a great many men *would*, and I see no point to punishing them for it. That would cause the army more problems than it would solve."

"What if the women they ravished were white?" the Consul from Croydon demanded.

"Violating women for the sport of it . . . No good officer can allow that. If white women had tried to kill our troops in combat, though . . . That would be the women's lookout, and their misfortune," Sinapis said.

He was consistent, anyhow—if he was telling the truth. If he wasn't, his face didn't know about it . . . which, if he was any kind of card player, meant nothing. "I had hoped for more cooperation from you, Colonel," Newton said reproachfully.

"I had hoped for more sense from you, your Excellency," Sinapis replied. "We do not always get what we hope for, though, do we?"

"Evidently not," Newton said. "Please make sure, however, that your soldiers do not molest these women again."

"Now that the heat of battle has cooled, I believe I can do that. Very well, your Excellency." Sinapis delivered a precise salute.

"And please issue orders that other women taken prisoner in combat are not to be violated," Newton continued.

The colonel's mouth twisted under the eaves of his drooping mustache. "I dislike giving orders sure to be ignored. It weakens discipline, which is the last thing any army needs."

"If you issue them strongly enough, the men will follow them," Newton said.

"You have never been a soldier. You have never tried to lead soldiers. This is as plain as the nose on your face—as plain as the nose on my face, even." Sinapis stroked his formidable proboscis. "I am very sorry, but issuing those orders is a waste of time."

Newton's voice went hard and flat: "Do it anyway."

"Yes, your Excellency." By contrast, Sinapis' voice held no expression at all. This time, his salute seemed more reproachful than anything else. Leland Newton didn't care. Some things he would not put up with, and this was one of them. Whether the orders really would do any good . . . he preferred not to think about.

A copperskin brought a hatchet down on a flapjack turtle's neck. Pouring blood, the turtle went into its death spasm. The head flew some distance from the body. Its fearsome jaws opened and closed, opened and closed. No one got anywhere near it. Like a snake's, it could bite for some time after being detached. And those jaws could easily take off a finger.

To white folks, flapjack turtle was something you ate when you couldn't get beef or pork or mutton or poultry. As a house slave, Frederick Radcliff had something of the same attitude. Field hands eked out the rations their masters gave them with anything they could get their hands on.

"I'll take this to the girls now," the copperskin said with a grin, picking up the turtle's carcass. The legs still flailed feebly; they didn't want to believe the beast was dead.

"Don't let them hear you call them that, Joaquin," Frederick said. "You won't like what happens if they do."

"I ain't afraid of them." Joaquin swaggered off.

"Any man who ain't afraid of women—he ain't as smart as he ought to be," Frederick remarked to Lorenzo.

"Yeah, there is that." Lorenzo's chuckle sounded distinctly wry. "Always knew they could fight—any fella ever had anything to do with 'em knows that. But I never reckoned they could fight like this, with guns and everything."

"Well, neither did I," Frederick said. "Don't suppose the white soldiers reckoned they could, either."

"Last surprise some of those bastards ever got," Lorenzo said. "Good thing, too."

"Oh, sure," Frederick agreed. "Kind of tough on the gals the whites catch, though."

Lorenzo nodded, but not with much sympathy. "They knew what they was gettin' into. And they knew what was liable to get into them if somethin' went wrong."

"White folks don't cornhole the ordinary fighters they catch," Frederick said. "We don't cornhole their fighters when we catch 'em. They shouldn't ought to fuck the gals."

"It's different," Lorenzo said, and Frederick found himself nodding. He couldn't have said just how it was different, but he also felt it was. Maybe because most men didn't enjoy cornholing other men, where any man who *was* a man would jump on a woman any chance he got.

"Still and all," he said slowly, "it doesn't seem right. We been fightin' straight up. So have the white soldiers, pretty much. Whole bunch of fellas jumpin' on a woman on account of she was carryin' a gun—that ain't straight up."

Lorenzo's eyes slid toward the cooking fires: the direction in which the younger copperskin with the flapjack turtle had gone. Slyly, he said, "You ought to go sing your song over there. You'd have all those pretty young gals crawlin' under the sheets with you faster'n you could—" He snapped his fingers.

"*That's* what I need, all right!" Frederick rolled his eyes. As any middle-aged man would have, he thought about an embarrassment of riches. Even were the spirit willing, the flesh was definitely weak. And his spirit wasn't so willing. "Reckon Helen'd have herself a thing or three to say about 'em."

"Give her one in the chops. That'll make her shut her big yap, damned if it won't." Lorenzo found simple answers for all worries except military ones. He'd lived with a lot of different women while he was a field hand—with none for more than a couple of years. Now that he was a general, or as close to a general as any man in the Free Republic of Atlantis was, he cut as wide a swath through the women who'd joined the insurrection as a man his age could hope to do.

But Frederick didn't want to live like that. "Helen and me, we done got along good for a hell of a long time. Why should I want to change now?"

"'Cause fresh pussy's more fun than the same old thing every God-damned time?" Yes, Lorenzo had an answer for everything.

One trouble: Frederick thought it was the wrong answer. If lying down with someone whose likes you knew and who knew what pleased you wasn't better than sleeping with a stranger . . . then it wasn't, that was all. Some men—and some women—preferred the one, some the other. Frederick saw no point to arguing about it. Would you argue about liking duck better than pork?

He did amble over toward the fires himself. Behind him, Lorenzo laughed a filthy laugh. In spite of himself, Frederick's back stiffened. That only made Lorenzo laugh harder.

"It's the Tribune!" one of the cooking women said.

"Stew won't be ready for a while yet," another one told him. Even as she spoke, chunks of turtle meat went into a big iron pot.

"It's all right. I'm just seein' how things are going, I guess you'd say," Frederick answered.

"How about that?" Admiration filled the copper-skinned woman's voice. By the way she eyed him, Frederick didn't think he'd have to work very hard to get her into his bed.

But, no matter what Lorenzo thought, that wasn't what he had in mind. All the people doing the cooking were women. Both they and the men seemed to take that for granted. Frederick wondered why. It wasn't as if men couldn't cook. Most boss cooks all through the slaveholding states were men. Frederick sadly remembered Davey. He'd been someone to reckon with, somebody who'd had a lot of influence on the master and mistress. The way to the heart did—or could—go through the stomach.

That had been fancy cooking, though. Women handled the plain job. Men cooked for superiors, women for equals. Maybe that was what was going on here. You couldn't get much plainer cooking, or cooking more intended for equals, than what went into feeding an army.

Frederick was ready to fight to the death to make Negroes and copperskins equal to whites in Atlantis. That women might be equal to men had hardly crossed his mind up till now. As it did, he shook his head. White men, black men, and copperskinned men were all the same under the skin. Anybody (well, anybody who wasn't a white slaveholder) could see that. But men and women? Men and women were *different*. Anybody could see that, too. Hadn't people of all colors been telling stories and making jokes about the differences since the beginning of time?

In the early days of the uprising, some of the men might have been hearing those old jokes inside their heads. They loudly doubted that women had any business picking up rifle muskets and taking potshots at white soldiers. And they plainly expected the women to break and run when soldiers fired at them.

Well, they knew better now. Some women had run when the shooting picked up—but so had some men. Women mostly weren't as big or as strong as men, so they had trouble fighting hand to hand. But the two sides didn't fight hand to hand all that often, which meant that mattered less than Frederick had feared it would. Wounded women shrieked on higher notes than wounded men. Still and all, though, no one who'd seen women in action would claim they couldn't fight.

Since they could . . . Didn't that argue that a lot of other differences were smaller than they seemed at first glance? Frederick rubbed his chin. Thanks to his famous grandfather, his beard was thicker than most Negroes'. He could have done without that part of Victor Radcliff's legacy.

What would his fellow fighters say if he told them that, after they won the war for freedom against the Atlantean army, they would have to give women the same freedom: freedom to vote, to hold property, to divorce for all the same reasons? They wouldn't like it, not even a little. Which argued that he should keep his big mouth shut.

And if you keep it shut, don't you slam the door on freedom, same as the whites want to do? That was an interesting question—no two ways about it. The way it looked to him, if he tried to win everything at once, he only increased his chances of winning nothing at all. Once he established the principle that Negroes and copperskins had the right to be something more than property throughout the USA, before too long someone should get around to establishing the principle that women had the right to be more than property.

Yes, that would be easy, wouldn't it? Of course it would. Frederick was sure of it. And, because he was, he decided not to try to push his followers any further than they were likely to want to go on their own. Equal rights for women could wait a while.

"Nigger equality? Mudface equality?" As usual, Jeremiah Stafford freighted the phrases with as much obscenity as they would carry, and a little more besides. "No white man from south of the Stour will put up with that nonsense for a minute, and you know it perfectly well."

Leland Newton only raised an eyebrow and rustled the latest batch of newspapers that had come into camp. "But there is more to the United States of Atlantis than white men from south of the Stour, and the rest of the people are getting damned sick of a war going nowhere," the other Consul said. "If they get sick of spending money on it, the states south of the Stour can fight it by themselves—and good luck to them."

After an outright triumph by the insurrectionists, that was what Stafford feared most. "If we don't get help from the rest of the country, why should we bother staying attached to it?" he said.

"Don't let the door hit you in the backside when you leave," Newton said cheerfully, which was also nothing Stafford wanted to hear. And that cheery tone rasped worse than the words.

Could the southern half of Atlantis—the smaller half, the poorer half, the less populous half, the half racked by servile insurrection—make a go of things on its own? Consul Stafford had no idea. "If we leave, and if we win our fight, how many niggers and mudfaces do you suppose we'll leave alive afterwards?" he said.

"I couldn't begin to guess," Consul Newton answered. "But if you murder them all, what happens to your precious social system then? I've asked you that before. Who brings in your crops? Who cuts your hair? Who cooks your supper? How soon before you're bankrupt because your wonderful whites from south of the Stour won't do nigger work to save their lives?"

Those were all ... intriguing questions, much more intriguing than Stafford wished they were. Even so, he said, "We'd be taking care of things our own way. Nothing else matters."

"Then what am I doing here? What are all the soldiers from north of the Stour doing here?" Newton asked. "If you don't want our help, we'll leave, believe me—and we'll be glad to do it, too."

"We want your help. We deserve it, by God," Stafford said. "But if you don't care to give it we'll go on by ourselves."

They scowled at each other. Stafford had the feeling they were talking past each other, as they had so often and for so long in New Hastings. He also had the feeling this was the worst possible time for them to be doing that. The trouble was, he didn't know how to fix it. Newton would not take him seriously; he didn't think Newton took himself seriously. And, doubting that, Stafford couldn't take Newton seriously, either.

Since he could, he saw only one thing to do: win the fight against the insurrectionists while the Atlantean army remained opposed to them. But that meant getting Colonel Sinapis to do something with it. And Stafford was unhappily aware how much he hadn't endeared himself to the colonel.

He tried to take a light tone when he asked Sinapis, "If you aren't using the army, may I borrow it for a little while?"

By the way the colonel's eyebrows came down and together, by the way his mouth tightened to a bloodless line, Stafford knew the approach had failed. "I *am* using it, your Excellency, in case you had not noticed," Sinapis answered in a voice like winter.

"You aren't using it enough," Stafford told him.

"There, sir, we differ," Colonel Sinapis said.

"Yes. We do," Stafford agreed grimly. Levity hadn't reached the somber officer. Maybe bluntness would. "See here, Colonel: do you want the United States of Atlantis to fall to pieces before your eyes?"

He was appalled when Sinapis obviously gave the question serious consideration. And he was even more appalled when the army commander shrugged his rather narrow shoulders. "Meaning no disrespect, your Excellency," Sinapis said, "but you will please believe me when I tell you I have seen far worse things."

Stafford almost asked him what could be worse than a republic—a republic often called the hope of both Europe and Terranova—dissolving into chaos. Only one thing made him hesitate. He feared Balthasar Sinapis would tell him. Instead, then, he tried a different road: "Let me put that another way, Colonel. Do you want to take the blame when the United States of Atlantis fall to pieces before your eyes?"

"And why should I?" Sinapis rumbled. "When these things happen, there is usually plenty of blame to go around."

He was a cool customer, all right. Well, Stafford had already discovered that, to his own discomfiture. "Why? I'll tell you why, Colonel. Because if this army does not put down the insurrection in a hurry, it's liable to be recalled. If it is, the southern states will go on fighting the war on their own, even if that means leaving the USA. That is what it *will* mean, too. Plenty of blame to go around, yes. But a lot of it will stick to you."

He waited. He'd told the truth as he saw it. How much that meant to Colonel Sinapis, or whether it meant anything at all to him ... he'd just have to see. He'd got Sinapis' attention, anyhow. The officer stroked his mustache. He'd done something that made Europe too warm for him. Stafford still didn't know what it was, but it must have been something juicy. If Sinapis got another big blot on his escutcheon, who would hire him after he left Atlantis? The Chinese, maybe? Maybe. Stafford didn't think even the most raggedy principality in southern Terranova would take the chance.

After a long, long pause, Sinapis said, "You have an unpleasant way of making your points."

"I tried a pleasant way, Colonel. You took no notice of it," Stafford answered.

Sinapis muttered to himself. Stafford didn't think it was in English. That might have been—probably was—just as well. What Stafford didn't understand, he didn't have to respond to. Another pause followed. Then the colonel returned to a language the Consul could follow: "What do you want me to do?"

Now we're getting somewhere. Stafford didn't say it out loud. If he had, he would have lost his man. Sinapis' pride was even touchier than that of a grandee from the state of Gernika. All the Consul said was, "This is what I've got in mind. . . . "

Rifle muskets cracked. Cannon thundered. Lorenzo's mouth twisted into a frown. "Damned white devils are getting pushy," he said.

"They are," Frederick Radcliff agreed. "How do we make them sorry for it?"

Now the copperskin smiled, and broadly. "You *do* know the questions to ask."

"I'm counting on you to know the answers I need," Frederick said. "If you don't, we've got trouble."

"I'll talk to people who know the ground, see what we can do," Lorenzo said. "Depends on what they tell me. And it depends on *how* pushy the soldiers are getting. If it's only some, chances are they'll give us more to worry about than they have been. But if they've decided they don't have to worry about us any more—"

"If that's what they've decided, it's up to us to show 'em how big a mistake they've made," Frederick said.

"*There* you go." Lorenzo smiled again. His lips were as thin as a white man's, which made this expression seem uncommonly cruel to Frederick. Lorenzo went on, "I reckon they're jumpy, all right. They think they've got to squash us today, this minute. The longer the war goes on, the more they figure they're losing."

He didn't say that the whites really were losing. That wasn't obvious. But if they thought they were losing, they might as well have been. Persuading them that they couldn't put down the insurrection was a big part, maybe the biggest part, of what Frederick wanted to do. It had worked for his grandfather against the English. How sweet if it worked for him now against the Atlanteans—against his grandfather's white relations.

Victor Radcliff hadn't had any white children who lived. Frederick was his only direct descendant. *A piece of property*, he thought. *That's all I am to the whites*. Had his grandmother been white, even if she weren't Victor Radcliff's wife ... Frederick sighed. He'd already been over that ground too many times in his mind.

A runner came back from the insurrectionists' picket line. A white soldier would have saluted before reporting. This Negro didn't bother. "White folks is bangin' away like nobody's business," he said. "Cannons blowin' holes in our line, soldiers comin' right on through 'em once they's blown. Either we needs more muskets down where the fightin's at or we needs to git outa there."

Frederick and Lorenzo looked at each other. Slowly, Lorenzo said, "We keep pullin' back, we lure 'em on, we get 'em to a place where we can really hurt 'em."

"Or maybe that's what they're after," Frederick responded, worry in his voice. "They're trying to get us to a place where they can really put the screws to us."

"Well, sure they are." Lorenzo sounded amused, which struck Frederick as taking optimism to an extreme. The copperskin went on, "We got to do it to them and not let them do it to us."

"So what are we supposed to do down there?" the messenger asked. "You want we should fall back?"

"Yes. Fall back." Frederick hoped that was the right answer. If it wasn't, he'd just hurt his own side.

He'd been thinking about the differences between men and women. His male fighters followed the orders he and

Lorenzo gave without much backtalk. The women who'd taken up arms against the white soldiers almost mutinied. "We want to kill them fuckers!" a copperskinned woman cried. "After what they done to us, we want to shoot their balls off!"

"Or cut 'em off!" a black woman added. The other women with rifle muskets and pistols shrilled furious agreement.

"We're gonna do that. Honest to God, we are." Frederick realized he sounded as if he was pleading. Then he realized he *was* pleading. He went right on doing it, too: "We've got to find a better spot, that's all. We've got to find a spot where we can punch a hole in them, not the other way around like they're doin' here. We can whip 'em. We will. This here just isn't the right place."

"You better be right," the copperskinned woman warned. "Yeah, you better be, else we gonna shoot *your* balls off." Again, her comrades ululated to show they were with her.

"I ain't worried about that," Frederick said.

"How come?" some of the women demanded, while others asked, "Why not?"

"On account of if we don't win, the white soldiers'll string me up, and Lorenzo here with me," Frederick answered. "Whatever happens to me after that, I ain't gonna care about it one way or the other."

"That's just it," said the Negro woman who'd complained before. "They catch you, they kill you, and then it's over. They catch us, our bad time's just startin'." The other women nodded.

But, after they'd had their say, they fell back with the men. "Hey, that was fun, wasn't it?" Lorenzo said. "Now I remember how come I never wanted to be Tribune."

"Fun? Matter of fact, no," Frederick said. Lorenzo laughed, not that he'd been joking. He went on, "One more thing I got to do, is all."

He did it. So did Lorenzo: the copperskin extracted the Free Republic of Atlantis' fighters as neatly and almost as painlessly as a dentist could extract a tooth using newfangled ether or chloroform. But the soldiers kept pushing after them, showing determination Frederick hadn't seen from them before.

"They mean it this time," he said unhappily.

Lorenzo nodded. "They do, damn them. Now we have to make them sorry for meaning it—if we can."

Frederick wished he hadn't added those last three words. He made himself nod, too. "Yes," he said. "If."

Leland Newton didn't know what his Consular colleague had done to light a fire under Colonel Sinapis. But Jeremiah Stafford must have done something. The Atlantean soldiers—and especially the militiamen who'd joined forces with Sinapis' regulars—advanced with more dash than they'd shown since crossing the Little Muddy. Part of that—no small part, Newton judged—came from their commander. Sinapis' heart hadn't been in the fight for some time. It was now.

And the whites were making progress. They were making more than Newton had thought they could, as a matter of fact. The insurrectionists skirmished and fell back, skirmished and fell back. How long could they keep falling back before they started falling apart? Consul Newton had wondered about that more than once, and each time the rebels' resilience surprised him. Could they surprise him again? He would be surprised if they could.

Sinapis' drive pushed the Negroes and copperskins back into some of the least known, least settled parts of Atlantis. Newton wouldn't have been surprised to see honkers grazing on some of these meadows. Audubon had, not many years before.

No one saw—or shot—any of the big flightless birds. But a red-crested eagle did tear up a soldier's back with its claws and fierce beak. If the man's friend hadn't driven it off with a fallen branch, it probably would have torn out his kidneys. Audubon and other, older, naturalists said honkers were the Atlantean national bird's favorite prey, though people or sheep would do at a pinch. One thing was sure: as honkers had declined, so had red-crested eagles.

As best they could, surgeons patched up the soldier this one had attacked. "Do you think he'll pull through?" Newton asked.

"If the wounds don't fester, he should," one of them answered. Seeing a splash of the soldier's blood on the back of his hand that he hadn't washed away, he spat on it and wiped it off with a rag.

"Not as deep as bullet wounds," his colleague agreed, tossing a scalpel into a tin basin of river water. "Nasty all the same, though. I'm not sorry we've killed most of those damned eagles—I'll tell you that. They're vicious brutes."

"Nothing but vicious brutes in this part of the country," the first surgeon said. He was a tubby man with mutton-chop whiskers that didn't suit the shape of his face. "The eagle, the niggers . . . " By the way he talked, he came from somewhere south of the Stour.

"I wouldn't be surprised if the insurrectionists say the same thing about us," Newton remarked.

"Well, your Excellency, people can say any tomfool thing they please," the surgeon answered. "But saying it doesn't make it so." His chest puffed out like a pouter pigeon's, so that it almost projected beyond his belly. He seemed to think he'd just said something wonderful.

Newton didn't. "As you demonstrate," he replied, and walked away. He felt the rotund surgeon's eyes boring into his back as if they were a red-crested eagle's claws. But the wounds they left behind tore only his imagination.

The army kept pushing ahead against resistance that seemed to fade more with each passing day. Jeremiah Stafford was inclined to gloat. "It may have taken longer than I thought it would at first, but we've finally got the insurrectionists where we want them," he declared.

"Even if we do, have we got the insurrection where we want it?" Newton asked.

Stafford sent him a look he would have been as glad not to have. "What are you going on about now?" the other Consul demanded.

"You know as well as I do," Newton said. "The slaves in Frederick Radcliff's army aren't the only ones in arms. There's fighting wherever men and women are enslaved."

He'd hoped that harsh way of putting things would make Stafford feel guilty, but no such luck. "Once we smash the head, the body will die. You wait and see," Stafford said confidently. "And I think we will smash it, too."

Newton was less sure they wouldn't than he had been a couple of weeks earlier. "How did you manage to, um, inspire Colonel Sinapis?" he asked.

"Trade secret," his colleague said smugly.

"Oh, come on! You sound like a drummer for a patent medicine," Newton said. "When they say their ingredients are a trade secret, they just mean they have more opium than the other fellow's potion does. If you'd put that much poppy juice into the good colonel, he'd be too sleepy to move, let alone fight."

He got a chuckle out of Stafford, anyhow. "Opium isn't the drug I used. I found something stronger."

"I didn't know there was anything," Newton said. "Opium really works, and that's more than you can say for most of the medicines the quacks have."

"Well, yes," Stafford allowed. "But threatening *dear* Colonel Sinapis' reputation turned out to work even better."

Had anyone ever used *dear* as less of an endearment? Consul Newton didn't think so. "What did you do?"

"I told him that if the southern states left the USA because he didn't go after the insurrectionists hard enough, he'd get the blame," Stafford said. "He would, too, by God. Who'd hire him after that?"

"Good question," Newton said slowly. And so it was. Well, a man who was a bad politician—which is to say, a man who didn't understand what made other men tick— wasn't likely to become Consul of the United States of Atlantis. Jeremiah Stafford might often be mistaken (as far as Newton was concerned, Stafford usually was), but that didn't make him a fool.

"I only wish I hadn't needed so long to see which lever to pull," he said now. "The insurrection might be over and done with if I'd figured it out sooner."

"Or we might have blundered into worse trouble than we really did find," Newton said.

"I don't think so." Stafford shook his head. "It's all over but the shouting. The insurrectionists will get what's coming to them, and high time, too."

XVIII

*A*head, to the northeast, Jeremiah Stafford could see the Green Ridge Mountains swelling up against the sky. They loomed taller than they had just a couple of days before. The insurrectionists kept giving ground. For a moment, Stafford almost forgot about the insurrectionists. He'd never dreamt he would see the mountains from this angle—from the back side, to any man who lived east of them, as most Atlanteans did—but here they were.

And here, almost in their rolling foothills, the Negroes and copperskins who'd caused the USA (to say nothing of Jeremiah Stafford in his own person) so much grief were making what had to be their last stand. Stafford had all kinds of reasons for thinking it had to be. If—no, when— the Atlantean army finished smashing them, they surely (please, God!) would be able to fight no more. And Atlantis needed it to be their last stand, too. Because if it wasn't, the army would likely be recalled. Not long after that happened, when it did, if it did, the country would probably start falling apart.

The insurrectionists seemed convinced this was their last chance, too. They'd run up earthworks at the far end of the low, wide valley that led toward the mountains. They might have been challenging the white Atlantean regulars and militiamen. *If you want us, you'll have to dig us out,* their actions said. *And if you try digging us out, you'll have to pay the price.*

Stafford turned to Balthasar Sinapis, who stood near him examining the trenches and ramparts through a spyglass. "How strong are they?" the Consul asked.

"Hard to tell," Colonel Sinapis answered. "The ground rises as you move that way—not much, but some. Enough so I have trouble seeing whatever they may be hiding there."

"It won't be much," Stafford said confidently. "Now that we've started driving them, they haven't been able to slow us down, let alone stop us. Have they?"

He waited. Sinapis couldn't very well do anything but dip his head in assent. The officer also couldn't help adding, "Because they haven't, your Excellency, doesn't mean they can't."

"Devil it doesn't," Stafford retorted. "They're whipped now. They have to know it, too, or they wouldn't hide behind earthworks. We go in, we slaughter them, and there's an end to it." *Let there be an end to it, O Lord!*

"Why are you so sure?" Leland Newton asked. By the way the words came out, he knew the answer as well as Stafford did. *Because this has to be the end. Because the country can't stand any more.*

Stafford didn't say that, not when the other Consul already knew it. He spoke to Sinapis as if Newton hadn't said a word: "They aren't waiting in the bushes to ambush us as we advance. You know they aren't—you ran enough scouts through the bushes."

"I needed to do it, too," the colonel replied with dignity. He waved toward the gently sloping sides of the valley: first to one, then to the other. "This is exactly the sort of terrain they are fond of using for an ambuscade."

"But they didn't, did they?" Stafford said. Colonel Sinapis couldn't very well claim the contrary. Stafford pressed his advantage: "And the reason they didn't is that they're too beaten down, too hard pressed. The foxes may have given us a good chase, but we've run them to earth. Now we'll bury them in it."

"You've always thought we would have an easier time against them than we turned out to," Newton said.

"Yes? And so?" Stafford answered coolly. "As soon as we root them out of their holes here, we've won. You never thought we could do it at all. It may have come later than I wanted, but not too late." *Don't let it be too late!*

If Newton wanted to argue, Stafford was ready. It was his own day to hold final authority, so the arguments didn't matter. But Newton didn't say anything more. As it had been when Caesar crossed the Rubicon, the die was cast.

"Form up the men, Colonel, and send them forward," Stafford told Sinapis. "We've come this far. Let's get it over with."

Sinapis gave back a precise salute. "As you say, your Excellency." He might have been a valet answering a rich Englishman. Then he gave the regular officers and militia commanders their orders. The regulars would follow them. The militiamen might or might not. Sinapis kept them on the wings and in the rear, where any failures ought to matter least.

Bugles blared. The regular soldiers moved to their places like marionettes on strings. The militiamen had improved over the course of this campaign. Despite profane shepherding from their officers and sergeants, they were still slower and sloppier than the men who made their living from war.

But so what? Stafford told himself. *They'll all roll over the insurrectionists, and then we'll glue things back together. We can still do it. I'm sure we can.*

How much work had the insurrectionists put into their earthworks? While they shoveled, one copperskin complained to Frederick Radcliff: "I don't reckon the overseers ever drove us this hard." Then he flung another spadeful of earth up onto the growing rampart in front of their trench.

And Frederick just looked back at him and answered, "Good." When the other man stared, Frederick had condescended to explain: "God-damned overseers never needed you as much as I do now." That seemed to satisfy the copperskin, who went back to digging without another word.

Now Frederick and Lorenzo looked out over the rampart at the white men mustering against them. "We can still do it," Frederick said. "I'm sure we can."

"I hope we can," Lorenzo said. "I hope like anything we can."

Frederick's head swung away from the Atlantean soldiers and toward his own amateur marshal. "You're the one who set this up," he reminded him.

"I know. I know. Now I'm the one who's worrying about it, too—all right?" Lorenzo said. "If it goes wrong, they'll roll over us."

"Ever since the uprising started, we've known that could happen," Frederick said. "As long as we can shoot ourselves or shoot each other before they get their hands on us, we'll be fine."

"Fine?" Lorenzo bared his teeth in something halfway between a smile and a snarl. "Is that what you call it these days? We'll be dead, is what we'll be."

"We've been dead ever since I took the hoe to Matthew and the rest of you followed me back to the big house 'stead of whompin' me to death with your spades," Frederick answered. "You know it as well as I do, too."

"Well . . . yeah." Lorenzo grudged a nod. "Don't mean I got to like it."

"If you liked it, they would've shoveled dirt over you by now. They would've shoveled dirt over us all by now," Frederick said.

Lorenzo stared out at the white soldiers. The discipline with which they formed their ranks was daunting. "It ain't like they've quit trying," the copperskin said.

"I know." Frederick raised his voice so all the fighters in the trench, Negroes and copperskins, men and women, could hear him: "We've got to hold them here. No matter what, we've got to. If they break through this line, we're screwed. So do whatever you can. You want to be free, you want to stay free, you want your children to be free if you've got any—or even if you don't yet—this here may be the place where you can make it real. You ready?"

"Yeah!" The answering shout wasn't so loud as it might have been. The fighters could watch the white men deploying out beyond rifle-musket range, too. It was intimidating. Beyond any possible fragment of doubt, it was meant to be.

A bugle rang out, ordering the Atlantean soldiers and

militiamen forward. The note was pure and sweet, almost like birdsong. Frederick spied a flash of gold that had to be sunlight sparking off the horn's polished bell.

"Here they come," somebody said. After a couple of heartbeats, Frederick realized that was his own voice.

The white men's cannon started roaring. Frederick hated artillery more than anything else—mostly because he'd never figured out how to match it. The white Atlanteans had it; the insurrectionists didn't—they just had to endure it.

In screamed the cannonballs. Some of them flew long. Others thudded into—and sometimes smashed through— the rampart in front of the trenches. A couple of them smashed into fighters after smashing through dirt. Screams rose up. The insurrectionists didn't have much in the way of surgeons. Herb women made poultices to keep wounds from going bad. Men who'd been butchers could lop off shattered limbs. Ether? They hadn't managed to steal any coming up from New Marseille. They relied on rum and thick leather straps to muffle pain.

If the Atlantean artillerists had had guns that could loft shells over the rampart and down into the trench, they would have hurt the insurrectionists worse. They did all they could with what they did have. Frederick thought the cannonading would never end. And, of course, one minute under fire seemed as long as a week of ordinary life, or maybe a year.

But the insurrectionists couldn't cower. They would die if they did. "Up!" Lorenzo yelled, reminding them. "Up and shoot! The more of 'em you shoot before they get close, the fewer you'll have to stick!"

The fewer who can get close and shoot you, he meant. Frederick could see why he didn't care to put it that way. Men who worried about what happened to their own precious flesh wouldn't be inclined to let gunfire come anywhere close to it. Who in his—or her—right mind would be so inclined?

Rifle muskets bellowed. Smoke rose in thick, fireworks-smelling clouds. Here and there, white men fell over— but only here and there. The rest kept coming. The bright morning sun shone off their bayonets, brighter than it had off the bugle but silver instead of gold.

"*Shoot* the bastards!" Lorenzo howled. "Can't let 'em come close, not with the numbers they've got. Kill 'em dead!"

The insurrectionists did their best. By now, they could fire almost as fast as the white regulars. Practice hadn't made regulars of the Negroes and copperskins, but it hadn't missed by much. And they were firing from behind the rampart, so they exposed only their heads and sometimes their shoulders to the white Atlanteans.

Not many of the whites were shooting. The regulars in the center trudged toward the ramparts as if they'd never heard of longarms. Here and there, a militiaman raised his piece to his shoulder and blasted away as he advanced. It wasn't exactly aimed fire, but that didn't exactly matter. With lots of bullets flying around, the law of averages said some wouldn't be wasted.

One cracked past Frederick, close enough so he felt, or thought he felt, the wind of its passage. His knees bent in the involuntary genuflection almost everyone accorded near misses. Fifty feet down the trench, a Negro half his age screeched, jumped in the air, and clapped a hand to his bleeding shoulder.

Whump! A cannon ball slammed into the rampart, throwing up a shower of dirt. The blacks and copperskins it had protected rubbed at their eyes and spat out grit—those who still had enough saliva to spit, anyhow. Those damned fieldpieces kept on pounding away.

"Hurrah!" the regulars shouted as they came closer. "*Hur*rah! *Hur*rah!" Some of the militiamen joined the rhythmic chant. Others howled like dogs baying at the moon or yelled "Honk! Honk!" If real honkers had sounded like that, they'd probably all laughed themselves to death.

For all the fierce and would-be fierce cheers, more and more white men fell as they neared the rebels' strongpoint. The rest of the soldiers leaned forward and slowed down, as if they were walking into a heavy wind. They were brave—hating them, Frederick knew that much too well. But not all the bravery in the world could bring troops up to a rampart if the fire from behind it was hot enough. The insurrectionists could deliver that kind of fire.

Their enemies' officers had seen charges fail before. They must have realized this one was liable to do the same. Almost at the same moment, several of them raised their voices to call out orders. The men obediently halted. You could really *do* things with soldiers like that. Yes, a couple of them fell over, one kicking, another ominously still. The rest of the first rank went to one knee. The second rank crouched above them. The third rank stood straight.

At another shouted command, they delivered a volley. Then they stood up as the next three ranks passed through them and delivered another one. After that, cheering, the regulars resumed their advance.

They hurt Frederick's men. Volleying at another army out in the open, odds were they would have ruined it and left it wide open for a charge. They couldn't bring that off here, no matter how much they must have wanted to. The rampart did its job, saving the insurrectionists untold dead and wounded.

Which might turn out to make no difference. If the regulars and militiamen got over the rampart and broke the defenders behind it, nothing would matter much. "When?" Frederick asked Lorenzo.

"Should be any time now," the copperskin said.

"Better be," Frederick said.

The Negroes and copperskins kept firing at the Atlantean regulars and militiamen. Despite the volleys, the regulars couldn't reach the rampart—not at the first try, anyhow. If they tried again . . . Frederick wanted to ask *When?* again. But he and Lorenzo had done what they could. Now they had to hope they'd done it right.

Consul Newton was getting sick of listening to Consul Stafford gloat about what would happen to the insurrectionists. Stafford cheered as the white Atlanteans came close to storming the low earthen wall Frederick Radcliff's followers had thrown up. "Next time they'll get over!" Stafford exulted. "And then—!" He made two-handed thrusting motions, as if wielding a bayoneted rifle musket.

He'd done that before, too. Newton was also sick of it. When he turned away from the other Consul, he might have been the first white man to spot the Negroes and copperskins coming over the low rise that topped one side of the valley. "Uh-oh," he said.

"Now what are you croaking about?" Stafford demanded. "You sound like a frog in springtime—know that?"

Instead of answering, Newton pointed. Then he looked toward the other valley rim. Insurrectionists were swarming down over that one, too. Somehow, he'd thought they might be.

"Uh-oh," Stafford said. Then, as if impelled by a lodestone, his head swung in the other direction, as Newton's had before it. "Uh-oh," he croaked again.

"Who sounds like a frog now?" Newton couldn't resist the gibe. Truth to tell, he hardly tried. Even when things looked to be coming to pieces, he could enjoy needling his opposite number.

Only trouble was, Stafford didn't notice he was being needled. "They tricked us!" he cried, fury and astonishment warring in his voice.

"I didn't know that wasn't in the rules," Newton answered. Part of him realized he was much too likely to get killed in the next hour. If you were going to die, shouldn't you die with a *bon mot* on your lips? Then again, why should you? You'd be just as dead one way as the other. And all the people who heard your last-minute wit seemed much too likely to end up dead with you. Who would send your cleverness on to your loved ones and to the history books?

The soldiers needed a few seconds longer than the Consuls to see that they were suddenly facing a flank attack. Their attention had been even more strongly focused on the fight in front of them, the fight at the rampart. The insurrectionists must have planned it that way. Jeremiah Stafford was absolutely right—no, dead right. The slaves *had* tricked the professional soldiers.

Now the professionals had to find some way to fix it—if they could. They didn't have long to think things over, either. The insurrectionists were already starting to pour enfilading fire into the militiamen on either wing of the Atlantean army. Bullets aimed at the end of a row of men were much more likely to bite than those aimed from the front.

Colonel Sinapis wasn't usually a demonstrative sort. He started hopping around and waving his arms and shouting like a man possessed—or possibly like a man with his trousers on fire. The artillerists frantically swung their guns toward the brushy, patchily wooded sides of the valley. They started banging away at the Negroes and copperskins on the army's flank.

Artillery was the one arm the Atlantean force had that the rebels lacked. How much good it would do here, though, struck Leland Newton as being open to doubt. The fighters on the slopes were in loose order. Cannonballs couldn't knock them over six or eight at a time, as they could against troops advancing close together over open ground. Maybe Sinapis hoped he could scare the insurrectionists away, or at least scare them into shooting badly. Or maybe—even more worrisome thought—he simply had no better schemes.

That turned out not to be true. He pulled the militiamen away from the assault on the rampart and sent them upslope against the flankers. But that exposed them to enfilading fire from the rebels behind the earthwork. The militiamen showed reckless courage. Many—maybe even most—of them were panting for vengeance against what they saw as their uprisen property.

None of that helped them much. Rifle muskets inflicted more punishment than flesh and blood could bear. Neither militiamen nor regulars had been able to get over the rampart. And the militiamen also weren't able to get in among the rebels on the slopes. They came close. The bodies they left there, marks like those of high tide on a beach, showed how very close they came. Close counted in horseshoes. In war, it sometimes proved worse than not trying at all.

Watching the militiamen reel down the slope, away from the concealed insurrectionists who murdered them one after another, Consul Stafford groaned like a man under the lash. "My God!" he said. "We are ruined—ruined, I tell you, Newton!"

"This whole valley is a killing ground," Newton said, which only put the same thing another way.

"Damn his fumblefingered soul, Sinapis blundered right into it, too," Stafford groaned.

"If he did, you helped push him along," Newton said. "You were bragging that you lit a fire under him. You told me how clever you were, how you got him to move when he might not have wanted to, when you threatened to blame him if Atlantis fell apart because he didn't break the rebellion. Right this minute, the rebellion is breaking us."

Stafford didn't call him a liar. He didn't call him a feebleminded twit, either. If that silence wasn't a telling measure of the other Consul's despair, Newton had no idea what would be.

Up a few hundred yards ahead of them, the regulars rushed the rampart again. If the white Atlanteans could break any part of the trap, they might be able to wreck the whole thing.

If. But muzzle flashes on the rampart spat toward the white men like tongues of fire shot from dragons' mouths. And bullets flew farther than dragonfire ever could. Again, the regulars had to sag back short of their goal.

An officer near Colonel Sinapis was trying to tell him something. The man's knees suddenly gave way. His hat fell off as he sagged to the ground. He wriggled for a little while, but not for long.

"They're murdering us! Murdering!" Stafford said.

"They are." Newton couldn't disagree. He did think the officer was liable to be lucky, as such things went. The poor fellow had died fast, and might not even have known he was hit. Not every man who stopped a bullet had such good fortune. Newton had seen too many ghastly wounds, and too many men suffering from them for too long, to hold any illusions on that score.

"If we can't stop them . . . Good Lord! What will become of the country after this?" Stafford choked out the words, but he did bring them forth. Newton had to respect him for that. Now the other Consul had found his *bon mot* in the face of death. How much good it would do him, and whether anyone hereabouts would survive to remember it tomorrow, were a couple of questions whose answers it seemed better not to contemplate.

Jeremiah Stafford had a bullet, a charge of gunpowder, and a percussion cap ready in each cylinder of his eight-shooter. How much good they'd do him against enemies armed with rifle muskets that far outranged his revolver, he didn't care to think about.

He and Consul Newton both went up to huddle close to the rear of the regular contingent. Maybe misery loved company. Maybe that was the safest place to be in these parts, not that any place in these parts counted as particularly safe, not if you were a white man.

Newton's accusation burned like vitriol inside Stafford's soul. Stafford *had* pushed Balthasar Sinapis as hard as he could. He *had* made the colonel go forward where Sinapis would have hesitated or even halted on his own. It *had* worked—up till now.

Up till now. Three of the most mournful and miserable words in the English language.

Then Stafford stopped thinking of mourning and misery in the abstract. A lieutenant about twenty feet away from him cried out, twisted an arm to try to clutch at the small of his back, and slowly crumpled to his knees and then to the ground.

A moment later, a private soldier went down, also shot in the back. Again, Newton realized what was going on before Stafford did. Newton didn't automatically assume the insurrectionists were stupid. "They've got men behind us, too," he said glumly.

And they did. The copperskins and blacks back there had done some quick, rough entrenching before they opened up on the white Atlanteans. No one had tried to stop them. No one had even noticed them till they started shooting. They could shoot at the whites with almost as much protection as the insurrectionists behind the ramparts had. And now they'd surrounded the whites.

A classical education came in handy all kinds of ways.

Even in this moment of despair, Stafford knew just what he and his comrades were facing. It wasn't as if such things hadn't happened before, even if that disaster might have stayed unmatched for two thousand years and more.

"Cannae!" Stafford groaned. "This is another Cannae!"

Hannibal had surrounded and slaughtered several Roman legions at Cannae during the Second Punic War. The battle was the Carthaginian's masterpiece. It was about as good a job as any general could do. And here, on a smaller scale, Frederick Radcliff had just re-created it.

Of course, Carthage didn't win the Second Punic War. But right at the moment, Jeremiah Stafford had no idea how the United States of Atlantis could hope to put down this great servile insurrection.

By the way things looked, neither did Colonel Sinapis. He turned to stare at the rebels firing on his men from behind. He raised his hands in horror. They seemed to fall limply back to his sides all by themselves.

He doesn't know whether to shit or go blind, Stafford thought. He hadn't heard the vulgar phrase in years, but he'd never known a time when it fit so well.

"Pull yourself together!" he shouted to Sinapis. "We've got to do something!"

"Something, yes, your Excellency, but what?" the colonel answered. "They have us in a modern Cannae."

So his classical training still worked, too, did it? Nice that something did, even if his generalship had let him—and everyone else—down. "Pull yourself together!" Stafford repeated. "Don't despair of the republic!"

Sinapis didn't answer. Maybe he wasn't despairing of the republic, but of his career. Stafford didn't know how he'd save that. Stafford didn't know how to save his own career, either, assuming he could get his own life spared.

Even then, the *non sequitur* made him laugh. *If you don't live through this, what happens in your career afterwards won't matter one whole hell of a lot*, he thought.

Bullets from all directions were flying around him now. He didn't know which way to duck. He did notice that Consul Newton and even Colonel Sinapis (whose courage was irreproachable, whatever one might say about other aspects of his military persona) also ducked at near misses. A few people, maybe the ones born without nerves, lacked that reflex, but only a few.

As Newton straightened, he touched the brim of his cap to Stafford. "Well, Jeremiah, I don't suppose you expected things to end up this way. I'd be lying if I told you I expected them to."

"I daresay you're happier about it than I am," Stafford answered. "Here's nigger equality, all right, and it will be the death of both of us."

"I don't want to die. I have too many things I still want to do," the other Consul said. "Trouble is, what I want doesn't matter right this minute."

"I blame it on Victor Radcliff," Stafford said. "Even diluted, his blood is better than the vinegar and horse piss in Sinapis' veins."

"As far as I know, the insurrectionists' number-one soldier, that Lorenzo, is pure copperskin," Newton said. "Will you tell me his blood is better than Sinapis', too?"

"Damned right, I will," Stafford answered. "My parrot could have done a better job leading this campaign than that stupid foreigner did—and I haven't got a parrot."

"Heh," Newton said—about as much laughter as the joke deserved.

In front of them, the Atlantean soldiers milled like ants stirred by a stick. Every time they turned any one way, they got shot at from the flank and behind as well as from the front. They weren't dying like ants, though. They were dying like flies.

The Negroes and copperskins didn't try to close with them. Why should they? They were doing fine carving up the white Atlanteans at a distance. Even as Stafford watched, the back of a militiaman's head exploded, the way a melon might after a sledgehammer came down on it. The man's rifle musket fell from fingers that could hold it no more. His knees buckled. He went down, and wouldn't rise again till Judgment Day.

Most of the militiamen owned slaves. How many of them would be left alive by the time this fight finished? Ironically, Stafford began to hope the insurrectionists made the massacre complete. That might horrify Atlantis into fighting the war seriously. If it did, the whites would win in the end. As Newton had pointed out, winning might entail making sure not a nigger or mudface remained aboveground and on his feet. That would play hob with the long-cherished social system south of the Stour.

Jeremiah Stafford found he didn't care. One way or another, the USA would sort things out. The Free Republic of Atlantis? That was an abomination, and had to be suppressed no matter what.

If I'm going to die, I may as well die usefully, he thought. He couldn't believe anything short of a massacre would galvanize the Senate and the people of Atlantis into giving the insurrectionists what they deserved. And, for the life of him—no, for the death of him—he couldn't see how the Atlantean regulars and militiamen had any chance of stopping a massacre.

Usefully, he thought again, and hoped it wouldn't hurt . . . too much.

"In the sack!" Lorenzo howled exultantly. "We've got the sons of bitches in the sack, and we just tied off the top. They can't even run away now. They're ours! Ours!—you hear me?"

"I hear you," Frederick Radcliff answered. "Looks to me like you're right. This went better than I ever dreamt it could." He'd wanted to surprise the white Atlanteans. He'd wanted to hurt them, too. To succeed beyond your wildest dreams . . . By the nature of things, you couldn't possibly expect that.

"All we've got to do is keep going now." Lorenzo mimed aiming, shooting, and reloading. "Before too long, won't be none of those white bastards left alive. Extra sweet blowing holes in the militiamen. The soldiers . . . They're just here working, you know? I don't have anything special against 'em."

"Except that they're trying to kill us." Frederick's voice was dry.

"Yeah. Except for that," Lorenzo agreed seriously. Then he came back to his favorite theme: "The militiamen, they're mostly out there on account of they wanted to get their property back. Turn us into slaves again, that means. Well, I got some news for them—it ain't gonna happen."

"Sure won't," Frederick said. The militiamen seemed to be falling even faster than the Atlantean regulars.

"Serves 'em right, too," Lorenzo said. "I want to kill 'em all, is what I want to do. And I reckon maybe we can do it, too."

"So do I," Frederick said. He never would have dreamt of *that* when the insurrection started, either. His dreams along those lines had been nightmares, almost without exception: nightmares of Atlantean regulars smashing through the rebels, shooting them, bayoneting them, hanging them, tormenting them in as many ways as his sleep-filled imagination could find. And it had proved ingenious in ways he never would have come up with awake. He hoped he wouldn't have, anyway.

"You know what'll happen when word of what we done gets to New Hastings?" Lorenzo said. "White folks'll shit, that's what!"

Frederick nodded gravely. "They sure will." Then he found a question Lorenzo hadn't yet: "And what happens once they get done shitting?"

"Huh?" The copperskin didn't even see that it *was* a question. "Who the devil cares what happens then?"

"We'd better," Frederick answered. What *would* the government of the United States of Atlantis do after a ragtag force of rebellious slaves slaughtered its professional soldiers and the white, mostly prosperous militiamen who fought beside those professionals?

Maybe the government would throw its hands in the air and decide the Free Republic of Atlantis was too strong to be put down. Maybe it would realize that blacks and copperskins were just as entitled to freedom as white men were. Maybe the government was looking for any reasonable excuse to liberate the men and women who'd labored in bondage for generations.

Maybe. But the more Frederick Radcliff thought about it, the less he believed it. The insurrectionists clearly could wipe this trapped force of white men off the face of the earth. Suppose they did. When word of the massacre got to New Hastings, wouldn't it infuriate the Senate? Wouldn't the Conscript Fathers decide the rebellion truly was dangerous? Wouldn't all the whites in Atlantis decide the same thing, regardless of whether they lived in Gernika or Penzance?

And if all the whites decided the insurrection was dangerous, what would happen next? Atlantis held many more whites than Negroes and copperskins. As much to the point, or maybe even more, those whites held far more wealth than their colored counterparts. If they decided they had to kill everyone in Atlantis who wasn't white so they could feel safe in their own beds, would they be able to do it?

No sooner asked than answered: of course they could. It might not be easy or quick or cheap, but they could do it. Frederick was sure of that. They might even feel bad about it afterwards, but afterwards would be too late to do anybody colored any good. Frederick was also sure of *that*.

Which meant . . . what? That slaughtering this trapped army might be the worst thing the insurrectionists could do? So it seemed to Frederick. One other thing also seemed all too plain: *not* slaughtering this trapped army had to be the second worst thing the insurrectionists could do.

"Lorenzo," he said.

"What d'you want?" the copperskin answered. "We've *got* these assholes. We've got 'em right where they belong."

Frederick explained what he wanted. He explained why he wanted it. Explaining made him more miserable, not happier. All the same, he finished, "We can't kill 'em all. We don't dare. Now that we've got 'em where we want 'em, we need to use that to get what we want. But we've got to call the cease-fire before they're all down."

Lorenzo spat in the dirt where the insurrectionists had dug their trench. "Then *you* go down and take a white flag and talk to the white folks. You done great stuff, Fred, but I will see you in hell before I do that here."

"All right. I will." Frederick didn't sound thrilled, but he nodded. Fair was fair.

"And what happens when the white sons of bitches

shoot you down like a hound even though you got that white flag?" No, Lorenzo didn't bother hiding his scorn.

"Get our men to stop shooting. I'll go down there. If the buckra kill me, go ahead and do what you want to them," Frederick answered. "You will anyway—and I won't be around to stop you."

"Damned straight you won't," Lorenzo muttered. He aimed a forefinger at Frederick's chest like a rifle musket. "You nigger bastard, you better be right. You fuck this up, nobody'll ever forgive you."

"Now tell me something I didn't know," Frederick said.

Slowly, the gunfire died away. Frederick scrambled up over the rampart and advanced on the whites armed with only a flag of truce. He wondered if one of his own people would shoot him in the back. That might almost be a relief.

XIX

*W*hen the firing from all around the white army slackened, sudden crazy hope flowered in Jeremiah Stafford. Maybe the insurrectionists were running out of ammunition! Maybe the whites could snatch victory from what had looked like sure disaster. Maybe . . .

Maybe Stafford was building castles in the air. That seemed much more likely when a stocky, middle-aged Negro scrambled none too gracefully over the rampart with a big white flag. The man held it up as he came toward the surviving whites.

"Boy, if he wants to parley, I'd talk till the cows come home," a soldier not far from Stafford said. "They can murder every fuckin' one of us, and they don't got to sweat real hard to do it, neither."

That was an inelegant way of summing up the situation, which didn't mean it wasn't true. Now that the shooting had paused, the moans and howls and shrieks of the wounded took center stage. Stafford wished a man could close his ears to shut out dreadful noises, the way he could close his eyes so he didn't have to see dreadful sights.

Colonel Sinapis limped back to the two Consuls. A blood-soaked bandage was wrapped around his left calf; he carried a stick in his right hand in place of his sword. Dipping his head to Stafford and Newton in turn, he said, "If

they wish to treat with us, your Excellencies, I must recommend that we do so. However much I regret to say so, we
are in no position to resist them."

"That does seem to be the case, doesn't it?" Leland
Newton was doing his best to stay calm: an admirable sentiment, as far as it went.

He and Sinapis both eyed Consul Stafford. "If Satan
wanted to talk to me right now, I do believe I listen respectfully," Stafford said. "That nigger there isn't the Devil—not
quite—but I'll hear him out."

"Thank you, your Excellency." Sinapis' voice seldom
showed much. But if he wasn't relieved right this minute,
Stafford had never heard anyone who was.

All the soldiers seemed glad the insurrectionists weren't
shooting any more. The regulars and militiamen also ceased
fire. Stafford saw a couple of them doff their hats to the Negro as he approached. Even without orders, some regulars
formed an escort for him and led him back to the Consuls
and Colonel Sinapis.

Stafford fought down the impulse to salute the rebels'
spokesman. Yes, the Consul was glad to be alive—and even
gladder he might stay that way a while longer. In lieu of the
salute, he asked, "Who are you?"

"My name is Frederick Radcliff." The Negro didn't
sound like a university man, but neither did he sound as
ignorant as many of his fellow slaves. Under dark, heavy
brows, his eyes flashed. "And who are *you*, friend?"

I am no friend of yours, Stafford thought, even as he gave
his own name. He studied the black man's face, searching
for traces of his illustrious grandfather. He didn't need long
to find them, either. The nose, the line of the jaw, the shape
of this Radcliff's ears . . . Yes, he did have a white ancestor,
and Stafford was willing to believe it was the man from
whose line he claimed to spring.

Consul Newton also introduced himself. Then he asked,
"Well, Mr. Radcliff, what do you want from us?"

The Negro eyed him with scant liking. "You ever call a
black man 'Mister' before?" he asked.

"Yes. There is legal equality in Croydon." Newton hesitated, then added, "I haven't done it very often, though."

Stafford wondered whether that would do more harm than good. Had someone admitted something like that to him, he wouldn't have liked it much. But Frederick Radcliff only grunted thoughtfully. "Well, maybe you'll talk straight to me," he muttered, before rounding on Stafford again. "How about you?"

"I doubt it," Stafford answered. Had he thought Radcliff would believe a lie, he would have tried one. But if the black man had the faintest notion of who he was and where he came from, a lie would prove worse than useless. Better not to trot one out where that was so.

Frederick Radcliff grunted again. "You don't reckon I'm dumb enough to believe any old story, anyways. That's somethin'." He waved back to the rampart from which he'd come, then to the sloping sides of the valley, and last of all to the insurrectionists who'd been pouring bullets into the white Atlanteans from behind. "You know we've got you. You can't hardly *not* know we've got you."

Both Stafford and Newton looked to Balthasar Sinapis. They weren't about to admit they could recognize military defeat—no, military catastrophe. That was what a colonel was for. Sinapis made a steeple of his fingertips. "The present situation is difficult," he allowed, which had to be the understatement of the year.

"Difficult, nothing." This time, Victor Radcliff's grandson didn't grunt—he snorted in fine derision. "If I wave my hand, you're all dead."

"If you think you would live more than a heartbeat after you did that, you're wrong," Stafford said.

"Oh, I know," the Negro answered easily. "As long as I have some other choice, I won't do it. If I don't . . . " He shrugged.

"If you think murdering all of us will help your cause, you may be making a mistake," Stafford told him.

"Yeah. I figured that out, too," said the Tribune of the Free Republic of Atlantis. Stafford had long been convinced Negroes had less in the way of wits than white men did. Dealing with Frederick Radcliff made him wonder, however little he wanted to. The leader of the insurrection nodded back toward the rampart.

"Lorenzo, he hasn't worked it through yet. He trusts me, but he doesn't see it for his own self. He wants you folks dead."

So you'd better deal with me. The Negro didn't say it, but it hung in the air nonetheless. Yes, he was a man of parts, all right.

Leland Newton said, "You wouldn't have come out unless you had something in mind besides killing us all."

"Think so, do you?" Frederick Radcliff had a very unpleasant grin. "Better not give me a hard time, or you're liable to find out you're wrong."

Colonel Sinapis stirred. "You have the air of a man who is about to demand a surrender and ready to put forth the terms on which he will accept it."

"That is just what I am, Colonel," the Negro said. "If you say yes, you get away with your lives. If you say no, we will wipe you out and then see what troubles jump up because we did. Up to you."

"Before we say yes or no, we had better find out what you are asking," Consul Stafford said.

Frederick Radcliff fixed him with a glare. "I am not asking one single, God-damned thing. I am telling you how it will be. If you don't like it, it's your funeral. Yes, sir, that's exactly what it is."

"If your terms are completely unacceptable, we can go on with the fight," Stafford said. Colonel Sinapis' horrified expression warned him they could do no such thing. Stafford pretended not to see it as he continued, "You may kill us, but we're liable to ruin your army while you're doing it."

"In your dreams, Stafford," Frederick Radcliff said. The Consul didn't think he'd ever had a colored man fail to give him his proper titles of respect before. He knew what he could do about it here: nothing. It rankled regardless.

"The terms," Consul Newton said.

"Right." The insurrectionists' leader seemed to remind himself that was why he'd come forth to talk with his enemies. "Terms. You can have your lives, and that's it. Give up all your rifle muskets and pistols. Give up all your artillery. Give up all your ammunition. Give up all your horses, too, except the ones you'll need for the wagons that haul your wounded. Then march away to New Marseille, and don't you ever come back again."

"That's outrageous!" Stafford exclaimed. "Once you have all our weapons, what's to stop you from starting the massacre again when we can't fight back?"

"Nothing," Frederick Radcliff answered. "If you'd licked us, we would've had to take whatever mercy you felt like giving us—and there wouldn't've been much, would there? Well, now the shoe's on the other foot, so see how you like it."

Consul Stafford liked it not at all. He took Newton and Colonel Sinapis aside to see how they felt about it. "What choice have we?" Sinapis asked bleakly, the wails from the wounded underscoring his words. "They can go back to killing us whenever they please."

"I don't believe they would violate the terms once made," Newton added. "They don't want to make themselves infamous in the eyes of Atlantis as a whole."

"You hope they don't," Stafford said.

"Yes." The other Consul nodded. "I hope."

They stopped talking. They didn't seem to have much else to say. When they turned back to Frederick Radcliff, he asked, "Well? What's it going to be?"—which made things no easier.

Consuls and colonel all looked at one another. Nobody wanted to say the fateful words. But someone had to. After a long, painful moment, Colonel Sinapis took the duty on himself. "We agree," he said, and then, sensing that that by itself wasn't enough, "We surrender."

When Cornwallis' troops surrendered to Victor Radcliff, their band played a tune called "The World Turned Upside Down." No bands played here, but the idea stayed with Leland Newton all the same.

Insurrectionists had come out to make sure the white militiamen and regulars held to the terms of the surrender Frederick Radcliff had imposed on Newton, Stafford, and Sinapis. Most of the Negroes and copperskins, though, stayed under cover. If the whites didn't go along, the rebels could always open fire again.

Once officers convinced the regulars that the insurrectionists would also abide by those terms, the professional soldiers were willing enough—even happy enough—to stack their rifle muskets and pile up leather cartridge boxes below them. The artillerists drove spikes into the touchholes on their fieldpieces, but nothing in the surrender terms said they couldn't. Frederick and Lorenzo hadn't thought of it, so the rebels would do without cannon a while longer.

That wasn't the truce's real danger point. Persuading the militiamen to hand over their guns was. The militiamen hated and feared their opponents much more than the regulars did. Many regulars, after all, came from north of the Stour; they might well be personally opposed to slavery. All the militiamen favored it. They all hated the idea that the insurrectionists might win freedom on the battlefield, and they all feared—no doubt with reason—that their former chattels might seek vengeance as soon as they caught their white foes unarmed.

Newton had to admit that Jeremiah Stafford did what he could to calm their fear, even if he was also bound to feel it himself. "They'll let us go," Stafford said, over and over again. "They'd be idiots if they did anything else."

"Damned right they're idiots!" a militiaman burst out. "Copperskins and mudfaces can't hardly be anything but!"

"Since we're stuck in their blamed trap, what does that make us?" Stafford inquired dryly. The militiaman blinked. That didn't seem to have occurred to him. Maybe he really was an idiot.

Hiding a rifle musket was next to impossible. When tipped with a two-foot bayonet, the weapon was taller than a man. Even without a bayonet, you couldn't very well stick one up your sleeve or down your trouser leg. Pistols—eight-shooters and old-style pepperboxes and even older flintlocks—were a different story.

"Not the end of the world, your Excellency," Colonel Sinapis said when Newton remarked on it. "Some of our men will be able to protect themselves from robbers or shoot game for the pot. You cannot make war with pistols, not against rifle muskets."

"I see the sense in that," Newton replied. "But will the insurrectionists? Or will they use a few holdout pistols as an excuse to treat our men more harshly than they would have otherwise?"

Sinapis' smile tugged up the corners of his mouth without reaching his eyes. "You think of such things, your Excellency. So do I, coming out of the cynical school of Europe. But that ploy never occurred to Frederick Radcliff or even to Lorenzo, who is less naive than the black man. When I mentioned it, they both promised they would not take it amiss, as long as the militiamen do not try anything foolish."

"That's good news." Newton tempered the remark by adding, "I hope so, anyhow."

"As do I," Sinapis agreed. "A few hotheads could greatly embarrass us by doing the wrong thing at the wrong time. I would not be sorry if the rebels made an example of them. I fear I would be sorry if those people made an example of all of us."

"Sorry. Yes." Consul Newton left it right there. The more rifle muskets went up in neat stacks of six, the more vulnerable the white survivors became. One thing was clear: even if the fighting continued after this disastrous battle, the insurrectionists would not lack guns, cartridges, or percussion caps for a long time to come.

Here and there, blacks or copperskins robbed disarmed white soldiers. A handful of militiamen—no regulars—died suddenly. Maybe they refused to take orders from men they still thought of as natural inferiors. Maybe slaves recognized owners they hadn't loved. Leland Newton found himself in a poor position to ask too many questions.

The whites started back toward New Marseille the next morning. They hadn't been able to bury all their dead. They had to rely on promises that the insurrectionists would see to it. And what were those promises worth? Anything? Newton had no idea.

He also had other, more immediate, worries. He kept looking back over his shoulder. If the Negroes and copperskins came swarming after the defeated Atlantean soldiers, what could the white men do? *Die*, Newton thought.

Stafford also kept looking over his shoulder. *Nervous, are you?* Newton couldn't twit him about it, not when he was nervous himself.

Some of the rebels, still carrying weapons, walked along beside the soldiers who'd surrendered. Newton didn't see anyone prominent. Frederick Radcliff wasn't coming along. Neither was Lorenzo. They had more important things to do with their time. *Probably taking charge of gathering up the loot,* Newton thought. Both the Tribune and his marshal were bound to think that was the most important thing they could do right now.

"Well," Stafford said, "we'll be marching like a couple of privates from the regulars by the time we get back to New Marseille."

"So we will. I know I'm in better shape than I was when I got on the train in New Hastings," Newton answered.

"So am I—here." Consul Stafford brushed his leg with the palm of his hand. "But here . . . ?" He brought his hand up to his heart for a moment, then sadly shook his head. "Everything I ever believed in is coming to pieces."

"Everything outside of church, you mean," Newton said.

"No. Everything." Stafford shook his head again. "I always truly thought it was God's will that whites should rule over niggers and mudfaces. Hell's bells, man, I still want to think so."

"The evidence would appear to be against you," Newton said carefully.

"Yes. It would. And I don't like that for beans." Stafford's voice was cold as an iceberg drifting past North Cape in dead of winter. "Maybe God has changed His mind about the way things work—the way they ought to work, I should say. And if He has, then we're all worse sinners than I ever thought we could be. That's pretty bad, too, believe me."

"I don't know anything about that. I leave God to the preachers. Taking care of myself seems hard enough most of the time," Newton said.

He won a thin chuckle from the other Consul. "It does, doesn't it? So you say you want to leave God to the Preacher? I didn't know you'd taken up with the House of Universal Devotion."

"That's not what I said, and you know it damned well."
A touch of irritation came into Leland Newton's voice.
No educated Atlantean could take the Preacher—even
when he got called the Reverend—or the House of Universal Devotion seriously. Atlantis had spawned its share
of sects and then some. That no educated man could take
the House of Universal Devotion seriously hadn't kept it
from becoming one of the more successful and prosperous
of those sects. No one had ever gone broke betting against
the ordinary fellow's good sense.

"All right." For once, Stafford didn't seem to feel like
arguing—or not about that, anyhow. He did have other
worries: "What do you suppose they'll do to us once we get
back to New Marseille and word of what happened here
gets to New Hastings?"

"I don't know," Newton answered. "Maybe they'll decide we were a pack of fools and send out a new army to
take a shot at the insurrection. Or maybe they'll try to turn
this cease-fire into a real peace. If they do that, we're the
people on the spot."

"On the spot is right." The prospect failed to delight
Stafford. "Make peace? I wanted to kill them all! Sweet,
suffering Jesus, but I still do!"

"I want all kinds of things I'm not likely to get. No matter how well I'm marching now, a carriage would be nice,
wouldn't it?" Consul Newton tramped on for a while. He
wondered what would happen if he wore through the soles
of his shoes before he got back to New Marseille. *You'll
start wearing through the soles of your feet, that's what.* After a furlong or so, he said, "That Frederick Radcliff is a
piece of work, isn't he?"

Jeremiah Stafford made a horrible face. "Oh, just a
little!" he answered. "Yes, sir, just a little. He's a chip off
Victor's block. I don't suppose anyone who ever met him
would tell you anything different."

"I expect his owner might have," Newton remarked.

"Yes, I expect the poor bastard might—and much good
it would have done him," Stafford said. "Long odds that
he's dead now. I wonder what he did to deserve it. I wonder
if he did anything."

"Some would say you deserve whatever happens to you if you buy and sell other people," Newton said.

"Some would say all kinds of damnfool things so they can fan themselves with their flapping jaws." Stafford used a flint-and-steel lighter to get a cheroot going. He tried to blow a smoke ring, but didn't have much luck.

"Frederick Radcliff . . ." Newton tried to bring things back to what he wanted to talk about: "If he were his grandfather's legitimate descendant, chances are he'd be Consul today instead of one of us. He knows his onions, no two ways about it."

"Onions," Stafford echoed disdainfully. "I half wish he would have killed us all. That would have set the country going in the right direction, anyhow. This way . . . It's humiliating, to know the damned insurrectionists could have killed you but decided not to on account of politics."

"In theory, I can see that," Newton said. "In theory."

"Reminds me of the Caudine Forks," Stafford continued, as if he hadn't spoken. Back even before the battle of Cannae, the Samnites had beaten a Roman army there and made the defeated soldiers pass under a slave's yoke before letting them go. Sharing a classical education with the other Consul, Newton understood the allusion. "Humiliating," Stafford repeated.

"It could be so," Newton agreed.

"Could be! My dear fellow—"

"It could be," Newton repeated, more forcefully this time. "But whether it is or not, I'm still damned glad to be alive. This way, at least I have a chance to sort things out later. If I were dead, I don't know how I'd manage that. Do you?"

Stafford opened his mouth. Then he closed it again. Newton had tried any number of things without obtaining that desirable result. He cherished it now that he finally had it.

Lorenzo admired the rifle muskets and the cartridge pouches and all the other impedimenta of war the white Atlanteans had to leave behind for their long march back to New Marseille—and their even longer march into disgrace. "Will you look at this shit?" the copperskin crooned. "Will you just fucking look at it?"

"I am looking at it," Frederick Radcliff answered. "Believe me, I like it as much as you do."

"You've got to go some to do that," Lorenzo said. Frederick believed him; Lorenzo might not have paid such careful, loving attention to a beautiful woman dancing naked before him. "We've even got cannon," he added.

"Can't do anything with 'em," Frederick said. "Now I know why people talk about spiking somebody's guns."

Lorenzo waved that aside. "We'll fix 'em. Won't take too long, neither, I bet. And even if we don't, so what? Damned white folks won't be able to shoot 'em at us."

"Yeah." Frederick had no trouble sounding enthusiastic about that. He'd never found anything he liked less than trying to stay nonchalant while roundshot screamed by. But, like most slaves, he had no trouble seeing the clouds that darkened silver linings. "Trouble is, these are the onliest cannons we've got. The damned buckra can go and pull more out of their assholes any time they please. It's the same deal as percussion caps—they can make 'em, and we can't."

"Won't have to worry about percussion caps for a hell of a long time, not after all the ones we took," Lorenzo said. Frederick wondered whether he'd missed the point. A moment later, Lorenzo proved he hadn't: "I bet some of our blacksmiths could make cannon if they set their minds to it."

"Maybe." If Frederick didn't sound convinced, it was only because he wasn't. "Sure wouldn't want to stand behind one the first time some poor damned fool fired it."

"Use a long fuse the first time," Lorenzo said. "After that, though . . . Hell, these guns the white folks make blow up every once in a while. Chance you take when you join the artillery."

"Reckon so," Frederick said. "With luck, though, won't be anybody shooting for a while now. Maybe the shooting's over. I hope so. Jesus! Do I ever!"

"Oh, I hope so, too. Doesn't mean I won't stay ready to fight," the copperskin answered. "White folks are likely

too muleheaded to quit just on account of we licked 'em
once. That's why I was so surprised you let 'em go when we
could've hurt 'em a lot worse'n we did."

"If they want to beat us bad enough, they can. They got
to decide to spend the money and spend the men, but we're
whipped if they do," Frederick said. "What we've got to do
is, we've got to make 'em decide not to do that stuff. If we
scare 'em too much, we're dead. It will take a while, but
we're dead. We've got to make 'em think, *These niggers and
mudfaces ain't so bad. Fighting them is more trouble than
it's worth. We let 'em go free, after a while they'll be just like
anybody else.*"

"Fuck 'em," Lorenzo said. "I don't want to act like Master Barford did, puttin' on airs like the fat fool he was."

"Not what I meant," Frederick said. "We got to make
'em figure we'll be peaceable once we're free. If they
reckon we'll keep on stealin' and burnin' and killin', they
won't give in no matter what."

Quite a few insurrectionists had found they liked the
outlaw life. That would cause trouble when peace came—if
it ever did. *One more thing to worry about later*, Frederick
thought. *First we've got to get peace.*

Negroes and copperskins and captured white soldiers
who weren't badly wounded dug long trenches in which to
bury the Atlantean regulars who'd died trying to get over
the rampart and up the gently sloping sides of the valley.
The stench of blood and shit and fear that hung over any
new battlefield was beginning to go off, to change to the
spoiled-meat stink that announced what the flesh was heir
to. The fight was only one day past; in the humid heat of
Atlantis' southwest, nothing stayed fresh for long.

"Good to get them underground," Frederick said.

"Sure is," Lorenzo answered. "And you'd best believe
our boys and girls'll go through their pockets one more
time, make damned sure nobody goes into a hole in the
ground while he's still got anything anyone can use."

"That's the way it ought to be," Frederick said. His fighters had already plundered the battlefield. Plenty of them
wore boots and socks that had graced white soldiers who
didn't need them any more. (Some of the white prisoners

walked around barefoot, too. If a man with a rifle musket wanted what you wore on your feet, would you tell him no?) Some of the copperskins and Negroes sported trousers or belts or tunics they hadn't owned a couple of days earlier. Some of the clothes were still bloodstained. Soaking them in cold water would get rid of most of those sinister marks.

Two copperskins led a skinny white man up to Frederick. One of them said, "This fella says he's a preacherman. He wants to say a prayer over the dead white men once they go in the graves."

"Oh, he does?" Frederick eyed the volunteer minister. "You ain't gonna do nothin' stupid, are you?"

"I hope not," the skinny man answered. "What do you mean, stupid?"

"Goin' on about how white folks're better than niggers and mudfaces, for instance," Frederick said. "Or about how they're sure to go to heaven 'cause they were fighting on God's side. You come out with shit like that, you're gonna end up *in* one of those trenches, not preachin' over it."

"That'd be just what you got coming, too, for bein' a fool," Lorenzo put in.

"I was going to recite the Twenty-third Psalm and the Lord's Prayer," the white man said. "I don't see how that can offend anybody."

Frederick thought about it, then nodded. "All right. Fair enough. Long as you stick to those, you can talk. I don't know that it'll do the white folks any good, but I don't see how it'll hurt, either."

His lack of zeal seemed to offend the would-be preacher, but the man had the sense not to open his mouth about it—a good thing, too. Lorenzo said, "As long as you stick to that kind of stuff, you won't get our fighters mad at you, neither. You do, it's the last dumb mistake you'll ever make."

"I understand," the prisoner said.

"You better," Frederick warned.

Most of the white captives turned out to hear the memorial service for their fallen friends. So did some of Frederick's Negroes and copperskins—more than he'd expected, really. One of the most successful tools whites had used to hold their slaves in line was a religion where God came down to earth as a white man. Frederick had taken years to realize that was what was going on. In spite of realizing it, he still thought of himself as a Christian more often than not. A lot of his fighters evidently felt the same way.

Still in a dirty gray uniform, the preacher stood in front of one of the filled-in trenches that scarred the meadow. Looking out over his audience, he said, "Let us pray."

Whites, blacks, and copperskins bowed their heads. Some of them clasped their hands or pressed palms together. As he'd promised, the preacher recited the Lord's Prayer and the Twenty-third Psalm. Everybody knew those. If you were going to draw comfort from a prayer, you'd find it in one or both of them.

Frederick thought the man would stop there. Had he stopped, he would have done well enough in an ordinary way. Instead, the fellow looked out over his audience and went on, "These soldiers gave their last full measure of devotion fighting for their country. And they will be repaid, for the House of God is a House of Universal Devotion, one where those who believe truly shall be made glad throughout all eternity—not just some eternity, mind you, but all of it!"

"What kind of shit is he going on about now?" Lorenzo asked.

All Frederick said was, "Uh-oh." He knew what the preacher was going on about. The House of Universal Devotion hadn't attracted many slaves, but he'd heard of it. He thought the Preacher and his followers were a flock of loons.

He wasn't the only one who did, either. A white prisoner threw a clod of dirt at the man preaching over the graves. "Shut your lying mouth!" the prisoner yelled.

"That's right!" another white man shouted. "The House of Universal Devotion is the doorway to hell!"

"Liar!" yet another captive said. "God talks to the Preacher, and the Preacher tells his people the truth!"

The preacher—without a capital letter ornamenting his calling—standing by the mass grave tried to go on, but his audience didn't want to listen to him any more. The white prisoners shook their fists at one another and bawled out curses and catcalls. They might have started brawling if not for the bemused insurrectionists standing guard over them.

"White folks are crazy. Crazy, I tell you." Lorenzo spoke with great sincerity. "Only one who cares which church you go to ought to be God. He's the only one with the answers, anyways."

"Of course white folks are crazy," Frederick answered. "They reckon they can keep slaves and keep 'em like beasts, and they reckon God loves 'em. You believe both those things at the same time, you got to be nuts."

"Yeah. Hadn't looked at it like that, but yeah." Lorenzo pointed at the angry prisoners. "What are we gonna do about those sorry bastards?"

"Long as they're just yelling, it doesn't hurt anybody. It's like a waddayacallit—a safety valve—on a steam engine," Frederick said. "They blow off steam against each other, they won't give us so much trouble."

One of the white men chose that moment to decide he didn't care whether the Negroes and copperskins were carrying guns. Full of crusading zeal, he decked another white who presumed to hold an opinion different from his about the House of Universal Devotion. A few seconds later, another enthusiast flattened the first fellow who'd used fists to make his point.

Frederick drew his eight-shooter and fired a round into the air. Nothing got people's instant, undivided attention like a gunshot. Christians who'd been about to swing on their fellow Christians suddenly had second thoughts.

"That will be enough of that," Frederick said into the pool of silence that spread as the echoes of the shot died away. "What you think about God is your business. When you punch somebody in the nose on account of what *he* thinks about God, that's my business. You leave other folks alone, and hope like hell they leave you alone, too. You start acting like mad dogs, you get what mad dogs deserve." Whites called slaves who dared rebel mad dogs. Frederick enjoyed throwing the phrase back in their faces. He pulled the trigger again. Another tongue of flame spat from the revolver's muzzle.

To his amazement, some of the prisoners wanted to argue with him. "I'm trying to save that ignorant fool's soul from hell," one white protested earnestly.

"He reckons you're headed that way yourself," Frederick answered. "What makes you so sure you're right and he's wrong?"

"Why, the Bible says so," the white man replied, as if to a fool.

"Suppose he reads it some different way? Or suppose he doesn't care about it at all?"

"Then he's surely bound for hell. And you'd better look to your own soul, too." The captive edged away from Frederick, as if afraid God would strike the Negro dead for presuming to ask such questions—and might singe him, too, if he stayed too near.

"I will. I do. I look to mine. You look to yours. Let that other fella look to his," Frederick said. "I promise you one thing: you start that kind of stupid trouble, we'll be the ones who end it."

Some of the prisoners thought the Preacher and the House of Universal Devotion were the fount of true doctrine. Many more were of the opinion that everything about them came straight from Satan. Frederick had heard that the Preacher opposed slaveholding. That inclined him toward giving the House of Universal Devotion the benefit of the doubt. Otherwise, he had a hard time caring one way or the other.

His main goal was to keep the captives from quarreling among themselves. Sooner or later, he hoped to exchange them for fighters captured by the white Atlanteans. Under the laws of war, both sides got treated the same way. What color a combatant was didn't matter. (The Europeans who put those laws together hadn't imagined fighting people of a different color. But that was all right—the laws had more stretch to them than their framers figured.)

Just by treating with Frederick and his fighters under the laws of war, the white Atlanteans granted them more equality than they'd ever enjoyed here before. If the whites won, that equality would vanish. Both sides recognized as much.

And, up till lately, neither side had seriously wondered what would happen if the Negroes and copperskins won. The whites hadn't dreamt it was possible. Neither had Frederick, not really. But dreaming time was over. Reality was here. Now both sides had to try to make the best of it.

BOOK IV

XX

*B*ack in New Marseille, the telegraphers were proud of themselves and their colleagues farther east. In spite of the insurrection, they'd managed to open a connection with New Hastings on the other coast. Most of the time, Jeremiah Stafford would have been proud right along with them.

Most of the time. When the news he had to give the capital was of a disaster, his heart wouldn't have broken had the line stayed down a little longer. As things were, he had no choice.

Neither did Consul Newton or Colonel Sinapis. Each man composed his own report and gave it to the telegraphers. Stafford collaborated with neither of the other leaders. As far as he knew, the other two didn't collaborate with each other. He wondered how much the reports differed. He wondered if anyone, reading all three, would be sure they talked about the same event.

He couldn't do anything about that. He thought he was telling the unvarnished truth. If Sinapis or Newton felt like lying, that wasn't his affair. If they thought he would stoop to lying, they didn't know him very well.

Besides, while you could write around the awful news as much as you pleased, you couldn't make it go away. The insurrectionists beat the Atlantean army. They made it surrender. In lieu of slaughtering it to the last man, they made it march away without its weapons.

No one responsible could deny any of that. If anybody tried, it wouldn't do him any good. No, the remaining interesting questions were two. First, who was to blame for the catastrophe? And, second, what the devil was the Atlantean government supposed to do about it now?

Newspapers in New Marseille had no doubt on that score. They printed highly colored interviews with soldiers they didn't name (and a good thing for the soldiers that they remained anonymous, or all the dreadful things they'd escaped in the battle would have landed on them in the aftermath). They also printed headlines like STRING UP THE CONSULS! and EXILE THE COLONEL!

"Nice to know we're loved," Leland Newton said, holding up one of the more inflammatory papers.

"Don't worry about it, your Excellency," Stafford answered as he corrected his breakfast coffee with a healthy splash of barrel-tree rum. "They loved you before we lost the battle."

"I'm sure they did." If the prospect dismayed Newton, he hid it very well. "After all, I disagreed with them, and what crime is more heinous than that?"

Stafford knew the answer to that particular question: losing the battle that was liable to mean liberty for all the copperskins and Negroes in the USA. Instead of saying so, he sipped his rum-laced coffee. The other Consul could see the answer as well as he could himself. The only difference was, Newton wouldn't think liberating slaves was a heinous offense. He was a northern man, after all, so what did he know?

A raised eyebrow said Newton guessed most of what was going on in Stafford's mind. The other Consul made a small production out of lighting a cigar. He said, "We both must be getting old. Seems too early in the day to quarrel, doesn't it?"

"Now that you mention it, yes," Stafford answered. "I will if you really want to, though. I don't want to disappoint you."

"I'll pass, thanks," Newton said. "The papers are quarrelsome enough, and whatever New Hastings has to say is bound to be worse. When do you suppose we'll hear from the Conscript Fathers?"

After someone flings water in their faces, because they're bound to faint when they get the news, Stafford thought morosely. "Are you really so eager?" he asked aloud.

"Eager? Well, as a matter of fact, no," the other Consul replied. "Say rather curious, in a clinical way, as if I'm wondering whether the dentist will tell me whether he has to pull one tooth or two."

Stafford winced. He'd had some agonizing encounters with tooth-pullers before they found out about ether. No one went to one of those quacks unless he was already in pain, and what they did to you only made you hurt worse— for a while, anyhow. Afterwards, you won relief. But that was afterwards. During was another story altogether.

And what sort of relief could the United States of Atlantis win from the abscess of insurrection? They'd tried to lance it, tried and failed. Now the poison was spreading through the country's system. Stafford had no idea how to stop it. He would have been amazed if the Senators on the far coast did.

He hadn't finished his ham and eggs and fried yams when a messenger who hadn't started shaving yet handed him one telegram and Consul Newton another. "Oh, joy," Stafford said as he unfolded his.

"Looking forward to it, are you?" Newton said.

"Well . . . no," Stafford answered. The other Consul managed a chuckle of sorts, but one with a distinct graveyard quality to it.

Senate expresses its disappointment at failure to suppress slave insurrection, the wire read. It wasn't quite *You clumsy idiot!,* but it might as well have been. The telegram continued, *Use any—repeat, any—measures necessary to end uprising. Manumission not mandatory but not—repeat, not—ruled out.*

That was all. That was quite enough. That was, as far as Jeremiah Stafford was concerned, much too much. "What does yours say?" he asked Newton.

"They want us to patch up a peace. That's what it

amounts to, anyhow," his colleague answered. "How about yours?"

"The same, more or less," Stafford said heavily. "By God, it frosts my pumpkin. If we fight a proper war, we can win it."

"Maybe we can, but how much more money will it cost?" Newton said. "How many more lives will we lose? How much longer will the Senate put up with that? How long will the Atlantean people put up with it?"

"Even Colonel Sinapis thinks we can win it." Stafford was clutching at straws, and he knew as much.

In case he hadn't, Consul Newton rubbed his nose in it: "Right now, how far will anyone follow Colonel Sinapis?"

Stafford didn't answer. No answer seemed necessary—or possible. Anyone who didn't blame the two Consuls for surrendering to Frederick Radcliff and the insurrectionists blamed Colonel Sinapis instead. Quite a few Atlanteans were sure there was plenty of blame to go around. That seemed to be the sense of the Senate's telegram.

Gently, Leland Newton said, "It won't be so bad. Truly, it won't. We've had free Negroes and copperskins in Croydon for more than a hundred years now. Our republic hasn't fallen apart. Your states won't, either."

"Easy for you to say," Stafford replied. "You may have freed them, but you never had very many for you to free. Things are different down here."

"They certainly are," Newton said. "The copperskins and blacks in Croydon are peaceful citizens, just like anyone else. They're up in arms here. Don't you see the connection? It's time to admit that what you've been doing here isn't working, even if it has made white people money."

That made Stafford scratch his head. As far as he was concerned, making money and working meant the same thing. At last, he saw, or thought he saw, some of what Newton had in mind: "You mean a few of the slaves don't fancy it."

"More than a few, don't you think? And 'don't fancy it' is like saying 'The ocean isn't small,'" Newton answered. "They 'don't fancy it' enough to pick up guns and risk their lives to try to do something about it. Shouldn't that tell you something?"

"You want me to say slavery is wicked and horrid, and everyone who has anything to do with it ought to be ashamed of himself, don't you?" Stafford said. "I'm very sorry, your Excellency, but I honestly don't believe that."

"I know. But whether you believe it isn't the point any more," Newton said.

That puzzled Stafford again. "How do you mean?"

"The point is, the slaves—the people who were slaves, I should say—do believe it. They would rather die than go on being slaves," Newton said. "A lot of them *have* died. They've made a lot of us die, too. Shouldn't *that* tell you something?"

"You're playing the schoolmaster here. Suppose you give me the lesson." Consul Stafford admired his own patience. Whether anyone else would admire it—or call it patience and not mulish intransigence—never crossed his mind.

And Newton seemed willing—maybe even eager—to do just what he'd asked. "The lesson is simple. If Negroes and copperskins go on being *them* and whites go on being *us*, Atlantis is ruined. We have to find a way for all of us to be Atlanteans together, or else we'll spend the next hundred years fighting."

"We *had* a way to live together," Stafford insisted.

"Yes, but too many people couldn't stand it. That's why we've got the insurrection now."

"Whites in the south won't like the way you have in mind. If blacks and Negroes can grab guns and fight, what makes you think white men can't?" Stafford said.

"That's simple enough." Newton aimed a forefinger at him as if it were a rifle musket. "You have to persuade them not to."

"We ought to try and grab New Marseille *now*," Lorenzo said. "We've got the white soldiers' guns. Besides, their hearts have to be down·in their shoes. We should hit hard and fast, before they get reinforcements and fresh supplies."

Frederick Radcliff drummed his fingers on the outside of his thigh. A few weeks ago, he might have agreed with his marshal. Now . . . everything had changed. Or, if things hadn't changed, the insurrection still had no hope. "Ask you a couple of questions?" he said.

One of Lorenzo's eyebrows rose. "How am I supposed to tell you no? You're the Tribune. What you say goes."

That wasn't how Frederick thought of his power—which didn't mean it wasn't useful here. "What happens if the white folks get riled enough to throw everything they've got into the fight against us?"

"Well . . . " The copperskin pursed his lips. As with the raised eyebrow, it wasn't a showy gesture; it was, in fact, hardly noticeable. That he'd made it at all counted for a good deal. So did his hesitation before he said, "Wouldn't be easy. They send everything, we'd have to be mighty careful fighting pitched battles. Raids, ambushes—we could keep on with that kind of stuff for a long time."

"Would we win in the end if we did?" Frederick persisted.

"Damned if I know." Lorenzo's answering grin was crooked. "Tell you the truth, when this whole thing started I figured we'd both be dead by now—dead or wishing we were."

"You ain't the only one," Frederick replied with feeling, and Lorenzo laughed out loud. "But the way it looks to me is, there's a time to push and a time to go easy. We showed 'em we could beat 'em, and we showed 'em we didn't aim to kill all the white men we could. Seems to me we got to let 'em chew on that for a while, see what they do next. If we push 'em now, we only tick 'em off—know what I mean?"

"Sure do. What I don't know is whether you're right." Lorenzo took a deep breath and let the air whuffle out between his lips. "What the hell, though? Like I say, you're the Tribune. You've got us this far. Seems like you know what you're doing."

I'm glad somebody thinks so. But Frederick didn't say that out loud. One of the tricks to leading he'd learned was never to let your followers know you had doubts. Sometimes you could get away with being wrong. With being unsure? No. That made you look weak, and how could a weak man lead? Not even Helen knew about some of the fears that knotted Frederick's insides. What you didn't show, you didn't have to explain. You didn't have to wonder about it so much yourself, either.

For once, he and his army didn't need to do anything right this minute. The white Atlanteans weren't pressing them—couldn't press them for a while, as Lorenzo had pointed out. Food wasn't a worry. Hardtack and salt pork and bully beef captured from the soldiers' supply weren't exciting, but kept body and soul together. And the hunting in this sparsely settled countryside was better than it would have been with more people around—though there wasn't much livestock to take here.

Just waiting around felt good. It took him back to his days as a slave. You weren't always busy, working for the masters. But you always had to be ready to get busy, and to get busy at someone else's whim. That was how things worked here, too. If he'd made a mistake about how the white men would respond after being defeated and spared, they would be the ones who let him know it.

Slaves always kept their eyes on masters and mistresses. They needed to know what the white folks were up to, sometimes before the whites were sure themselves. And the Negroes and copperskins still slaving it in New Marseille were the insurrectionists' eyes and ears there.

Frederick Radcliff didn't think the Consuls' army could move without his knowing about it beforehand. The slaves in New Marseille saw no signs that it was getting ready to move. Frederick took that for a good omen.

So did Lorenzo, who heard about it as soon as he did, or maybe even sooner. "Looks like you know what you were talking about," the copperskin said.

"I'm as happy about it as you are—you'd best believe I am," Frederick said.

"How long you aim to give 'em?" Lorenzo asked.

"Till it feels right. Don't know what else to tell you," Frederick answered.

To his surprise, that got a smile from the marshal. "We're all makin' this up as we go along," Lorenzo said.

"Ain't it the truth!" Frederick never would have admitted it if the other man hadn't come out with it first, but he wasn't about to deny it once Lorenzo pointed it out.

After a while, fighters started slipping out of camp. They thought they'd already got what they wanted. And they didn't think the Free Republic of Atlantis had any business telling them what to do any more. They were free, weren't they?

Lorenzo and Frederick took a different view of things. With Frederick's approval, Lorenzo posted guards around the encampment to catch deserters and bring them back. The United States of Atlantis didn't let their soldiers walk away whenever the men happened to feel like it. As far as Frederick was concerned, the Free Republic of Atlantis shouldn't, either.

That highly offended some of the men who wanted to go home. "Who you think you are, playing the white man over me?" a black fighter demanded when he was hauled before Frederick. "You ain't nothin' but a nigger, same as me. You got no business tellin' me what to do!"

"If I had me ten cents for every time I heard that, I'd be the richest nigger in Atlantis," Frederick said.

"It's the truth, damn it," the other Negro said. "If I'm a free man, ain't nobody can make me do nothin' I don't want to."

"It doesn't work that way," Frederick answered. "Nobody can buy you or sell you. That's what bein' free means. But you're in the army now. Nobody made you join up. You did it your own self."

"That's right. And that means I can leave whenever I please, too," the prisoner said.

"Means no such thing. If people left whenever they wanted to, pretty soon we wouldn't have an army any more. You go in, you got to stay in till the job is done unless you made a deal beforehand to get out sooner," Frederick said.

"Nobody told me I could make a deal like that!" the other Negro exclaimed.

Frederick smiled sweetly. "Then it looks like you're in till the job is done, doesn't it? That's how my granddad did things, and that's how I'm gonna do 'em, too."

"Your granddad was nothin' but a white man, and he didn't set no niggers free," the other man retorted. "Look where you was at 'fore we rose up. House nigger, that's all you was, an' I bet you felt all jumped-up about it, too."

How right he was! Frederick was embarrassed to remember the way he'd looked down on field hands before he got stripes on his back and became one himself. He was also damned if he'd admit any such thing. Instead, he answered, "You've got to start somewhere. Everybody's got to start somewhere. Before Victor Radcliff done what he done, nobody in Atlantis was free. White folks had to do what the King of England and his people said—"

"An' black folks an' copperskins had to do what the white folks said," the other Negro broke in.

"That's right." Frederick nodded. "My granddad made it so white folks were free, anyways. My grandma used to say he wished he could do more—"

"He done plenty with her, didn't he?"

"Shut up!" Frederick said fiercely. "If I was a white man an' you talked to me like that, I'd make you regret it—bet your sorry ass I would. But he figured out you can't have an army 'less you got people who have to stay in. He was right. All the white folks' countries do it that way. We're gonna win, we got to do it that way, too."

"I'll run off again. You wait an' see if I don't," the prisoner declared.

"I know who you are, Humphrey," Frederick said. He hadn't till one of the guards whispered the man's name in his ear, but he sure did now. "This time, you don't get anything but a talking-to, on account of you didn't know no better. We catch you again, you'll be sorry for sure."

The prisoner—Humphrey—stripped off his shirt and turned his back. His scars made Frederick's look like a beginner's. "What you gonna do to me that the white folks ain't already done?" he asked as he faced Frederick once more.

And what do I say to that? Frederick wondered. To his surprise, he found something: "White folks whipped you 'cause you did stuff they didn't like. You run off from us, they'd thank you for it. Chances are they'd pay you for it, same as the Romans paid Judas. You want their thirty pieces of silver, go ahead an' run, you bastard."

That shut Humphrey up, anyhow. Maybe he'd stick around. Maybe he'd try to desert again. If he succeeded . . . Frederick couldn't do anything about that. If Humphrey failed, he couldn't say he hadn't been warned. Freedom had limits. It had to have limits, or it turned into chaos.

Frederick hadn't understood that before tasting freedom himself. But there was nothing like running a revolution to drive the lesson home. His grandfather could have told him the same thing—if Victor Radcliff wasn't fighting on the other side.

Colonel Sinapis emptied New Marseille's arsenal to equip most of his regulars with rifle muskets—and with some ancient flintlock smoothbores that had gathered cobwebs there for God only knew how long. There weren't enough weapons for all the regulars. There weren't enough for any militiamen. They were loudly unhappy about that.

Sinapis stuck by his guns, and by the way he handed them out. Leland Newton backed him. "It's not a state arsenal— it's an arsenal of the United States of Atlantis," Newton told a self-appointed militia colonel. "It's only right that the guns go to troops from the national government first. If we had more, you'd get your share."

"Or maybe we wouldn't." The colonel—who decked himself out in a uniform far fancier than Sinapis'—had a pointy nose, a whiny voice, and a suspicious mind. "Reckon you're afraid we'd do us some real fightin' against them damned niggers."

Newton *was* afraid they'd try, and would shatter the fragile tacit truce that still held. Since he didn't care to admit that, he answered, "I haven't seen your men win any more laurels than the regulars."

"We never got the chance!" the militiaman complained. "That damnfool foreigner you've got in charge of your soldiers wouldn't turn us loose and let us fight the way we wanted to."

What did that mean? Newton feared he knew. The colonel wanted to rape and loot and burn and slaughter. He would have made a fine freebooter from western Atlantis' piratical past. A soldier? That looked to be a different story.

"Your private war against the men and women who were your slaves is not the only thing at stake here," the Consul said coldly. "The fate of the United States of Atlantis rides on this, too."

"You reckon they don't go together?" The militia colonel made as if to spit, then—barely—thought better of it. "If you do, you're even dumber'n I give you credit for, and that's saying something." He clumped away, disgust plain in every line of his body.

Staring after him, Newton sighed. Then he swore under his breath. The militiamen didn't have to stay under Colonel Sinapis' command. If they grew desperate enough, and if they got their hands on some muskets (which they could probably manage if they grew desperate enough), they could storm off against the insurrectionists on their own. Newton didn't think they would cover themselves in glory. He knew he might be wrong, though. And even if he was right, that might not stop them.

He started to go warn Sinapis. But what would that accomplish? The most the regular officer could do would be to put the militiamen under guard. That would only complete the breach Newton wanted to prevent. The militiamen wouldn't listen to reason from Sinapis, any more than that damned colonel had wanted to listen to Newton.

What then? Reluctantly, Newton hunted up Jeremiah Stafford instead of the regular colonel. He feared the other Consul wouldn't listen to him, either. Still, if Stafford didn't, how were they worse off?

Stafford did hear him out. Then he asked a reasonable enough question: "What do you want me to do about it, your Excellency?"

"We aren't fighting Frederick Radcliff's men right now," Newton answered. "I'd like to keep it that way if we can."

"Right this minute, the militiamen have damn-all to fight with," Stafford said. "That's the biggest part of what's eating them."

"Not the biggest part," Newton said. The other Consul

looked a question at him. He went on, "What's bothering them is the same thing that's bothering you. They don't want the Negroes and copperskins to get their freedom."

"Yes, that's about the size of it," Stafford said. "Why do you think I'd want to slow them down, then?"

"Because they'll only spill sand in the gears, and you know it as well as I do. God knows the two of us don't agree, but you're not a stupid man. That militia colonel . . . " Newton shook his head. "He couldn't cut his way out of a gunnysack if you gave him a pair of scissors. Your Excellency, we have a chance to end this peacefully. We—"

Stafford interrupted: "Peacefully, maybe, but not the way I'd want it."

"To end this the way you want it, we'd have to soak Atlantis in blood. Even that might not do it, because killing all the Negroes and copperskins leaves the country without slaves, which isn't what you have in mind, either. Or it might not end at all—there might be murders and burnings and bushwhackings a hundred years from now. You can have peace, or you can have slavery. I don't think you can have both any more. It's not just cooking and sewing and barbering these days. Will an overseer ever be able to turn his back on a slave with a shovel in his hands again?"

"You . . . God . . . damned . . . son . . . of . . . a . . . bitch." The words dragged from Stafford one by one, as if dredged up from somewhere deep inside him.

"Your servant, sir." Newton made as if to bow.

The other Consul started to say something else, then broke off with an expression of almost physical pain—or maybe of true hatred. Now Stafford was the one who shook his head, like a horse bedeviled with flies. He tried again: "You *are* a son of a bitch. You know how to rub my nose in it, don't you?"

"I'm sorry." Newton lied without hesitation. "The thing is there. You know it's there, even if you don't like it. That's the difference between you and the colonel of militia. If I make you see it or smell it or whatever you please, you won't go on telling me it's not."

"I wish I could," Stafford said bitterly.

"I'm sure you do. But it's too late for that, isn't it? The Senate wants to get this over with. By the way the wires sound, it doesn't care how we do it. People south of the Stour—white people, I mean—will get used to the idea of freeing slaves faster if someone they respect tells them they don't have much choice any more."

"Some of them may. The rest will stand in line to shoot me. It'll be a long line, too." Stafford didn't sound like a man who was joking.

"What will things be like if they go on the way they have? Better? Or worse?" Newton asked. If anything would keep Stafford thinking about what needed doing—whether he liked it or not—that was it.

By the way he screwed up his face, he might have been passing a kidney stone. "This is not the way I wanted things to turn out when we left New Hastings," he said. "But you're happy now, aren't you?"

"'Happy' probably goes too far," Newton replied. "I've always thought the slaves deserve to be free. I hoped we wouldn't need bloodshed to free them."

"It may not be over yet, or even close to over," Stafford said. "Do you remember what I told you before? No matter how happy"—he used the word again, with malice aforethought—"you are that niggers and mudfaces get to ape white men, plenty of people south of the Stour won't be. A lot of them will be like the militia colonel you don't care for—they'll want to keep fighting no matter what."

"I do remember. We've been over this ground before. What's the most they can hope for? I can think of two things." Newton held up two fingers. He touched one with the index finger of his other hand. "Maybe they'll kill off all the blacks and copperskins down here. Then they won't have any slaves left, whatever they were fighting for will be pointless, and their grandchildren will ask them, 'How could you do such a horrible thing?'" He touched the other finger. "Or maybe they'll win. I don't think it's likely, but you never can tell. But even if they do, will they trust slaves around anything sharp from then on out? I asked you that a couple of minutes ago, and you swore at me."

"You deserved it, too," Stafford said.

"Which still doesn't answer my question, your Excellency."

What Stafford called him then made everything the other Consul had said before sound like an endearment. It would have made a hard-bitten regular sergeant, a twenty-year veteran, blush like a maiden aunt. Even on the receiving end, Newton admired it. When his colleague finally ran down, he inclined his head. "Your mother would be proud of you," he said.

"If she knew what you had in mind, she'd call you worse than that," Stafford said.

"The worst of it is, I believe you—which also doesn't answer my question," Newton said. "For God's sake, Jeremiah, if you think that hero from the militia will get you what you want, turn him loose. But if you think he's the biggest jackass this side of a stud farm, you ought to slow him down before he makes a bad spot worse."

He wondered whether Stafford would ream him out yet again. The other Consul didn't. He just gestured wearily, as if to say he wanted nothing more to do with Leland Newton and his impertinent questions. Knowing when not to push any more could be even more important than knowing when to keep pushing no matter what. Newton touched a finger to the brim of his tall beaver hat and left Stafford alone with his conscience—assuming he had one.

And the militiamen did not march off against Frederick Radcliff's fighters on their own. Newton didn't know whether Stafford had anything to do with that. Nor did he try to find out. What difference did it make, anyhow? In politics as in sausage-stuffing, the result often proved more appetizing than what went into producing it.

Frederick Radcliff had never dreamt his word would be as good as law in much of the state of New Marseille, as well as being heard in states east of the Green Ridge Mountains. People all over Atlantis had paid attention to his grandfather, but what did that have to do with anything? Victor Radcliff had enjoyed the enormous advantage of a white skin. For a man who had to do without one, Frederick had come further than he'd ever imagined he could.

"I hope to Jesus you have!" Helen exclaimed when he remarked on that. He could always count on his wife to keep him from getting a big head. With a sly smile, she went on, "Beats the daylights out of being Master Barford's house nigger, don't it?"

"Oh, you might say so," Frederick answered—she didn't know Humphrey had mocked him for his former post. "Yeah, you just might. And I was all puffed up about that when it was what I had. I sure was. Seems like a thousand years ago."

His cheeks heated. For once, he was glad his skin was too dark to show much of a flush. Humphrey had known the difference between house slaves and field hands, all right. So far, Humphrey hadn't tried to run off again. Or, if he had, the word hadn't got to Frederick.

Those weren't the same—not even close. One of the things Frederick had learned was that being a leader didn't mean knowing everything that was going on. You could be pretty sure of what you saw with your own eyes. Past that, you had to rely on what other people told you.

That sounded better than it really was. As any slave knew, people lied whenever they thought it would do them some good—or sometimes whenever they felt like it. They kept quiet about things that made them look bad. If nobody found out about things like that, they won the game.

Or they thought so, anyhow. Trouble was, the things people lied about or swept under the rug were often the things a leader most needed to learn. Frederick didn't like using side channels to find out about things his lieutenants should have told him. That didn't mean he didn't do it. Back on the plantation, Henry Barford had done the same kind of thing. In the end, it didn't save him—the uprising was too sudden, too swift, to be sidetracked. But it had helped him run things for years. And it helped Frederick now.

"A thousand years ago," his wife echoed. "It does, but it seems like day before yesterday, too. I reckoned I'd die a slave—I really did."

"So did I," Frederick said. Considering who his grandfather was, he thought that fate seemed even more bitter to him than it did to Helen. He'd never had the nerve to tell her that, though. His best guess was that she'd call him a stupid, uppity nigger if he dared do such a thing. Sometimes you didn't want to find out how good your best guess was.

"Ain't gonna happen now," Helen said in wondering tones.

"No. It won't. We'll die free," Frederick agreed, adding, "And it's startin' to look like that won't happen in the next ten minutes, neither."

"Wouldn't have believed that when you clouted Matthew," Helen said. "I reckoned you was dead. I reckoned I was, too. And not just the two of us—the whole work gang."

"Things turn out right, fifty years from now old niggers'll go on about how tough things were in the work gangs, and young niggers listenin' to 'em won't have any notion of what they're talkin' about. That's what I'm aimin' for," Frederick said.

While he was a house slave, he hadn't understood what a hard life field hands led. He'd known, but he hadn't understood, not till he lived it himself for a little while. It was even harder for him, because they got used to it from childhood while he was dropped into it as a middle-aged man with soft hands and with welts from the lash on his back.

"Be somethin' if we got it," Helen said. His disaster had turned her out into the fields, too. She'd never blamed him for it, not out loud, which surely made her a princess among women. She asked, "Any news about what the white folks in New Marseille're up to?"

Not altogether comfortably, Frederick shook his head. "Only thing I know for sure is, they haven't come out against us. And some of the militiamen done gone home, on account of they can't get their hands on any guns."

"Aw, toooo bad." Helen didn't sound brokenhearted.

Frederick laughed. "Ain't it just?"

"They ain't comin' out to fight. But they ain't comin' out to talk with us, neither," his wife said.

"That's about the size of it. You'd know if they were," Frederick said.

"Well, I hope so," Helen said, which reminded Frederick of his own thoughts about how hard it was to be sure of what was going on. Then she asked, "What if they don't do either one?"

"If they don't fight *or* talk?" Frederick said. Helen nodded. He scratched his head. The white folks had to do one or the other ... didn't they?

"Maybe they try an' wait us out, see if our army falls apart," Helen said. "They know how to hold things together better'n we do."

Once more, that reminded Frederick of his unpleasant encounter with Humphrey. "You're right," he said in somber tones. "They do. They've had more practice doin' it."

"Think we ought to, like, push 'em, then?" Helen asked. "Be harder for them to make like they don't want to talk with us if we try an' talk with them right in front of all the newspapers an' everybody."

"It would," Frederick murmured. *Damned if it wouldn't*, he thought. Saying no or saying nothing was easy in private. Doing it where people who wanted you to say yes could listen in ... That was another story.

"Dunno if you ought to go yourself. Talkin' with 'em face-to-face when we had guns all around, that was fine. Stickin' your head in the lion's mouth in New Marseille ... Maybe they listen to you. But maybe they shoot you instead. Even if the Consuls don't tell 'em to, maybe they do it irregardless," Helen said.

"Uh-huh. Same goes for Lorenzo." Frederick could easily imagine a militiaman pulling out an eight-shooter and blazing away. The white men from south of the Stour loved rebellious slaves no more than the Negroes and copperskins loved them. The militiamen were having trouble getting firearms in New Marseille. That might count for very little. A length of rope might suit them better, in fact. Yes, watching a leader of the insurrection kick away his life might make them laugh like hyenas.

Frederick had never heard a hyena, or seen one. Atlanteans often said things, or thought them, for no better reason than that they were embedded in the English language. He supposed his African ancestors and cousins knew all about hyenas.

"Lorenzo." Helen's nostrils flared. "Don't know if you

oughta trust that copperskin. He's liable to want to be the top fella, not the second one."

It wasn't as if that thought hadn't also occurred to Frederick. But he said, "If he aimed to kill me, he could've done it a hundred times by now. White folks are the ones we got to worry about, not our own kind."

"You hope," Helen said.

So Frederick did. If he remembered that Lorenzo *was* a copperskin, *wasn't* exactly his own kind . . . If he remembered that, the insurrection would eat itself up. Quite deliberately, he made himself forget it.

XXI

*J*eremiah Stafford might have been happier to see the arrival of the Antichrist at New Marseille than he was when Frederick Radcliff's emissary rode into town. On the other hand, he might not have. On the other other hand—assuming people came with three—he wasn't sure there was much difference between the Antichrist and a spokesman for the Free Republic of Atlantis.

Had he had any choice, he would have ignored the Negro named Samuel. But Samuel made sure Stafford and Newton and Colonel Sinapis had no choice. Carrying a flag of truce, he rode into town with a guard of half a dozen insurrectionists. Two of them had captured Atlantean cavalry carbines, three had eight-shooters, while the last bore the Free Republic's flag.

Up till then, Consul Stafford hadn't known the Free Republic had a flag. It hadn't shown one in any of its fights with Sinapis' soldiers. But it did now—one in stark contrast to the USA's crimson red-crested eagle's head on blue. The Free Republic's flag showed three vertical stripes: red, black, and white.

Samuel was only too happy to explain its meaning to New Marseille's newspapermen (and parading through town with it made sure the newspapermen noticed him). "It shows the three folks of the Free Republic," the Negro told anyone who would listen. "Copperskins, Negroes, and whites can all live together there in equality."

Not a single reporter asked him what had happened to the whites in the Free Republic, or why so many militiamen hailed from land it held. That the reporters didn't ask such questions infuriated Stafford. "The black bastard might as well have cast a spell on them!" he complained.

"He's clever," Leland Newton said, which only irked Stafford more. The other Consul went on, "And that flag is a master stroke. It makes the Free Republic look to be the same kind of thing the United States are."

"One more lie!" Stafford said. "He's trying to force us to treat with him."

"He's doing a good job, too, wouldn't you say?" Newton answered. "If we don't treat with him—or treat with his principals, which is what he's come to arrange—we have to start fighting again."

Although Stafford was ready for that, he and the militiamen seemed to be the only people in New Marseille—maybe the only people in the USA—who were. "He's arranged things so we have no choice," he said sourly.

That didn't get the response he wanted, either. "Well, your Excellency, if you think so, too, let's meet him and get it over with," Newton said.

Stafford didn't want to, which was putting it mildly. But he'd done all kinds of things he didn't want to do since leaving New Hastings. The more of them he did, the easier the next one seemed to become. Meet with a nigger fronting for a slave insurrection? Before leaving the capital, he would have laughed at the idea—if he didn't punch whoever was mad enough to suggest it. Now . . . Now he let out a wintry sigh and said, "All right. Maybe it will make those jackasses with pens shut up, anyhow. That would be worth a little something."

It didn't. Samuel made sure it wouldn't. He wanted to meet while New Marseille's reporters listened in. "Why not?" he said. "The Free Republic's got nothing to hide." That only made the scribes like him better.

And so they sat down together in the eatery attached to New Marseille's second-best hotel, the Silver Oil Thrush.

Foreigners, no doubt, would have found the name peculiar. Consul Stafford cared little for what foreigners thought. Oil thrushes had grown scarce, even here in the southwest, but he'd eaten them often enough to know how tasty they were.

Samuel, on the other hand, was a stringy old buzzard, his woolly hair frosted with gray. He must have been somebody's butler, or something of the sort, before the insurrection: he spoke almost like an educated white man, with only a vanishing trace of a slave accent. Letting niggers and copperskins learn to read and write was a big mistake—Stafford had always thought so. It gave them ideas above their station.

Too late to worry about that now. "Tribune Radcliff and Marshal Lorenzo want to meet with you folks to end the war," Samuel said. Off to one side of the table where he talked with the Consuls and Colonel Sinapis, a sketch artist took down their likenesses. Soon, a woodcut of the scene would grace some New Marseille newspaper.

"If they think we'll recognize their crackbrained titles, they'd better think again," Stafford snapped.

Samuel only shrugged. "Talk to them about that, your Excellency. Talk to me about talking to them." His use of Stafford's title of respect annoyed the Consul instead of mollifying him.

"If I had my way—" Stafford began.

"You'd whip me within an inch of my life. I know that, your Excellency," Samuel broke in, with perfect accuracy. "But you don't have your way here, not any more you don't. Shall we talk instead?"

"Yes. Let's." That was Newton, not Stafford.

"I would still sooner fight it out," Stafford said. Knowing he would get no support from the other Consul, he looked to Balthasar Sinapis instead. He got no support from the colonel, either. He feared he knew what that meant: Sinapis didn't want the insurrectionists to humiliate him again. In a way, Stafford sympathized. In another way . . . "What good is having an army if you don't dare use it?"

To his surprise, Sinapis answered him: "To keep someone else from using his army against you."

"So that's why the niggers aren't in New Marseille, is it?" Stafford snarled.

"Yes. That is exactly why," Sinapis said.

"And on account of we don't want to come into New Marseille any old way," Samuel said. "We don't want to fight any more. We want peace. You gonna tell all the people in Atlantis you don't want peace?"

You sneaky son of a bitch, Stafford thought, watching the reporters scribble. Samuel knew how to play to the gallery—Frederick Radcliff must have understood what he was doing when he sent out the other Negro. Damn it, the people of Atlantis, or too many of them, *didn't* want anybody telling them their leaders didn't want peace.

"If you think the people of Atlantis—of the United States of Atlantis—will let the so-called Free Republic of Atlantis stand, you'd better think again," Newton said. Stafford blinked, the way he did whenever he and the other Consul agreed about something.

Samuel only spread his pale-palmed hands. "I'm not the one to talk about that, either," he said. "You've got to see what the Tribune and the Marshal have to say."

Consul Newton nodded. He was willing to do that. Colonel Sinapis was also willing to do it, or at least resigned to the prospect. If Stafford said no, all the blame would land on him. There was probably enough to crush him.

If only . . . ! *If only a lot of things*, he thought. They started with wondering why Victor Radcliff had to get a slave with child and went on from there. Too late to do anything about any of them now. Stafford was stuck with the world as it was.

He didn't say yes. He couldn't make himself do that. But he didn't say no, no matter how much he wanted to.

Approaching the hamlet of Slug Hollow, Leland Newton wondered how it had got its name. The answer proved altogether mundane: it sat in a depression, and the trees thereabouts were full of cucumber slugs, some of them half as long as a man's arm. The settlers had had the imagination of so many cherrystone clams, but they'd told the truth as they saw it.

No whites were left in the hamlet. Maybe they'd fled. Maybe they hadn't had the chance. Newton didn't ask—he didn't want to know. Jeremiah Stafford did ask, pointedly. He made sure he did it where the reporters could hear him, too. Newton thought about teasing him for taking lessons from Samuel, but decided not to. He didn't think his colleague would appreciate it.

When Stafford asked, Samuel only shrugged and spread his hands again. "I don't know what happened," he said. "They were long gone by the time I came through here— that's all I can tell you."

"A likely story," Stafford said. "How do you suppose so many buildings burned down? Lightning?"

"I don't know," Samuel repeated. "If I don't know, I can't tell you."

"Would we find bones if we dug in the ruins?" Stafford asked.

"Maybe you would, your Excellency," the Negro said. "You got to remember, though—a war went through here."

Newton was ready to make allowances for that. Stafford didn't seem to be, which surprised the other Consul very little: "It's war when you do it, eh? But it's nasty and villainous when we fight back."

"You said it, your Excellency. I didn't," Samuel answered. Stafford sent him a murderous glare.

The Consuls and the soldiers they'd brought along camped west of the ruined Slug Hollow. Samuel and his smaller retinue camped east of the place. When Frederick and Lorenzo came down to join them, they would bring enough fighters to equalize the numbers.

Colonel Sinapis had a good-sized force within easy reach of Slug Hollow. He wasn't supposed to, but he did. Leland Newton would have been amazed if the same weren't true for the insurrectionists. If the talks failed—or maybe even if they succeeded—the war could start again any time.

Frederick Radcliff and Lorenzo walked into Slug Hollow two days after the men from New Marseille got there. The Negro and copperskin would have cut a fancier figure had they ridden. Maybe they didn't care. Or maybe they didn't ride. Why would they have learned while they were slaves?

Stafford greeted them with, "If you keep up this nonsense about the Free Republic of Atlantis, we have nothing to say to one another."

"If you call everything that's ours nonsense before we even start talking about it, maybe you ought to send in your soldiers again," Lorenzo answered. "You want to settle things by fighting, I reckon we can do that."

If Newton hadn't got it for free, he would have paid a hundred eagles for a glimpse of Stafford's face. The other Consul plainly *did* want to settle things by fighting. Just as plainly, he knew he couldn't. The United States of Atlantis had ended up with egg on their face when they tried. No matter how much he despised the idea, he had to sit down and talk with the insurrectionists now. And he did despise the idea, and made only the barest effort to hide it.

Frederick Radcliff said, "If we can get what we need inside the United States of Atlantis, we don't need to worry so much about the Free Republic. If we can't . . . Well, that's a different story." He made hand-washing motions to show how different it was liable to be.

"What *do* you need?" Newton asked. "Can you put it into words for us?" If Radcliff couldn't, the Consul feared the talks would end up going nowhere.

But the Negro leader didn't hesitate. "You bet I can," he said. "We want to be free. We don't want anybody, no matter what color he is, to buy us and sell us any more. We want the law in Atlantis to forget about color, matter of fact. Whatever a white man can do, a Negro or a copperskin ought to be able to do. Whatever a white man gets in trouble for, one of us ought to get in trouble for, too—as much trouble, but no more."

Consul Stafford seemed bound and determined to make himself as difficult as he could. "You want the right to miscegenate with white women!" he exclaimed.

"To do what?" Lorenzo asked.

"To screw 'em," Frederick Radcliff explained, which wasn't the whole answer, but which came close enough.

"Oh. That." To Newton's surprise, Lorenzo laughed out loud. "What makes you think we think white women are pretty enough to be worth screwing?" he asked Stafford.

Again, Newton would have paid money to look at an expression he got to see for nothing.

"White folks always get hot and bothered about that," Frederick said gravely. "They spent all this time screwin' our women, so naturally they figure we got to pay 'em back the same way."

Consul Stafford finally quit spluttering and gasping like a newly landed trout. "Will you have the infernal gall to claim you've all been chaste throughout this uprising? I hope not, by God, because I know better."

"No, I don't say that. You don't like it so much when it happens to your womenfolk, do you, your Excellency?" Frederick Radcliff answered. "But I say this—put us under fair laws and we'll live up to them. My woman's about the same shade I am. We been together lots of years. I don't want a white woman—I want her to be my legal wife. What's so bad about that?"

"A lot of men from south of the Stour will tell you it's the wickedest thing they ever heard," Newton said.

"A lot of men from south of the Stour are damned fools," Lorenzo said, and then, "Hell, it ain't like we didn't already know that."

"If you provoke us, we *will* keep fighting," Consul Stafford warned. Colonel Sinapis stirred, but he didn't come right out and call the Consul from Cosquer a liar.

Can we go on fighting? Newton wondered. He supposed it was possible. He didn't think it would be easy or cheap or quick. What would the United States of Atlantis be like after a generation of nasty campaigning and ambushes? Would they be any kind of place he wanted to live? He didn't think so. Would they be any kind of place where a Negro or copperskin *could* live? He also had his doubts about that.

"You don't love us, and we don't love you," Frederick said. "Might be better if we went our own way in a chunk of this country."

"A minute ago, you claimed you would follow our laws," Stafford said. "If you make your own country out of ours, do you aim to pay for what you take away from us?"

Frederick rubbed his chin. "That might cause some trouble," he admitted.

"Oh, maybe a little," Stafford said. "For that matter, how do you propose to compensate all the slaveowners in the USA for having their property forcibly stolen from them?"

"You know what, your Excellency? That ain't my worry," Frederick Radcliff said.

"Why not?" Stafford pressed.

"On account of any man who's been a slave will tell you slavery's wrong to begin with," the Negro answered. "Why should you get paid 'cause you can't do now what you never should have started doing?"

"Isn't that an interesting question?" Newton murmured.

"Shut up," Stafford told him. He turned back to Frederick Radcliff. "Will you tell me slavery is illegal?"

"Not yet," Frederick answered. "But it sure ought to be."

"You'll find plenty of people who disagree with you," Stafford said.

"Damned few who've ever been slaves," Lorenzo told him.

"This is what we're here to talk about," Newton said. "What we have now plainly isn't working." He waited for the other Consul to quarrel with him, but Stafford didn't. Thus encouraged, if that was the word, he went on, "We want to see what we can work out that will leave almost everyone not too unhappy."

This time, Jeremiah Stafford looked like nothing so much as a stray dog vomiting in the middle of the street. But Frederick Radcliff slowly nodded. If that wasn't a politician's nod, Consul Newton had never seen one. And if that was a politician's nod . . . In that case, the Negro leader was—or at least might be—a man with whom it would be possible to deal.

Newton dared hope so.

"Almost everybody not too unhappy!" Lorenzo not only mocked the sentiment, he did a rotten job of imitating Leland Newton's accent. To Frederick's ear, the copperskin sounded like a man trying to talk around a mouthful of rocks.

"Have you got a better idea?" Frederick asked. "What are we supposed to do if we can't find a bargain the white folks will live with?"

"What we ought to do is kill the Consuls and that damned foreign colonel," Lorenzo said. "After that, they'd all thrash like a pullet that just met the chopper." With the flat of his hand, he mimed a hatchet coming down on a skinny neck. Then he did an alarmingly accurate impression of a chicken that had just lost its head.

But Frederick held up both hands in horror. "They would act like that—for a little while. Then they'd decide they could never trust us again, even a tiny bit, and they'd hunt us down no matter how long it took or what it cost."

"Let 'em try, and good luck to 'em," Lorenzo said.

"Do you *want* to live like a hunted animal the rest of your days?" Frederick asked. "If you do, you found the fastest way to get what you want."

"Me? I want to live like the fancy masters wish they could," Lorenzo said. "I want to have servants fan me with those big old feathers—"

"Ostrich plumes," Frederick put in. Sure enough, such fans were in great demand among the richer plantation owners. Or they had been, till the people who would have done the fanning decided they didn't care for the work.

"Yeah. Them," Lorenzo agreed. "And I want pretty girls to drop grapes in my mouth whenever I get hungry, or maybe thirsty."

Frederick didn't know whether to laugh or to be appalled. "How do you propose to get that without turning into a master yourself?"

"Maybe we could make the Consuls slaves instead of killing 'em." Lorenzo was full of ideas today. Not necessarily good ideas, but ideas all the same.

"And where would you get the pretty girls?" Frederick asked, with the air of a man humoring a lunatic.

"Oh, what pretty girl wouldn't want to come to Slug Hollow?" Lorenzo said, and if that wasn't the most lunatic thing Frederick Radcliff had ever heard, he didn't know what would be. No one in his—or her—right mind would want to come to Slug Hollow. No one would have wanted to come here if the place were named Silver Nugget. Slug Hollow by any other name would have been a place people tried to get away from, not one they flocked to.

"They could drop cucumber slugs into your mouth when you got hungry," Frederick said.

"Ain't like I never ate 'em before," Lorenzo answered. "Don't know many field hands who haven't. Maybe it's different with house slaves."

"I know what they taste like," Frederick said, which was true enough. If the copperskin wanted to claim field hands ate such delicacies more often than house slaves did, Frederick couldn't argue with him.

But Lorenzo chose to change the subject instead: "Reckon we'll get what we're after here?"

"Don't know," Frederick answered uneasily. "We don't want to keep fighting forever, though, we gotta try."

"Fighting forever'd be better'n going back to where we were. Damned if I'll ever pick any more cotton for a white man," Lorenzo said.

"That, I know," Frederick said. He felt the same way, and he'd done it for days, not for years. All the Negroes and copperskins who followed him felt the same way. If the whites camped on the far side of Slug Hollow didn't understand that, these talks would fail. And if they failed . . . fighting forever was what would come next.

He tried to picture what Atlantis would look like after ten years of skirmishing, or twenty, or thirty. Like a restive horse, his mind shied away from what that called up. Would anyone, white or colored, care to live here after something like that? Frederick flinched at all the unpleasant possibilities he could see. And they weren't just possibilities—they struck him as being likelihoods.

Lorenzo said, "Ain't many women here gonna let white men do what they want with 'em no more, neither."

"Uh-huh," Frederick said. That shot hit much too close to the center of the target—much too close to the heart of who he was. What *had* things been like between his grandmother and Victor Radcliff? Her owner lent her to the other white Atlantean for his pleasure; Frederick knew that. Had she taken any of her own? Had they even liked each other? As far as Frederick knew, his grandmother had never said anything to his father about his father's father beyond letting him know who that famous father was.

Had the insurrection come two generations earlier, would Frederick's grandmother have picked up a musket and tried to blow out Victor Radcliff's brains for using her the way he did? Again, Frederick had no idea.

Lorenzo pressed ahead: "So we've got to get free, or else we've got to keep fighting. No other way we can go." He looked at Frederick. Frederick understood exactly what that look meant, too: no matter what he said about it, if the talks failed the fight would go on with him or without him.

But he didn't disagree with Lorenzo, not here. "Nope. No other way," he said. The copperskin seemed satisfied. The white men camped on the far side of Slug Hollow wouldn't be so easy to placate. *Well, if we go back to shooting at each other, how are we worse off?* Frederick wondered. He saw no way. And if that wasn't a judgment on the United States of Atlantis, what would be?

Jeremiah Stafford scowled across the table at Frederick Radcliff and Lorenzo. Pretending even for a moment that a Negro and a copperskin had any business treating with him as equals was galling enough. Remembering that they could have killed him but hadn't didn't make him feel any more kindly toward them—not now, when he no longer lay in their grasp.

The table also reminded him what a travesty this was. Back in New Hastings, he'd dickered with Senators across tables ornamented with marquetry so fine and intricate, it must have left the woodworkers shortsighted for life. This one was of roughly planed boards hacked from the local pine. It stood in the taproom of a tavern abandoned when the insurrection flooded over Slug Hollow. Since that day, spider webs had grown thick up near the ceiling and in the corners of the room—or maybe they'd been there all along. In a miserable place like this, who could tell?

"You seem to think turning all the slaves south of the Stour loose will be easy," Stafford said to the leaders of the insurrection. "Wave our hands—abracadabra!—and it's done. I have to tell you, it won't be like that."

"Oh, we know," Frederick Radcliff answered. "You better believe we know."

"If it was gonna be easy, we wouldn't've had to start killing people," Lorenzo added.

Bloodthirsty savage, Stafford thought. "You had no business doing that any which way," he said.

"Oh, yes, we did," Frederick Radcliff said. "It was the only way we could make you notice we were there. White folks *don't* notice slaves, except to make money off of 'em or to lay the women." Bitterness edged his voice. Considering who his grandfather was, that was understandable enough.

As far as Stafford knew, he'd sired no colored babies himself. Not for lack of effort, though. Admitting as much probably wasn't the smartest thing he could do. Instead, he said, "If we turn you loose, it will break a lot of white families. You said it yourself—people do make money from slaves. That's one of the big reasons they won't want to give them up."

"Good luck making money off of slaves now," Frederick Radcliff said. "The devil's come out. You can't put him down again so easy."

"That is an unfortunate fact, but a fact we must face," Leland Newton said. Stafford sent his fellow Consul a sour look. Much as he wished he could, though, he didn't contradict him. This rebellion had succeeded all too well. It warned that others could succeed, too. Slaves might be ignorant, but they weren't too stupid to see that. If only they were!

"One reason you don't want to turn slaves loose is money," Lorenzo said. "What are the others, Mr. Consul, sir?" He turned the titles of respect into sneers.

Before either Stafford or Newton could answer, Frederick Radcliff said, "C'mon, friend—you know why. White folks reckon they're better'n niggers and mudfaces. Gives 'em somebody to look down their noses at."

"I knew they had those long, pointy ones for some kind of reason," Lorenzo said, even if his was almost as long and sharp as the average white man's. Frederick Radcliff's was lower and flatter. He didn't take after his grandfather there, anyway.

But the Negro hit a nerve with Jeremiah Stafford, all right. "We think so because it's true," Stafford growled.

"Everything says so, from the Bible to the most modern scholars. It must be so."

To his amazement—and fury—the Negro and copper-skin both burst out laughing. "It's your Bible," Frederick Radcliff said. "They're your scholars. What are they gonna say? 'No, we're just a bunch of stupid cows next to these other folks'? I don't think so!"

That had never occurred to Stafford. It disconcerted him, but only for a moment. "The Bible is the word of God," he said sternly. "God would not lie, and you face hellfire if you say He would."

Lorenzo went right on laughing. "Devil'd have you on the fire right now if we didn't turn you loose."

No, Jeremiah Stafford didn't care to be reminded of that, not even slightly. This time, Frederick Radcliff spoke before Stafford could say anything: "That's about the size of it. Bible doesn't matter, not for this. I don't care if white folks reckon they're better'n we are. That doesn't matter, either. What matters is, you aren't strong enough to hold us down any more, and now we know it."

"Realpolitik," Colonel Sinapis murmured. It sounded almost as if it ought to be an English word, but not quite.

Consul Newton's thoughtful grunt said he understood it. Stafford believed he did, too, which didn't mean he liked it. But then Newton spoke to the insurrectionists: "You can't leave what white men think out of the way you think. If your horses rose up against you—"

That was precisely how Stafford saw things. It was also precisely calculated to enrage the Negro and the copper-skin. "You call me an animal, you can kiss my ass," Frederick Radcliff said.

"I didn't. I don't." Newton held up a hand, as if to deny everything. "But most white men south of the Stour are liable to. More than a few from north of the river, too, I have to tell you, but maybe not so many. If you forget that, or if you try to pretend it isn't there, you're missing something important."

Stafford stared at his colleague in amazement. "He said it—I didn't," Stafford said. "I agree with every word of it, though."

"Well, I've got two words for those damnfool white folks," Lorenzo said: "Tough shit."

"*Realpolitik*," Colonel Sinapis repeated, louder this time. He looked across the table at the rebels. "The Consuls are right. White men in Atlantis do feel this way. You cannot ignore it because you do not care for it."

"Maybe us winning this fight here has gone a ways toward changing their minds," Frederick Radcliff said.

Balthasar Sinapis politely dipped his head. "Maybe," he said. "I would not bet on this anything I was not ready to lose."

"Most white men will go to their graves sure they are better than any copperskin or Negro ever born," Stafford added.

"If that's what it takes, we'll send 'em there," Lorenzo said. He started to get up from the table.

"Wait." Frederick Radcliff and Consul Newton said the same thing at the same time. They both blinked, then smiled almost identical sheepish smiles. Lorenzo blinked, too, and did sit down again. Newton went on, "We need to bring back something like peace. We can't go on the way we have been. The country will fall to pieces if we do, and that won't help anyone."

"I was thinking the same thing," Frederick Radcliff said. "We keep fighting the rest of our lives, we've got nothin' worth havin'."

"Slaves don't get set free, we've got nothin' worth havin', either," Lorenzo said.

"What have you got if you make the white men south of the Stour want to fight you to the death?" Stafford asked. "The way you're going, that's just what you're doing."

"We have to be free. Have to be," Frederick Radcliff said. Lorenzo nodded.

"Freeing you will break hundreds of thousands of white men, maybe millions," Stafford said. "They won't put up with it. Neither would you, not in their shoes."

This time, both Lorenzo and Frederick Radcliff got up. Newton started to say something. Then he stopped—he seemed to have no idea what would call them back. They walked out of the tavern together.

Newton and Colonel Sinapis both turned on Stafford. "A bad peace is worse than none at all," Stafford insisted. Neither of the other two men said a word. He didn't think that was because he'd convinced them.

Leland Newton held on to his temper with both hands. "It's either free them or fight forever," he said.

"Suppose I asked you to bankrupt yourself. Suppose I asked every fifth man in the state of Croydon to do the same," Stafford returned. "How eager would *you* be?"

"It won't be so bad as that," Newton said.

"Like hell it won't," the other Consul replied. "We won't do it. I know my people. Why won't you listen to me?"

"Negroes and copperskins were 'your people,' too," Newton said. "Why wouldn't you listen to them?"

He took a certain malicious pleasure in watching the other Consul's mouth fall open. "They don't vote!" Stafford sputtered. He needed a moment to gather himself. Then, his voice strengthening, he added, "And they've got no business voting, either!"

"It doesn't seem to do any harm in Croydon," Newton said. "No great pestilences—we don't even have the yellow jack up there, the way you do in Cosquer. God hasn't chosen to drop the city into the sea."

"I don't know why not," Stafford said. In the south, people thought Croydon and Hanover were dens of iniquity, full of sin and degradation. What Stafford didn't understand— one of the many things he didn't understand—was that people in Hanover and Croydon felt the same way about the states south of the Stour, and all because of slavery.

"You need to ask God about that," Newton said. "But you can't really believe you'll be able to put all the insurrectionists back in bondage . . . can you?" The question said he didn't want to believe Stafford could believe any such thing.

His colleague's mutinous countenance declared that Stafford wanted to believe it—wanted to with all his heart and all his soul and all his might. It also said Stafford wanted to kill as many men and women as he needed to in order to bring the rest back to submission. But then, slowly, the other Consul's features crumpled. "No," he said. "I can't." No bombastic tragedian playing Hamlet could have packed more anguish into three words.

Hearing them made Newton want to jump for joy. He didn't—nor did he show that he wanted to. Showing Stafford any such thing would only have further stiffened his colleague's already stiff back. So Newton spoke as if it were nothing but a matter of practical politics: "Well, then, how do we do what wants doing?"

"Good question," the other Consul said. "I warned you before—the whites south of the Stour won't put up with nigger freedom, let alone nigger equality."

"The way it looks to me, their only other choice is going on with this war, and that hasn't worked so well, either," Newton said.

"A lot of them won't care," Stafford said bleakly.

"Well, the militiamen we had with us can help spread the word," Newton said. "And they can help spread the word that the copperskins and Negroes could have killed every last one of us, but didn't."

"Good God!" The Consul from Cosquer looked at him as if he'd taken leave of his senses. "Do you think those people will do anything on account of *gratitude*? You know what that's worth."

So Newton did, much too well. Anyone who counted on gratitude in politics wouldn't stay in politics long. "No," Newton insisted. "But people all over the south need to know the insurrectionists aren't devils with horns and barbed tails."

"Are you so sure? What about the ones who slaughtered their masters and violated their mistresses when the uprising started?" Stafford said. "Shouldn't they hang for murder?"

"It was a war. Bad things happen in wars—that's what makes them what they are," Newton replied. "I think we will have to declare an amnesty. Otherwise the fighting starts again, doesn't it?"

"Amnesty." Stafford spat the word back at him. "So they get away with all their crimes? Makes me wish I were a nigger myself."

"Don't be silly, Jeremiah. Nothing could make you wish you were a nigger," Newton said with great assurance. His colleague couldn't deny it, either. Newton went on, "And can you see any way around it? As far as the slaves are concerned, everything their masters ever did to them was a crime."

"Oh, piffle," Stafford said. *He owns slaves, too*, Newton reminded himself. "What about masters who keep slaves on when they're old and useless?"

That did happen. Newton knew as much. He also knew something else: "What about the ones who don't? There are plenty of them, too."

Stafford waved that aside. "From now on, I can see broken-down copperskins begging in the streets and dying in the gutter. Too many slaves can't make a living unless somebody tells them what to do."

"How do you know? How does anyone know?" Newton said. "They deserve a chance, just like everybody else."

"You'll find out. And when they do start starving, do you know what will happen? They'll blame us for turning them loose," Stafford said.

That didn't sound as improbable as Leland Newton would have wished. All the same, he said, "Freedom isn't easy for every white man, either. But how many whites do you know who want to be slaves?"

"You make everything sound so simple," Stafford said. "It won't be. You wait and see—it won't."

"So what?" Newton said. "We've got to start some-where, unless we go back to the war. Can we do that?" To his vast relief, Stafford shook his head.

XXII

*J*eremiah Stafford was drunk. Even though Slug Hollow had that miserable wreck of a tavern, the place no longer held spirits or wine or beer. The insurrectionists—or maybe the locals, as they decamped—had made off with its stock in trade. Such impediments did not stop a determined man. Stafford had paid a cavalry sergeant half an eagle for a jug of barrel-tree rum, and proceeded to get outside of as much of it as he could.

It was harsh stuff. It burned all the way down. He would feel like death come morning, or maybe a little worse than that. Right this minute, he didn't care.

He did care that the cheap, fierce rum wasn't doing what he wanted it to do. Like so many men, he drank to forget. But he still remembered. The more he poured down, the more sharply he seemed to remember, too.

He'd told Leland Newton the slaves would have to be free. Worse, he'd been cold sober when he did it. *I can take it back*, he thought. Newton would never be able to prove the words had come out of his mouth. Prove it or not, though, they would both know. And it was true. It might be loathsome—it *was* loathsome! sweet Jesus, was it loathsome!—but it was true.

"They'll kill me," he mumbled as he staggered through Slug Hollow's narrow, fern-choked streets. "They'll murder me." No one had ever murdered a Consul of the United States of Atlantis. No one had even tried to assassinate one. There'd been brawls on the Senate floor, but that wasn't the same thing. No, not even close.

Of course, no Consul of the USA had ever tried to tell half his country that it couldn't go on the way it had for the past two hundred years and more. If—no, when—Stafford tried to do that, how many people would start loading their muskets?

How many people lived south of the Stour? How many of them weren't Negroes or copperskins? Stafford laughed raucously. An easy calculation, even for a drunk man: enough to make pretty sure one of them would get him. You couldn't stop a determined man. Stafford laughed some more. Frederick Radcliff, damn his black hide and blacker heart, sure had proved that.

"Radcliffs!" Stafford muttered. "Radcliffes!" He pronounced the *e* the second time. He laughed some more. He was part Radcliff himself. So was Newton. Few prominent people in Atlantis weren't. Few indeed—no matter what color they were!

Why couldn't Victor Radcliff have kept it in his trousers? Stafford took it out of *his* trousers and watered some of the ferns that had sprung up since Slug Hollow was abandoned. Or maybe the ferns had been here all along—in a pisspot hole in the ground like this one, who could say for sure? Come to that, who cared?

A big green katydid, long as one of his fingers, hopped away and disappeared under a rotting board. This was the back of beyond, all right. In most towns, mice and rats had supplanted the native Atlantean bugs. Not here, not yet. Maybe not for a long time, either. By all the signs, Slug Hollow was going back to the wilderness from which it had sprung.

Stafford veered around a corner. He stopped short—so short that he almost fell over. Someone else was promenading through the streets of Slug Hollow. The nerve of the fellow!

A second look told the Consul *promenading* wasn't the right word. The other man listed like a ship on a windswept sea. He was as drunk as Stafford was. He might have been drunker, if such a thing was possible.

Evidently it was, because he needed longer to notice Stafford than Stafford had to notice him. When he did, a sozzled grin slowly spread across his copperskinned face. "What are you doing here, you shun—*son*—of a bitch?" he asked.

"I could ashk—*ask*—you the same question, Lorenzo," Stafford said.

"I can come here," the insurrectionists' war leader replied. "Slug Hollow isn't yours."

"It isn't yours, either," Stafford said. "It doesn't belong to anybody any more."

Lorenzo's grin got wider. "Who'd want it?" He pulled a small, flat bottle from the waistband of his trousers. "Have a snort?"

"Take one of mine." Stafford held out the larger jug he was carrying. Each man drank from the other's liquor. Lorenzo's bottle held whisky every bit as raw and snarling as Stafford's rum.

"Whoosh!" Lorenzo wiped his mouth on his sleeve. "That's fine stuff!" He had to be drunk as a lord to say such a thing. Stafford at least knew he was drinking slop. It didn't stop him, or even slow him down, but he knew it.

I could kill him, Stafford thought. Lorenzo wouldn't expect a sudden attack. But what good would it do? The rebels would only find someone else, and the new man might prove smarter.

And Stafford realized the copperskin was eyeing him in a peculiar and unpleasant way. "I could cut your heart out like I was butchering a shoat," Lorenzo said.

"You could try," Stafford said, trying to steady his feet under him.

"Ahh, what's the use?" Lorenzo said. "You bastards might find somebody who really knows what he's doing."

That set Stafford laughing. "I was thinking the same thing about you," he said.

"Well, fuck you, then!" the copperskin exclaimed. A couple of seconds later, he started laughing again, too.

"You *son* of a bitch. God damn me to hell and gone if we ain't pretty much alike after all."

"Fuck *you!*" Stafford said—what could be more offensive than hearing you were like a rebel slave?

But what if it was true? They were both drunker than a leader had any business getting. Their thoughts had been running down the same track, as if in lockstep. Maybe copperskin chiefs in Terranova and black kinglets in Africa had to worry about the same kinds of things as white Consuls and emperors in Atlantis and Europe. And, when they worried about them, maybe they came up with the same kinds of answers. If they did . . .

"Sweet, suffering Jesus," Stafford whispered. If that was true, maybe—just maybe—liberating the slaves in Atlantis wouldn't be the catastrophe he'd always dreaded. Which didn't mean it wouldn't turn into some other catastrophe. And which also didn't mean he could convince the rest of the whites south of the Stour that it wouldn't be exactly the catastrophe they'd always feared.

But it did mean he would have to try.

White men always said copperskins drank like fish. Frederick Radcliff knew he had good reason to distrust anything white men said about the people they'd enslaved. That didn't mean he hadn't seen the same thing: not from every copperskin he'd known, and not all the time, but from a good many, and more often than from Negroes or whites.

He couldn't remember when he'd seen anyone of any color worse for wear than Lorenzo was now. The copperskin's hands trembled. The whites of his eyes were almost as yellow as egg yolks. Like fertile egg yolks, they were tracked with red. Even inside Frederick's tent, Lorenzo squinted as if the dim light were much too bright. He spoke in something close to a whisper—the sound of his own voice seemed enough to hurt his ears. He moved very carefully, as though pieces might break off if he bumped into anything.

"Hell of a spree," Frederick remarked, his tone as neutral as he could make it.

"And so?" Lorenzo replied. Frederick had never heard a whispered snarl before.

"You be able to talk to the white folks when we start dickering again?" Frederick asked. That was the only question that counted.

Lorenzo gave back the ghost of a grin. "Yes, Mother."

"Ahhh ... " Frederick made a disgusted noise, down deep in his throat. No matter what Lorenzo thought, he did need to know such things.

But the copperskin went on, "Matter of fact, I've been talkin' with 'em while I was drunk."

"What? With one of their soldiers in Slug Hollow?" Frederick was glad his marshal felt like talking with a white man instead of trying to murder him. Even drunk, Lorenzo was much too likely to succeed. And if he did, that was much too likely to touch the fighting off again.

Lorenzo shook his head, then winced: sure as the devil, moving anything must have hurt. "Nah," he said. "With one of the big fellas—that Stafford asswipe."

"You ... talked with ... Jeremiah Stafford?" Disbelief clogged the way Frederick's words came out. The Negro couldn't imagine why the war leader hadn't hurled himself at the southern Consul's throat.

No matter what Frederick couldn't imagine, Lorenzo nodded ... gingerly. "Sure did," he said. "He was as toasted as I was, pretty near. Had some rum that'd strip the paint off a wall in nothin' flat." He smacked his lips, remembering.

"How about that?" Frederick said. Along with *Isn't that interesting?*, it was one of the handful of phrases that wouldn't land anybody in trouble. A plantation owner's black butler often found a use for phrases like that.

"Yeah. How about that?" In Lorenzo's mouth, by contrast, the phrase became one of wonder. "You know something else? He ain't such a bad fellow."

"How about that?" Frederick repeated. Now wonder filled his voice, too. Lorenzo couldn't have surprised him more if he'd said that Jeremiah Stafford was really a woman under his clothes.

"It's a fact. Damned if it ain't," the copperskin declared. It was no such thing. It was what Lorenzo thought right this minute. Frederick understood the difference, whether Lorenzo did or not. What Frederick didn't come within miles of understanding was *why* Lorenzo thought so right this minute. Since he didn't, he asked him.

"Why? I'll tell you why—on account of him and me, we think the same way," Lorenzo answered.

If that wasn't a judgment on the copperskin, what would be? Frederick had no idea. "How do you mean?" he inquired.

"Well, I'll tell you—it was like this," Lorenzo said. "When I seen him, first thing I thought was *I ought to murder this stinking shithead.*"

"I believe *that*," Frederick said. It was almost the first thing Lorenzo'd said that he did believe.

"And you know what?" the war leader continued. "First thing *he* thought was *I should murder this God-damned copperskin.*"

"I believe that, too," Frederick said. As far as he could see, the only reason Consul Stafford didn't want to murder every Negro and copperskin in the USA was that, if he did, nobody would be left to do the hard, sweaty work white folks didn't care to do for themselves. Stafford scared him more than any of his other opponents. He asked, "Why didn't you try? Why didn't *he* try?" If they were both falling-down drunk, what could possibly have held them back?

Lorenzo proceeded to tell him: "I didn't, on account of I was worried that, if I just left him there dead, the white bastards were liable to come up with somebody who's smarter and meaner."

"Mm," Frederick said—even *How about that?* wouldn't do. Stretching his mind, he could imagine the whites coming up with somebody smarter than Stafford, though the Consul from Cosquer was nobody's fool. But meaner? Frederick didn't think such a thing was possible. He hoped it wasn't.

"And do you know what?" Lorenzo said. "Do you know?"

"No. What?" Frederick said.

"He told me the only reason he didn't go for me was

because he was afraid *we'd* find somebody better. Is that funny, or is that funny?"

"That's funny, all right," Frederick agreed, though he didn't feel like laughing. *Could* he replace Lorenzo at need? If something happened to the copperskin, he'd have to try. Would any other insurrectionist make as good a general? Frederick Radcliff feared the answer was no.

"He gave me some of his rum to drink, and I gave him some of the tanglefoot I had." Lorenzo shook his head again: small motions this time, ones that might not hurt so much. "I was a fool to mix 'em. My damned head wouldn't want to fall off so bad if I stuck to whiskey."

"You drink enough of it, and it'll get to you any which way," Frederick said.

"Well, yeah, but . . . " Lorenzo sighed. "You know what I want now? I want the scale of the snake that bit me, that's what. Got any?"

"Not in here," Frederick said.

"I'm gonna go get me some, then." Lorenzo turned back toward the tent flap.

"Take it easy this time," Frederick warned.

"Yes, Mother," the copperskin said once more. He added, "I pour down that much shit two days in a row, I'm liable to wake up dead tomorrow morning."

"Doesn't stop some people," Frederick said. More than a few of the people it didn't stop were copperskins.

But Lorenzo said, "I bet Stafford's lookin' for the scale of the snake right now, too. Like I say, he's quite a fella." Away he went, muttering a low-voiced curse at the bright sunshine outside.

"Quite a fella," Frederick echoed. He wished he did have something strong inside the tent now. He didn't feel like getting drunk, but he sure could have used a knock.

Things were going better than Leland Newton had dreamt they could. His colleague from Cosquer had stuck to his agreement that the slaves in the USA would have to be freed. Newton hadn't really expected that. He knew Stafford had got head-over-heels drunk after agreeing, but he hadn't thought even getting drunk would make him go on.

Go on Stafford did, though. Something might have happened *while* he was drunk. If it had, the Consul from Cosquer didn't want to talk about it. Newton had probed a couple of times, as discreetly as he knew how. He wasn't discreet enough. Stafford rebuffed every query.

Newton did notice Stafford and Lorenzo the copperskin eyeing each other whenever the two sides met in the tumbledown tavern. They still differed, often loudly, but they didn't seem ready—no, eager—to go at each other with knives any more. Newton asked Stafford about that, too.

"Oh, he's a rotten copperskin, but he's not such a bad fellow," the other Consul answered.

"You never said anything like *that* before," Newton observed.

Stafford only shrugged. "If we're going to make this work, we need to make it work," he replied, and Newton couldn't very well quarrel with that.

Agreeing that Negroes and copperskins needed to be free turned out to be the easy part of the bargain. Agreeing on what that freedom meant and how far it should stretch proved much harder.

Frederick Radcliff knew what he wanted. "If we're gonna be equal, we gotta be *equal*," he said, over and over again. "Anything a white man can do, a black man or a copperskin has to be able to do. If you can vote, we can vote. If you can make contracts, we can make contracts. If you go to school, we go to school with you. We especially need to go to school, on account of you people wouldn't let us do that for so long."

That *especially* made Consul Stafford stir. "If you want to be equal, you shouldn't get to claim you especially deserve to do something."

Radcliff looked back at him. "Haven't you been saying we especially can't marry white folks?"

Stafford turned red. "Miscegenation is contrary to nature."

"Who told *you*?" the leader of the insurrection retorted. "Sure never bothers white men when they feel like laying colored women. If you don't believe me, you oughta ask my grandfather."

That made Stafford turn redder. "There's a difference," he mumbled.

"How come?" Lorenzo asked him. "Miscegenation either way, ain't it? Don't matter whether a white man sticks it in or a white woman gets it stuck into her."

"You are crude, sir," Newton told him. His own ears felt as if they were on fire—he wasn't used to such blunt talk.

"Fucking is crude," Lorenzo answered. "Don't need fancy clothes to do it in. Hell, clothes just get in the way."

Newton did his best to turn the subject: "Maybe we can make a bargain. If you give up the right to intermarry, we can consider granting you preferential access to schooling."

"Yes. That might be possible." Stafford almost fell over himself agreeing. He didn't like the idea of educated Negroes and copperskins in the USA. But he liked the idea of their walking down the aisle with white women even less. That was what politics was all about: yielding something you didn't care for so you wouldn't have to accept something you really couldn't stand.

The proposition made Frederick Radcliff and Lorenzo hesitate, anyhow. They put their heads together and argued in low voices. At last, Radcliff said, "Let's talk some more in the mornin', if that's all right by you. We got to take this back to our people, see how they feel about it."

"Fair enough," Newton said before Stafford could respond. The other Consul didn't object. Newton hadn't thought he would: Stafford might recognize the need for these bargaining sessions, but that didn't mean he cared for them.

After Radcliff and Lorenzo had left, Stafford turned to Newton and asked, "How would you like your sister or your daughter marrying a nigger?"

"I wouldn't like it much," Newton answered honestly. "I don't think any of the women would like the notion very much, either. I doubt whether many white women would. That's why I hope the insurrectionists will give up their claim to intermarriage in exchange for schooling."

"Hmp. You've got some sense, anyhow. Who would have thought so?" Stafford managed a crooked grin.

"May I speak to this point?" Colonel Sinapis asked.

Newton and Stafford both eyed him in surprise. Neither intermarriage nor education had much to do with soldiering, which was his province. But Newton said, "By all means, Colonel," and Stafford nodded.

"Thank you, your Excellencies," Sinapis said. "In Europe we have only a handful of copperskins and Negroes—not enough for people to get excited about. What we have instead is a great plenty of Jews."

"We have some here, too," Newton said. "We treat them more or less like any other white men." Consul Stafford nodded again. Newton finished, "My secretary, Mr. Ricardo, is a Jew, and a very able man."

"I have seen what you do here. Even in your army you have some officers who are Jews—not many, but some. In Europe, this would never happen." By the way the colonel sounded, he approved of the European practice. But he went on, "I understand why this is so, too. You have not so many Jews here. And you have so much dislike for colored people, not much for Jews is left over."

"That's an ... interesting way of looking at things," Consul Newton said uncomfortably. It made more sense than he wished it did.

"But what's your point, Colonel?" Stafford asked.

"Ah. My point, yes." Before coming to it, Balthasar Sinapis made a small production of lighting a cigar. Once it was drawing well, he went on, "In my lifetime, European laws against intermarriage with Jews have mostly fallen into disuse. Some people said the sky would fall or the Antichrist would come after this happened, but the world still goes on as it always did. Maybe things would turn out the same way here."

"Maybe they would," Newton said thoughtfully. "We can hope so, anyhow."

"I wouldn't bet anything I wasn't ready to lose," Stafford said. "Marrying Jews, at least you're marrying money. Marrying a nigger ... " His disgusted look told what he thought of that.

"No one would *make* anybody marry someone of a different color," Newton said. "The question is whether it ought to be legally possible."

"I know what the question is," Stafford replied. "I know what the answer ought to be, too."

"When you make a treaty to settle a war, you do not always get everything you want," Colonel Sinapis said.

"I understand that. But I'd like to get some of what I want," Consul Stafford said.

"So would the Negroes and copperskins," Newton reminded him. Stafford's expression said he didn't need—or, more likely, didn't want—reminding.

Every time Frederick Radcliff walked into the tumble-down tavern to talk with the white Consuls and colonel, he felt like a trainer sticking his head into a tiger's mouth. He'd come away safe every time up till now, but things only had to go wrong once and. . . .

He felt doubly nervous walking in there this particular morning. It must have shown, because Lorenzo said, "Don't worry. This is what we decided. If the white folks don't like it, that's their hard luck."

Frederick shook his head. "Liable to be everybody's hard luck. That's what I'm worried about."

"We whipped them," Lorenzo said. "Let them sweat."

With an effort, Frederick made himself nod. The white men sat there waiting for him and Lorenzo to join them. Frederick didn't trust any of them. Consul Stafford was an open enemy. Consul Newton was less of one, at least openly, but Frederick wondered what he thought down deep of Negroes and copperskins. As for Colonel Sinapis . . . Maybe it was Frederick's imagination, but he thought the foreign officer looked down on the two Consuls almost as much as they looked down on the uprisen slaves they faced. That puzzled Frederick. Did coming from Europe count for so much? He thought Colonel Sinapis thought it did.

"Good morning," Newton said as Frederick and Lorenzo sat down across the table from him. "What have you decided about my proposal?"

After a deep breath, Frederick answered, "Sorry, but we aren't going to take it."

Newton looked as if he'd bitten into something sour.

"Are you sure? Many—even most—of your people would benefit from education. Only a handful would take advantage of intermarrying, and chances are some of them would end up sorry they'd ever tried it."

"You may be right. You likely are. But that isn't the point," Frederick said.

"Oh? Suppose you tell me what is, then." Newton's voice was light and clear, as usual, but the Consul was provoked enough to show the iron underneath, which he seldom did.

Frederick took another deep breath. He needed one. He tried to hold his own voice steady as he answered, "Point is, if we're gonna be equal with white folks, we got to be equal every way there is. We deserve to get schooled same as white folks if we're equal. And we deserve the right to marry no matter what color somebody is. If we say you can take that away from us, what are we sayin'? We're sayin' you're better'n we are, an' all the talk about bein' equal is just that—talk."

The white men glowered at him and Lorenzo. Lorenzo glowered right back. Frederick only sat there waiting. Slowly, Consul Newton said, "It's hard to negotiate with you if you give us nothing to negotiate about."

"That's what I'm trying to tell you. That's why we rose up," Frederick said. "How can you negotiate about freedom? Either a man's free, or he ain't. If we got to be free, we got to be all the way free."

"A matter of principle." Consul Stafford sounded less scornful than he often did.

"That's right. A matter of principle." Frederick nodded. The white man had come out with what he was trying to say.

"We have our own principles, you know," Stafford said.

"Sure you do." That was Lorenzo, answering before Frederick could speak. "You can buy us and sell us and lay our women whenever you've got a stiff dick you don't know what to do with. Only you can't, not any more. That's how come we rose up, too."

Stafford didn't explode, the way Frederick thought he

might. All he said was, "Getting this past the Senate will be harder than you seem to think."

"Tell 'em you're doing what's right," Frederick said. "It's the truth."

"As if *that* matters," Leland Newton muttered, more to himself than to anyone else.

"It better matter," Frederick said. "If it don't, we got to start over. An' startin' over means the Free Republic of Atlantis an' lots more shootin'."

"I told you before—we can start shooting again if you push us hard enough. You won't like what happens if we do," Stafford said.

"You won't like it, either," Lorenzo promised, and exchanged more glares with the Consul from Cosquer. But they weren't the same kind of glares as they had been before the two leaders drank together on the overgrown streets of Slug Hollow. Then, Stafford might have been scowling at a dangerous dog, Lorenzo eyeing a fierce redcrested eagle. Now each recognized the other as a man. That much was plain. Whether such recognition improved things was, unfortunately, a different question.

"We rose up on account of freedom," Frederick said. "If we could've got it without fighting, we would've done that. But it wasn't about to happen—you folks know it wasn't, and you know why, too."

"Do you see the day, then, when one of the Consuls of the United States of Atlantis will be a Negro and the other a copperskin?" Jeremiah Stafford didn't sound as if he saw that day, but he didn't—quite—sound as if he were mocking Frederick, either.

Since he didn't, Frederick judged he deserved a serious answer: "Not any time soon. More white folks than there are colored, and people just naturally vote for their own. But maybe the day will come when nobody cares what color a man is, as long as he's a good man and he knows what he's doin'."

"A noble sentiment," Consul Newton said softly.

"Well, so it is," Stafford agreed. He looked across the table at Frederick. "You'd better not hold your breath waiting for that day, though."

Frederick looked back at him. "No need to worry about that, your Excellency. I don't aim to."

"I don't care if a copperskin gets to be Consul," Lorenzo said. "What I care about is whether it's against the law for him to try. Long as he *can* try—long as nobody ties him to the whipping post and stripes his back for even thinking about it—I won't fuss. Same with marryin' out of your color: I don't reckon it'll happen real often, but there shouldn't be a law against it."

"That's right," Frederick said. "That's just right. That's how it ought to be."

"Easy enough for you to say so, out here in the middle of nowhere," Consul Stafford said. "As I told you a little while ago, it won't be so easy to convince the Senate in New Hastings."

"Do we have to bring the war across the mountains, then? We can do that." Frederick wasn't really sure the insurrectionists could do any such thing, but he wanted to keep the white men worried.

By the looks on their faces, he did. "Even if we give you everything you say you want, you may not end up happy with it," Newton said.

"If the law says we're free, we'll be happy with it," Frederick answered.

"If the law says we're equal, we'll be happy," Lorenzo added.

Colonel Sinapis suddenly spoke up: "No matter what the law says, white men will keep running Atlantis for a long time to come. You are right—there are more of them than there are of you. And they have more money. They have more experience running things, too. You may not be slaves in law any more, but you will not at once become equals, no matter what the law says."

Frederick Radcliff glanced over at Lorenzo. The foreign colonel's words seemed much too likely for comfort. Lorenzo spread his hands, as if to say he felt the same way. But what came out of his mouth was, "Chance we've got to take."

"I think so, too," Frederick said. "We have to start somewhere."

*   *   *

Leland Newton had drafted the accord that would, with
luck, put an end to what almost everyone these days was
calling the Great Servile Insurrection. He wrote it in language more simple than he would have used most of the
time. He was a barrister; keeping things simple wasn't
something he normally did. But, while Frederick Radcliff
could read and write, he wasn't trained in the law. Newton
didn't want him to be able to claim he'd signed something
he didn't fully understand.

"Why not?" Stafford said when Newton remarked on
that. "It'd serve the damned nigger right."

"We came to Slug Hollow to stop trouble, not to stir up
more of it," Newton said.

"We came west to stamp out the insurrection," Stafford
replied, "and look what a good job of it we did."

"If we bring home a peace the whole country can live
with, we will have done well enough here," Newton said.

"If." The other Consul bore down heavily on the word.
"And if the whites south of the Stour rebel because of the
peace we've brought home, how well will we have done
here? That may yet happen, you know."

"I do intend to propose that they be compensated for
the loss of what has been their property," Newton said.

"That may do some good. Then again, it may not," Stafford replied. "If living in houses were to be made illegal tomorrow, how happy would you be to get money for a house
you had to leave?"

"Happier than if I didn't get any, I suppose," Newton
answered.

"You would still be angry, though, wouldn't you? You
might be angry enough to go to war about it," Stafford said.

"I hope not." Newton heard less conviction in his own
voice than he would have liked. He gathered strength as
he went on, "White men south of the Stour can't go back
to living in the house they had before. Their neighbors will
burn it down around their ears if they try. You know that's
so."

Unwillingly, his colleague nodded. "But a good many of
them don't understand that it's so," Stafford said.

"We've got to convince them. *You've* got to convince them," Newton said. "They admire you. They respect you. They believe you. They believe *in* you."

"And much good any of that will do me. As soon as I tell them they really do have to give up their slaves, they'll start plotting to assassinate me. And if you think I'm exaggerating, you'd better think again," Stafford said.

Newton didn't think the other Consul was. He knew how high passions ran among slaveholders. "Maybe what's happened to our army—and what's happened to some of them—will give them the idea that times have changed," Newton said hopefully.

"Maybe." Stafford didn't sound as if he believed it for a minute.

"If you feel the way you do, why are you signing the agreement?" Newton asked.

"This will be bad. Not signing would be worse," Stafford said. "I can see that much. I'm not a blind man, no matter how often you've called me one on the Consuls' dais. But you and the insurrectionists seem sure angels will sing hosannas as soon as everyone's name goes on that paper. I am here to tell you things won't be so simple."

Do I think everything will be wonderful once we have an agreement? Newton wondered. Maybe he did. And maybe Stafford was right to have his doubts. But he was also right about something else: "Not signing *would* be worse."

"I said so." Jeremiah Stafford gestured impatiently. "But that doesn't mean signing will be good. It just means signing won't be so bad. You can say right away that a man is free. How long does it take before he truly believes he's free, though? And how long before his neighbors believe it?"

He was full of hard questions this morning. Newton wished he himself were as full of answers. He said, "All we can do is find out." He handed the other Consul the paper he'd been working on. "Does this say everything we need to say? Is it clear? Have I forgotten anything?"

Stafford perused it. He suggested two or three small changes. The points he raised were cogent; Newton made the changes without a murmur. His colleague sighed.

"Now I suppose it is as good as it can be. Whether it should be . . . " Stafford sighed again. "I think not, but events have overtaken me."

"General Cornwallis must have said the same thing when Victor Radcliff trapped him in Croydon," Newton remarked.

"He ended up doing well for himself—and for England—in India," Stafford said. "Atlantis can't send me so far away. When the country learns what we're about to do here today, it may wish it could."

"The Treaty of Slug Hollow, or perhaps the Slug Hollow Agreement. Schoolchildren from now till the end of time will have to learn about it, and about the people who signed it," Newton said.

"But what will they learn?" Stafford asked. "Will teachers say we were heroes, or will they call us a pack of fools and thrash all the little brats who can't remember how we made a hash of things?"

More hard questions. Newton could only shrug. "We'll have to do it and then find out, that's all," he said. "Are you ready?"

"No, but we're going to do it anyhow," the other Consul answered. "Then we have to persuade the Senate not to crucify us because we did it. And good luck on that score, your Excellency."

"We'll both need all the luck we can find," Newton said. "So will the United States of Atlantis." He carefully folded the Slug Hollow Agreement and put it in a jacket pocket. It meant nothing till it was signed. But that moment was only a few steps away now.

XXIII

*F*rederick Radcliff studied the paper in front of him with more care than he'd ever given any other piece of writing. No other piece of writing he'd ever seen would affect his life so much, or affect the lives of so many other people.

"Is it all right?" Lorenzo asked anxiously. The copperskin couldn't read, and had to trust his judgment. With much effort, and with his tongue wagging from a corner of his mouth like a hard-working schoolboy's, Lorenzo could write his name. Even that little put him ahead of most slaves.

"I . . . think so," Frederick answered. He glanced across the table at Consul Newton, who'd given him the document. Newton was a white man, a barrister, and a politico, and so triply not to be trusted. He smiled back blandly now. Frederick discounted that. His gaze swung to the other Consul, the southern Consul. The less happy Jeremiah Stafford looked, the more relieved Frederick felt. Stafford was bound to have seen the agreement beforehand. If he didn't like it, it was less likely to hold hidden traps that would limit the future liberty of blacks and copperskins.

"As you will see, we have already signed the document,"

Newton said. "It needs only your signature, and that of your marshal, for us to submit it to the Senate and end this insurrection that has discommoded everyone."

"Not everyone, your Excellency. Oh, no. Not everyone," Frederick said. "You see freedom in front of you, you don't reckon you're—what did you call it? Discommoded, that's right." He filed the word away so he could use it again if he ever found the need.

Consul Stafford sniffed. "You see a chicken coop in front of you, you don't care who owns it."

"I expect that's so, your Excellency," Frederick said. "You're hungry enough, I expect it's so no matter what color you are. You want to get free bad enough, I expect you rise up no matter what color you are, too. Back in the old, old days, weren't white men slaves? And didn't they rise up whenever they saw the chance?"

"Spartacus," Newton said.

"That's the fella!" Frederick nodded. He knew little more about the ancient slave insurrectionist than his name. He hadn't even been able to come up with it a moment before. All the same, lots of Negroes and copperskins knew there'd been plenty of slave revolts before their day. Whites didn't want them learning such things, which was all the greater incentive for doing so.

Plainly, Consul Stafford also knew about Spartacus. Just as plainly, he didn't like what he knew and didn't want colored men knowing it. But that was his hard luck, nobody else's.

Frederick went through the agreement one more time. He might miss something because Consul Newton was too clever for him. You took that chance in any dicker. He was damned if he would miss anything because he hadn't been diligent enough, though.

"Is it all right?" Lorenzo asked again. He respected and feared the written word all the more because he had no control over it.

Reluctantly, Frederick nodded. He had his own fears: that damaging clauses still hid under the surface, the way crocodiles waited underwater for whatever might be rash enough to step into their river. But on the surface everything seemed as it should. "It *is* all right," he replied, more firmly than he had the last time.

"May I offer you a pen?" Consul Newton took one from his pocket and held it out across the table.

"Got my own, thanks," Frederick said, not without pride. He pulled it out. It was at least as fine as the white man's, likely finer.

"Where did you steal it?" Stafford asked.

"I don't have to tell you that, and I don't aim to," Frederick said. "Take a look at Article Four here." His finger stabbed down onto it. "There's an amnesty for things that happened during the war. If it covers killin' folks, I reckon it covers gettin' my hands on an ink pen."

He waited to see if Stafford would call him a liar. By all the signs, the Consul from Cosquer wanted to. Since Article Four said exactly what Frederick maintained, Stafford couldn't. He fumed instead. Leland Newton kept his face studiously blank. Colonel Sinapis looked amused, but only for a couple of heartbeats. Then his features also went impassive again.

Newton slid a bottle of ink across the table. That Frederick did accept, opening it with a nod of thanks. He dipped his pen, then signed his name on the line waiting for it. His signature wasn't so fancy and florid as any of the white men's—Sinapis', in particular, was a production—but so what? You could tell it was his name, and nothing else mattered.

He pushed the paper over to Lorenzo and handed him the pen. "You sign it here." He pointed to the only remaining blank line.

"By God, I'll do it," Lorenzo said, and he did.

"We have an agreement. The Great Servile Insurrection has ended at last," Newton said.

"The Free Republic of Atlantis is no more." Consul Stafford took what comfort he could from that.

"*We* have an agreement," Frederick said. "But the Senate back in New Hastings still has to say everything's all right, doesn't it? Till then, it's just what we've done. It's not official, like."

"That's true. Consul Stafford and I will do all we can

to make sure the Senate *does* approve what we've done here," Consul Newton said. "We don't want the fighting to flare up again. And our own prestige is on the line here, you know. If the Senate rejects this agreement, it's the same as rejecting our leadership."

Stafford made a wordless noise, down deep in his throat. Maybe his heart wouldn't break if the Senate did reject the agreement. It might be the same as rejecting his leadership, but it might also keep slavery alive—for a little longer, anyhow. That was part of the reason Frederick said, "Reckon I'll come back to New Hastings with you, me and my wife. Nobody's got more reason to try and make the Senate see things the right way than the two of us."

"Are you sure that would be wise?" Newton said slowly. "Your presence there might do more harm than good." Consul Stafford's face said—shouted—that he thought the same thing.

But Frederick answered, "I'll take the chance, your Excellency. Honest to God, sir, I will. Let the Senate see that a Negro can be a civilized fella, or pretty close. Let the Senate see that a Negro and his woman can love each other just like a white man and his wife. Ain't no proper reason our folks can't get married, same as yours."

"Copperskins, too," Lorenzo added.

"Copperskins, too," Frederick agreed. "An' let the Senate see one more thing. Let the Senate see a Negro can be named Radcliff. That's what happens when white men get to go tomcatting around with the slave women. And I'm here to tell you it ain't right."

"God bless my soul," Leland Newton murmured. For a moment, Consul Stafford looked as if someone had hit him in the face with a wet fish. For an even briefer moment, Colonel Sinapis looked amused again. Then, as before, he donned the mask of impassivity.

"You gonna tell me I *can't* come? What's this piece of paper worth if you say somethin' like that?" Frederick tapped the agreement Lorenzo had just signed.

"Come ahead. By all means, come ahead," Stafford said. "It will be something out of the ordinary, at any rate. But you must understand: there is no guarantee the Conscript Fathers, even the ones from the north, will love you."

"Like I said, chance I take." Frederick hoped he sounded calmer than he felt. "And why shouldn't they love me, or at least like me some? I bet I'm kin to half of 'em, maybe more."

For some reason, neither Stafford nor Newton seemed to want to answer that. Colonel Sinapis, by contrast, laughed out loud. If looks could have killed, the ones both Consuls sent him would have left the USA looking for a new army commander. But nobody tried any more to tell Frederick he shouldn't accompany the Consuls back to New Hastings.

Jeremiah Stafford had shared railway cars with Negroes before. Porters fetched food and drink and pipeweed to passengers who needed them. He'd always taken those porters as much for granted as seats or windows: they were part of the railroad's accouterments. It wasn't as if he had to treat them like human beings.

Sharing a railway car with Negro *passengers* was something else again. During the course of the fighting and the talks, he'd come to respect Frederick Radcliff. Maybe that respect grew not least because of Frederick's famous white grandfather. Regardless of the reason, it was real.

But Frederick's woman—Stafford didn't care to think of her as his wife—was nothing but a dumpy, rather frumpy, middle-aged nigger. Frederick might have reasons for loving her. Whatever they were, Stafford couldn't see them.

She didn't put on airs, anyhow. That was the one good thing he could find to say about her. But, as the train rattled and jounced east toward the Green Ridge Mountains, he became more and more certain he could smell her—and Frederick. What white man didn't know that niggers stank?

He wanted to say something. Had more southerners sat in the car with him, he would have. If either Leland Newton or Balthasar Sinapis had two working nostrils, though, neither man gave any sign of it. Sinapis smoked cigar after cigar, and the pipeweed he favored smelled worse than any Negro ever born. Stafford wanted to open a window, but didn't want wood smoke and soot flying in.

And so he stayed where he was and stayed quiet, sizzling inside. Neither Frederick Radcliff nor Helen—Stafford supposed he ought to think of her as Helen Radcliff, but the idea of real slave marriages was as repugnant to him as the idea of slaves with surnames—gave him any open cause to complain. All they did was look out the window and exclaim at the scenery every so often. A white couple on their first journey by train might have acted the same way.

"What kind of reception do you think we'll get when we come into settled country?" Newton asked as the train started into a pass that would take it through the mountains.

"The terms we made will have gone before us, eh?" Stafford said.

"Well, of course. We wired them to New Hastings, after all," the other Consul replied. "Wherever the wires reach, people will have heard about them."

Stafford nodded. He knew as much—who didn't? But he was trying to pretend ignorance. And he had his reasons: "In that case, your Excellency, we should count ourselves lucky if they don't drag us off the train and lynch us."

By Newton's gulp, he hadn't expected Stafford to be so blunt. "You are joking, I hope," he said.

"I only wish I were," Stafford said.

He hadn't intended that Frederick Radcliff should hear him, but the Negro did. "Welcome to the club, your Excellency," Radcliff said.

"Huh? What club?" Stafford asked.

"Any time a black goes out amongst whites, he knows he's a dead man if he gets out of line," said the leader of the insurrection. "Same goes for copperskins, too. Now you know how it feels."

"He's got you there," Newton said with a sly chuckle.

"Huzzah," Stafford answered sourly. He feared he'd feel like a hunted animal till the train got north of the Stour—if he lived that long. He didn't care whether slaves felt that way all the time—or had felt that way all the time—till his own signature on that damned sheet of paper acknowledged that they were slaves no more. You needed to keep such people in line. Keeping them afraid went a long way toward doing just that. But white men had always been the lords of creation in Atlantis. Stafford hated feeling any other way.

He tensed when the train stopped in a hamlet called West Duxbury for wood and water. No ravening mob appeared. West Duxbury didn't have enough people to make a ravening mob. But someone flung a rock through a window as the train pulled out of the station.

Frederick Radcliff and Helen sat there with the air of people who'd been through worse in their time. Consul Stafford counted himself lucky to have got off so lightly. Leland Newton was the one who let out a startled yip. He almost jumped out of his seat. All in all, he reminded Stafford of a cat that had just made the sudden and unwelcome acquaintance of a rocking chair.

Sure enough, smoke did pour into the car. It masked whatever odor the Negroes in there might have had. It also made Stafford's eyes water and made him cough. He felt as if he'd been puffing on a pipe without letup for a week, the only difference being that he didn't get the little lift pipeweed brought with it. All things considered, he would rather have kept the window intact . . . he supposed.

More towns, bigger towns, and more stops lay ahead. How long would it be before somebody decided a rock wasn't good enough? How long before somebody pulled out an eight-shooter, or maybe a rifle musket? No, Stafford hadn't been joking about any of that. He knew how white people down here would feel about setting slaves free.

Life was a miserable bastard, all right. But what other choice did you have? At the moment, Stafford knew exactly what other choice he had. Outraged southern men could pull him from the train and hang him or burn him or simply tear him to pieces. Living seemed better . . . if he could get away with it.

A conductor whose wool jacket was resplendent with polished brass buttons strode into the car and bawled, "New Hastings! Coming into New Hastings!"

"Thank God!" Leland Newton said. No one in the battered railway carriage seemed angry that he came close to taking the name of the Lord in vain. He knew why not, too: the others were just as glad to make it to the capital in one piece as he was.

Stafford had warned that it would be bad. Newton had thought his colleague was exaggerating to make liberating Negroes and copperskins seem a worse idea than it really was. But the Consul from Cosquer turned out to know what he was talking about. White men south of the Stour really were up in arms at the idea of turning their bonds-men loose.

White women, too. Newton shuddered at the memory of all those screaming, furious faces. Some of the things they called him would have made a deep-sea sailor blanch. Some of the things they called Frederick Radcliff made what they called him seem endearments by comparison.

Senators were chosen because they had a longer view and were better able to deliberate than ordinary people. So Atlantean charter theory said, anyhow. In practice, as Newton knew too well, Senators often became Senators because they were better able to say what most people in their state already thought. If southern Senators were better able to say what those women had been screaming, they would meet this train with bayonets and with cannon loaded with canister.

It pulled into the station. Gray-uniformed Atlantean soldiers did stand on the platform with fixed bayonets. But they faced away from the train, not towards it. They were there to protect the Consuls and Frederick Radcliff and his wife, not to mete out summary justice on them.

The captain commanding the soldiers called, "Don't you worry, folks! Nothing's gonna harm you, not while I'm around." He spoke like a man from Hanover, from the north, which meant—Newton hoped it meant—he had no use for slavery. The Consul presumed that was Colonel Sin-apis' doing. He hoped so, at any rate. Sinapis had got off the train early. Maybe he had a good idea of what they'd go through on the way to New Hastings. Or maybe he just wanted to buy himself a little more time before he had to explain to his superiors at the Ministry of War why he hadn't crushed the insurrection.

Consul Newton breathed a sigh of relief once he got off the train. As soon as he was traveling by himself, he would be pretty safe. Consuls were the highest magistrates in the USA, yes, but how many people knew what they looked like? They didn't put their faces on coins like European sovereigns or Terranovan strongmen. They were citizens of the republic over which they presided.

As far as Newton was concerned, things were supposed to work like that. He worried about the way photographs— and woodcuts and lithographs based on them—would change politics. Wouldn't they make it impossible for anyone who wasn't handsome to serve his country? And wouldn't they make it easy for a good-looking scoundrel to subvert freedom?

All that would be trouble for another day, though. The day they already had brought plenty of trouble of its own.

Consul Newton got a better notion of how much trouble it brought when he spent a few big copper cents on the day's newspapers. The papers in New Hastings were always unrestrained—which was putting it mildly. Today they out-did themselves. Some of them called him and Consul Stafford heroes. To others, they were the worst traitors since Habakkuk Biddiscombe, who'd gone over to King George in the middle of the struggle for freedom and fought harder against the Atlantean Assembly's army than most of the redcoats.

The *New Hastings Chronicle* showed a front-page cartoon of a Negro who looked something like Frederick Radcliff and something like a gorilla. The caption was NEXT CONSUL OF THE USA? Presumably to no one's surprise, the *Chronicle* didn't care for the notion.

Even if everything went well, how long would it be until more than a handful of white men were willing to vote for a Negro? Frederick Radcliff himself didn't think the day would come any time soon. Newton agreed with him. That might be too bad, which made it no less true.

He found more guards around the Senate building, which also housed the two Consuls. They, or at least some of them, knew who he was. "You really gonna turn them people loose?" one of them demanded, in accents identical to Consul Stafford's.

"Yes, we are, and you just told me why," Newton answered. The corporal sent back a blank stare. Newton spelled it out for him: "Because they *are* people, and for one man to own another is wrong."

"Huh," the man in gray said—a noise full of nothing but skepticism. "Ain't like they're *white* people, for cryin' out loud."

"How would you feel about that if they owned whites and not the other way around?" Newton inquired.

"Huh," the two-striper said again. After some deliberation, he went on, "Reckon there'd be some niggers and mudfaces who needed killing, and pretty God-damned quick, too . . . your Excellency."

Newton had never heard a less respectful title of respect. Even so, he said, "They decided the same thing—about white people. And now, if you will excuse me . . . " He didn't want to spend all day arguing with an underofficer about what he'd done. Sure as the devil, he'd be spending day after day arguing with one Senator after another after another.

Behind him, the corporal and his men started arguing among themselves. Some of them thought Newton had a point, anyhow. That made him feel a little better about what he and Stafford had done in Slug Hollow. Down south of the Stour, everyone seemed to want the Consuls' scalps.

Men from Croydon and other northern states greeted Newton like a conquering hero as he walked the winding corridors of the Senate House. Yes, he did have some support, at least. A Senator from Hanover asked him, "How did you manage to get the Great Stone Face to do what was right?"

That description of his Consular colleague made Newton chuckle in spite of himself. The Great Stone Face wasn't there any more. It had been a rocky profile—a cliffside, really—on the eastern slopes of the Green Ridge Mountains not far west of Croydon. *Had been* was the operative term: when Newton was a young man, an avalanche turned the Great Stone Face into the Great Stone Rubble Heap. But the memory of it, like memories of moles and wolves and lions, lingered on modern Atlanteans' tongues.

And, if old paintings and woodcuts told the truth, that rocky profile did bear a certain resemblance to Consul Stafford's. Newton feared telling the other Consul as much wouldn't be the smartest thing he could do.

"Well, how *did* you?" the politico from Hanover persisted.

Newton chuckled again, this time on a rueful note: the distilled residue of terror. "The insurrectionists beat us," he answered. "They didn't just beat us, either—they could have massacred us. But they held off. Nothing like that for concentrating the mind, believe me."

"It must be true. So the newspapers weren't turning out their usual rubbish when they said the slaves won?" the Senator said.

"No. They weren't." With three words, Newton tried to conceal the fear he remembered much too well. Listening to himself, he found he was mournfully certain he'd admitted it instead.

"Well, well," the Hanover man said. "Is the black Radcliff a man his grandfather would have approved of?"

"Do you know, I rather think he is," Consul Newton said slowly. "You'll see Frederick Radcliff for yourself before long, and one of the things you'll see about him is that he knows what he wants and he doesn't aim to turn aside till he gets it, no matter what's in his way. To me, that sounds a lot like Victor Radcliff in the old days. How about you?"

"I suppose so," the Senator answered. "One of the things Victor must've wanted was a nigger wench, eh? Might've been better for everybody if he hadn't got her. We would have bought more time to work out how to deal with this mess without tearing the country apart."

"It could be," Newton said, but he didn't believe it for a minute. The United States of Atlantis had been busy quarreling about slavery for longer than he'd been in public life, with no sign they were getting anywhere. The insurrection was only one more proof that they hadn't been. And . . . "If Frederick Radcliff were never born, my guess is that some other Negro or copperskin would have kicked up an uprising anyway before very long."

The Senator blinked. "Now there's an interesting notion. Did the slaves rise up because this fellow Radcliff led them into insurrection, or would they have gone off anyway if he weren't around?"

It *was* an interesting question . . . as long as you didn't start chasing it round and round like a puppy in hot pursuit of its own tail. "I hope you don't expect me to prove anything, as if we were back in plane geometry at college," Newton said.

"God forbid!" the other man replied. "My cousin's friend taught geometry himself. If he hadn't tutored me, I never would have got through it."

"Well, all right. I know how you feel, believe me," Newton said, remembering his own struggles with Euclid's axioms and theorems. "My guess is, we got the insurrection we got because of Frederick Radcliff. If he'd never been born, we would have got a different one before too long. How different? A little? A lot?" He spread his hands. "I couldn't begin to tell you."

"Seems reasonable," the Senator from Hanover said after some thought of his own.

"It does, doesn't it?" Newton said. "All of which, again, proves exactly nothing."

New Hastings held more people than Frederick Radcliff would have dreamt could live together. It dwarfed New Marseille, the biggest town he'd seen up till then. And Croydon was supposed to be bigger, and Hanover was supposed to be bigger still.

Frederick had trouble believing any such thing was possible. But then, he'd also had trouble believing a city like this was possible. He didn't know everything there was to know—a fact he'd got his nose rubbed in time after time. He suspected everybody ever born had that happen.

The Consuls put Helen and him up in a hotel. That had to cost a lot of money, but they didn't seem to worry about it. People waited on the two Negroes as if they were important whites. Not all the hotel staff consisted of Negroes and copperskins, either. Some of the waiters and sweepers and what-have-you were white men and women, most of whom spoke English with one odd accent or another. They were as professionally deferential as the colored people beside whom they worked.

"I could get to like this," Frederick remarked as a white man in a boiled shirt bowed him and Helen to their table at the hotel restaurant.

"Don't let it go to your head," she said, even as the servitor pulled out a chair so she could sit in it. "Talks don't work out the way folks hope, we're nothin' but a couple of no-account niggers again."

Her pungent good sense made Frederick smile. "Oh, I know," he said as he sat down himself. "But look how they fuss over us now. They *can* treat us like real people if they want to bad enough."

"Sure. You treat a coral snake or a lancehead polite, too, long as it's got a chance to bite you," his wife answered. "Soon as it can't, though, you try and figure out how you're gonna smash in its head."

That also seemed more sensible than Frederick wished it did. The other thing that seemed sensible was enjoying himself while other people were paying for it. He ordered roast duck with loaf sugar and a wine the waiter recommended. The wine came all the way from France, and was almost as tasty as its price proclaimed it ought to be.

"Master Barford, he didn't know about stuff like this," Helen said after she tried it.

"Even if he did, he didn't have the eagles to buy stuff like this," Frederick answered. He'd known some other planters had more money than his master. Just the same, all slaveholders had seemed rich to him.

From a slave's perspective, all slaveholders *were* rich. What Frederick hadn't realized was that there were plenty of people richer than any of the backwoods planters out near New Marseille. He suspected that among their number were both the Consuls and most Atlantean Senators.

He was also beginning to suspect that, if he played his cards right, he could end up rich himself. He was, after all, the man who represented Negroes and copperskins to the rest of the USA. If the man who did that didn't end up dead, he would end up prominent. And didn't a prominent man always have influence to sell?

Do I want to get rich? Frederick wondered. But that was the wrong question. Anybody who wasn't an idiot knew having money was better than not having it. No one wanted to go hungry or barefoot or to wear rags or live in a leaky, tumbledown shack. The real question was, did Frederick want to get rich badly enough to sell himself, to sell out the people who counted on him, so he could pile up stacks of golden eagles?

The sweetened roast duck suddenly tasted like carrion in his mouth. If he did something like that, wouldn't he still be a slave? And wouldn't he be a slave who'd willingly—no, eagerly—sold himself to his new masters when he might have stayed free? How could you look at yourself in the mirror after you did something like that? Every time you lathered up to shave, wouldn't you want to cut your throat instead?

"Well, then, I won't do nothin' like that," he muttered.

"Won't do nothin' like what?" Helen asked. Even if it often seemed as if she could, she couldn't read his mind after all.

"Never mind," Frederick said. They'd been together all these years; she'd earned the right to push him. She used it, too. It didn't do her any good, not this time.

"You traitorous son of a bitch!" That was what most of Jeremiah Stafford's friends called him these days. The rest called him "You treasonous son of a bitch!" The only difference lay in their erstwhile friends' attitude toward the language, not in their attitude toward him.

They all seemed to hate him. And the more they pushed him and mocked him and called him a jackass, the more they provoked him to push back. When his train pulled in at New Hastings, he'd still despised liberation and everything that went with it. They kept telling him it was impossible and he'd had no business agreeing to it in the first place.

Naturally, he defended what he'd done. "You would have signed that paper, too, if you were there," he told anyone who would listen. But nobody wanted to listen to him. That was a big part of the problem.

Supporters of slavery organized marches through the streets of New Hastings. The marchers made the city almost unlivable with drums and horns during the day. At night, they used their noisemakers and carried torches as well. Stafford feared they would burn down the capital over his head.

He didn't think his fears were misplaced. Whenever the marchers came upon a copperskin or a Negro, they beat him within an inch of his life. Colored men in New Hastings were free, not slaves. That worried the marchers not a cent's worth. If anything, it only inflamed them more.

New Hastings had no real police force. As far as Consul Stafford knew, London was the only city that did. The few watchmen on the city payroll here were no match for the marchers—or for the marchers' white foes, who waded into them whenever the odds seemed decent. They weren't content with clouting one another over the head with placards. Knives came out. So did pistols.

And so did soldiers. Stafford never found out who gave the order. Afterwards, no one seemed to want to admit it. But hard-looking men in gray uniforms who carried bayoneted rifle muskets appeared on street corners at sunup one morning. When the antiliberation marchers disobeyed their orders in any particular, they opened fire without warning.

That probably wouldn't have worked in a southern city like Cosquer or Nouveau Redon or Gernika. It would have stirred up more trouble than it put down. But it served its purpose in New Hastings. The marchers rapidly discovered they didn't have enough popular backing to take on the soldiers. Making the discovery cost them more casualties. Order returned to the capital.

Order failed to return to the Senate floor. Stafford and Newton had presided over tempestuous sessions before. Those were as nothing compared to what the Consuls met now. Shaking his fist at Stafford, a Senator from Gernika cried, "You've changed!"

"Indeed," Stafford replied. "No matter what the honorable gentleman may believe, it is not against the rules of this house."

He might as well have saved his breath. "You've changed!" the Senator repeated, as if it were forbidden in the sterner books of the Bible. "We haven't, and we aren't about to."

"Fools never do," Stafford said.

That, of course, only poured oil on the fire. Several Senators screamed abuse at him in English, French, and Spanish.

Bang! Bang! Consul Newton plied the gavel with might and main. "The honorable gentlemen are out of order," he said—you could sound all the more insulting when you were exquisitely polite. "They would do well to remember to look toward the future, not the past."

Take your heads out of the sand, Stafford translated to himself. Did ostriches really stick their heads in the sand? He had no idea. He'd never seen an ostrich. They were supposed to be pretty stupid, just like honkers. He'd never seen a honker, either, even though they were Atlantean birds. As far as he knew, nobody'd seen any honkers since Audubon found some to paint . . . which probably meant backwoodsmen had shot and eaten the last few survivors.

Back around the time when the United States of Atlantis freed themselves from England, there'd been proposals to set land aside as a preserve for Atlantis' native creatures. Nothing ever came of those proposals—no state cared to give up land from which it might one day draw taxes. It was probably too late for honkers now, anyhow. It might not be for some other creatures. . . .

But even if it wasn't, Consul Stafford had more urgent things to worry about at the moment. "My colleague is right," he said—a sentence that hadn't crossed his lips very often before the failed campaign to put down the slave insurrection. "We may not like going forward, but we have no other choice—not unless you would rather spend the rest of your lives fighting a war we are unlikely to win, and one that will not bring us the benefits we seek even if we should win."

"If you hadn't buggered up the fight against the niggers,

you'd sing a different tune now," a Senator from Nouveau Redon said.

"You wouldn't go along with everything the Croydon man says," another southern Senator added.

"We did the best we could," Stafford answered. "We faced danger together, and we made the agreement with Frederick Radcliff together, too."

"And you get the blame together!" shouted the Senator from Nouveau Redon.

"The credit, you mean," Leland Newton said. "History will justify us. It always justifies people who believe in progress."

Did it? Stafford had his doubts. But the way his former friends howled made him have doubts about his doubts, too.

XXIV

$\mathcal{T}$he clerk of the Senate eyed Frederick Radcliff with as much warmth as he would have given a cucumber slug in his salad. "Do you solemnly swear the testimony you are about to give will be the truth, the whole truth, and nothing but the truth, so help you God?" he droned.

"I do," Frederick said.

"Are you aware that perjury is a felony punishable by fine or imprisonment or both?"

"I wasn't, but I am now," Frederick answered. A couple of Senators chuckled. A few more smiled. All of them were northern men. The dignitaries from south of the Stour seemed affronted that a Negro should testify before them at all. *Well, too damned bad*, Frederick thought.

As for the clerk, he was impervious. All he said was, "State your name for the record."

"I am Frederick Radcliff," Frederick said. That probably affronted the southern Senators all over again. A Negro with any surname would have been bad enough. A Negro with the most prominent surname in Atlantis was more than twice as bad. A Negro grandson of the famous First Consul was much more than twice as bad.

Even the clerk's eyes said as much. If he wasn't from a slaveholding state himself, Frederick would have been mightily surprised. But all that came out of his mouth was, "You may be seated."

Frederick sat in the witness' chair. The angle at which it was turned let him see the two Consuls on their dais as well as the Senators on the floor of the chamber. Consul Newton said, "For the record, you are the man who was styled Tribune of the Free Republic of Atlantis, are you not?"

"That's right," Frederick replied.

"Treason!" three Senators shouted at the same time.

"No such thing," Frederick said, though that wasn't a question. "Was it treason when my grandfather rose up against England?" *My grandfather.* If they didn't care for that, too damned bad again.

"It would have been treason, if Victor Radcliff and the Atlantean army had lost," Newton said.

"And it would have been treason if you and your army had lost, too." By the way Consul Stafford sounded, he was still sorry it hadn't been.

"But we didn't, and so it ain't—isn't." Frederick corrected himself. Quite a few Senators would think of him as a dumb nigger no matter what he did, but he didn't want to give them extra ammunition.

"Treason doth never prosper: what's the reason? For if it prosper, none dare call it treason." Newton seemed to be quoting something. By the ring of it, it was old-fashioned. Shakespeare? Frederick had read some, but didn't remember seeing it there.

"If you say that about my grandfather, you can say it about me. If you don't, saying it about me isn't fair," he said.

"I'm not saying it about anyone, because, by the terms of the agreement we signed, there is no such thing as the Free Republic of Atlantis any more. The slave insurrection is over and done with—isn't that right?" Newton said.

"Yes, sir, long as the rest of the agreement gets carried out," Frederick answered. "Long as the slaves get freed, and we get the same rights in law as any other Atlanteans."

Several southern Senators started yelling abuse at him. Several northern Senators applauded him, trying to drown out the southerners. Newton and Stafford both used their gavels. No one seemed to want to pay any attention to them. "The Sergeant at Arms will restore order by any means necessary," Stafford warned.

That worthy looked at him as if he'd taken leave of his senses. Frederick sympathized with the functionary. Quite a few Senators carried stout sticks, more often as weapons than as aids to keeping them on their pins. And how many more hid a dirk or a pistol under their waistcoats? Frederick didn't know. He wouldn't have wanted to find out the hard way, either.

Finally, something like order did return. "Why do you suppose Consul Stafford and I agreed to terms like those?" Newton asked. "Was it out of the goodness of our hearts, say?"

"Not likely . . . sir," Frederick said, which startled laughter out of Senators from both sides of the Stour. He went on, "Probably because we had you in a place where we could've slaughtered you, but we didn't do it."

"Yes, you did have us in a place like that," the Consul agreed. "Why did you let us go, then?"

"So we could get terms instead of fighting forever," Frederick said.

"And now you have those terms," Newton said.

Frederick nodded. "We sure do."

"What do you think of them?"

"They're fair. We can live with them."

"They're an outrage! They don't punish you for what you did in the insurrection!" a southern Senator shouted.

Newton and Stafford used their gavels again. Frederick talked through the sharp thuds: "They don't punish the slaveholders for everything they did before the insurrection, either."

That set the Senator to spluttering without words. "Both sides agreed that recriminations were pointless," Consul Newton said. Frederick nodded once more, though he'd learned the word *recriminations* after the talks with the white men started.

"We did," Consul Stafford agreed. "I don't believe that made anyone happy. I know it didn't make me happy. But I also know doing anything else would have made everyone even more unhappy."

"I want all the Conscript Fathers to think about that," Newton said. "I understand that you may not wish to ratify the agreement we made in Slug Hollow. Believe me, though—the consequences of rejecting it are far worse than the consequences of accepting it."

"Easy for you to say—you aren't losing half your property!" that stubborn southerner cried.

"We intend to arrange compensation for slaveholders—after the agreement is accepted," Newton said.

The southerner only jeered: "You say now you intend to. But when will we see cash for our niggers and mudfaces? When pigs fly, is my guess. You'll get what you want, and you won't give us what we need."

He sounded like a girl trying not to give in to a man who wanted to go to bed with her. Noting how much the Senator sounded like that kind of girl, Frederick had all he could do not to laugh out loud. "We will meet all our obligations," Consul Newton insisted. *Of course I'll marry you afterwards*, he might have been saying. And maybe a man who told a girl something like that meant it, and maybe he didn't.

"May I say somethin', your Excellency?" Frederick asked.

"Go ahead," Newton said. Stafford nodded.

"Thanks. What I want to say is, nobody's giving us anything for all the stuff slaves have to go through. If slaves didn't have to go through things like that, I wouldn't have me Victor Radcliff for a granddad. I don't reckon there's enough money in Atlantis to pay us for all that. Just let us be free, and we'll call it square. If white folks get somethin' 'cause they can't own people and buy people and sell people any more, they better reckon they're the lucky ones, not the other way around."

That got him another hand—from Senators from north of the Stour, he presumed. It also got him more fury from Senators from states where owning slaves remained legal. His guess was that most of those Senators would be wealthy men, which meant most were likely to own slaves themselves. No wonder they didn't love him. Some of them brandished their sticks at him. But, if any of them were armed with more than sticks, they didn't show it. That was something . . . Frederick supposed.

He turned to the Consuls. "Ask you something?"

"We're supposed to be questioning *you*," Stafford said with a thin smile. But then he nodded. "Go ahead."

"Black man or a copperskin ever talk in front of the Senate before?" Frederick asked.

"It's possible." Consul Newton answered after a pause for thought. "Not certain, but possible. In the states north of the Stour, colored men have been free for a long time. They've been able to get an education. Some of them have done very well for themselves, and become experts on this and that. So they may have testified. I'm not sure going back through the records would say one way or the other."

"All right." Frederick hadn't thought of that. "Reckon folks won't have any doubts from here on out."

"I . . . reckon you're right." By the way Newton paused before coming out with the word, he didn't use it very often. "And your testimony has been intelligent and to the point. Let the record show also. You have testified like a man."

"I am a man," Frederick said. The Senators from south of the Stour might not like that, but it was true. And he'd just proved it on the most important stage Atlantis had.

Senators from south of the Stour hadn't cared for Leland Newton before he went off to face the insurrectionists. They liked him even less now that he'd come back with an agreement they saw as a surrender.

"Why'd you sell the country down the river, you son of a bitch?" one of them growled as he came up to Newton in a hall.

"Would you ask Consul Stafford the same question the same way?" Newton inquired.

"I've already done it," the politico replied—he might be a fool, but he was a consistent fool.

Right at the moment, Newton didn't see consistency as

a virtue. He snapped, "Well, what did he tell you, you dumb shitheel?"

The Senator's jaw dropped. He was more used to dishing out insults than to taking them. "I ought to cut your liver out for that, God damn you to hell."

"When I have to deal with oafs like you, I think He has already sent me there," Newton replied.

"Why, you—!" The Senator drew back a meaty fist.

As if by magic, an eight-shooter appeared in Newton's hand. He'd practiced drawing it in front of a mirror. Practice might not make perfect, but it definitely improved things. "I will tolerate the rough side of your tongue, sir. But I suffer no man to lay a hand on me."

"Pull the trigger! You wouldn't dare!"

"You have already made a great many mistakes. I promise you, you will have made your last one if you swing on me." Newton aimed the pistol at the middle of the Senator's chest. The politico was a beefy man; if Newton did fire, he couldn't very well miss. A lead ball almost half an inch across—or more than one—would make almost any man thoughtful.

Even the Senator? Even him. He took one careful backwards step, then another. As if he hadn't, he snarled, "I still say you're screwing the country."

"Say whatever you please." Newton didn't lower the revolver. "For now, why don't you go say it somewhere else?"

Swearing under his breath, the Senator edged past him. Newton held on to the pistol till he was sure the other man was going away. Then he tucked it back into his belt under his jacket. Only as he was putting it away did he let his hand shake—or rather, lose the ability to keep it from shaking. He came much too close to shooting himself in the leg.

"That must have been fun." Frederick Radcliff came out of another Senator's office.

"Now that you mention it," Newton said, "no."

"Is this what running Atlantis is like all the time? Is this what my grandfather had to do?" the Negro asked.

"If Victor Radcliff ever drew a pistol on a Senator in a hallway, history does not record it," Leland Newton answered. "Plenty of people called him everything they could think of, though, and a little more besides. By everything I've read, and by everything old men told me when I was young, he gave as good as he got, or maybe a bit better."

"Huh," Victor Radcliff's grandson said thoughtfully, and then, "Well, I worried some of my people might shoot me, too."

"Did you?" Consul Newton said; Frederick hadn't admitted that before. "So things weren't all sweetness and light in the Free Republic of Atlantis?"

"Are you kiddin' me? Only place it's all like that is heaven—'cept I bet they argue there, too," Frederick said. "Somebody brags his halo's shinier'n the other fellow's, or this lady doesn't like it on account of that other lady over there, she's playin' her harp too loud."

"If some of the Conscript Fathers heard you, they would call you a blasphemous skink." Newton had to suck hard on the insides of his cheeks to keep from cackling like a laying hen. He had no trouble at all picturing Frederick's querulous angels, and hearing them inside his head. Chances were that made him a blasphemous skink, too. He didn't intend to lose any sleep over it.

And Frederick Radcliff passed from the ridiculously sublime to the serious in a single sentence: "If all the southern Senators are like that big-mouthed bastard, how will you ever pass the agreement?"

"Not all of them are, thank God," Newton said. "I doubt they will love you any time soon, but some of them can see reason if you hit them over the head with a rock. Consul Stafford did, after all."

"Happy day. That makes one," Frederick said.

"There will be more. There must be more." Was Newton saying that because he really believed it, or to try to convince himself? He didn't care to inquire into the question too closely. To his relief, Frederick Radcliff didn't seem to care to, either.

No one banged on the door to the hotel room Frederick Radcliff and Helen shared. They had guards out in the hall to make sure no unwelcome and possibly armed visitors barged in on them. Given the emotional and political climate in the Senate, and in New Hastings generally, Frederick was glad those guards were there.

When someone tapped on his door, then, he didn't hesitate to open it. One of the guards handed him a newspaper, saying, "A Senator gave me this. He asked if you'd seen this story here." A callused forefinger showed which story.

Frederick would have found the headline even without the helpful digit. What else would a Senator want him to read but a story headlined SLAVE REVOLT IN GERNIKA SPREADS!?

He quickly read the piece. The revolt had broken out near St. Augustine, a sleepy subtropical town on the east coast south of the city of Gernika, the state capital. Local planters had had no luck crushing it; neither had the state militia. The state of Gernika had been Spanish Atlantis till the USA bought it from Spain thirty years earlier. Both before and after coming into the USA, Spaniards had an evil reputation among slaves. Better to be owned by an English Atlantean than a Frenchman, but better a Frenchman than a Spaniard any day—or so Negroes and copperskins said.

Maybe that was true, maybe not. If the slaves down in Gernika believed it, they would fight harder against the men who'd claimed the right to own them. Frederick gave the paper back to the guard. "All right. Now I've seen it. What does the Senator want me to do about it?"

"He didn't tell me," the guard answered. "But if I was him, I'd want you to stop it. That's what you're here for, right?"

That's what you're here for, right, nigger? The guard didn't say it out loud. He and his friends were doing their job well enough, so maybe he didn't even think it. Maybe. But Frederick had trouble believing that. He could hear slights in a white man's tone of voice. If he sometimes heard them even when they weren't there, well, who could blame him?

Regardless of whether *nigger* was in the guard's thought, what he did say made obvious sense. It had equally obvious problems. "How am I supposed to stop something down in Gernika if I'm here in New Hastings?"

"Beats me." The guard tapped the two stripes on the left upper arm of his tunic. "I ain't nothin' but a dumb corporal. You should ought to talk to the Senator."

"It would help if I knew which one," Frederick pointed out.

"Oh, sure. That makes a difference, don't it?" Laughing at himself, the underofficer thumped his forehead with the heel of his hand. Perhaps all men really were brothers under the skin. Frederick had used that same gesture when he was feeling more stupid than usual. The corporal went on, "This here was Senator Marquard, from Cosquer."

From Consul Stafford's home state, just north of Gernika. A Frenchman, by his name. A sly fellow, whatever his name and background—he didn't want trouble spilling up over the border. Slaves everywhere south of the Stour seemed suspended in a state of limbo. If the Senate approved the Slug Hollow agreement, they would be free. If the Senate didn't, they would explode, and Frederick didn't think he or anyone else would be able to stop them or even slow them down.

The Negroes and copperskins down by St. Augustine must not have been able to wait. Or else some master had done something intolerable even by the loose standards of masters in a state where Spanish rules still held sway. The newspaper story hadn't said what touched off the uprising. Maybe the reporter didn't know. Maybe, when he was writing about slaves, he didn't care.

Frederick didn't remember any particularly hostile questions from Senator Marquard. The little the Negro knew of him suggested he could see sense. He supported slavery—what Senator from south of the Stour didn't?—but he was less fanatical than most of his colleagues. Which meant . . .

"I'm going to have to see him," Frederick told Helen after summarizing the newspaper story and his conversation with the guard.

"How come? All he wants to do is get you killed," his wife said.

That hadn't occurred to Frederick. He hadn't thought of himself as naive, but maybe he should have. If he went down

to Gernika to try to settle things and either the whites or
the rebellious slaves didn't want to listen to him, he could
easily end up dead. But if he didn't, what was he worth as a
leader? What was the Slug Hollow accord worth?

Sighing, he said, "I got to see the Senator. Where I go
from there . . . Well, we'll find out."

Senator Abel Marquard was ready to see Frederick.
Frederick would have been astonished if he weren't. Marquard looked both debauched and clever. His eyes were
red-tracked and pouchy; he combed a few strands of coal-
black hair across a vast expanse of scalp. But he had the
air of a man who calculated and who remembered—favors,
yes, but also slights.

He shook hands with Frederick with no visible qualms:
a courtesy not all southern Senators seemed willing to extend to a black man. When he said, "I am pleased to make
the acquaintance of the man of the hour," Frederick could
hear no sarcasm—which, with a customer as smooth as
Marquard, didn't mean it wasn't there.

"Pleased to meet you, too, sir," Frederick said, wondering if he meant it. "What can I do for you?"

"Not what you can do for me—what you can do for Atlantis," Senator Marquard answered.

Frederick decided to stop beating around the bush.
"Why should I do anything for Atlantis? What the devil
has Atlantis ever done for me? Plenty to me, I will say that,
but not much for me."

"Not yet, maybe," Marquard agreed blandly. "But how
would you expect the Senate to approve the Slug Hollow
agreement"—he named it with obvious amusement—
"when slaves are still in arms against the country in spite of
the truce you promised?"

"Oh, come on . . . sir," Frederick said with a snort. "I've
never been to Gernika. I've never been anywhere near it.
If you think I'm in charge of slaves down there the way
a colonel in New Hastings is in charge of soldiers in New
Marseille, you better think again."

"I see. Well, let me ask you another question, then: if you
are not in charge of these people, if they pay you no heed,
why should anyone here take the Slug Hollow agreement

seriously?" Marquard said. "Does it not promise more than you can deliver?"

"Mmp." Frederick made an unhappy noise. He parried the question as best he could: "If you go along with it, the slaves won't have any reason to rise up, on account of they won't be slaves any more."

"It could be." Marquard didn't call him a liar to his face, but he might as well have. "On the other hand, we are entitled to proof that you are a leader who can get your people to follow you wherever they happen to be."

By *your people*, he couldn't mean anything but *Negroes and copperskins*. Frederick wanted to argue with him about that. He thought the Slug Hollow accord was good for everyone in Atlantis, regardless of color. But that would sidetrack the argument. Instead, he stayed direct: "Suppose I do that for you, then? What will you do for me in exchange?"

Senator Marquard looked pained. Such straightforwardness held little appeal for him. "You would not find me ungrateful," he murmured, pasting a delicate smile onto his thin lips.

Frederick's lips were far from thin, his smile far from delicate. "If I do this, and I come back alive—or even if I don't—will you back the Slug Hollow agreement? Will you do everything you can to get your friends to back it, too?"

The Senator looked pained. "You ask me to put my political future in your hands."

"Well, you're askin' me to risk my neck," Frederick retorted. "You think I'm gonna do that for nothin', you better think twice."

"I could tell you yes and then do exactly as I please," Marquard said. "You are no Senator yourself. You have no power to enforce a bargain."

"No, huh?" Frederick smiled again, as unpleasantly as he could. "How many slaves have you got, sir? If you renege on me, how long do you reckon you can go before you have an accident? Or you can turn your slaves loose, I guess—but if you do that, you may as well go along with Slug Hollow, right?"

Senator Marquard opened his mouth. Then he closed it again. After a long silence, he said, "It is not to be doubted that you favor your grandfather. The Radcliffs have always been famous for their stubbornness."

"I don't know anything about that. I never got to meet him. He never came to see my grandma again, or my pa." Frederick didn't try to hide his bitterness. "All I know is, you want me to do this, and I want something from you. If I play your game, will you play mine?"

Another silence followed the question. Abel Marquard made a steeple of his fingertips. Over his hands, he stared across his desk at Frederick. "Had you been born white, you would assuredly have been chosen Consul by now— more than once, unless I miss my guess."

"Who can say?" That thought had also occurred to Frederick. "But I never had the chance, on account of I'm black instead. Maybe some other Negro or copperskin will get it one of these days—if you go along with what I worked out with the Consuls Atlantis has got now."

By Marquard's expression, he wasn't convinced that would be good for the country. His chuckle wasn't enthusiastic, either. But he said, "All right. If you go and pour oil on the troubled waters of Gernika, I will do what I can to have the Senate ratify the Slug Hollow agreement. Does that suit you?"

Frederick thought about asking him to put it in writing. Before he did, he realized Marquard would refuse. Frederick tried a different question: "Your word as a gentleman, sir?"

He knew the southern planter's code. Other than a southern planter, who knew it better than a house slave? If Marquard gave his word as a gentleman, even to a Negro, he would keep it. A man who broke his word showed he was no gentleman, and a southern planter who showed he was no gentleman had no reason to go on living.

Those same thoughts had to be passing through Abel Marquard's mind. If they were, his much-lived-in face gave no sign of it. His answering nod held no trace of hesitation. "My word as a gentleman," he said, and held out his right hand. Frederick took it again. One man risked his life; the other, his influence. Each probably would have said he chanced too much.

Jeremiah Stafford had been on the point of demanding an army to put down the new spark of insurrection in Gernika when Frederick Radcliff said he would go down there and try to do the job himself. That took the Consul by surprise. He wondered if the rebellious slaves in Gernika had even heard of Frederick Radcliff. They'd heard there was trouble, and they'd decided to start some more. That was how things looked to him, anyhow.

Part of him wanted the Negro to go down there, fail miserably, and prove to the world that the Slug Hollow agreement wasn't worth the paper it was written on. What surprised him was that part of him didn't. The world had changed, and Stafford had changed with it. Frederick Radcliff's slave army could have carried out a massacre worse than any in Atlantean history. It could have, but it hadn't. Stafford remained among the living because of the Negro leader's restraint. And so . . .

A life for a life, Stafford thought when he summoned Frederick to his office. Things weren't so simple, of course. Atlantis owed the black man far more than one life. But Stafford was doing what he could.

Dressed in white shirt, black trousers and jacket, and black cravat—dressed like a prominent white man, in other words—Frederick Radcliff cut an imposing figure. Amazing what wearing a jacket with black buttons rather than a butler's brass ones could do: the Negro no longer seemed the least bit servile.

The figure he cut made it easier for Stafford to treat with him as an equal. "If you go down to Gernika, you lay your life on the line," the Consul warned.

He hadn't expected Frederick to look amused. "You aren't the first one to say so," the Negro answered dryly. "Even if I couldn't cipher it out for myself, my wife made it real clear." He paused, chuckled, and repeated himself: "*Real* clear."

"Why are you going, then?" Stafford asked.

"On account of it needs doing," Frederick said. "If you send in soldiers, you're liable to stir up everything south of the Stour. But if I can calm things down, like, that goes a long way toward showing things can work out the way we hoped when we talked in Slug Hollow."

Stafford hadn't hoped things would work out when they talked in Slug Hollow—just the opposite, in fact. But, having signed the agreement, he had to support it. All the abuse heaped on him because of it only put his back up. He was a stubborn man himself . . . and he had Radcliff blood of his own, on his mother's side.

"If you don't calm things down—" he began.

"Chance I take," Frederick Radcliff broke in. "If I deliver, the Senate's liable to look at the Slug Hollow agreement a whole different way."

If I deliver, I'm the man of the hour. Stafford understood what the black man meant but didn't say. If Frederick delivered, he would be more powerful than any Senator: arguably more powerful than either Consul. And who would have chosen him to hold such power? Not the people. Only himself.

Yes, the kind of power the Negro would have lay altogether outside the Charter. Somehow, that worried Consul Stafford less than it might have were Frederick a different man. Back around the turn of the century, the slaves on one of the islands south of Atlantis had risen up and overthrown their French overlords. They hadn't just overthrown them, either—they'd slaughtered them. Since then, they'd had a dizzying series of generals and kings and untitled strongmen, all grabbing for power for its own sake. Stafford didn't think that was what Frederick Radcliff had in mind.

Of course, if he was wrong . . .

"It'll work out, your Excellency," Frederick said. "Or I hope it will. My biggest worry isn't the Negroes and copperskins. My biggest worry is some angry white man with a rifle musket. But he's the kind of fella I've got to worry about here in New Hastings, too."

"You're well protected here," Stafford said. "Staying safe in Gernika will be harder, I'm afraid."

"Chance I take," the Negro repeated. "It should be all

right ... unless some Senator is hiring those fellas with the rifle muskets."

What am I supposed to say to that? Consul Stafford wondered. "Do you want me to tell you they'd never do anything like that?" he asked aloud. "Do you want me to tell you they're too honorable to get those ideas?"

"Nah." Frederick shook his head. "You'd be lying, and we'd both know it. Hell and breakfast, your Excellency, some of 'em'd shoot a white man who said anything about slavery. Most of 'em'd shoot an uppity nigger, or fix it up so somebody else did the shooting for 'em."

Stafford didn't argue the point. How could he? He did say, "Don't you think that's a good argument for staying right where you are?"

"I won't lie—I'd like to," Frederick Radcliff answered. "But if I do, what do you think the chances are the Slug Hollow agreement'll go through?"

"It would still have some chance, I think," Stafford said judiciously.

"Uh-huh. That's about what I think. It'd have some—not too much," Frederick said. "If I do go, if I can calm things down, odds get a lot better. You white folks have already had plenty of chances to kill me. What's one more?" His laughter was not filled with mirth.

Neither was the chuckle Stafford returned. "It's not as if copperskins and Negroes never took a shot at me."

"No, huh?" This time, Frederick Radcliff did sound amused. "If you didn't sign that paper, there'd be plenty of 'em who'd still want to let the air out of you."

"You mean there aren't any now?" Stafford asked.

"Oh, maybe some," Frederick allowed. "But there would be more." He cocked his head to one side. "Nobody here but us chickens right now, your Excellency. How come you didn't back away from Slug Hollow soon as you had the chance? I would've bet my shirt you would—an' I would've lost it, too."

"I thought about it," Stafford said—that wouldn't surprise the black man. The Consul went on, "But what good would it have done me if I had? The fighting would just have started up again. Maybe we would have won it. I think we would, once you provoked us enough to make us push back hard. What would winning mean, though? It wouldn't turn the clock back to where it was before the insurrection started. I think we would have had to kill most of the blacks and copperskins in the country to make the rest quit. The new rising in Gernika says the same thing."

"Yes, I think so, too," Frederick Radcliff agreed quietly.

"All right, then." Consul Stafford spread his hands. "If we killed most of our slaves, we couldn't go on living the way we could when we had them all. And going on the old way would be the only point to repudiating Slug Hollow."

"You can't put Humpty Dumpty together again," Frederick said.

"No, you sure can't." Stafford nodded. "All the king's horses and all the king's men . . . and since the old way won't work any more, we'd better try to make the new ones work as well as they can."

"That's how it looks to me, all right. I didn't reckon it'd look that way to *you*," Frederick said.

"No, eh?" This time, Stafford's chuckle was distinctly wry. "The other thing that happened was, as soon as the terms we agreed to in Slug Hollow got out, every idiot in New Hastings started telling me what kind of idiot I was. When a damned fool starts screaming at you, you know he's got to be wrong. And if he's wrong, what does that mean? It means you're right. You follow me?"

"Oh, yes. *Ohhh*, yes," Frederick answered. The canniest Senator could have sounded no more convincing. "One of the sweetest things in the world is rubbing some dumb son of a bitch's nose in just what a dumb son of a bitch he really is."

"Now that you mention it—yes," the Consul said. Drunk, he'd seen that Lorenzo was a man not so very different from him. Now, sober, he realized the same thing about Frederick Radcliff. Which meant he and his ancestors, back to the earliest days of slaveholding in Atlantis, had been wrongheaded through and through. Which meant the Slug Hollow accord was probably the least the USA should be doing, not the most. But that was a worry for another day. Today had plenty of worries of its own. Among them . . .

"I *do* wish you the best of luck coming back safe from St. Augustine."

"I believe you," Frederick replied. "I wouldn't have a few months ago, but I do now."

"That's all right. I wouldn't have meant it a few months ago," Stafford said. "Things change. Either you change with them—or you don't, and they roll over you. I don't like that, Lord knows, but it's the only game in town." No, he didn't like it one bit, which, as he'd said, mattered not even a cent's worth.

XXV

*F*rederick Radcliff thought he knew everything there was to know about living in a warm, muggy climate. As soon as he got off his steamship—another first—and rode inland from St. Augustine, he realized he was an amateur. Sweat sprang out on his skin. But it didn't cool him, because it didn't—it couldn't—evaporate. It just clung, leaving him hot and wet.

One of the men in the cavalry escort the national government had given him wore spectacles. The trooper took them off and polished them with a rag, then set them back on his nose. Ten minutes later, he did it again. "Goddamned things keep steaming up," he grumbled.

The ground was flat and swampy. Frederick saw shades of green he'd never imagined before. Ferns grew everywhere. They even sprouted from the sides of brick walls. Herons—blue and gray and white, some of them almost as tall as a man—stood in shallow pools. Every so often, one of those bayonet beaks would plunge into the water. A wriggling fish or frog or salamander would vanish at a gulp.

Vultures spiraling down out of the sky drew Frederick's notice to carrion before his nose caught the sickly-sweet reek. The men from his escort smelled it about the same time he did. "Something's dead," one of them said.

"Something big," added the trooper with the eyeglasses.

He tried to wipe the condensation off them one more time. By the way he swore under his breath as he stuffed the rag back into his tunic pocket, he wasn't having much luck.

They rode around a corner, and then all reined in at once. A corpse hung from the branches of a cypress tree. Frederick thought it was a Negro's, but it might have been a copperskin's. Not easy to be sure: it was bloated and blackened, and the carrion birds had already been at it. A turkey vulture perched on the branch, not far from where the noose was tied. It sent the travelers a beady jet stare.

So battered was the body that it might even have been a white man's, hanged by the insurrectionists. It might have been, but it wasn't: a placard tied to it warned SLAVES STAY QUIET. They were still in country white men controlled, then.

"How much longer till we get to where the slaves have kicked off the traces?" Frederick asked.

"Should be pretty soon," a cavalryman answered. "When they start shooting at us from ambush, that's a pretty good sign."

Was it? Frederick wasn't so sure. Rebellious slaves might want to fire at government soldiers, yes. But disgruntled white men could also want to shoot at a Negro who'd already led a much-too-successful uprising.

You knew that before you came down here, Frederick reminded himself. And so he had, but the knowledge hadn't seemed so immediate in New Hastings. What would keep a white man from hiding in the ferns near that tree and potting the fellow who'd helped turn his world inside out?

The stink would, you fool. Frederick wouldn't have wanted to wait in ambush here. Maybe one of the vultures would have, but he couldn't think of anyone else who was likely to.

Then they rode past the hanged man. With the way the breeze was blowing, that took the stench away. Frederick started looking apprehensively at every clump of ferns or bushes, every stand of squat barrel trees, every fence and slave cabin. If somebody wanted to take a shot at him, it would be easy, guards or no guards.

Before long, the death reek returned. They'd passed

from land the whites controlled into country the rebels held. Here and there, animals lay bloating in the fields. There were only a few of those, though. Frederick understood why: most of the beasts would have been butchered and eaten. But he wouldn't have seen any in a peaceful countryside. Human bodies lay in the fields, too. His nose told him many more people had died somewhere out of sight.

Slave cabins stood empty, some with doors yawning open. So did big houses, the ones that hadn't burned. Many of the planters' houses had had their windows smashed, so that they stared out at the muddy road like so many skulls with big, black, blind eye sockets.

In rebel country, several cavalrymen held up white flags of truce. Frederick wondered how much good they would do—and whether they would do any. Then he decided they had to do some. Without them, he was sure his party already would have been attacked.

"How do we get them to come out and to us talk?" asked the lieutenant who commanded his guards. Maximilian Braun's side whiskers had gray in them; he spoke with a heavy German accent—*like a Dutchman*, most Atlanteans would have said. Like Colonel Sinapis and a good many others, he'd washed up on these shores because of some European political upheaval. He would be grayer yet before he got a captain's third small star on either side of his collar.

One thing Frederick was sure of—like most Europeans, Braun had no use for slavery. "Maybe we should stop and stay in one place a while," the Negro said.

"Why not?" Braun said. "That will them a better chance give to surround us and wipe us out." No matter what he thought about slavery, he had an acute sense of self-preservation. Well, who didn't?

But the officer gave the necessary orders. His men set about making camp. They ran up a large Atlantean flag. The scarlet red-crested eagle's head on dark blue had never meant much to Frederick—he was *in* Atlantis, but not *of* it. Now that might change. He hoped it would.

Along with the national flag, the soldiers also went on flying a large flag of truce. Frederick hoped it would do some good. If it didn't . . . If it didn't, he was liable to discover in short order that Lieutenant Braun hadn't been joking. The immigrant didn't sound as if he had been.

Braun set out sentries at the cardinal points of the compass. The rest of the troopers tended to their horses. Having watched cavalrymen before, Frederick knew they worried about the mounts ahead of themselves. As soon as the animals were brushed and fed and watered, the troopers sat or squatted on the ground and started shooting dice. One of them glanced up at Frederick. "Want to get into the game?" he asked, sounding friendlier than white men commonly did.

Frederick needed only a heartbeat to figure out why: the trooper saw him as a victim to be fleeced—or, more likely, skinned. It wasn't as if Frederick had never made the little ivory cubes spin himself. But . . . "Sorry," he said. "I've got me a rule against gambling with the other fella's dice."

"You ain't so dumb," the trooper said, not without regret. "Too bad. I was kinda hopin' you were." He eyed the Negro in a different way. "You really think you can get these rebels to behave?"

"I'm here to try," Frederick answered.

"Sure, sure." The cavalryman nodded as he rattled the dice in his right hand. "But what are the odds?" He threw the dice. "Seven!" he said happily, and scooped up the money on the ground.

What *were* the odds? Frederick shrugged. "We'll just have to find out, that's all."

"Wonderful," the trooper said. "We're liable to find out they'd sooner kill us than talk to us. What do we do then?"

"Try and fight them. Try and stay alive," Frederick replied. He could have given the answer in one word, but he preferred not to say that word out loud. *Die.* Yes, they could easily do that.

Leland Newton wished he were down in Gernika. He couldn't remember the last time such a longing had overtaken him. He didn't think such a longing had ever overtaken him before, come to that. Ever since Atlantis acquired it from Spain, the new state had drowsed under the subtropical sun. If its Senators were more impassioned about slavery than men from other states south of the Stour, it didn't send many of them to New Hastings: its free population was small. Newton understood that; he wouldn't have cared to make his home in the midst of such humid heat, either.

Ten or twelve years earlier, a great cyclone had chewed across Gernika's southern peninsula. Not all the damage from it was repaired, even yet. Nothing happened fast down in Gernika. Up till now, that might as well have been a law of nature.

But times changed. If that wasn't a motto for the bustling, driving nineteenth century, Newton didn't know what would be. When he was a boy, steam engines had been rare, expensive novelties. Now steamships plied the seven seas. Railroads with steam-driven locomotives tied the land down under an ever-tightening web of iron. And another web, this one of copper wires almost as thin and insubstantial as gossamer, brought news from one place to another as soon as it happened. Who at the turn of the century would have dreamt of any of that?

Who at any time in all the prior history of the world would have dreamt of change fast enough to be visible in one man's lifetime? No one. Now the nineteenth century, and the men of the nineteenth century, had to try to cope with it.

Some tried to cope by denying that that change was real. Slavery's diehard defenders seemed to Newton to be such men. But the change was there whether they liked it or not. Even a sensible conservative like Jeremiah Stafford could see as much. That he could finally see as much went a long way toward making him sensible in Newton's eyes.

And some tried to push change along even faster than Newton thought it ought to go. He was pretty sure Stafford and he could eventually get the Slug Hollow agreement through the Senate. The slaves in Gernika didn't want to wait. They'd had enough of waiting at white men's orders for white men's profit. Newton didn't know what they aimed to do on their own. He suspected they didn't, either. But it would be of their choosing, which was what they wanted.

If Frederick Radcliff could calm them down and persuade them to wait, the prestige he gained in so doing would surely help the Slug Hollow accord. According to Stafford, that was Frederick's calculation. But if things didn't go the way the Negro hoped, the cost was unlikely to remain only political. Chances were Frederick wouldn't come back to New Hastings again.

He had to know it, too, know it better than anyone. But he'd gone all the same. Some whites still insisted on calling the insurrectionist slaves a pack of cowards. Newton hadn't believed that before he saw his first battlefield. In all the fights against the Negroes and copperskins, he hadn't seen them perform any less bravely than their white foes. And going forward into the face of what was much too likely to be death in Gernika took a courage of its own.

So Leland Newton thought, at any rate. Several Senators from south of the Stour saw things differently, and weren't shy about saying so on the Senate floor. "The sooner that Radcliff nigger's disposed of, the better off everyone will be," declared a diehard slaveholder from Nouveau Redon.

"By 'everyone,' no doubt, the honorable gentleman means the entire population of Gernika except for whites, copperskins, and Negroes," Newton observed dryly.

"Yes. I mean, no!" Too late, the Conscript Father realized he'd stuck his foot in it. Not only did Consul Newton mock him from the dais, but jeers rose on the floor both from northern Senators and also from men who would normally have supported him. With a baleful stare, the Senator from Nouveau Redon shook his fist at Newton. "You tricked me!"

"It wasn't hard," Newton answered. "That may perhaps—only perhaps, note—indicate that the honorable gentleman was talking through his hat."

The honorable gentleman didn't believe he was doing any such thing. Somehow, Newton hadn't thought he would. The honorable gentleman tried to demonstrate he was doing no such thing by talking through his hat some more—at interminable length.

Interminable, at any rate, till Consul Stafford terminated the torrent of verbiage with several sharp raps of his gavel. "That will be quite enough of that. Quite a bit too much of that, in fact. The gentleman is out of order."

"By God, sir, I am not!" the Senator shouted furiously.

"I'm afraid you are," Stafford said, more in sorrow than in anger—for the time being, at any rate. "You are so far out of order that it would take a most superior watchmaker to pop off your back, tighten your mainspring, oil you up, and generally get you running again as you should."

"Watchmaker?" the Senator spluttered. "What nonsense are you spouting now? God-damned watchmaker? And you said *I* was talking through my hat?"

"No, he didn't. I did," Newton said. "And you were. And you are. And it looks like you'll keep right on doing it unless you sit down and shut up. So why don't you do that instead . . . sir?"

"Hear! Hear!" As the laughter had before, the cry rose from northern and southern Senators together. Outraged but even more downcast, the Senator from Nouveau Redon sank into his chair and resentfully fell silent.

Newton turned to Stafford. "Thank you, your Excellency."

The other Consul nodded back. "Thank *you*, your Excellency." They smiled at each other. Newton couldn't remember that happening up on the dais before the Slug Hollow agreement. However little Stafford might want them to, they found themselves on the same side now . . . and on the same side as Frederick Radcliff.

That would all fall apart if the Negro came to grief in Gernika. *I should be down there helping him*, Newton thought again. But, for the life of him, he didn't see what he could do *to* help. Frederick Radcliff's position and power might lie outside the Charter, but they were no less real for that.

They'd been camped west of St. Augustine for three days before a rebel slave showed himself. Lieutenant Braun had a bad case of the fidgets by then. Frederick Radcliff didn't. Far better than the white officer, he understood how leery of authority the insurrectionists were. He'd wondered whether any of them would appear at all, or whether they would melt off into the swamps and the barrel-tree thickets till he and the Atlantean soldiers went away.

But a copperskin did come out of the greenery. The flag of truce he carried had been hacked from a bedsheet. *A planter's bedsheet*, Frederick thought—the cloth was too white and too fine ever to have belonged to a slave.

"You really Frederick Radcliff?" the copperskin called to him, plainly not wanting to come any closer than he had to.

"I really am Frederick Radcliff," Frederick shouted back. "Who are you?"

"My friends call me Quince," the other man answered, pronouncing it in two syllables—*keen*-say—not like the name of the fruit. "It means 'fifteen' in Spanish."

"Why do they call you that?" Frederick asked, as he was obviously meant to do.

"Oh, maybe it's because that's how many white men I've done for," Quince said, eyeing the cavalrymen with Frederick. "Or maybe it's because—" He glanced down at himself with unmistakable male complacency. He wore baggy slave trousers, so it was impossible to be sure what he had in mind, but. . . .

A trooper got the same idea Frederick did, and at the same time, too. Frederick was constrained by what he saw as diplomacy. The trooper wasn't, and hooted in derision. "Now tell me another one!" he bawled in Quince's direction. "My God-damned horse ain't that big!"

"Poor creature," Quince said. If he was joking, he joked with a straight face—or something. Frederick shook his own head like a man harassed by mosquitoes. At the moment, he wasn't that kind of man, but in Gernika he was liable to turn into that kind of man any second now. He had some gauzy netting to sleep in—and he had some bites.

"I don't care how you're hung," he told Quince. "Come on in and talk with us if you don't want to get hanged."

The trooper who'd doubted Quince's attributes groaned.

Several other cavalrymen sent Frederick reproachful stares. Maybe they hadn't thought Negroes could make such bad puns. If they hadn't, it only proved they hadn't been around Negroes much.

As for Quince himself, he gaped at Frederick. Then he threw back his head and yipped. He sounded more like a fox barking at the moon than a man laughing, but the grin on his face declared that that was what he had to be. "Nobody told me you were a funny fellow," he said, walking toward Frederick and the troopers.

"Don't worry about it," Frederick answered. "Nobody told me I was, either." That drew more yips from Quince. Frederick went on, "Can you speak for all the slaves who've risen up in these parts?"

"If I can't, nobody can," Quince declared. The trouble was, maybe nobody could. As Frederick Radcliff had reason to know, insurrectionists lacked the Atlantean army's neat chain of command. The army relied on hundreds of years—thousands of years, some officers said—of military tradition. Every band of rebels made things up as it went along.

Lieutenant Braun's thoughts must have run along a similar track. "*Can* you for these slave rebels speak?" he demanded, as if he were contemplating seizing Quince for impersonating a spokesman rather than for any of the real crimes the copperskin must have committed. For all Frederick knew, the Dutchman was contemplating exactly that. He seemed a very . . . orderly officer.

But Quince nodded back at him. "I can. I do. I will," the copperskin said, an enumeration thorough enough to satisfy even Maximilian Braun. Casually, as if the matter were of no great importance but did need mentioning, Quince added, "Anything bad happens to me, it'll happen to you people, too—only slower." He walked into the encampment.

"*Ja, ja.*" Lieutenant Braun sounded impatient, not afraid. Frederick admired his coolness, unsure he could imitate it himself. The Negro's eyes surveyed the ferns from which Quince had emerged. He saw no other fighters, which proved nothing. They *would* be out there.

A sergeant muttered something to one of the troopers. The man looked surprised, but nodded. He brought Quince a square of hardtack, some chewy army sausage that was about half salt, and a tin mug of coffee. "For now, we're friends," the soldier said. He sounded none too friendly, but sometimes actions spoke louder than words.

Quince eyed the food as if wondering if it was laced with rat poison. In his place, Frederick would have wondered— had wondered—the same thing. Trusting the men who'd bought and sold you didn't come easy for a slave in Atlantis. But the Gernikan rebel leader ate. He showed no great enthusiasm, but who could get enthusiastic about rations? After washing down the bite of hardtack with some coffee, he nodded back at the trooper who'd fed him. "For now," he agreed.

"Maybe for longer. I hope so," Frederick said. "You know about the Slug Hollow arrangements, the ones they're talking over now in New Hastings?"

"Heard little bits—that's about all," Quince said. "Masters don't like that kind of news getting to slaves, so they sit on it as hard as they can."

Frederick Radcliff nodded. Back in his days on the Barford plantation—only last year, though they seemed as far away as China or Japan—he'd seen the same thing. Slaveholders weren't fools. And, like the army, they had lots of experience on their side. If slaves didn't hear news that had to do with them, they couldn't get all hot and bothered about it. And so slaveholders did their level best to keep their two-legged property in the dark.

"What it comes down to is, the Senate's working up toward saying these arrangements are the way things ought to be in Atlantis from here on out," Frederick told him. "Slaves'll be free—free as white men. They'll have the same rights—all of 'em. They'll get to own property. They'll get to vote. If somebody elects 'em, they'll get to go to state-houses or to the Senate. Their kids'll go to school, same as white boys."

"And you say the Senate's gonna do this?" Quince didn't call him a liar, not in so many words, but he might as well have. "How'd that happen?"

"On account of the slaves I led whipped the snot out of the Atlantean army the Senate sent out against us, that's how," Frederick said proudly.

Quince's eyes lit up. "And you killed all the fuckers? Nigger, you're my kind of man!"

Frederick Radcliff was far from sure he wanted to be Quince's kind of man. But he did want Quince to be his kind of man here. "No, we didn't," he replied. "The government never would've let us alone if we had. We took their guns and let them go and made terms with them. There won't be any slaves left in Atlantis after the Slug Hollow agreement goes through—if it does."

"But those God-damned asswipes in New Hastings won't let it happen, huh?" Quince said. "Sounds like them, by Jesus!"

"No, that's not what was going on," Frederick answered. "I think they would have passed it sooner or later. But then they got word of this uprising. They got to wondering if I could bring slaves along in the deal, or if folks'd just keep on fighting."

"Can you blame us for rising up against these fucking dons?" Quince said. "And the shitheads who came down after Atlantis bought Gernika are just as bad." He paused, then shook his head. "Nah, they're even worse, on account of they don't know when to quit and the Spaniards do. Well, sometimes."

"How can I blame you for rising up when I rose up, too?" Frederick said. "But there's a good time to do that stuff, and there's a time that ain't so good. You could've picked a better one."

"Huh." If Quince was impressed, he didn't show it. "And what happens when we put down our guns? White devils jump on us with both feet, that's what." He answered his own question before Frederick could.

But Frederick said, "No, that's not how it'll work. You put down your guns now, it'll be like it was a war, and nobody'll come after you later on."

"Give me a new story, why don't you?—one I'll believe." Scorn filled Quince's voice.

"If the government in New Hastings has to, it'll send

in soldiers to keep white folks off your back," Frederick insisted.

"Go on! You're tryin' to fool me," Quince said.

"No such thing. Honest to God, Quince, I mean it." Frederick raised his right hand, as if taking an oath. "But you got to do it pretty quick. If you don't, if the important white folks back in New Hastings decide I can't deliver the goods—"

"I got you." The copperskin stabbed a forefinger in his direction. "You want to be a big fella himself, and you want to get big on account of us."

"I'm already a big fella," Frederick said. "What I want is for slaves to get free. That's the size of it. You keep doing what you're doing, you could mess that up for niggers and mudfaces all over Atlantis."

"Says you."

"Yeah, says me," Frederick answered. "And the reason I say so is, it's true. You go on killing people and burning stuff, they'll send lots of soldiers after you, and I won't be able to do anything about it."

"So we'll lick 'em. You say you did." Quince seemed stubborn enough to make a proper leader for a rebel band. He might have got on well with Lorenzo.

"We did. And maybe you will. But even if you do, you'll still be hurting all the other slaves in Atlantis," Frederick said.

"Why should we care? When did them other fuckers ever care about us?"

Before Frederick could answer, Lieutenant Braun unexpectedly broke in: "One of your poets in English wrote, 'No man an island is.' He was wise, in spite of an Englishman being. Whatever you do, to other folk it makes a difference. Whatever they do, to you it matters. Believe me, I would not be in this strange land a stranger if this were not so."

"Huh," Quince said. "I can't decide here on my own. I got to go back and talk with some other people, know what I mean?"

"Sure," Frederick said. "Do that, then."

"Strange. Even insurrectionists find it needful to invent

again the committee," Braun said. "This may God's judgment upon us be."

"Huh," Quince repeated, not knowing what to make of that. Frederick Radcliff didn't know, either. Still scratching his head, the copperskin eased away from the people who'd entered his territory and slipped off into the woods.

"It could be that you him convinced," Lieutenant Braun said.

"Could be, yeah," Frederick said. "Could be you helped, too. Hope so." He shrugged. "Now we wait and see what happens next, that's all."

For Jeremiah Stafford, waiting and seeing what happened next was the hardest part of having Frederick Radcliff go off to Gernika. If the Negro persuaded his fellow slaves to abandon their revolt, he would be a hero. If the slaves kept fighting, whites in the Senate would decide Frederick couldn't keep his own side in line—which would doom the Slug Hollow agreement. And if some angry white man down by St. Augustine shot Frederick, Negroes and copperskins in the rest of the country would explode—which would also doom the Slug Hollow agreement.

Dooming the Slug Hollow agreement would also doom Consul Stafford—politically, anyhow. Frederick Radcliff was liable to be doomed in the far more literal sense of the word. He'd understood that when he set out for Gernika, but he'd gone anyhow. That was admirable or stupid, depending on one's point of view. Stafford wanted to think the black man was nothing but the usual dumb nigger. He wanted to, but he couldn't. Whatever Frederick was, usual he wasn't.

And the two of them were bound together now, like those occasional sets of twins that seldom lived long. If Frederick failed, he pulled Stafford down with him. That was part of what went with signing the accord at Slug Hollow. For the life of him, though, Stafford still didn't see what else he could have done.

Some of his Senatorial colleagues from states south of the Stour understood why he'd done what he'd done. Not all of them were willing to admit it where a reporter—or even a waiter—might overhear them and quote them, but they would when they talked with him in private.

Others understood nothing and didn't care to be enlightened. A Senator from Gernika with the euphonious name of Storm Whitson thundered against "that interfering nigger" with every breath he took. And Storm Whitson had taken a lot of breaths. He was up past ninety. As a youth, he'd carried a musket against King George's redcoats. Later, he'd moved south to Gernika and made his fortune in indigo and rice—and in clever slave-dealing. Stafford wished he could blame Whitson's intemperance on senile decay. But, while the old man wore thick glasses and cupped a hand behind his ear to get the drift of what other Senators were saying, his mind was clear. He'd been thundering about Negroes and copperskins for as long as anyone could remember.

He stood up on the Senate floor now—leaning on a stick, yes, but despite that straighter than many younger men—and shouted, "These inferior breeds must remain under our thumb! God has ordained it, and we would go against His will if we were to change the way we have done things for so long!"

Heads bobbed up and down. Not so long before, Stafford's would have been one of those nodding heads. He too had believed the slaveholders' course was ordained by God. But, if it was, why had God let the insurrectionists beat the stuffing out of the Atlantean army in the backwoods of New Marseille?

Before he could ask the question, his comrade on the dais found a different one. "I realize the honorable Conscript Father is a man of remarkable experience," Consul Newton said—loudly, to make sure Senator Whitson heard him. "But will he tell this house he was present at the Creation and heard from Jehovah's lips this onus laid upon the darker races?"

Senators from north of the Stour laughed. So did some from south of the river. Storm Whitson simply stood there, a living illustration of the third part of the riddle of the

Sphinx. "Beware, your Excellency, lest God punish you for your iniquity," he said.

"If you are so sure He will, then He must speak to you, eh?" Newton said.

"God will speak to any man who opens his heart and listens," Senator Whitson replied.

"Any man who opens his mouth and talks can say God speaks to him," Newton observed. "But saying something doesn't make it so."

"As you have proved time and again," Whitson snapped. He might be getting frail, but his wits had indeed stayed sharp—sharp enough to make Newton wince.

Stafford used his gavel. "Discussions of God and His purposes do not belong in the Senate," he said. "As the Atlantean Assembly ordained even before we won our freedom from England, our people may follow any faith they choose. Or, if they choose, they may follow none."

"The Lord will punish them if they choose to follow none," Whitson declared.

"Maybe. As a matter of fact, I think so, too. But"—Stafford shrugged—"neither of us can prove it. It's between them and God, not between them and us."

"I always thought the Atlantean Assembly made a mistake," Whitson said. "A proper Christian country has no business putting up with Jews and freethinkers and other unrighteous folk."

"By law, the United States of Atlantis are not a proper Christian country," Stafford said. "Follow the Bible in your own life if you want to. No one will tell you you may not. But in the Senate, we will follow the law."

"Follow it even when it takes us straight to ruination," Whitson jeered.

"Change isn't ruin. We need to get used to that. We need to remember it," Consul Newton said. "I've had reason to think about that quite a bit lately. Change is only change. It can be good or bad. It doesn't have to be either one."

"When you've seen as much change as I have, young fellow, you'll know it's mostly bad," Senator Whitson said. "And this change you want to ram down our throats is the worst one yet. Nigger equality? Pah!" He made as if to spit.

"The way it looks to me, we have one choice besides liberating our slaves: we can kill them all, or try," Jeremiah Stafford said. "We can't trust them to go on serving us the way they did before. The Slug Hollow agreement may not be a wonderful bargain for Atlantis. It is the best bargain we could get, things being as they are."

"Nonsense!" the Senator from Gernika said.

"It isn't," Stafford answered. "Even now, part of me wishes it were, but it isn't."

Frederick Radcliff couldn't have been any more bored waiting for Quince to step out of the undergrowth again. He knew the copperskin might tell him the rebels didn't intend to lay down their arms. He knew Quince might not come back alone, but at the head of a swarm of slaves. If Quince did, Frederick wouldn't see New Hastings or Helen again.

But he couldn't do anything about any of that. He also couldn't worry about it all the time. And so . . . he was bored.

He was so bored, he did get into the cavalry troopers' seemingly unending dice game. He lost five and a half eagles in less time than it takes to tell. After that, he got out of the game again.

"Sure we can't talk you into sticking?" one of the horsemen asked, rattling the bones as temptingly as he could.

"Nah. I've already been as much of a sucker as I can afford to be, and some more besides," Frederick answered.

"You might win this time." The trooper rattled the dice again.

"Slim odds." Frederick left it right there. He didn't *know* the game was crooked. He didn't want to waste any more money on a voyage of discovery, either. A lifetime of slavery had convinced him each and every gold eagle—each and every silver ten-cent piece—was precious. Losing so many so fast . . . What Helen would say if she ever found out . . . No, he didn't want to play any more.

Then the troopers quit coaxing him. They all grabbed

for their eight-shooters. One of them pointed. "Here's that mudfaced son of a bitch again!"

Sure enough, there stood Quince at the edge of the open ground. Lots of dirt in the southern states (though not that of Gernika) was reddish, which was how copperskins got their nasty nickname. Quince waved his big white flag. "Come on in!" Frederick called. "The truce holds no matter what you tell us."

Maybe so, maybe not. If the cavalrymen decided plugging Quince would help them, they'd do it. How could Frederick stop them? He couldn't. He knew it, and Quince had to know it, too.

But the rebel leader did come in. Along with the flag of truce, he had a pepperbox pistol on his right hip. Chances were it had been some planter's prized possession . . . and chances were that planter needed it no more and would never need it again. Ceremoniously, Quince laid the fancy pistol at Frederick Radcliff's feet. "We're gonna try peace," Quince said, as if it were a dangerous, possibly poisonous, medicine, like mercury for the pox. "If we can put down our guns and still get free . . . That's worth doing. But if it don't work out, nigger, you'll answer to me."

One black could call another *nigger* without a jolt. The word packed some in a copperskin's mouth, as *mudface* did in a Negro's. Quince had used it before, mostly in admiration. Frederick didn't think he intended malice this time. "Fair enough," he answered. "But if it don't work out, you got to stand in line. Plenty of other folks'll want to nail my hide to the wall."

"I believe *that*," Quince said. "Nobody's gonna come down on us 'cause we rose up, or 'cause of stuff we did while we were fighting?"

"That's the deal," Frederick said. "Nobody'll go to law with you on account of any of that." White survivors might try to take private revenge. If they came to trial, white juries might—likely would—acquit them. Frederick didn't know what he could do about that. So far, he hadn't come up with anything. But it was outside the law, and Negroes and copperskins could also play those games once they were free.

"They for true gonna pass that arrangement up in New Hastings?" Quince asked.

"If they don't, we *all* start fighting again," Frederick answered. "They got to know that, too. Chances that they *will* pass it just got better, too, if your people honest to God do quit fighting."

"Still a couple of snowball cocksuckers I wouldn't mind finishing, but I guess I can let 'em live," Quince said. Frederick nodded. Those whites were just as sure to want Quince dead. Well, they and he would have to forgo the pleasure . . . if the Slug Hollow accord passed. *It has to now*, Frederick thought. *Doesn't it?*

XXVI

*J*eremiah Stafford hated waiting. When you had to sit there twiddling your thumbs, what you were waiting for usually wasn't anything you wanted. It might be something you needed, but that was a different story. If you had a toothache, you waited for the dentist to get to work on you. Then you waited for whatever horrible things he was doing to be over. Ether was supposed to help with that torment, as it did with so many others. Stafford hadn't had to visit a tooth-drawer since the stuff came into use. He wasn't so eager to test its virtues that he wanted to visit one, either. Nobody with a full set of marbles *wanted* to visit the dentist.

What the Consul waited for now wasn't the cessation of pain. If the news here proved bad, though, it could end up causing more pain than all the toothaches he'd ever had put together. Bad news here could split Atlantis like a jeweler splitting a sapphire—or, less neatly, like a drunk falling out of a second-story window and breaking his leg. The second comparison seemed to Stafford to fit better. He wished it didn't.

Ever since the redcoats sailed away, New Hastings had been *the* place where important things happened in the USA. Now, all of a sudden, it wasn't. As history had been made in Slug Hollow (Stafford did his best to forget all the fighting preceding that bit of history), so now it would be made somewhere outside of St. Augustine, in the heat and humidity and insignificance of Gernika.

But what kind of history would be made there? That was what Stafford waited to discover, along with the rest of official New Hastings. He didn't have a flannel rag tied around his head to keep a swollen jaw from tormenting him quite so much, but he might as well have.

He was pretending to go through paperwork in his office when his secretary stuck his head in and said, "Your Excellency, a soldier wants to see you."

"A soldier?" Stafford echoed, and the secretary nodded. With a shrug, the Consul said, "All right, Ned. Send him in." Whatever the soldier wanted, talking to him was bound to be more interesting than a report on the previous fiscal year's revenues and expenses pertaining to canals.

The soldier strode in and delivered a salute as stiff as a marionette's. He was a young second lieutenant, so new in his uniform that he all but squeaked. "Your Excellency!" he said, and saluted again. "I am Lieutenant Morris Radcliffe, and I have the honor to bring you a report Colonel Sinapis has just received from Lieutenant Braun, who commands the security detail assigned to Frederick Radcliff in Gernika."

Stafford wondered which twig Morris Radcliffe represented on the family's huge, many-branched tree. He wondered how the lieutenant was related to him, and how the youngster was related to Frederick Radcliff. He also wondered what Morris Radcliffe thought of being related to a Negro.

But he wondered none of those things for more than a split second. "News from Colonel Sinapis? From this Lieutenant Braun?" he barked. "Well, out with it, man!"

"Sir? Uh, yes, sir!" Startled by Stafford's outburst, Lieutenant Radcliffe had to compose himself before he could remember what he was supposed to say. "Colonel Sinapis told me to tell you that Lieutenant Braun told him that Frederick Radcliff has arranged an end to the hostilities between whites and slaves in and around St. Augustine."

"He *has* arranged that?" Stafford wanted to make sure

he'd got it straight. Sometimes you heard with your heart, not your ears.

"Yes, your Excellency, he has." Young Radcliffe confirmed it. "At the present moment—or at the moment Lieutenant Braun sent the telegram—there is, uh, was no fighting in Gernika. The Negroes and copperskins who had rebelled against established authority are coming in from the woods and swamps."

What else would they be coming in from? As far as Stafford knew, Gernika had precious little territory that *wasn't* woods or swamps. He forced his wandering wits back to the matter at hand. "Well," he said, and then "Well" again. On the third try, he managed something better: "It's a great day for Atlantis."

"Yes, sir. I think so, too." Lieutenant Radcliffe looked confused. "Colonel Sinapis told me he thought you would say something like that. What with where you come from and all, I wasn't so sure he was right."

By the way the lieutenant talked, he'd been born north of the Stour. Some northerners thought anybody who favored slavery had been issued horns and pitchforks by Satan himself. (Some men from Stafford's part of the country felt the same about people who opposed slavery. Stafford had himself, not so long before. He declined to dwell on that now.)

Wearily, the Consul answered, "Even when you wish they would, things don't always last. When they wear out, you've got to patch 'em up or get rid of 'em and try something new. Doesn't look like we can patch slavery. Since we can't, we'd better figure out how to get along without it, don't you think?"

"Me? Uh, yes, sir." Lieutenant Radcliffe gulped and blushed like a girl. "That's my *personal* opinion, you understand, your Excellency. My opinion as a soldier . . . Well, soldiers aren't supposed to have opinions about stuff that has to do with politics."

"Of course," Stafford said dryly, and the junior—very junior—officer turned pinker yet. But it was a sound rule. Soldiers were supposed to do what the people who did concern themselves with politics told them to do. They weren't supposed to give their superiors any back talk about it, either.

If opinions got hot enough, the system would break down. If commanded to put down slaveholders, some soldiers from south of the Stour would refuse. As Stafford had seen for himself, fewer from north of the river would refuse to fight slaves. That had been true before the Slug Hollow agreement, anyhow. Maybe it wasn't any more. Northerners were liable to figure the south had had its chance for a tolerable peace, and to refuse to help it any further if it turned its back on that chance.

He hoped that wouldn't come up. If there was any justice in the world, it wouldn't. "Whether you have opinions about politics or not, Lieutenant, I do, and I will give you one of mine," Stafford said. "If I can't get the Slug Hollow agreement through the Senate after this, I will go home."

While Leland Newton was campaigning against the slave insurrectionists, the newspapers called him and Consul Stafford and Colonel Sinapis every kind of idiot under the sun. They called Frederick Radcliff worse than that. Now, conveniently forgetting what they'd said then, they sported headlines with words like *peace* and *justice* and *dignity* and *statesmanship* prominently displayed. They applied those words not only to Frederick but also to the two Consuls, who got credit for sending him south to St. Augustine.

Even Sinapis came in for praise. The papers said generous things about his common sense and restraint. Those same qualities had been conspicuously absent in his conduct of the campaign against the rebels west of the Green Ridge Mountains—again, if you believed the newspapers.

Newton didn't, which didn't stop him from reading them. If you added them all together—the ones that loved you and the ones that loathed you—you might come within spitting distance of the truth. Even if you didn't, you would find out what editors—and the men who paid them—thought to be the truth. And, in politics, what people thought to be true was at least as important as what was true.

The Consul from Croydon also found his colleague from Cosquer as eager as he was to get the Slug Hollow accord through the Senate. The only problem was, southern Senators kept using every delaying tactic they could find. Newton had known fools like Storm Whitson would go right on being foolish. He had expected canny politicos like Abel Marquard to see which way the wind was blowing.

"Didn't you make some kind of arrangement with Frederick Radcliff before he left for Gernika?" Newton asked. "Aren't you reneging on it now?"

Marquard's expressive nostrils flared. "I would never make an arrangement with a Negro—except the kind his grandfather made with his grandmother. How could I renege on an arrangement I did not make?"

"What if he claims you did?" asked Newton, who knew better than to take everything the slippery Senator said at face value.

"What if he does?" Senator Marquard answered easily. "People claim all kinds of things they can't prove."

"He may not need to prove it. He'll be a very popular man when he comes back from St. Augustine," Newton said. "If he tells the papers you said this, that, or the other thing, don't you think most people who read that will believe it?"

"People not of our profession may, but who worries about what people not of our profession believe? Only other people not of our profession." Marquard snapped his fingers to show what he thought of such people.

"They elect the burgesses who'll vote on whether to reelect you," Newton said. Senator Marquard snapped his fingers again. He seemed bound and determined to stay unimpressed.

And, on the Senate floor, he seemed bound and determined to keep the Slug Hollow agreement from ever reaching a vote. He had friends, too, friends Newton hadn't expected him to have. "Can't you do anything about those people?" Newton asked Jeremiah Stafford. "Most of them come from your state."

"I'm trying," Stafford said.

"So are they," Newton answered. "Exceedingly trying."

"Heh," the other Consul said. "Let me put that another way: I am doing everything I know how to do."

"Well, then, you'd better come up with something new, because what you know how to do isn't working," Newton said.

Stafford glared. "I don't see that I'm getting much help from you."

"From me? Any Senator from south of the Stour would just as soon cut me as look at me." Newton exaggerated, but not by much. "Maybe we really do need to wait and see if the Negro can bring them to their senses."

"Maybe we do." But Stafford didn't seem convinced, for he went on, "Have you any idea—any idea at all—how strange relying on a Negro for anything at all seems to me?"

"Perhaps not. In Croydon, though, Negroes—and copperskins—have been citizens for longer than I've been alive. They've been citizens longer than Atlantis has been free of England. We—whites, I mean—don't always love them, but we're used to treating them like men, not like children or farm animals," Newton said.

"And how often do they leave you sorry you've treated them that way?" the other Consul asked.

"Well, I don't have statistics at my fingertips, the way the Minister of the Fisc does with his accounts. My impression is that they're about as reliable as white men—not much worse, not much better," Newton replied.

"Fair enough," Stafford said. "Is it any wonder I'm worried, then?"

"When you put it that way ... no." Consul Newton wished he could give a different answer, but any politico learned early in the game not to count on other people too much, regardless of their color. If he didn't learn that, he didn't stay in the game long enough to learn much else.

When Frederick Radcliff came back to New Hastings, he got a parade through the town's old, old streets. People cheered him—whites, blacks, and copperskins. He waved to the crowd. As a brass band thumped behind him, he took off his tall hat and waved it, too. Sitting beside him in the open carriage, Helen seemed ready to burst with pride.

The next day, Frederick called on Senator Marquard at

Marquard's offices in the Senate House. Marquard's white secretary gravely told him the politico was indisposed and could not see him. Frederick said, "Oh, too bad," and went away. But when Abel Marquard was also "indisposed" the following day and the day after that, the Negro began to suspect a trend.

He went to the house Marquard rented in New Hastings, only a couple of blocks from the Senate House. The Senator's Negro butler received him there. "Pleasure to meet you, Mr. Radcliff," said the other black man, whose name was Clarence. "Everybody's proud of you—you'd best believe that."

"Thank you kindly," Frederick said. By *everybody*, Clarence doubtless meant *everybody our color*. He had to be a highly trusted man, or the Senator wouldn't have brought him to a state where he could run off if he chose. Frederick went on, "Can I see himself?" He hadn't had such a prominent master, but he'd done Clarence's job for Henry Barford.

"He's here. I'm sure he'd be glad to see you. Wait just a minute," the butler answered.

"Obliged." Frederick wasn't so sure of that, but he didn't say so.

Clarence came back almost as fast as he'd promised. His smile had disappeared, though. "Well, he *will* see you," he said, and took it no further than that.

Senator Marquard's study would have made Master Barford jealous. The Senator did shake hands with Frederick, but didn't look happy doing it. "I kept my half of the bargain, sir," Frederick said without preamble. "Now it's time for you to keep yours."

"Bargain? What bargain?" By the way Marquard said the word, it might have come from Russian or Chinese. "We made no bargain that I recollect."

Frederick stared at him. He'd known some pretty fancy liars in his time, but for straight-faced gall the Senator from Cosquer took the prize. "You know damned well what bargain . . . sir," Frederick said, and proceeded to spell it out in words of one syllable.

By Abel Marquard's manner, he might have been hearing of it for the very first time. "My dear fellow!" he ex-claimed when Frederick finished. "When you were down in Gernika, you must have eaten some of the mystic mush-rooms that grow there—you know, the ones that can make men think they see God or the Devil sitting in front of them till they get better. You are imagining things."

"Oh, I am, am I?" Frederick said grimly. "If I think I see the Devil sitting in front of me now, it's on account of I'm looking right at you." He stormed out of the Senator's study.

"Something wrong?" Clarence asked him.

"Oh, you might say so. Yeah, you just might." The story poured out of Frederick.

"Is that what happened?" Clarence said when he fin-ished.

"That's *just* what happened. So help me God, it is." Fred-erick raised his right hand, as if to swear it.

"I believe you. He's an old serpent, the master is—a sly old serpent, but a serpent even so." Senator Marquard's butler spoke with a certain somber pride. After shaking his head, Clarence went on, "He ain't gonna get away with it, though, not this time. Slug Hollow's too important to let him."

"Well, I think so, too," Frederick Radcliff said. "But what can you do about it?" He paused, grinning. "That kind of stuff?"

Clarence laid a finger by the side of his broad, flat nose and winked. "Yeah, that kind of stuff. You leave it to me, friend."

Frederick nodded and left Senator Marquard's resi-dence. He'd warned the Senator that Marquard's own slaves wouldn't let him get away with such double-dealing. Now he had to hope he was right. He intended to give Clarence a week before going to the newspapers himself. He feared that would put the Senator's back up instead of bringing him around, but it was the only weapon he had.

He turned out not to need it. Four days after Abel Mar-quard had denied making any agreement to back the Slug Hollow accord if Frederick quelled the uprising in Gernika, the Senator publicly announced his support for the accord. "It may not be a perfect bargain," Marquard declared in ringing tones on the Senate floor, "but it is the best one we are likely to get."

Marquard was an influential man. When he lined up behind Slug Hollow, he brought a good many other Senators with him. Frederick had hoped he would do exactly that. The Negro almost sought out the Senator to ask him why he'd changed his mind. But Frederick didn't need long to decide not to do that. He sought out Clarence instead.

They didn't meet at Marquard's house. That might have proved embarrassing to all concerned. A tavern and eatery that catered to Negroes, copperskins, and poor whites served better than well enough. Over fried fish and mugs of beer, Frederick asked, "What did you do?"

"Who, me?" Clarence might have borrowed that blank look from his master. "I didn't do anything. I didn't do anything at all, even the things I was supposed to do. You ever listen to a white man who has to find his own cravat and black his own shoes?"

A slow grin spread across Frederick Radcliff's face. "I like that!"

"Oh, it gets better, too," Clarence said. "It sure does. He had to give his own washing to the laundry gal, too. An' she made a mess of it—just by accident, of course."

"Of course," Frederick agreed. They both chuckled.

"Socks and drawers got starched. Shirts an' trousers didn't. A jacket got washed in hot water, so it shrank like you wouldn't believe. Such a shame!" Clarence rolled his eyes. "And I ain't even started on what the cook's been up to."

"No?" Frederick asked eagerly.

"No, sir." Clarence shook his head. "The bread was scorched one day. The next day, it didn't rise. The shrimp in the stew were a little off—just a little, but enough." He held his nose. "The master's were, anyhow. What we got was first-rate. Something in the salad gave the Senator the runs. After that, he got word things weren't goin' real well down on his plantation, neither. Soon as he heard *that*, he started wondering if something funny was goin' on."

"Now why would he think anything like that?" Butter wouldn't have melted in Frederick's mouth.

"Beats me. I haven't got the slightest idea." Anybody listening to Clarence would have been convinced he too was one of God's natural-born innocents. "But then he had a little talk with me. You hear him talk, he figures niggers and mudfaces, they never heard of Slug Hollow or what led up to it."

"Likely tell!" Frederick burst out.

"Uh-huh." Clarence nodded. "You can't believe how surprised he acted when I turned out to know as much about it as he did. 'Clarence,' he says, 'Clarence, you really want to be free and have all that trouble taking care of your own self?' And he looks surprised all over again when I go, 'I sure do, Master Marquard. An' I don't know me one single slave who don't. There may be some, but I don't know none.'"

"What did he say then?" Frederick asked eagerly.

"He says, 'If I want to live long enough to go home again once I'm done in the Senate, reckon I better go along with Slug Hollow, huh?' An' I say, 'Senator Marquard, sir, I hope you live a real long time. But if you want black folks an' copper folks to stay happy with you, you got to know we is all for Slug Hollow.' We had to get his attention, like, but we finally went an' done it."

"Good for you," Frederick said. "When he made out like I was a liar, looked to me like the only way to . . . to wake him up, like, was to hope his own people could get him thinkin' 'bout things."

"We did that, all right. Don't reckon a white man would've thought of it, but you ain't no white man, even if your granddaddy was," Clarence said. "Takes a fella who was a slave hisself to know how things really work with a planter and his niggers. He votes for Slug Hollow, he gets his friends to do the same, we gonna be free for true?"

"For true," Frederick said firmly. "Don't know what happens after that. Don't know if there's any happy endings."

"You know what? Me, I don't care," Clarence said. "Long as there's a happy beginning, long as I got a chance, I'll make it some kind of way."

"You ain't the first fella who told me that kind of thing," Frederick said. "Lots of us're figurin' we can make it some kind of way."

"Some of us won't," Clarence predicted.

"Expect you're right. But some white folks don't make it, either, even with everything goin' for them," Frederick answered. "You said it—long as we've got the chance, that's what really counts."

"Yeah." Abel Marquard's butler nodded. His eyes went dreamy and far away. "A chance. Just a God-damned chance . . ."

"Honest to God, Clarence, I think it'll happen now," Frederick said. "And you've helped make it happen. You know that, an' I know that, an' the Senator, he sure knows that, too, but I bet you anything it never shows up in the history books."

"I ain't gonna touch that bet. I may be dumb, but not *so* dumb," Clarence said. "When did anything a nigger did *ever* show up in the history books?"

"One of these days, that may happen, too," Frederick Radcliff said. "One of these days—but not quite yet."

Leland Newton glanced over at Jeremiah Stafford, who nodded. Newton brought his gavel down smartly on the desk in front of him: once, twice, three times. "The Clerk of the Senate will call the roll," he said.

"Yes, your Excellency," the Clerk of the Senate replied. How often had the functionary called the roll? Hundreds—more likely thousands—of times. He'd held his post longer than Newton had been in New Hastings. Newton couldn't remember his ever acknowledging that command from a Consul before. But now poorly suppressed excitement filled his voice, as it filled Newton's.

New Hastings hadn't known a moment like this since . . . when? Since the Atlantean Assembly reconvened here after the redcoats went home, reconvened and hammered out the system of government the USA had used ever since? No doubt that was an important time, but Newton thought this one topped it. Wouldn't you have to reach all the way back to the fifteenth century, when the Battle of the Strand ensured that no local kings, no local nobility, would lord it over the populace? Newton thought so.

The Clerk of the Senate did his best to return to his usual emotionless tone: "The question before the Conscript Fathers is, Shall the Senate ratify the agreement made by the two Consuls with one Frederick Radcliff and his supporters in the village of Slug Hollow, state of New Marseille?" No matter how hard he tried to sound dull, he didn't quite succeed.

Avalon voted first: the state north of New Marseille headed the alphabetical list. Within each state's contingent, the Senators also voted in alphabetical order. One of Avalon's six Senators voted no. Slavery wasn't legal in Avalon, but it had been up until twenty-five years earlier. Some sympathy for slaveholding lingered yet.

Cosquer came next. It had more Senators than Avalon did, since it held more people; as far as Newton knew, every one of its Conscript Fathers owned slaves. Some of them defiantly voted against the Slug Hollow accord. Consul Newton waited tensely till Abel Marquard's name came up.

"Senator Marquard!" the Clerk of the Senate intoned at last.

"Aye," Marquard said. Newton and the Clerk might have failed to keep their voices emotionless, but the Senator from Cosquer succeeded. Could machines have been made to speak, his voice might have come from one of them.

He had opposed the agreement. Frederick Radcliff had claimed the two of them had an arrangement whereby, if the Negro brought peace to Gernika, Marquard would support Slug Hollow. The Senator denied everything. But, no matter what he'd denied, he'd changed his mind. He'd announced he would support the accord, and now he'd gone and done it.

Newton wondered how and why it came to pass that Abel Marquard had changed his mind. Nobody seemed to know. Or, if anyone—Frederick Radcliff, for instance— did know, he wasn't talking. Something out of the ordinary must have happened, but who could say what?

And, in the end, what difference did it make? As long as

Marquard voted the right way (which he did) and as long as
he brought some Senatorial colleagues with him (which he
also did), everything else was a matter of details.

"The state of Croydon's delegation will now vote," the
Clerk of the Senate declared after the last man from Cosquer spoke a defiant nay. One by one, the Clerk polled
Croydon's Senators. All of them voted to accept the accord
and make slavery a thing of the past. Leland Newton would
have been horrified and astonished had they done anything
else.

On the Consular dais, Stafford turned and whispered to
him: "Next up is the compensation bill, the way we agreed."

"Oh, yes. Of course." For a moment, Newton was
tempted to imitate Senator Marquard and say something
like, *We did?* The look on Stafford's face would almost be
worth it. But the operative word was *almost*. Compensation would make freeing the slaves, if not delightful to the
whites who owned them, at least possible for those whites.
Freeing slaves without compensation would touch off a
revolt that would make the one just past (Newton hoped
it was just past) seem a children's spat by comparison.

That seemed as obvious to Newton as it did to Stafford.
The other Consul's warnings about the country breaking to
pieces in the absence of such measures weren't idle. Now
Newton would have to persuade northern Senators that
their states, their constituents, needed to see their taxes
rise to placate a group of people who, they were convinced,
were morally wrong.

*Southern Senators went out on a limb for you and for
Atlantis.* He could already see in his mind's eye the shape
his argument would take. *Now it's your turn to do the same
for them.*

Newton hoped the northern Senators would keep their
country in mind, not just the next election at their local
statehouse, the one that might send them back to New
Hastings or hurl them into private life again, rejected by
their own people. Yes, the kind of revenge the states south
of the Stour could take would be far worse than even the
Great Servile Insurrection.

Like Avalon, Freetown lay on the border with the slaveholding states. Two Freetown Senators voted against the Slug Hollow agreement. Newton winced. He'd expected to lose one vote there, but not two. Even though Abel Marquard had come through in the end, this would be closer than he wanted.

Storm Whitson looked ready to burst in anger and astonishment when the majority of the delegation from Gernika voted for Slug Hollow. "Brutus, Judas, Habakkuk Biddiscombe, and you sons of bitches!" he cried. "Traitors all!"

"That remark will be stricken from the record," Consul Newton declared. "And you are out of order, Senator."

"Well, sir, if I am, I don't much care to be *in* order," Whitson shot back.

"While you are on the Senate floor, you *will* abide by the Senate's rules," Newton said.

Whatever Whitson said after that, the gavel overrode. Then it was on to Hanover, the most heavily populated of the United States of Atlantis and also one of the states staunchest against slavery. As Croydon's had, Hanover's delegation voted unanimously for the Slug Hollow accord.

After that—before that, really, but the unanimous vote made it clear to even the dullest and the most partisan— the result was plain. When the last Senator had voted, the floor erupted in cheers and boos and applause and catcalls. A northern Senator punched a southerner in the nose. "I've wanted to do that for fifteen years!" he yelled. Then, before the Sergeant at Arms could get to them, the southerner picked himself up and decked his uncollegial colleague with a chair.

Eventually, the Sergeant at Arms and nearby Senators untangled them. On any other day, such behavior would have been a great scandal. It would have made headlines in papers on both sides of the Stour. When tomorrow came, though, it might not make the papers at all. The slaves were free! This side of the Second Coming, what news in Atlantis could be bigger than that?

The line that led to the justice of the peace's chambers stretched around the block when Frederick Radcliff and

Helen took their places in it. Most of the couples in the line were Negroes and copperskins: the reliable slaves of people who'd come up from south of the Stour to do business of one kind or another in the capital. It hadn't been legal for citizens of New Hastings to own slaves for many years. Southerners could bring them up here, though, the risk being that, if the slaves escaped, nobody would do much to help the owners recover the property that had absconded with itself.

A few white couples—people who'd decided to get married today before so many newly free slaves rushed to make their unions official—stood in line with the copperskins and Negroes. Some seemed nervous about becoming the minority element in that long ribbon of colored people. Others made the best of it. That the Negroes and copperskins were all in high spirits lent everything a quality of easiness. A white man pulled a flask out of a jacket pocket and took a nip. He passed it to his sweetheart, a redhead with skin so pale it was almost phosphorescent. She also drank, then handed it to the copperskinned woman standing behind her. The copperskin smiled and sipped and gave the flask to her man. It went down the line till it ran dry, which didn't take long.

But that wasn't the only flask or bottle going around. Frederick and Helen had a swig of distilled lightning. "Somebody in line's gonna get too pickled to be able to say his 'I do's,'" Frederick predicted, smacking his lips.

"Well, if he is, his woman'll set him straight." Helen spoke as if that were a law of nature. To her, it probably was.

When the line didn't move as fast as Frederick thought it should have, he said, "How come they didn't hire more judges who could hitch people?"

"Don't be silly. They're white folks," Helen answered. "They're too dumb to see we'd all want to do this."

"Yeah," Frederick said with a sigh. A lot of whites honestly believed Negroes and copperskins were no more than animals that happened to be especially useful because they walked erect and had hands. And the whites had done their best to ensure that slaves stayed animal-like by making it hard—sometimes impossible—for them to learn to read and write and cipher. Then, seeing how ignorant their colored workers were, they had no trouble deciding slaves truly were stupid.

When he and Helen finally got into the justice of the peace's parlor, they had forms to fill out before they could go through the ceremony. A secretary did stand by to help illiterate couples. That wasn't because of the influx of newly freed slaves; quite a few whites who intended to marry also lacked their letters (though far fewer, proportionally, than was true among copperskins and Negroes).

Frederick and Helen also had to pay the one-eagle fee required to make things official. Frederick proudly dropped a fat silver coin onto the tabletop. Its sweet ring told the world—and the secretary—it was genuine. The functionary filled in the blank lines on a form in a receipt book, tore it out, and handed it to Frederick. "Here you are, Mr. Radcliff," he said, for all the world as if he were dealing with a white man, and an important white man at that.

"Thank you kindly," Frederick answered, as if he *were* an important white man. Hearing and understanding that tone, Helen set a hand on his arm. They beamed at each other.

The newly married couple in line in front of them—he a mulatto, she a copperskin with strong cheekbones and long, lustrous blue-black hair—came out of the justice of the peace's chamber hand in hand. Both of them were beaming, too. "Congratulations," Frederick said.

"Thanks, friend. Same to you," the man replied.

From within, the justice of the peace called, "Who's next? Got to keep things moving today."

"Here we come, your Honor," Frederick said. He and Helen walked in together.

Books filled the shelves behind the justice's desk. The half-empty glass of amber liquid on the desk said he'd already needed fortifying. But his motions were steady and his voice had no slur as he said, "Raise your right hands and set your left hands on the Bibles there."

"Yes, sir," Frederick said. He didn't mind giving respect

to a white man whose position deserved it. Helen nodded to the justice of the peace as she obeyed.

"I perform this marriage ceremony by virtue of the authority vested in me by the sovereign state of New Hastings," the justice of the peace intoned, as he already had so many times before on this special day. He looked at Frederick. "Repeat after me: I—state your name—"

"Frederick Radcliff."

The white man's eyebrows rose, but he didn't miss a beat. He led Frederick through his part of the brief proceeding, then took Helen through hers. When they'd both said everything required of them, the justice of the peace went on, "By virtue of the said authority vested in me by the sovereign state of New Hastings, I now pronounce you man and wife." To Frederick, he added, "You may kiss your bride."

It wasn't as if Frederick hadn't been kissing Helen, and going to bed with her, for all of their adult lives. But kissing his bride? That was a different story. White men's laws—slaveholders' laws—hadn't let them be man and wife till the Slug Hollow agreement passed the Atlantean Senate. He made the most of the kiss.

With a cough, the justice of the peace said, "Don't like to hurry you along, folks, but I've got to do it. Big long line there behind you. I want to get through as many folks as I can. Nobody's going to hold things up, not today."

"Sorry," Frederick said. "Not sorry I kissed her, but—"

"Oh, come on," Helen told him. "His Honor knows what you mean."

Without a doubt, his Honor did. Frederick Radcliff and his wife, Helen Radcliff, left the white man's chamber together. This was the first time she'd had a surname to call her own. For that matter, Frederick's surname had been highly unofficial. No more. Ex-slaves who didn't have surnames would need to acquire them as fast as they could. State governments and the government of the United States of Atlantis would want to keep track of their new citizens: if for no other reason then to tax them more efficiently.

Taxes. Frederick's lip curled. He'd never had to worry about those while Henry Barford owned him. Freedom had some rough spots, sure as the devil. Nobody took care of free men who were down on their luck or too old and feeble to work, either. But, compared to the alternative . . . "Come on, Mrs. Radcliff," Frederick said. They walked past the secretary and out into the street together.

NEW IN HARDCOVER

FROM

NEW YORK TIMES BESTSELLING AUTHOR
HARRY TURTLEDOVE

ATLANTIS AND
OTHER PLACES

A famous naturalist seeks a near-extinct species of bird found only on the rarest of lands. A young American on a European holiday finds himself storming an enchanted German castle. Centaurs take a sea voyage to a land where they encounter a strange and frightening tribe of creatures known as man. London's most famous detective travels to Atlantis to investigate a series of murders.

This collection includes these and more amazing stories of ancient eras, historical figures, mysterious events, and out-of-this-world adventure from the incomparable Harry Turtledove.

"The maven of alternate history."
—*San Diego Union-Tribune*

R0058

NEW YORK TIMES
BESTSELLING AUTHOR

HARRY TURTLEDOVE

The United States of Atlantis

England has driven the French from Atlantis, giving King George leave to tighten his control over the colonies. The Redcoats have seized the continent's eastern coastal towns as part of a strategy to bend the colonists to their will.

Instead, England's tactics have only strengthened the Atlanteans' resolve to be free. As leader of the revolutionaries, Victor Radcliff will make the English pay for each and every piece of land they dare to occupy, and will stop at nothing to preserve the liberty of his people as a new nation is born—a nation that will change the face of the world.

**Available wherever books are sold or at
penguin.com**

ALSO AVAILABLE

FROM

NEW YORK TIMES **BESTSELLING AUTHOR**
HARRY TURTLEDOVE

OPENING ATLANTIS

Atlantis lies between Europe and the East Coast of
Terranova. For many years, this land of opportunity lured
dreamers from around the globe with its natural resources,
offering a new beginning for those willing to brave the
wonders of the unexplored territory.

It is a new world indeed: ripe for discovery, for plunder,
and eventually for colonization—but will its settlers
destroy the very wonders they had
journeyed to Atlantis to find?

"The unchallenged master of alternative
history touches on a common myth in his latest
retelling of the history of the world."
—*Library Journal*

THE ULTIMATE IN SCIENCE FICTION AND FANTASY!

From magical tales of distant worlds to stories of technological advances beyond the grasp of man, Penguin has everything you need to stretch your imagination to its limits.

penguin.com

ACE
Get the latest information on favorites like
William Gibson, T.A. Barron, Brian Jacques,
Ursula K. Le Guin, Sharon Shinn, Charlaine Harris,
Patricia Briggs, and Marjorie M. Liu,
as well as updates on the best new authors.

ROC
Escape with Jim Butcher, Harry Turtledove, Anne Bishop,
S.M. Stirling, Simon R. Green, E.E. Knight, Kat Richardson,
Rachel Caine, and many others—plus news on the
latest and hottest in science fiction and fantasy.

DAW
Patrick Rothfuss, Mercedes Lackey, Kristen Britain,
Tanya Huff, Tad Williams, C.J. Cherryh, and many more—
DAW has something to satisfy the cravings of any
science fiction and fantasy lover.
Also visit dawbooks.com.

*Get the best of science fiction and fantasy
at your fingertips!*